Dodging into
hyperfocused
terrified blonde.

He watched Bree step away from the car with a horrified look on her face.

"Bree!" Scott called.

A car horn screamed.

Brakes squealed.

Scott glanced to his left in time to see a compact car skidding toward him. The driver spun the wheel at the last second and the small car slid past Scott and slammed into a parked car. Scott turned back to the dark sedan and was about to reach for the door when the driver peeled away, burning rubber on the street.

Without hesitation, he went to Bree and placed gentle hands on her shoulders. "Are you okay?"

She nodded, but he could tell she was traumatized.

"The man in that black car threatened me," she said.

"Threatened you how?"

"He told me to get in, then he flashed a gun."

Scott automatically pulled Bree against his chest into a gentle hug. "It's okay. He's gone."

For now, he added silently.

Hope White
and
Elisabeth Rees

Guardian's Watch

Previously published as *Covert Christmas* and *Covert Cargo*

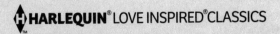

HARLEQUIN® LOVE INSPIRED®CLASSICS

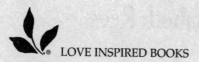

LOVE INSPIRED BOOKS

PLEASE RECYCLE
THIS PRODUCT IS RECYCLABLE

Recycling programs
for this product may
not exist in your area.

ISBN-13: 978-1-335-14310-5

Guardian's Watch

Copyright © 2019 by Harlequin Books S.A.

Covert Christmas
First published in 2014. This edition published in 2019.
Copyright © 2014 by Pat White

Covert Cargo
First published in 2016. This edition published in 2019.
Copyright © 2016 by Elisabeth Rees

www.Harlequin.com

Printed in U.S.A.

CONTENTS

COVERT CHRISTMAS   7
Hope White

COVERT CARGO   259
Elisabeth Rees

An eternal optimist, **Hope White** was born and raised in the Midwest. She and her college sweetheart have been married for thirty years and are blessed with two wonderful sons, two feisty cats and a bossy border collie. When not dreaming up inspirational tales, Hope enjoys hiking, sipping tea with friends and going to the movies. She loves to hear from readers, who can contact her at hopewhiteauthor@gmail.com.

Books by Hope White

Love Inspired Suspense

Hidden in Shadows
Witness on the Run
Christmas Haven
Small Town Protector
Safe Harbor
Baby on the Run
Nanny Witness

Echo Mountain

Mountain Rescue
Covert Christmas
Payback
Christmas Undercover
Witness Pursuit
Mountain Ambush

Visit the Author Profile page at Harlequin.com.

COVERT CHRISTMAS

Hope White

God is our refuge and strength,
an ever-present help in trouble.
—*Psalms* 46:1

This book is dedicated to Washington State Search and Rescue volunteers. A heartfelt thanks to those who answered my many questions: Chris, Guy, Bethany and Brenda from Snohomish County Search and Rescue K9 Unit, along with Andrew from Everett Mountain Rescue, and Justin from Bellingham Mountain Rescue.

ONE

They were close, dangerously close.

Scott Becket sprinted up the trail, hoping to disappear in the brush ahead. He wasn't sure how long he could keep up this pace considering the abuse he'd sustained at the hands of his captors. He was lucky to have gotten away, although without his backpack he wouldn't survive long out here in the Cascade Mountains.

Scott needed the perfect spot where he could camouflage himself until they passed, if they passed, because he knew they were nothing if not determined to find Scott and kill him. After they finished what they'd started earlier—"persuading" him to admit where he'd hidden the proof of criminal activity that could destroy them all.

As long as he had sole possession of the documentation, Scott would breathe another day or two, long enough to gather the last bit of evidence he needed to end this thing.

Eyeing the trail ahead, he hoped he wouldn't run into innocent civilians out for an afternoon hike. Scott didn't want to put others in jeopardy and wasn't sure how far his pursuers would go to secure the information and eliminate Scott, the only person cynical enough to question their plan.

He winced at the pain of bruised ribs as he gasped to fill his lungs with air. Scott berated himself for not catching on sooner. What a fool. Just like he'd been a fool to think he could get water samples to the EPA without being caught. But then he hadn't been thinking clearly for a while now.

They'd distracted him with the illusion of love and happiness. Christa had been so good, too, an expert at making him feel safe and loved. He should have known better. Sweet, perfect women like Christa did not fall in love with damaged goods like Scott Becket.

They'd also distracted Scott with threats against his boss and veiled threats against Scott's sister. He hoped Emily took his message seriously and got out of town. If anything happened to his baby sister—

Crack! He ducked at the sound of a gunshot echoing through the woods. Now they were shooting at him? They wouldn't find zip if they killed him first and asked questions later.

He glanced over his shoulder to see how close they were—

His boot hit a tree root sticking up from the trail and he slammed chest-first against the ground, air ripping from his lungs.

It couldn't end like this, with Scott dead in the mountains, the notes and emails he'd collected never making it to the proper authorities.

Junior would continue his plan, and eventually ascend to an even more powerful position as a governor or senator. Scott knew if the guy made it into office people would die from his greed.

Scott scrambled to his feet, his hiking boots getting a solid grip on the soft earth. He wouldn't give up the fight until he was, in fact, dead.

With renewed focus he took off, eyeing a switchback up ahead.

"Stop!" a man shouted.

Sure, stop running and die. Not a chance.

Another *crack* echoed across the mountain range. He hoped someone heard the gunshot and called 9-1-1.

Scott should have called the cops before now, maybe even called his former partner at the Chicago P.D. Right, and have Joe lecture Scott about his screwup with the Domingo kid and subsequent resignation?

Scott didn't have much pull left with law enforcement, which is why being named head of security for Global Resources International had been such a confidence builder.

Or had that been the plan all along, employ a scapegoat like Scott Becket as a fail-safe, someone to take the heat if it all went south?

He hadn't seen it coming.

Approaching another switchback, Scott reached for a tree to steady himself as he made the turn. His momentum put him dangerously close to the edge of the trail overlooking a steep drop. If he could just make it around the corner and out of sight—

Crack!

Pain seared across his upper arm.

He instinctively grabbed it and stumbled, slipping over the edge and skidding down the lush terrain.

Whack! He came to a sudden stop and gasped for breath. His head throbbed, his arm burned and his ribs ached. He blinked, struggling to focus but his vision wouldn't clear. All he could see was a blur of green above him; all he could hear was the sound of angry voices.

Closer, louder.

A high-pitched ringing cut through the echo of voices.

And darkness consumed him.

Breanna McBride dangled her feet from her position twenty feet up in a tree and gazed at the vast mountain range. The air smelled fresh and invigorating, and the Douglas fir and Western Hemlock scattered across the countryside reminded her that Christmas was only weeks away.

She heard what sounded like a gunshot and wondered if it was a blank fired off to signal the end of the training exercise for the Echo Mountain Search and Rescue K9 unit.

Some might accuse Bree of being overly enthusiastic for hiding out up here; others might call her crazy. But Grace Longfellow, the SAR group leader, asked Bree to plan an exceptional challenge for today's candidates and handlers, so she found this camouflaged spot high off the ground in Woods Pass.

It could happen, Bree mused. A hiker could fall from a trail up above and land in a tree, maybe. Bree figured they should be ready for anything. Today was the final test, the graduation for three more dogs hoping to join the SAR K9 team.

She waited. Turned up the volume on her radio so she wouldn't miss the announcement. The exercise wouldn't have ended until the dogs found Bree, right?

A second shot echoed across the mountains and she

ripped her radio off her belt. "This is Bree. Has the training exercise ended, over?"

"We're still looking for you and one other victim, over," Grace answered.

"But I heard—" Sudden movement caught her eye. A body tumbled onto the trail below, landing maybe twenty feet from her tree. "I think we have a real victim, over."

"He's gotta be down there!" a man's voice called from the distance.

Bree raised her lightweight binoculars and spotted two men heading down the trail.

One of them was carrying a gun.

Her heart raced as her mind clicked off possible reasons why a man would be carrying a handgun in the national park. Hunting was illegal here, and the last time someone was shot in the park it was a private investigator shot by a criminal involved in a theft ring.

Bree's eyes darted from the two armed men to the unconscious one on the trail. She was torn between staying concealed and safe or helping him. Maybe if someone would have helped her when she was with her ex-boyfriend Thomas....

"Don't be foolish," she whispered. How could she possibly defend herself and an injured man against two men with guns?

"Grace, I've got a situation here," she said into the radio. "We may need the police. There are two assailants, one is carrying a handgun, and a third man who is wounded, over."

"Location?"

Bree gave her the coordinates. "I'm turning down the radio so they don't hear you."

"Stay hidden," Grace ordered.

"Copy that."

Bree took a slow, deep breath to calm her frantic heartbeat. She hadn't felt this kind of adrenaline rush, this kind of fear since…

"Thomas," she hushed.

No, she'd left that behind when she'd fled Seattle, returned to Echo Mountain and rebooted her life. She thought she'd erased the fear and trepidation from her mind. From her soul.

The wounded man groaned and managed to stand up.

And that's when she saw the blood seeping between his fingers as he gripped his upper arm.

She glanced to her right. The gunmen were heading straight for him. She snapped her attention to the wounded man. He stumbled a few feet.…

In the direction of the gunmen!

Her gaze snapped back and forth from the gunmen to the wounded man back to the gunmen. With a groan, the man fell to his knees and collapsed on the ground. Unconscious, exposed and so utterly vulnerable.

"No." She flung her leg over the branch and climbed down from the tree, unable to sit here and watch a man be brutalized. She had to help him.

She must be out of her mind.

Hitting the ground, she called in. "Grace, the gunmen are headed my way. I need to help the wounded man, over."

"Bree, don't—"

"I can't watch them kill the guy, over."

She turned down the volume on the radio and rushed to the man's side. He was in his thirties with brown hair and a slight beard, and wasn't carrying a backpack. His shirt was ripped in spots and she noticed a nasty gash above his right eye.

She felt for a pulse. Strong and steady.

Now what? The man was solidly built and probably weighed close to two hundred pounds. His pursuers were five, maybe six minutes away.

"Sir, we have to move. Sir?" She gave him a gentle shake.

He opened his eyes. They were a dulled shade of blue that she suspected were more vivid on a normal day.

"I… Emily?" He blinked a confused expression at her.

"Come on, you're not safe here."

She encouraged him to get up and put his arm around her shoulder. Although worried about his blood loss, she couldn't take the time to dress the wound until they were safely out of sight. Bree led him to the edge of the trail where she'd seen a plateau maybe five feet below. She'd noticed it from her spot in the tree, and made a mental note that it would serve as good cover if someone got caught out here in a storm.

She didn't imagine using it to save a man's life.

"We're going to climb down there." She pointed. "Think you can do it?"

He glanced down below, but didn't answer. He seemed out of it. She touched his cheek and his gaze drifted to her eyes.

"Watch me." She shifted onto her belly and grabbed a tree root. "Hold on to this and edge your way down. It's not far."

She dropped onto the plateau and motioned to him. "Your turn."

At first he didn't move. Instead, his gaze drifted across the lush forest in the distance.

"Hey, Blue Eyes." She clapped her hands.

He looked at her.

"Come on, buddy. Please?"

He sat down and for a second she thought he'd given up. Instead, he shifted onto his stomach.

"That's it, now grab the tree root—"

He dropped down and wavered. She grabbed his jacket, yanking him away from the ledge.

"Good job," she said, releasing him and taking off her pack.

He leaned against the mountainside and sat down, his eyes half closed, his breathing quick and shallow. She wondered if he were going into shock.

"What's your name?" she whispered, joining him.

"My…name," he said, his eyes drifting shut.

Voices echoed across the canyon. She plastered herself as close to the mountain wall as possible to stay out of sight. The stranger leaned against Bree's shoulder. Concerned that the men above might be able to see his legs sticking out, she encouraged Blue Eyes to sit parallel to the mountain wall, hidden from view. She sat cross-legged, and eased him back to cradle his head in her lap.

She stroked his hairline, assessing his head wound, trying to block out the fear and panic of being discovered.

It was at that moment she realized neither her friends nor police would make it here in time to save them. A familiar knot of helplessness coiled in her stomach.

She was the only one she could depend on, the only one this wounded man could depend on.

No, that wasn't totally true.

Our Father, which art in Heaven, Hallowed be Thy name, she thought, reciting the Lord's Prayer in her head to calm the anxiety threatening to take hold.

This all seemed so surreal, like she was watching someone else go through the motions of climbing out of a safe spot in a tree to help a stranger.

"I won't..." the man whispered. "I won't let them hurt you, Emily."

"Shh," she soothed. She needed him to stay quiet, yet she wondered if the pain from his arm wound or head injury was making him agitated.

"He's here! I know he's here!" a man's voice echoed.

They were getting close.

The gravity of her situation suddenly hit her. The wounded man had been shot in a public park in the middle of the day. These men were brutal killers undeterred by anything or anyone.

Her mind started down that terrifying road, the one that led to panic, so she took a slow deep breath and counted to five. Then exhaled, also counting to five. This wasn't just about Bree protecting herself anymore. This was about a wounded man being hunted like an animal.

With her free hand she fingered the silver locket she had bought with her first check as groundskeeper for Echo Mountain Resort. To Bree the dove engraved on the front not only represented the Holy Spirit, but also freedom, freedom to live her life without the cloak of fear clouding her mind, fear of being hurt, fear of making a mistake.

She hoped this wasn't her biggest mistake, she

thought, stroking the blue-eyed man's hair to keep him calm.

"You can't run forever!" a man threatened from above.

Bree stilled. Held her breath.

"He's probably dead," another man with a husky voice said.

"We need proof."

"Forget it. We don't have proper gear to go climbing down mountains."

"Then we'll get gear and come back."

"Are you nuts?" the husky voice challenged. "By tomorrow his body will be torn apart by wild animals. Done."

"He's gonna want proof."

"Wait, what's this?"

Her breath caught in her throat. Had they found something that exposed Bree's hiding place?

"Blood," the husky-voiced man said.

"I told you I nailed him."

"There, it leads over the side."

"You think he's down there?"

Bree closed her eyes and prayed they weren't looking directly down at the plateau. She couldn't be sure that she and Mr. Blue Eyes were completely hidden from view.

"Look down there."

Bree's mind cataloged everything she had in her backpack: water, snacks, compass, map, fire starter, extra clothes and first-aid kit. Wasn't there something she could use to defend herself?

"I don't see anything," the husky voice said.

Blue Eyes groaned, gripping his injured arm.

"Shh," she soothed as best she could, considering the terror filling her chest.

"Did you hear that?"

Silence rang in Bree's ears. She waited. Patted the wounded man's forehead, hoping her touch would soothe him, quiet him.

"You're imagining things," the husky voice said.

"I'm not imagining that blood."

"He went over the edge and hit bottom."

"Or he's right down there."

"Where?"

Bree stilled. They'd figured it out.

With unusual calm, she dug quietly in her pack, her hands searching for something, anything she could use as a weapon.

Rely on yourself and only yourself. That had been her mantra for at least six months following her breakup with Thomas. It had been an isolated existence, but good training for emergency situations.

Like this one.

"You want to go down there and check?" the husky voice said. "Go ahead. I didn't hear anything."

"Then you need to get your hearing checked."

Bree's fingers grazed across her snack bag and water bottle, then brushed across the canister of pepper spray she'd purchased after the mugging.

It was dumb luck that she'd forgotten to take it out of her backpack after moving back to the country. She slipped it out and put her finger on the button.

Calmed her breathing.

Prepared herself for the worst. Although she had martial arts training, this small area wasn't the ideal space to spar with a violent man.

"You got rope?" a male voice said.

"It's not that far," Husky countered. "But I think you're wasting your time."

Bree's pulse sped up. Her heart pounded against her chest.

She could do this. She could defend herself and Mr. Blue Eyes from his attackers.

You naive little country girl, Thomas's words haunted her.

"Emily," Blue Eyes whispered.

"I heard it," Husky said. "Go get him."

Bree held her breath and prayed.

TWO

With a shaky finger on the canister, Bree reminded herself to breathe. Would there be enough pepper spray to immobilize two men if they both came down?

I can do this. I am a strong woman.

The echo of barking dogs sparked relief in Bree's chest. The SAR team was closing in on her location.

"Wait, listen. Dogs, a pack of them," the husky-voiced guy said.

"Wild dogs?"

"No, idiot, search-and-rescue dogs. I saw their van at the trailhead. We've gotta get out of here."

"What about—?"

"Forget it. Let's go."

A few minutes passed, silence ringing in Bree's ears. The gunmen weren't coming down to investigate; she and Blue Eyes were safe for the time being. Now, to make sure he didn't lose too much blood while they waited to be rescued.

The thought snapped her into action. She radioed her position to Grace and dug in her pack for her first-aid kit.

"Grace, the victim will need medical assistance, over," Bree said.

"What's his condition, over?"

"Head injury and gunshot wound. I can deal with the head injury, over."

She pulled out an antiseptic wipe and winced as she cleaned the man's head wound. It was pretty bad and would probably need stitches. In the meantime she applied a butterfly bandage.

His eyes fluttered open. "Who…are you?"

"Breanna, but you can call me Bree."

"Bree…anna," he whispered and his eyes fluttered shut.

"Now comes the hard part," she said to herself. His arm. She'd taken first-aid classes, sure, but a gunshot wound wasn't exactly standard practice.

"Bree, this is Trevor. How's his airway and breathing, over?"

"Seems okay. He's in and out of consciousness. He suffered a head injury, but I'm more worried about the gunshot wound to his arm, over."

"Apply pressure to slow the bleeding," Trevor said. "If it's a through-and-through apply it to both entry and exit wounds. If he goes into shock, cover him up if his skin's cold or remove outer gear if he's hot, over."

"Thanks, over."

"We're a few minutes away. Hang in there, over."

"I'm actually about five feet below the trail, over."

"Copy that," Trevor said.

Bree refocused on tending her patient. She pulled out two spare T-shirts and a scarf. She slid his jacket off, and ripped the material away from his wound, which wasn't as bad as she'd originally thought. It looked as though the bullet had grazed the skin of his upper arm, but didn't pass through his flesh. She wrapped one of the shirts around his arm and secured it with the scarf.

Rinsing blood from her hands with water and antiseptic, she caught herself humming, a coping mechanism she'd developed to stay calm. Only now did she realize what she'd done: saved a man's life, and her own, from armed gunmen.

Up to this point she'd been going through the motions in a detached state, as if she were watching a movie. She'd felt this kind of detachment before. It had been a tool to numb herself to a brutal, violent scene. And there were plenty of those when she'd dated Thomas.

"No reason to think about that," she said, shaking off the unpleasant memories.

Right now, at this moment in time, she was okay, the stranger was relatively okay, and help was close. She could fully freak out and process all this later when she got back to her cottage at the resort.

She pressed the back of her hand against the man's cheek to determine if he was going into shock.

"You're cold, all right." She pulled a thermal blanket out of her pack and covered him up. "Hang in there, buddy. Help's on the way."

The most beautiful sound floated across his mind.

The sound of a woman humming.

She hummed a familiar Christmas song, only he couldn't remember the title. He cracked open his eyes but all he could see through blurred vision was a bright mass of gold.

"Hey there," she said.

He thought she smiled but couldn't tell for sure. Her

voice sounded throaty, yet feminine, and he wanted to hear more of it.

"I…" is all he could get out.

"You're going to be okay."

She was wrong, of course. He knew she was wrong, yet he couldn't explain why. They were both in serious danger and had to get out of here.

"Trip…"

"I would have tripped too if I'd been chased by those goons," she said.

"Have to…go." He struggled to sit up but a firm hand pressed against his chest.

A firm, yet calming hand placed directly over his heart. "It's okay. Those guys are gone. We're safe and help is coming."

He believed her. He didn't know why. He was not the type of man to trust easily or believe strangers, especially not a woman.

"What's your name?" she asked.

He blinked a few times, struggling to make her face come into focus.

"My name?" he said.

"I'm Bree, remember?"

He didn't remember Bree, he didn't remember much of anything.

"I can't… Don't remember."

"Not even your name?"

He shook his head, exhaling a quick breath of panic.

"Hey, hey, it's okay. We'll figure it out."

Her soft warm hand stroked his cheek in a soothing gesture. He closed his eyes, fighting to remember who he was, where he was from and why he was here with this woman.

"You've probably got a concussion. With a little time it will come back to you." She ran her fingers down his hairline to his jaw. Once, twice. "It's going to be okay," she whispered.

But it wouldn't be okay, not unless he… What? What was he supposed to do?

Blinking his eyes open, his gaze landed on her smile. His vision was clearing. That had to be a good sign, right? This view was definitely a good thing. A beautiful woman stared down at him, offering a warm and caring smile. She wasn't glamorous like a cover model. She was adorable, a girl-next-door type of beautiful you read about in novels but wondered if they really existed.

"Your eyes look better," she said, withdrawing her hand from his face.

He wanted to beg her to continue the nurturing gesture, but he couldn't bring himself to say the words. Begging a woman for anything felt wrong, and downright stupid.

"I can see you," he said.

"That's awesome. How's the pain on a scale of one to ten?"

"Pain?"

"Your arm, your head?"

"Were we…hiking together?"

"No, I was out here for a search-and-rescue training mission and saw you fall."

"I fell?"

"Yes."

He struggled to remember why he'd come out here in the first place. His gaze drifted beyond the woman to the brilliant shades of green surrounding them. It was so peaceful out here, so serene.

"One to ten?" she prompted.

He redirected his attention to her. "What?"

"Your pain?"

"Seven?"

"There's no wrong answer. Just be honest and it will all work out."

Honest? Was she kidding?

"That bad, huh?" she said.

"What?"

"The pain. You made a face like someone shoved a lemon in your mouth."

"Yeah, I guess it hurts," he said, concerned that she was able to read him so easily.

"Well, it'll probably get worse before it gets better. We're going to have to lift you out of here and carry you down the trail to an ambulance."

"No hospital." He'd be an easy target for sure. But for whom?

"Sorry, Blue Eyes, but a gunshot wound warrants a trip to the E.R., and probably a meet-and-greet from the local police."

"But—"

"Save your strength."

She placed her hand against his chest again, this time gently patting him in a rhythm that soothed him into a state of relaxation. His eyes drifted shut.

Pain speared down his arm to his fingertips.

"Ah, God," he breathed.

But God couldn't help him, not after everything he'd done.

"Take it easy," a woman's stern voice said. "You're hurting him."

It was the blonde from before. What was her name again?

He opened his eyes. Struggled to focus. But everything seemed to bounce around him. The sky, the trees, the blonde beauty.

"Hey, Blue Eyes," she said. "We're almost there."

He wanted to reach out but his arms were bound to a board of some kind. He must have looked panicked because she slid her hand into his and squeezed.

"We had to secure you to the litter so you'd remain as still as possible. We don't want you losing any more blood than necessary. Okay?" She smiled.

"Okay," he thought he said. Closed his eyes. Listened to the conversation around him.

"Why can't they send a helo?" the woman said.

"No place to land up here. The ambulance is waiting," a male voice answered.

"I'm afraid he's losing too much blood."

"His vitals are good."

"Will they—"

"Bree, take a breath. He's alive. You're alive. All is well."

Something pinched his arm. He opened his eyes. "What, ouch."

"Hello, Mr. Smith," a young female paramedic said. "I'll call you Mr. Smith because we couldn't find any identification and it seems more dignified than calling you Mr. Blue Eyes." She sneered at the cute blonde woman standing on the other side of him.

Her name, he desperately needed to remember the blonde's name.

"Are you allergic to any medications?" the para-medic asked.

"I don't…think so."

"Can you tell me what day it is?"

His gazed drifted past her to the lush forest in the distance. They were outside, surrounded by green. How did he get here again?

"Sir?"

He glanced at the paramedic, a twenty-something brunette with a tattoo of a butterfly on her neck. "It's daytime."

"Do you know what day it is?"

He glanced at the blonde beauty. She offered an en-couraging smile. It didn't help.

"How about your name?" the paramedic said.

"I told you he doesn't remember," the blonde said with an edge to her voice.

"Sir, do you know where you are?" the paramedic tried again.

"Mountains," he gasped, hating the sound of his voice. Weak. Defeated.

"What city or state?" she asked, administering some-thing into his IV.

"I… Washington?"

The blonde beauty offered a bright smile. He could look at those green eyes, that joyful smile all day long.

"Do you remember the trailhead or mountain you went climbing this morning?"

He glanced at the blonde. She started to mouth some-thing.

"Bree!" the EMT scolded. "No cheating."

"Sorry." Bree put up her hands.

Bree, that's right. A charming name.

"Okay, let's get you into the ambulance." The paramedic nodded at someone behind him. The stretcher shifted slightly, then he was lifted up into the ambulance.

"Bree," he said, panicked. He reached out hoping to touch her again, feel her calming presence.

"It's okay. I'll meet you at the hospital," she said.

He may not make it to the hospital. He didn't know the brunette with the butterfly tattoo. He didn't trust her.

"Bree." He struggled to sit up.

"Easy there, Mr. Smith. You don't want to pull out your IV."

"Bree," he croaked, desperate, trying to roll off the stretcher.

Suddenly she was beside him, holding his hand.

"Right there is fine," the paramedic ordered Bree, then said to the driver, "Okay, Roscoe, let's go."

He turned his head to the left, needing to see Bree, look into her green eyes. Green like the forest. Her image started to blur again. He was losing focus, losing consciousness.

"I can't… Bree…"

He closed his eyes, but felt her squeeze his hand.

"What's happening to him?" she asked.

"It's probably the pain meds," the paramedic said.

"But he should stay conscious, shouldn't he? Especially if he has a head injury?"

"Calm down, cuz. He's stable. It's all good."

He was drifting in and out, picking up only pieces of conversation.

I couldn't let him die.

Two gunmen?

He wasn't with them; they were after him.

That was foolish.

I don't care. He needed me.

You don't even know him.

He squeezed her hand, struggling to stay connected, to stay conscious.

"It's okay," a woman whispered against his ear.

It was Bree's voice. He'd know it anywhere.

He couldn't remember his own name, where he'd been or how he'd ended up in an ambulance. Those three things should drive him to the brink of despair.

But they didn't because Bree was here. He took a deep breath, clung to her hand and drifted.

"You've upset him," Bree snapped at her cousin Maddie.

"Right, so it's not the bullet wound or head injury that's got him freaked out," Maddie said, sarcastically. "Look, I shouldn't have let you ride along in the first place, so stop busting my chops."

"I'm worried about him." She noted Mr. Blue Eyes' skin looked pale.

"He's not your problem."

Bree ignored the comment and stroked the back of his hand.

"Bree?"

She glanced at her cousin, who frowned with concern.

"You didn't see him, Maddie. He was so—" Bree glanced at the bruise forming around his head wound "—broken."

Maddie reached over and touched Bree's shoulder. "I'm sorry."

With a nod, Bree glanced back at the stranger. They both knew Maddie's words referred more to Bree's terrible Thomas past than the current situation.

"He's okay," Maddie said, pausing as she unbuttoned his shirt. "Whoa."

"What?"

"He's got a lot of redness on his chest and stomach, like he was beaten up."

They pulled up to the hospital.

"This is as far as you go, sorry," Maddie said.

The back door opened. Two sheriff's deputies stood there, along with Echo Mountain Police Chief Lew Washburn, and Wallace Falls Police Chief Charles Trainer, who Bree's family fondly called Uncle Chuck.

Two officers and two police chiefs? Blue Eyes must be in big-time trouble.

"Bree," he groaned, opening his eyes.

Maddie shot Bree a disapproving look.

"I'm here," Bree said, squeezing his hand.

The other paramedic came around and helped Maddie lift the stretcher out of the ambulance. Blue Eyes didn't release Bree's hand.

Uncle Chuck approached. "Breanna, we need to—"

"I'll be right back," she interrupted.

She walked alongside the stretcher, offering words of comfort to Blue Eyes. "You'll be okay. They'll take care of you here."

"Don't leave."

"I'll stay close, promise."

"You've got to let him go, Bree," Maddie said as they wheeled him into the E.R.

Bree released his hand.

"No, Bree," he gasped, and the look in his eyes nearly

tore her apart inside. Pure and utter devastation coupled with fear. She'd seen that look...in the mirror.

She motioned for her cousin to stop the stretcher and Bree leaned close to the stranger. "I'll be right outside. Let them fix you up so you can get out of here and do something fun."

"With you?"

Bree shot a quick glance at Maddie and looked back at the stranger. "Sure."

"You won't leave me?"

"I won't leave you."

He released her hand and they wheeled him into the examining area. Bree automatically reached for her locket, praying for guidance. Had she done the right thing by making that promise? Of course she had, because it had calmed him down enough to release her and get much needed medical attention.

"Breanna?"

She turned to Uncle Chuck and Chief Washburn.

"Hey, hi, Uncle Chuck." She gave him a hug. Chuck had been a friend for years and helped out after Dad had passed away.

They broke the hug and she nodded at Lew Washburn. "Hey, Chief."

"Let's sit down and you can give me your official statement." Chief Washburn motioned her to the waiting area.

Breanna hesitated, not wanting to break her word to Blue Eyes.

"We'll be close to the examining room," Chief Washburn said.

With a nod, Breanna accompanied them to the waiting area, positioning herself so she could keep an eye on the door.

"Do you know the victim?" Uncle Chuck asked her.

"No." Although she felt oddly connected to him in a way she couldn't explain.

"Tell us what happened," Chief Washburn said.

As Bree retold the story, she clicked into that distancing mode, the place where it felt as if she was talking about someone else.

"You jumped out of the tree to help him, knowing he was being pursued by two gunmen?" Uncle Chuck said.

She didn't miss the disbelief in his voice, nor the disapproval.

"They would have killed him," she said.

"They might have killed you," he scolded.

His tone sparked shame through her body, but she pushed it aside. She would not feel ashamed for saving a man's life.

"They were far enough away that I didn't feel I was in immediate danger," she said. "I thought I had enough time to help the man hide until authorities arrived."

"When I tell your mother—"

"Please let me do it. I'll call her as soon as we're done."

Bree surely didn't want people tattling on her, although considering how many people had probably heard about the morning's events, Bree suspected Mom already knew. Small towns were like that.

"What else can I tell you?" She directed her question to Chief Washburn.

"A description of the gunmen."

She described what they looked like, trying to recall details from when she viewed them through the binoculars.

"One of the men said 'he's gonna want proof,'" Bree said.

"You were so close that you could hear what they were saying?" Uncle Chuck's voice pitched.

"Uncle Chuck, I've been through a traumatic event. It's just now hitting me how dangerous it was and you're not helping."

"I'm sorry, you're right, I'm sorry."

But it was natural for him to worry. He was protective of the McBride clan.

"Let's all take a breath," Chief Washburn said. "Breanna's okay, but we have two gunmen on the loose and we need to involve as many law enforcement personnel as possible to track them down so no one else gets hurt."

"They had accents," Bree said.

"Foreign or…?" Chief Washburn asked.

"Midwest, Chicago. You know that nasal A sound?"

"Okay, that's good." The chief wrote something in his notepad. "As I understand it, there was no ID on the victim?"

"That's right."

"Did he tell you his name?" Chief Washburn asked.

"He doesn't seem to remember it."

"Convenient," Uncle Chuck muttered.

"He's got a nasty head wound," she said defensively.

The E.R. doors opened to the outside and she spotted a familiar group of people: the SAR K9 team, along with Bree's brother, Aiden, and their mom. So much for Bree calmly breaking the news to Mom about today's events. Bree's best friend, Billie, and her fiancé, Quinn, were also with the group.

Aiden marched up to Bree, who put out her hand in a stop gesture. "I'm fine, but I need another minute to give my statement."

She didn't miss Mom's worried frown, or the angry twist of Aiden's mouth. He'd better not be angry with her or she'd let him have it. Bree had been holding it in these past few hours, trying to remain calm and levelheaded for Blue Eyes. It wouldn't take much for her to lose her cool, especially with family who she knew loved her no matter how cranky she got.

Bree finished describing the two men. Chief Washburn asked, "About the gunshot victim, any idea who he is or why he was assaulted?"

"No, sir. He didn't say much, although he said a name, Emily, and that he'd keep her safe."

The chief jotted something down. "Did he have a backpack?"

"No, sir. Maddie the EMT made a comment about his chest and torso looking red, too, like he'd been beaten up."

"And he said nothing that would give us a clue what he was doing out on the trail?"

"No, sorry."

"It seemed like he's bonded with you," Chief Washburn said.

Mom and Aiden were within earshot, but she didn't care. "Yes, sir, I believe he has."

"He trusts you?" Chief Washburn said.

"He's scared. He can't remember anything, even his name, and he's in a strange hospital with multiple injuries. He needs to trust someone."

"And you're okay with that?" Chief Washburn said.

"Yes, sir."

"Even though this could be a dangerous man?"

"We don't know that."

"Someone was shooting at him," Uncle Chuck interjected.

"I know," she said, glancing at him, "I was there, remember?"

Bree wasn't usually a smarty-pants, but she was tired of people passing judgment on her. They'd passed judgment on her relationship with Thomas, which is one of the reasons she'd stayed silent about the emotional abuse for so long.

A few people had also given her a hard time about no longer doing hair when she'd moved back to town, instead choosing to be a groundskeeper, working for her brother who managed Echo Mountain Resort. Everyone seemed to have an opinion about Bree's life. Some days she wished they'd all spend their energy worrying about themselves.

"I can't make any sense out of your behavior today," Chuck said.

"Why don't you go check on Margaret?" Chief Washburn suggested to Uncle Chuck.

Chuck had obviously lost objectivity in regards to this situation because of how much he cared about Bree's mom. It was the worst kept secret in town.

Chief Washburn closed his notebook. "I'm going to assign an officer to watch over the victim. I'm sure your family is going to encourage you to detach from this situation."

"I can't," she said.

"Because?"

"I feel a connection to him."

Chief Washburn studied her and waited for more.

"I know what it's like to feel lost and vulnerable,"

she said, "to feel so scared and there's no one to help you. I've been there."

"Well, truth is your connection to this man could be my best lead, but I won't be responsible for stirring up trouble between you and your family. If you stick close to him and discover anything that might help with my investigation, please call me." The chief handed her a business card with his office and cell numbers.

"Of course."

He hesitated before standing. "Breanna, you are a remarkably brave woman."

"Thank you, sir."

She glanced past him at the group of family and friends in the waiting area. They probably wouldn't call her brave or applaud her decision to help the stranger.

Bree had survived a violent event, yet had kept it together long enough to give her statement to police. She needed time alone to regroup, a few minutes to let the reality of her situation wash over her—but in private so she wouldn't get emotional in front of her family.

"Hey, Chief, I need to use the washroom. Would you mind telling my family I'll be right back?"

"Sure."

Bree slipped away, hurried down the hall into the single-stall bathroom and locked the door.

She was okay; everything was fine. She studied her reflection in the mirror. The chief would circulate a description of the attackers, and Blue Eyes would get his memory back and help them figure out why someone had tried to kill him.

No matter what her family said, she knew in her heart she'd done the right thing by helping him. She wouldn't allow her overly protective brother to make her feel guilty or ashamed by her actions.

Splashing cool water on her face, Bree considered the words she'd spoken to Blue Eyes. *I'll stay close, promise.*

Maybe she shouldn't have said that, but she desperately wanted him to get medical attention and it seemed as though promising to stay close was the only way to make that happen.

"Looks like I'm hanging around for a while," she whispered to herself, because Bree didn't break promises, even to strangers.

This should be fun, explaining to her family and friends why she was sticking close to a man she barely knew. Make that a man she didn't know at all, heck, she didn't even know his name.

She pulled her hair back, spread gloss on her dry lips and applied a little blush to look healthy, not exhausted. They'd be waiting and wanting details, a reason as to why she'd jump into the midst of gunfire. The only explanation she could offer was that it was the right thing to do.

"Don't second-guess yourself," she said to her reflection in the mirror. That behavior had gotten her into trouble before.

She grabbed her pack and left the bathroom. As she ambled down the hall, she took a deep breath and touched her necklace for strength.

Her family and friends were passionate about keeping her safe because they loved her.

Love, a complicated emotion.

She glanced up and noticed a man leave the E.R.

examining room heading in her direction. Boy, it was busy tonight at the Echo County E.R.

She politely smiled at the man as he passed, and he nodded in return. Distracted by thoughts of defending herself from her family, it took a few seconds before she realized he looked familiar.

"I was about to come find you," Aiden said, walking up to her.

In a flash it hit her: the man she just passed was one of the gunmen.

And he'd come out of the examining area where they'd taken Blue Eyes.

"No, no, no," she muttered, shoving her brother aside.

"Bree?"

She rushed past him and flung open the doors to the examining area. The curtains were pulled back and all the beds were empty.

THREE

"Can I help you?" a nurse asked Bree from the corner of the room.

"A man was brought in, thirties, dark hair, blue eyes, slight beard."

"Mr. Smith?"

"Yes, where is he?"

"They moved him."

"Bree, what are you doing?" Aiden said, following her into the examining area.

She turned to him. "Is Chief Washburn still here?"

"Yes, he's—"

"Go tell him I just saw one of the shooters."

"He's here? Are you sure?" Aiden's face reddened.

"Yes, go."

Bree turned back to the nurse and focused on speaking as calmly as possible as she fought the panic building in her chest. "Mr. Smith's in danger. You need to tell the police where he's been moved so they can protect him."

"Sure, okay, let me check the computer." She went to a terminal and tapped on the keyboard.

"Did anyone else ask about him?" Bree pressed.

"I don't think so, but I just got here."

Chief Washburn rushed into the examining area. "Where did you see him?"

"He passed me in the hallway just now," Bree said.

"Description?"

"Black jacket, maroon shirt. It was the older one, in his sixties, with salt-and-pepper hair, wearing a blue baseball cap with a red *C* on it." Bree shook her head in frustration. "I smiled at him because I didn't realize who he was at first."

"That's a good thing," the chief said. "He won't know we're onto him, and he won't suspect that you recognized him."

The chief spoke into the radio on his shoulder, giving instructions to his officers. He glanced at the nurse, "Room number?"

"Still checking."

"Are you done with my sister, Chief, because I'd like to take her home," Aiden said.

"I can't leave," she said.

"Breanna—"

"They moved him to room 214 on the second floor." The nurse interrupted Aiden.

"Closest stairs?" the chief said.

"Around the corner on the left," the nurse said.

Bree started to go with him, but the chief blocked her. "Please stay with your family where it's safe."

"I have to make sure he's okay."

"That's our job." He nodded at Aiden. "Take her to the waiting area, but don't leave the hospital."

"Yes, sir."

The chief spoke orders into his radio as he rushed

out of the examining area. The doors closed behind him and Bree fingered her necklace.

"Hey," Aiden said.

She glanced at him.

"Mom's freaking out. You should probably…" He motioned toward the waiting area.

With a nod, she went to the door and pushed it open, facing her family and friends. Mom rushed to her and offered a loving hug, holding on as if she feared Bree might disappear. Understandable given Bree's history. It had been almost two years since she had abruptly packed up and moved to the city on a quest for more excitement in her life. She had learned the hard way that excitement was overrated.

"I'm okay, Mom." Bree broke the hug and squeezed Mom's hands. "Really, I'm good."

As the rest of the group started firing off questions, Bree put up her hand to silence them.

"I appreciate your support, especially you guys." She nodded at the SAR K9 team members who'd come to the hospital: Grace, Trevor, Christopher and Luke.

"Bree, what happened?" Bree's best friend, Billie, asked with worry in her eyes.

As Bree described the events of the past few hours, she watched her family and friends' expressions change from disbelief to shock to concern.

"She did a brave thing," Trevor offered.

"A potentially deadly brave thing," Aiden said.

Tears welling in her eyes, Mom studied her daughter like she'd never seen her before.

Billie gave Bree a hug. "Quinn and I are headed to California on business tomorrow, but I think I should stay and keep you company."

"No, don't you dare stay back on my account. I'm fine."

"That's debatable," Aiden muttered.

"What do you mean?" Mom said.

Aiden narrowed his eyes at Bree, probably expecting her to confess she'd developed an unhealthy and inappropriate connection to a stranger with a gunshot wound.

"I'm okay," Bree confirmed. "No injuries."

"Good, then we can go home," Mom said, reaching out to take her hand.

"I can't leave the hospital," Bree said.

"Why not?" Mom asked.

"Here we go," Aiden muttered.

"Chief Washburn asked me to stay, and even if he hadn't, I want to be here for Mr. Smith when he wakes up."

"Breanna—"

"Mom, he has no one, no friends, no family here at the hospital. He doesn't even remember who he is. I was able to comfort him and he needs me."

"You don't even know him," Aiden snapped.

"That doesn't make his pain any less real," Bree countered.

"This isn't your responsibility."

"No one should be so scared and alone."

"Are we still talking about that guy or you?" Aiden accused.

"Aiden, that's enough," Mom said.

He planted his hands on his hips and glanced at the floor, shaking his head.

"Breanna is right. The stranger has no one." Mom scanned the group of friends surrounding them. "We have the wonder of love and friendship." Mom cracked a proud, gentle smile at Bree. "And the Lord would want us to share our gift."

Surrounded by gray, floating in a mass of nothingness, he couldn't be sure he heard the voice. Where was he again?

I'm going to kill you, slowly, painfully.

An inferno of panic exploded in his chest, the pressure causing him to gasp for air. He wanted to call out but could barely stay focused, much less shout for someone to help him.

I'll beat you until you give it up, the voice threatened.

He struggled to form words, willing his vocal cords to kick into gear. If only he could get his mind to grab on to something other than the paralyzing anxiety coursing through him.

Then I'll smother you with a pillow.

"Can I help you?" a woman's voice said.

The blonde woman? Right, because he'd made her promise to stay close. No, please God, this couldn't be her. If the man threatened to suffocate him with a pillow he'd surely have no problem hurting the woman.

The woman? Bree. That was her name.

"Bree," he gasped, remembering her beautiful green eyes, her grounding smile.

A hand gripped his fingers and squeezed. "I'm here."

No, she shouldn't be here. His attacker was close, in the room, poised to smother and kill him. Which put Bree in the way because she was tending to him, holding his hand. He tried to pull away, wanting to let her go so she'd be safe.

"What is it?" she said.

He opened his eyes and she came into focus, her sparkling emerald eyes and heart-shaped face framed with golden hair.

"Danger," he rasped.

"It's okay. There's no danger."

"He said…was going to…kill me."

"No one's here but me." She glanced above him. "And the nurse."

He shifted his head to the side and spotted a brown-haired nurse fiddling with a machine beside his bed. She smiled down at him.

"See, you're A-okay," Bree said.

He turned back to Bree. "He was here."

"In your room?"

He nodded.

She exchanged a glance with the nurse.

"I'll go get the officer," the nurse said.

He didn't take his eyes off Bree. "Officer?"

"A police officer was assigned to your room last night because I saw one of the shooters."

"In my room? You were here when he…?" His voice cracked before he could finish.

"It's okay." She stroked his arm with one hand while still holding onto him with her other. "He passed me in the hallway, that's all." She offered a tender smile. "Are you sure you saw him in here?"

"I heard him."

"He threatened you?" she said.

He nodded.

"I'm so sorry." She sighed. "That must have been terrifying."

Not as terrifying as the thought of the guy hurting Bree.

He was suffering a major head injury all right. Why else would he be more concerned with this woman's well-being than his mission? His mission, which was what again? He couldn't remember. He wasn't even sure how he'd ended up in the hospital.

"What's wrong?" she asked, as if she sensed his anxiety.

"I don't remember how I got here or, sorry, but I don't remember how I know you."

"You don't remember being shot?"

He shook his head.

"Do you remember your name?"

"Scott."

"Nice to meet you, Scott," she said with a relieved smile.

He wondered why she cared so much about him.

A police officer marched up to his bedside. "Ma'am, I should be asking the questions."

"Of course, sorry." She didn't move, still clinging to Scott's hand.

"If you wouldn't mind," the officer said, and motioned for her to leave.

"I don't, go ahead and ask your questions."

The cop narrowed his eyes at her in frustration. "Breanna."

"Ryan," she challenged back.

The cop shook his head, figuring he'd lost this round, and refocused on Scott.

"Sir, I'm Officer McBride with the Echo Mountain P.D. I've been assigned to keep you in protective custody tonight. Would you mind answering some questions to help us with the investigation?"

"Very professional, A plus," Bree teased.

Officer McBride glared at her.

"Sure," Scott said, trying to shift up in bed.

Bree released his hand and adjusted his pillow behind his back. When she sat back down, he automatically reached for her hand, he wasn't sure why, and she gave it willingly. That got another narrowing of eyes from Officer McBride.

"Let's start with your name," the cop asked, pulling out a small notebook.

"Scott, Scott…" He hesitated. A voice in his head warned that sharing his last name would put him in more danger. "I don't know, Scott something."

"Age?"

"Thirty-one."

"Your occupation?"

"I'm…" He wracked his brain, searching for work or even family-related memories. "I'm a cop," he said, but it didn't feel right. "I think."

"You're not sure?"

"No sir."

"Where do you live?"

"A big city. Detroit? Chicago?"

"What brought you to Echo Mountain?"

"I needed to…"

They would die. He needed to save them.

"I don't remember." He closed his eyes.

He felt Bree squeeze his hand in a supportive gesture, but he couldn't look at her without feeling the shame of failure. Was she one of the people who would die because he couldn't see this through to the end?

"Scott?" the cop said.

He opened his eyes.

"What *do* you remember?"

An image flashed across his mind of a teenager splayed on the ground clinging to a flashlight.

"I don't…" He shook his head. "I'm not sure."

"Anything could help."

"It's all jumbled."

"Do you remember being chased in the mountains?"

"I think so."

He remembered being chased but couldn't be sure if it was a recent memory or a distant one.

"Why do you think those men were chasing you?"

"I don't know."

"You didn't have any identification on you. Did they take it?"

"I guess."

"You sustained trauma to the torso area. Do you remember them assaulting you?"

"I…" He caught glimpses, flashes of images.

"Scott, why did they shoot you?"

"Enough, Ryan," Bree snapped. "You're upsetting him."

"It's my job to get answers, Breanna."

"Well, he's obviously not up to giving you answers, so back off."

"I'm calling the chief." He turned and walked out.

"You do that," she muttered.

It was like they were ten-year-olds fighting over the last peanut butter cookie. A rush of memories filled his thoughts. Scott cracked a smile. They reminded him of he and Emily when they were kids, always competing with one another.

"What's so funny?" she challenged.

"You guys remind me of me and my sister."

"Hey, you remembered something, that's great."

"Yeah, memories from twenty years ago," he said. "So what's the deal with you and the cop?"

"Ryan practically grew up at our house, so he's more like a brother than a cousin. And one thing I do not need is another overly protective brother-type in my life."

"It's not their fault."

She cocked her head in question.

"There's something about you that makes us want to take care of you."

"Well, you shouldn't. I've taken karate and carry a wicked can of pepper spray in my bag, police grade." She cocked her chin.

Yet he sensed trepidation behind her confident words.

"Can I ask you something?" he said.

"Sure."

"Why are you here?"

"Do you want me to leave?"

"No, of course not. I'm just trying to figure out how I got so lucky."

"You were shot, sustained a concussion and bruised ribs. What's so lucky about that?"

"The fact that a beautiful woman is sitting beside my bed."

She blushed and glanced at their hands. "You're embarrassing me."

"Sorry, it was meant to be a compliment." Scott didn't remember a lot, but he knew that most women appreciated compliments.

Wasn't it obvious Bree wasn't "most" women?

"How's Mr. Smith?" a doctor said, coming into the room.

"Actually, he remembered his name," Bree offered.

"Excellent." The doctor extended his hand to Bree. "I'm Dr. Vann and you are who, his girlfriend?"

"No." She blushed again. "Just a friend."

She looked even more adorable when she blushed. Scott's chest ached with wanting something he could never have—a gentle, nurturing woman like Bree in his life.

"Let's take a look." Dr. Vann flashed a penlight in Scott's eyes and examined his head wound. "Head injuries are tricky. I suspect you're suffering from retrograde amnesia, a condition where a patient forgets the events preceding and immediately following the head injury. The severity of the injury will affect how far back you can remember. Do you recall what happened leading up to your injury?" The doctor jotted something on a clipboard.

"No, sir," Scott answered.

"What is the last thing you *do* remember?"

A memory sparked in his mind of he and his partner, Joe, interviewing a witness. "I remember a case I was working on."

"And when was that?"

"I'm not sure."

"Do you know why you're in the hospital?" the doctor asked.

"Someone shot me."

"So, you remember the shooting?"

"Not really."

Dr. Vann glanced at Scott.

"I told him what happened," Bree said.

"We should probably let him remember on his own," the doctor said.

"Oh, okay, sorry."

Scott did not want her feeling badly because of him and he knew the sooner he got out of here and away from Bree, the safer she'd be. "How long do I have to stay in the hospital?"

"Overnight to keep an eye on the head injury." Dr. Vann glanced at a pager on his belt. "I'll check in later. The best thing for the patient is rest." The doctor nodded at Bree and left the room.

A phone vibrated in Bree's pocket and she pulled it out, glanced at the text and frowned.

"You need to go," Scott said. "It's okay."

"It's not critical. It's my brother pulling his boss card to get me away from," she hesitated, "the hospital."

"You mean away from me?" He cracked a half smile.

"Pretty much. Don't take it personally. The perks of having an overprotective family."

"Sounds nice." And it did, especially since he'd grown up in a single parent household with a mom who had to work two jobs to support Scott and his sister. There had been no extended family, no protective adults to keep an eye on Scott and Emily.

He suddenly grew tired and couldn't hold back a yawn.

"I should let you sleep," she said.

"Okay," he said, but he didn't let go of her hand. His eyes drifted shut and his mind wandered, his imagination landing on a peaceful, majestic view of a valley from the top of a mountain.

And beside him stood the adorable Breanna with the enchanting smile.

Bree decided to spend the night at the hospital. Her family and friends followed Mom's lead and supported

Bree's decision to help the stranger. Once the police determined the gunman was no longer in the hospital, Bree sent everyone home while she hovered at Scott's bedside. She was even able to convince Aiden to feed and walk Bree's dog, Fiona, but not without a lecture.

At first Bree wasn't sure hospital staff would let her hang out all night, but Chief Washburn said it was okay and left 24-hour police protection outside Scott's room. Bree felt safe and was where she needed to be—beside Scott's bed.

When they'd come in to check his vitals he'd wake up with a panicked look, asking where he was and what had happened. Bree would tell him he was safe, everything was okay, and he'd drift back to sleep.

But morning came and Aiden demanded she show up at work by noon or find another job. It was an empty threat, of course, but she respected his position and did as ordered, leaving Scott alone. She hoped he'd sleep most of the day to give his body a chance to heal.

She didn't like being away from Scott, but couldn't rationalize blowing off an entire day of work to babysit a grown man, a stranger. Still, when she thought about the vulnerable look on his face she knew she'd get back to the hospital. She only wished it was earlier than eight in the evening.

Thanks to big brother Aiden, she had extra holiday lights to string along the split rail fence bordering Resort Drive. No surprise that he'd told the other part-timers to go home at three because he was watching his payroll numbers.

Truth was, he was doing his best to keep her busy and away from the hospital. Since Aiden was tied up with a guest when it was time for her to leave, she avoided lecture number seven, or was it seventeen?

Pulling into the hospital lot, she parked near an overhead light and glanced out her window before getting out of the car. She hoped tonight's staff knew she was on the list of people allowed to come by after visiting hours.

As she marched across the lot, she started to wonder if everyone was justified in worrying about her attachment to Scott. She didn't have the best track record with romantic relationships; make that a dismal track record.

But this wasn't about romance, it was about helping someone in need, a man she felt a visceral connection to when she looked into his wary eyes.

She rode the elevator to the second floor and when she got out she noticed the absence of a police officer outside of Scott's room. She fought the panic ringing in her ears. Perhaps Scott had remembered something and the officer on duty was in his room taking his statement.

Her pulse quickened as she stepped into the doorway. "Scott?"

The bed was empty.

"Can I help you?" a nurse said coming down the hall.

"Scott's gone" was all Bree could get out.

"Are you a relative?"

"Where is he?"

"A police officer took him away."

"Took him where?"

"I'm assuming to lockup. He was arrested."

FOUR

"Arrested?" Bree said. "How long ago did they leave?"

"Maybe ten minutes?"

"Where were they taking him?"

"I'm not sure."

Bree spun around and rushed toward the stairs. As she passed the elevators, the doors opened and her cousin Ryan marched out. Bree hesitated.

"Why did the police arrest Scott?" she asked.

"What are you talking about? I was sent to relieve Officer Waters."

"Then Waters arrested him?"

"No one arrested him that I know of."

"He's gone, Ryan. The nurse said he was arrested."

"That's not right." Ryan motored to the room as if he couldn't comprehend Bree's words. When he spotted the empty bed, he shot her a concerned frown and pressed the button on his shoulder radio. "This is Officer McBride. Where did Officer Waters take Scott Smith, over?"

Bree and Ryan stared at each other, both dreading the response about to come through the radio. Was this a mix-up or had something nefarious happened?

"Officer Waters said he was relieved twenty minutes ago by a sheriff's deputy, over."

Ryan went to the nurse's station. "Who authorized the patient in room 214 to be released into police custody?"

The two nurses turned to the doctor standing behind them.

"Not me," the doctor said.

"Please check the patient's chart," Ryan said, calmly.

The redheaded nurse typed something into the computer. A few nerve-racking seconds passed, then she said, "Dr. Vann released him."

"Please page him for me," Ryan instructed the redheaded nurse.

Bree turned and headed for the elevators.

"Where are you going?" Ryan called after her.

She shook her head, frustrated.

"Stay out of this, Bree."

Man, she was tired of people telling her what to do. Ever since the Thomas trauma people treated her like a fragile doll, breakable by the slightest touch.

The elevator doors opened but she decided she needed to walk instead and took the stairs. She was worried, beyond worried, suspecting that whoever was after Scott in the mountains had managed to kidnap him from the hospital to finish what they'd started.

Or was she overreacting because she'd developed an unhealthy attachment to the stranger with the striking blue eyes? She got to the ground floor and was about to open the door to the main hallway, when she heard a voice drift up from the basement level. She leaned against the railing, but couldn't see the source of the voice.

"I got him released, but he was fighting it. I couldn't overmedicate him or he wouldn't be able to walk out on his own…. No one is in delivery at this time of night. It's fine."

Bree stepped back, whipped open the door and took off into the hospital. She spotted an orderly.

"Delivery entrance?" she asked.

"Why do you want to know?"

She didn't have time for a lengthy discussion so she rushed past him and found a map on the wall. Pausing long enough to figure out the location of the delivery entrance, she ripped her phone out of her pocket and called her cousin Ryan. It went into voice mail. He probably kept the ringer off during his shift. She hung up, fearing by the time he got her voice mail it would be too late.

Scott would be gone, maybe even dead.

Her phone vibrated. Ryan was calling her back.

"They took him out the delivery entrance," she said, without waiting for him to speak. "I'm headed there now."

"No, Bree, don't—"

She ended the call and focused on getting to the entrance and…and…what? Once again she was throwing herself into a potentially dangerous situation in order to save Scott. Mom would be upset; Aiden would be furious. What was Bree supposed to do, let the gunman kidnap Scott against his will?

The mystery voice, which she suspected was Dr. Vann, said Scott was fighting his captor. Good, that meant they might not have left the hospital. She hoped. She prayed.

She got to the delivery area and flung open the door. A long storage aisle led to a dock where they dropped off supplies for the hospital. She yanked a fire extinguisher off the wall as a weapon, and rushed to the end of the dock.

Heart racing, she peered across the back lot into the woods bordering the hospital. She saw nothing, heard no one.

She was too late.

"Scott!" she cried.

Two police cars, lights flashing, sped into the lot.

"Breanna," her cousin said, coming up behind her. "You should have stayed back."

"He's gone," she said, looking into Ryan's brown eyes. "They got him, and they're going to kill him."

He glanced down at her hand, her fingers digging into his arm, then back at her face. "We'll find him."

"Officer McBride!" one of the cops called.

Bree and Ryan both glanced at him. He held up what looked like a hospital ID bracelet. "Found this at the edge of the woods."

"Stay here," Ryan said.

He went to help the other two officers search the surrounding woods. She put down the fire extinguisher and paced, fretted and nibbled her fingernail. Not able to stand it any longer, she hopped down to aid in the search.

"Breanna, I said get back," Ryan ordered.

She froze, but didn't retreat. She needed to be close in case they found Scott. They had to find him or else that meant...

She struggled to calm her breathing, the sound of silence ringing in her ears as she watched them fan out to search the perimeter.

"I've got blood here," one of the officers announced. "It leads this way."

Without waiting for permission, she took off into the woods.

"Bree!" her cousin called.

Scott collapsed in a pile of wet brush and gasped for air. The guy had convinced everyone, including Scott, that he was a legitimate deputy responsible for bringing Scott in for questioning.

Only when they got to the guy's car did Scott suspect something was off. Way off. The supposed deputy had parked in a dark corner of the back lot as if he didn't want to be seen. Through somewhat blurred vision, Scott realized he wasn't getting into a typical cruiser but a rented, high-end luxury vehicle.

Wrong. There's no way a county deputy or small-town P.D. would spring for such an expensive car. Scott got into the back and when the "deputy" slid behind the wheel, Scott darted out the other side, racing for the woods.

The lush evergreens seemed close one minute and miles away the next.

The fake deputy caught up to him and they struggled, but Scott managed to nail him with an uppercut that brought the guy down. Scott sprinted as fast as his exhausted body could take him, deep into the dark woods where he could hide from his kidnapper. He assumed it was one of the guys from yesterday, one of the guys Bree had told him about, but didn't know for sure.

Scott couldn't remember much about the past few days or months, except for the obvious: he'd gotten himself into a world of trouble.

As he stumbled through the woods, he barely felt the branches scraping his cheeks and hands as he forged ahead into the mass of trees.

He staggered to a downed tree trunk, climbed over it and collapsed on the other side, using it for cover. He hated this, hated hiding like a coward, but with his limited brain function he'd be stupid to go on the offensive. Instead, he'd hide out and wait. For what, to be rescued?

Not likely. He was rescued yesterday by the adorable blonde and her friends but no one was lucky enough to be rescued twice in two days. He closed his eyes, waiting for the inevitable, trying to think of another strategy to buy himself a little more time.

Time to finish something important, but what?

He heard the crunch of footsteps against fallen twigs as his attacker closed in. Scott was going to die. The man had said as much when he'd threatened him in the hospital.

Scott.

But it was *her* voice, the beautiful, gentle voice that awakened him yesterday, calmed him when he thought he'd go mad. In his last minutes on earth he was hallucinating, hearing the gentle voice of Breanna calling out to him.

"Scott!" Her voice carried across the dense forest.

He blinked open his eyes. It wasn't a dream.

"I'm here," he croaked, his voice raw and weak.

"Did you hear that?" a man said.

Scott shrank lower into the earth. Maybe her voice wasn't real, after all. Had he imagined it to keep from falling into a pit of despair?

"Scott, it's Breanna. Are you out there?"

Bree was here? But why was she with the man who tried to kidnap him from the hospital?

"Scott, it's Officer McBride from yesterday. I'm with your friend, Breanna. We're here to help. Where are you, buddy?"

"Breanna," Scott said with as much force as he could manage. "Over here."

He tried sitting up, but his body felt as though someone had pumped lead into his veins. He could hardly move. "Breanna."

A light flashed above him, and then pinned him with its powerful beam.

"Scott." She came into view, a frown of worry creasing her forehead.

"You're here," he said.

"I'm here." She smiled, a smile that made everything right.

Relief drifted over him like a thick blanket on a cold winter's night. He studied her green eyes, and a sense of calm washed over him.

"Are you okay?" she said. "Did he hurt you?"

"I… I'm tired."

"It's okay. We can talk later."

She stroked his hair. He leaned into her touch knowing he was safe as long as she was near.

Bree spent the next day sticking close to Scott, more like hovering, until he was discharged in the afternoon. She didn't trust the hospital to keep him safe from his attackers after the incident last night. The men who were after Scott were terribly bold to impersonate a deputy and attempt to kidnap him from the hospital.

Bree had told Chief Washburn she thought she'd

heard Dr. Vann's voice in the stairwell, but it turned out the doctor was off duty so it couldn't have been him.

Rather than ruminate about what had nearly happened, she focused on the positive—Scott was okay. She held his hand and comforted him when he thrashed in his sleep, and hoped that he'd wake up and remember something that could help him defend himself against these men.

When he finally awoke, he didn't remember much more than he had when they'd first brought him in. Thankfully someone had recognized him from photos the local police were circulating and identified him as Scott James, a guest at Echo Mountain Resort. Bree heard from Ryan that Chief Washburn was checking with Chicago and Detroit police departments to confirm Scott's identity.

Dr. Vann wasn't convinced Scott should be discharged considering he'd been drugged last night, but Scott wanted out of the hospital and Bree couldn't blame him.

Chief Washburn sent Officer Carrington to escort them to the resort, probably at the urging of her uncle Chuck, who still worried that she was developing an unhealthy attachment to Scott.

The hospital volunteer pushed Scott to the exit door in a wheelchair and he stood, tentatively. Bree gripped his arm for support.

"Thanks," he said, gazing down into her eyes.

It was that look, a look of deep appreciation tinted with fear that kept her close. He shifted into the front seat of the SUV and she shut the door. Fiona started barking in the back, so Bree tapped on the window. "Stop."

Fiona sat and stopped barking. What did Bree expect? There was a new person sitting in the front seat and Fiona hadn't been officially introduced. How dare Bree allow a stranger into her car.

Into her heart.

She buried that unwelcome thought and got behind the wheel. "Sorry about the dog. She's protective."

"A good thing," he said. "You're lucky to have her."

Bree pulled away from the hospital and spotted Officer Carrington in the rear view mirror following close behind.

"Breanna?"

"Yes?"

"I have no idea what's going to happen next, but I wanted to make sure I said thank you for everything you've done."

"You're welcome."

"I'd probably be dead if it weren't for you."

She knew firsthand that focusing on the darkness only made things worse so she tried to lighten things a little.

"Right, a good thing I'd been hanging out in a tree, trying to outwit the K9 dogs."

"Is that why you were there?"

"Yep, it was the final test to approve them for duty."

"And you were in the tree because hikers climb trees after they're wounded and immobilized?" The corner of his mouth curled.

Good, he had a sense of humor. That would get him through the tough road ahead, both the physical recovery and the violence that seemed to be hounding him.

"A hiker could fall and get stuck in a tree, or a paraglider could miscalculate his landing, or—"

"I get it, I get it," he said with a smile.

Her heart skipped. His genuine smile was the first pleasant interaction they'd had. Everything else up to this point had been tainted with worry or panic on his part, and determined protection on hers.

"What?" he said, studying her.

"What, what?"

"You look, I don't know, pleased."

"You smiled." She glanced back at the road. "It's nice to see you smile."

A few seconds of silence passed. Breanna couldn't help but wonder who this man really was and if he had family, or a wife. It didn't matter. She would offer assistance until his family showed up to care for him.

"Can I ask you something?" he said.

"Of course."

"Why are you doing this?"

"Driving you to the resort? That's where you're staying. Don't you remember?"

"I meant, why are you helping me?"

"Because it's the right thing to do."

"Why do I sense there's more to it?"

Interesting that he could read her so easily when she'd been told by plenty of people that she often came off as aloof and detached. Well, ever since her time under Thomas's rule, anyway. That's when she'd learned to hide her true feelings so he wouldn't be able to use them against her.

"I'm sorry," Scott said.

She snapped her attention to him briefly, then refocused on the road. "Excuse me?"

"Your expression turned terribly sad. I sense it's my fault."

"It's not you. I was remembering something."

"Bad, huh?"

"An old boyfriend and how he controlled me."

"You're kidding." He chuckled.

"You're laughing at me?" she said, her tone more hurt than angry.

"Wait, no, I'm sorry, it's just, the way you ordered hospital staff around, the demanding tone you took with sheriff's deputies—"

"That was one deputy and he's my cousin."

"Trust me, from where I'm sitting, you're definitely in control."

"Thanks, I'll take that as a compliment."

"Good. I would not want to get on your bad side. You know karate." He winked.

"You really are remembering things."

"I remember stuff since the accident, but not what happened leading up to it." He glanced out the passenger window. "That would be the most helpful right now."

"It'll come back to you."

"I hope it's not too late."

"Too late for what?"

He glanced at her and frowned. "I'm not sure."

She exited the expressway and headed for the resort.

"After you drop me at the resort, we can't see each other again," he announced.

"Whoa, I've heard brain injuries can cause rude behavior, but that was a little over the top."

"I'm trying to protect you."

"First things first. I'll help you get settled in your room, then we can argue about breaking up," she joked.

"You seem awfully cavalier about this."

"I don't mean to come off that way, but focusing on the negative stuff only stresses us out more."

She parked in the back lot and pointed at her two-bedroom cottage in the distance. "That's my place, if you ever need anything." She opened her door. "Come on, Fiona and I will get you settled."

She got out of the car and shook off the odd, painful sting she'd felt when he said he never wanted to see her again. He was only considering her well-being.

Officer Carrington pulled his cruiser into the spot next to Bree's.

She opened the hatch and let Fiona out of the back of the truck. The dog immediately ran up to Scott to check him out. Although most golden retrievers were happy pups, Fiona tended to be wary of people. Yet she wasn't wary of Scott. Fiona did her hip wiggle dance, wagging her tail enthusiastically. Scott reached down and stroked her head. Fiona posed in a perfect dog sit and looked up at him.

"She's a sweetheart," he said.

"She has her moments." Bree smiled down at her puppy. She still considered the two-year-old dog a pup since she could play for hours and never get tired. A good trait for a rescue dog.

Officer Carrington joined them as they headed for the building. "I'd like to go in first," he said.

"Whatever you think is best." Bree motioned him ahead. "He's in room one twelve, on the right."

They went into the building, Fiona trotting between Bree and Scott like a proud pup. Scott seemed to be walking steadily, not like before at the hospital.

"You're feeling better?" she asked.

"Head still hurts, but my vision's pretty clear and I don't feel like the floor is shifting on me."

"That's a good sign," she encouraged.

They got to his room and she handed the key card to the officer.

"Please wait out here," he said.

"Of course." She leaned against the wall and sighed.

Scott studied her. "You have to be beat."

"What makes you say that?"

"Every time I opened my eyes you were there, so I'm assuming you haven't gotten much sleep in the past two days."

"I can function on very few hours of sleep."

"Then why haven't you finished cleaning up around the tennis court?" Aiden said, walking up to them.

Fiona started to rush Aiden, but Bree gave her the command to stay.

"Scott, this is my brother Aiden."

"The manager of the resort," Scott said, shaking Aiden's hand.

"One and the same. And being manager, I can decide if a guest has overstayed his welcome."

"Aiden," she said in a scolding tone.

He ignored her and leveled Scott with a threatening squint of his eyes. "After they find your ID and wallet, I'll expect you to be checking out."

Bree grabbed his arm and pulled him away from Scott. "What's the matter with you?"

"It's dangerous for him to be here."

"It was dangerous when those men were after Billie, but you let her stay here."

"That's different. She's family."

"It's okay," Scott said. "He's right. I'll leave as soon as I can."

The door to his room opened and Officer Carrington motioned them inside. "All clear."

Scott went into the room and Bree followed.

"Bree, where are you going?" Aiden said.

"Someone in our family should be hospitable. Fiona, come."

The golden rushed to her master's side, they went into the room and shut the door on her brother.

She bit back her embarrassment at Aiden's behavior and took in her surroundings. It was a mini-suite complete with kitchenette, living room and separate bedroom. These rooms were designed for extended stays.

"I've been ordered to keep you under surveillance, Scott," Officer Carrington said. "If nothing else, the sight of the cruiser in the lot and me outside your door might deter the assailants from returning."

"Great, thanks." As Scott ambled to the sliding glass door he touched a suit jacket stretched across a chair as if it looked foreign to him.

"I'm going to patrol the grounds out back." With a nod, Officer Carrington left.

Bree didn't like the odd look creasing Scott's features but before she could question him her phone vibrated with a call. She glanced at the screen. "It's my mom."

"Your brother is right," he said, staring out across the grounds. "You should go."

She went to him and touched his shoulder. "I'm not going anywhere until I know you're okay, but I need to take this call."

He nodded, not looking at her.

"Hey, Mom." She went to the kitchenette.

"Honey, I got a call from Aiden."

"Wow, that was fast." Bree glanced inside the fridge. It had a carton of orange juice and a few to-go containers.

"He's worried about you. We're all worried."

"Thank you for that. I'm blessed to have such a loving family."

She glanced at Scott, who disappeared into the bedroom.

"Don't get me wrong," Mom said. "You're doing a wonderful thing, Breanna. But your brother and I are concerned that Scott's problems will become your problems, that the danger will spill onto you."

"Scott's been assigned 24-hour police protection so he's safe. Also, since we're at the resort we'll get Harvey to help keep an eye on things."

"Yes, well that makes me feel a little better. Harvey would never let anything happen to you."

True enough. Bree shared a special bond with Harvey, the resort's security manager. She considered him more of a father figure than a coworker.

"Everything will be fine, Mom."

"You sound so sure of yourself."

"You're going to have to trust that I wouldn't put myself in unnecessary danger."

"I… I'd like to believe that."

Bree could hear the question in Mom's voice, probably because she was remembering all the months when Bree claimed to be fine, when in fact she was not.

"Don't worry," Bree said.

Hoping to assuage Scott's worry about Bree's safety

as well as her mom's, she wandered toward the bedroom and said, "I'm perfectly safe."

Bree stopped short in the doorway.

Scott sat on the bed gripping a pistol in his hand.

FIVE

"I'll call you later, Mom." Bree pocketed her phone and took a deep breath to calm her frantic pulse.

"Scott?"

"I found this on the nightstand." He glanced at her with confusion in his eyes. "Why do I have a gun?"

"I'm sure you had a good reason."

"I'm not a cop anymore, I know that much."

"Why do you say that?"

"A cop would never carry a .50 caliber cannon like this. It's overkill."

He placed the gun on the bed beside him. "Call Officer Carrington, or your cousin, or the police chief. I need to be arrested."

"For owning a firearm?" she said, walking over and sitting next to him on the bed. "Lots of people own guns."

"Don't try to make this okay, Breanna." He stood and paced to the window. "It's not okay."

A few seconds of silence passed between them. She wanted to help, but wasn't sure how. Telling him everything was going to be okay didn't seem to comfort him.

"Call the sheriff's office and have them take me in to be fingerprinted."

"Don't you think you should rest first?"

He turned to her, his eyes now dark with anger. "Call them, or I'll call 9-1-1."

She ignored his threatening expression because she sensed the anger was directed at himself. "I'll get Officer Carrington."

She plucked the gun from the bed by its grip, walked it into the main living area and placed it on the breakfast bar. Although her words were meant to calm them both, she realized this changed things. If he didn't have a permit for the gun, which he probably didn't since his wallet had been stolen, then could he be arrested for illegal possession of a firearm?

Grabbing the wall phone, she called the security office to enlist Harvey's help.

"Security," he answered.

"Harvey, it's Breanna."

"Hey, Bree, how's our amnesiac guest?"

"Word travels fast. Harvey, I have a situation and need your help."

"Name it."

"I have to track down the police officer assigned to Scott. He's on the grounds somewhere and I need him to come to Scott's room."

"I'll find him. Everything okay?"

"Sure." She glanced into the bedroom. Scott flopped down on his back, his good arm draped over his face.

"Let me know when you find him, and maybe you'll want to come by, too."

"I'm on it."

She ended the call and went into the bedroom to sit

beside Scott. He must have felt the bed shift because he opened his eyes and looked at her. "You need to go."

"Scott—"

"Now! Get out of here!" He got up, marched into the bathroom and slammed the door.

Scott stared into the mirror at his harried expression: his cheeks red with anger, his eyes wild with fear. If the woman had any sense at all she'd be gone when he opened the bathroom door because the way he looked right now scared even Scott.

If only he could escape himself, he mused, flipping on the tap. He splashed his face with cold water. This self-pity was starting to wear on him. He wasn't that guy, the kind of man who let things happen to him without trying to defend himself. Yet with only part of his brain functioning, he felt more than a little frustrated.

And lost.

Except when he was looking into Bree's beautiful green eyes.

"That's a side effect the brain trauma," he told himself.

It had to be. Women were not something you relied on for strength, at least that had been Scott's experience. He practically raised both his mom and little sister after Dad had left, and as far as romantic relationships... He pinched his eyes shut, trying to remember something, someone.

But only a high school girlfriend who broke it off when she went to college, and a few fleeting trysts filtered into his thoughts. Yet he thought there had been a more serious relationship.

His head started to pound. "What difference does it

make?" he muttered. Once the cops came and retrieved his gun, he'd be arrested for sure.

He felt himself being sucked into the self-pitying vortex again and fought it. There was more at stake than Scott's personal situation, a lot more.

The doctors had warned him that a head injury could cause emotional highs and lows, anger issues and even symptoms of depression. Whatever. He didn't have the luxury of suffering from such ailments.

It was time to pull himself out of this funk and face his situation head-on, without the help of his beautiful and caring crutch named Breanna.

He finger-combed his hair back off his face and took a steadying breath. Somehow he needed to get his memory back. That had to be his primary focus.

He opened the door to an empty bedroom. Good, she left as he'd requested. Still, he went into the main living area to be sure.

An older man in his mid-sixties glanced up from analyzing the gun on the breakfast bar. "I'm Harvey, the resort security manager. Officer Carrington should be here shortly." Harvey walked over and shook Scott's hand. "Sorry to hear about your situation. Bree told me you don't remember anything leading up to the assault."

"Bree, is she…?"

"Gone. Got a SAR call."

"SAR?" Scott asked.

"Search and rescue. A kid went missing on a field trip into the mountains. They called in the K9 team to assist, hoping the dogs could track her quickly. So—" Harvey sat at the breakfast bar "—want to tell me about this gun?"

"Wish I could."

"Don't remember much, huh?" Harvey pressed.

"No, sir, although, I was a cop. I remember that much."

"Well, we have that in common."

"You were on the job?" Scott shifted onto a bar stool.

"Yep, Seattle P.D. This is my official retirement." Someone knocked on the door. "That'll be Officer Carrington." Harvey went to let him in.

"Where is he?" an angry voice said.

"Aiden, cool your jets."

Bree's brother stormed around the corner and came at Scott. "You brought a gun into my resort?"

Aiden grabbed Scott by the arm, ripped him off the bar stool and shoved him against the wall. Pain reverberated down Scott's arm from the gunshot wound to his fingertips.

"My sister was in this room, with a gun?" Aiden slugged him in the jaw and stars crossed Scott's vision.

"That's enough!" Harvey pulled Aiden off of Scott.

Scott swiped at his lip with the back of his hand and eyed his attacker. "I'm sorry."

That only infuriated him more. Aiden broke free of Harvey and pinned Scott against the wall yet again. This time he hesitated before striking.

"Do it," Scott said. "Just do it."

Scott deserved the beating and then some. He'd failed so many people in his life, and was about to fail a bunch more.

Aiden glared, his jaw twitching with his struggle for self-control. Instead of hitting him, he let go with a jerk that banged Scott's head against the wall.

Stars fluttered across Scott's vision again and his legs buckled.

"Whoa, whoa," Harvey said, gripping Scott's arm and guiding him to the couch.

Nausea rolled through Scott's stomach as the room spun.

He must have passed out because the next thing he heard was a rather intense interrogation of Bree's brother, Aiden.

"How hard did you hit him?"

Scott cracked open his eyes. Officer Carrington was firing off the questions.

"Not hard, I didn't hit him that hard. At least I didn't mean to."

"But you did, and now we've got two armed assailants running around Echo Mountain, a questionable firearm and the only one who could shed light on this case is out cold because of you. Give me your hands." Officer Carrington ripped the cuffs off his belt.

This was wrong. Scott understood Aiden's motivation and didn't blame him for being furious. Scott had put Bree in danger by letting her into his room, into his life.

Aiden slowly offered his wrists to the officer.

"No," Scott croaked, sitting up and gripping his head. It ached worse than before. "It's not his fault."

"He admitted to assaulting you," Officer Carrington said.

Squinting, Scott glanced at the officer. "A misunderstanding. I'm not pressing charges."

Aiden cocked his head as if trying to figure out Scott's angle. But there was none. Scott wouldn't be responsible for Bree's brother being charged and taken into custody. She'd never forgive him, and for some reason her opinion of Scott meant a lot right now.

Someone knocked at the door and Harvey opened it. "Chief," he said in greeting.

Chief Washburn marched into the room. "What's going on?" he asked, glancing from Officer Carrington to Aiden, to Scott.

"Supposedly a misunderstanding," Officer Carrington said. "This is what I called about." He handed an evidence bag to the chief with the gun tucked inside.

"A .50 caliber Desert Eagle? Is it registered?" the chief asked.

"I have no idea." Scott massaged his temples. "If I carried registration it would have been in my wallet." Scott glanced up. The chief and Officer Carrington hovered over him, wanting answers. Scott had none.

He glanced at Aiden who sat in a chair studying the floor.

"I would have done the same thing," Scott blurted out.

Aiden glanced at him.

"That's your job as a big brother. I get it. I've been there."

"Focus on the gun, Scott," the chief said.

Scott redirected his attention to the chief. "Sir, if I knew anything I'd tell you."

The chief's phone beeped. He glanced at it and shook his head. "As long as you're being honest," the chief started, then pinned Scott with a serious frown. "You said you were a cop?"

"Yes."

"Then how about telling us why the name Scott James doesn't come up in any law enforcement databases?"

* * *

Bree and Fiona headed into the national park, teamed with Will Rankin. Will would focus on the map while Bree watched Fiona, looking for tell signs. Grace and her lab, Dodger, were accompanied by Griffin Swift, and three other SAR members followed along as well in case the missing child needed to be carried out on a litter. Bree had strapped on her mission-ready pack and was at the trailhead in a matter of minutes.

As they hiked toward the last spot the child was seen, Bree inhaled the crisp mountain air, glad she'd noticed the text on her phone when she had. It gave her something to do, something productive and helpful after being ordered to leave by Scott.

She suspected he pushed her away because he feared for her safety, which only made her respect him more. She knew how strongly he relied on her, so pushing her away must have been extremely difficult.

"So how is he?" Grace said over her shoulder.

"Who?"

"The mysterious Scott? That's who you were thinking about, right?"

"That obvious, huh?"

"Pretty obvious."

Grace was a lovely fortysomething woman with auburn hair, who acted like an older sibling A non-meddling older sibling.

"Scott's better, I guess."

"Must be scary, not remembering anything."

"It puts him in a very vulnerable position," Bree said.

"I can imagine." Grace pulled out her topographical map encased in plastic and reviewed the area. "Should be right up here."

"The rest of the kids came down already?"

"Yes, sheriff's office didn't want to risk more kids wandering off to find their friend so they ordered them to come back down. Here it is." Grace hesitated and glanced back at her team. "Heather was last seen forty-five minutes ago in this general area. Ready?" Grace offered the article of clothing with Heather's scent to each of the dogs.

The three K9 handlers split up, heading into the thick brush of blackberries, devil's club and rotting logs. Bree was glad to have Will as her partner. He had both field EMT experience and little girl experience, since he had two girls of his own.

Fiona was unusually excited today, perhaps because she didn't get her twice-daily walks for the past few days and had extra energy.

"That's it, Fiona. Good girl," Bree encouraged.

"Heather!" Grace called out, although they all suspected the little girl must be unconscious or she would have answered to her teachers and friends calling out her name earlier.

Bree glanced at the sky. They had plenty of daylight to work with, which was good.

"At least it's decent weather," Will commented. "On my last mission it poured nonstop for five hours."

"Yikes, which one was that?"

"The hiker that got separated from his buddies in Crystal Pass."

"Oh, right. That was a nasty day to be out."

"Bet you're sorry you missed it."

"Very funny. Would have been there, but had a family thing."

"Well, my girls weren't too happy with me when I

went out on the call. I said I'd avoid SAR missions for the next month."

"Yet here you are."

"They're with their grandparents."

"Why do you do this, anyway?" she asked. "I mean you're so busy with work and your girls."

"I like to help, you know, find people."

Yes, she understood completely. It felt good to focus on helping someone else rather than ruminating about your own miseries and losses. Will had suffered his share of loss. His wife died of cancer, leaving him to be a single parent.

And Bree? Adopting Fiona and joining SAR when she moved back to town kept her busy and focused on helping others instead of wallowing in her own shame.

"It's certainly a good feeling to be proactive and help people," she offered.

They'd been searching for a good half hour when Fiona started pulling hard on the leash and stuck her nose to the ground.

"What is it, Fi?" Bree said.

A splash of pink stuck out from the dark green brush up ahead. Bree stomped over wild blackberry bushes in an effort to get to Heather.

Please, God, let her be okay.

Fiona rushed to the little girl, sniffing and nudging. "Okay, girl, okay. Grace, we've located Heather, over," Bree said into her radio.

"Coordinates?"

Will rattled them off and kneeled beside Heather to examine the little girl. She was curled up in a ball, but he was able to slide her mitten off to take her pulse.

"It's strong," he said. "Maybe she hit her head."

Fiona went in for a kiss on Heather's cheek. "Fi, no." Bree pulled her back.

"Heather, honey? Can you hear me?" Will said.

She whimpered. Will and Bree shared a look.

"Can you open your eyes?" Will said.

She shook her head no.

"Why not?"

"I'm scared," she moaned.

"Are you hurt?" Will asked.

She shook her head again.

Bree nodded at Will, then at Fiona.

"Good idea," Will said softly.

"Heather, honey, I need your help," Bree said. "My dog, Fiona, is scared, too. You know why?"

Heather nodded she didn't.

"Because she's worried about you. Can you open your eyes and tell Fiona you're okay?"

The little girl blinked a few times, and opened her eyes. Bree relaxed the leash and Fiona went in for a sniff. Heather giggled and reached out to pet Fiona.

"Thank you so much," Bree said. "You ready to go home?"

"Can Fiona come with me?"

Bree smiled. "No, honey, she's got to stay at my place and be ready to find more missing kids like you. But I'll tell you what, she'll walk you down to the trail where your mom and dad are waiting."

"Heather, before you get up, are you sure you didn't fall and hurt yourself?" Will asked.

Heather offered her hand, scratched from a thorny bush.

"How about I clean that out and wrap it?" Will said.

"Will it hurt?"

"Not too much."

"Here." Bree led Fiona to the other side of the little girl. "You can pet Fiona while Will fixes your cut, okay?"

"Okay."

Bree commanded Fiona to lie beside the little girl, and Heather reached out to stroke Fi's head. Bree pressed the button on her radio. "The victim doesn't seem to have any serious injuries, over," she said. "We'll meet you where we split up, over."

"Roger," Grace said.

Fiona crawled closer to Heather and sniffed her cheek. Heather giggled. The golden knew exactly how to distract her from Will's first-aid efforts.

In a few short minutes, he was finished. "Okay, let's get you up," Will said. He put his hands under her armpits and lifted her with ease. Bree suspected he'd done this many times with his girls. "How does that feel? Legs working okay?"

"Yes," she said, not taking her eyes off Fiona, who also stood.

"Great, then let's get you home," Will said. "It's kind of messy out here. Do you think you can walk?"

"Can Fiona carry me?" she said.

"She wishes she could," Bree said. "Here," she handed Heather the leash, and picked her up.

"You sure?" Will asked Bree.

"I'm good." With the little girl in her arms, and both of them holding Fiona's leash, they headed back to the trail.

It had been an emotional afternoon to say the least. She pulled into the driveway of her bungalow and put Fiona into the fenced yard. Harvey jogged up to her.

"Hey there," she said.

"Got word you found her," Harvey said, raising his hand.

She slapped him a high five. "Fiona found her, I just happened to be tagging along."

"You're too modest."

"How's Scott?" she said.

"Scott, he, uh…" Harvey glanced down.

Her blood pressure spiked. "What? He's okay, right?"

"He's okay, but they took him in for questioning."

"Because of the gun?"

"And he's been lying."

"Lying about what?"

"They couldn't find any record of a cop named Scott James."

"I'm sure there's an explanation."

"Probably not a good one."

"Where'd they take him?"

"Bree, leave it alone."

"Wish I could." She pulled open the driver's door and got behind the wheel. "Where?" she said.

"Chief Washburn took him to the station."

"Thanks."

Harvey blocked her from shutting the door. "Be careful."

"If you're worried about Scott, don't be. He'd never hurt me." She pulled the door shut and backed out of the driveway. Fiona was fine outside, and if it started to rain she had the doggie door that gave her access to the kitchen.

As Bree raced into town, she checked the speedometer. She didn't want to get delayed because of a speeding ticket. No, she needed to get to the police station and…and…

What? What was she doing, exactly? One thing for sure, she wasn't thinking straight. She'd told Harvey that Scott would never hurt her. Was she delusional? She didn't know Scott that well. How could she make such a bold statement?

His eyes.

There was something about the look in his eyes that touched her core, reminding her what it felt like to be scared and alone. She'd promised herself she'd never feel that way again, and she surely wouldn't stand by and watch another person be brutalized and not try to help.

Or maybe she was losing her mind.

The emotional afternoon had taken its toll: worrying about a lost girl, praying for her safety, finding her, and at first thinking she was…dead.

And then Bree had carried her out of the brush, emotions tangling up even more at the feel of a little girl depending on Bree, needing her so badly. Would Bree ever have a child of her own? Hold a child of her own?

Wow, talk about an emotional volcano. Bree was all over the place. Maybe so, but she knew one thing: Scott was being interrogated and had no one in his corner.

That is, until she got there.

Ten minutes later she pulled onto Main Street and looked for a spot in the lot, but it was full. She parked across the street and glanced out her window. The chief was escorting Scott out of the building. Now where were they taking him? She flung open her car door.

"Scott!" she called.

She thought he spotted her, but looked quickly away

as the chief led him to a squad car. She glanced both ways to safely cross the street.

"Hey!" she called out again and took a step.

The squeal of tires made her glance over her shoulder. A black car sped up and stopped abruptly in front of her. The passenger door opened and a man wearing dark sunglasses and a low-hung baseball cap said, "Get in."

Was he nuts?

"No, thank you," Bree said.

"I said—" he placed a gun on the driver's seat in a not-so-subtle threat "—get in."

SIX

"Something's wrong," Scott said to the chief, eyeing Bree as she spoke with the driver in the black sedan.

There was something about her expression that made Scott head in her direction.

"Where are you going?" Chief Washburn said.

"She's in trouble."

Scott took off, not considering what he'd do once he got to the car, or how embarrassed he'd be if his instincts, like his brain, were off-line.

He wanted to call out, let her know he was coming to help, but he couldn't even speak, panic strangling his vocal cords.

"Scott!" Chief Washburn called.

Scott hoped the chief followed him. At least the guy had a firearm. Scott had nothing but a sincere desire to protect Bree.

Dodging into the street, Scott was hyperfocused on the lovely but terrified blonde who stepped away from the car with a horrified look on her face.

"Bree!" Scott called.

A car horn screamed.

Brakes squealed.

Scott glanced to his left in time to see a compact car skidding toward him. The driver spun the wheel at the last second and the small car slid past Scott and slammed into a parked car. Scott turned back to the dark sedan just as the driver peeled away, burning rubber on the street.

Without hesitation, he went to Bree and placed gentle hands on her shoulders. "Are you okay?"

She nodded, but he could tell she was traumatized.

"What was that about?" Chief Washburn said, rushing up to Scott and Bree. He led them between parked cars to the sidewalk as he spoke into his radio. "We need an officer on Main Street. There's been an accident." He redirected his attention to Bree. "You okay?"

"The man in that black car threatened me."

"Threatened you how?"

"He told me to get in, then he flashed a gun."

"Did you recognize him?" the chief asked.

"No, sir."

Scott automatically pulled Bree against his chest into a gentle hug. "It's okay, he's gone."

"Did either of you get a plate number?" the chief asked.

Bree shook her head.

"I think the first three letters were AGE," Scott offered.

The chief took a few steps away and spoke into his shoulder radio again, telling officers to be on the lookout for the black sedan. Scott stroked Bree's soft hair in a calming gesture. "You're okay."

She leaned back and looked up into his eyes. "Thanks to you."

"I wouldn't go that far."

"I would. If you hadn't drawn attention to him I might have been in his car headed to who knows where."

"But you didn't get in his car. Smart girl."

"We'll keep an eye out for him," the chief said.

Bree broke the hug, but Scott kept a protective arm around her shoulder.

"Scott saved my life, Chief."

The chief nodded at Bree. "How about you come into the station and give an official statement about what happened?"

"Sure."

"Head back inside while I check on the driver over there."

"Tell her I'm sorry for running in front of her," Scott said.

With a nod, the chief jogged across the street and spoke with the teenager who stared at her crushed front bumper, with her hands framing her face.

"Come on, let's go," Scott said.

Bree stepped away from Scott's protective hold and he wondered if she thought it inappropriate, or if she was worried about town gossips. There were plenty of gawkers out here getting a look at the fender bender. He respected her need for space and didn't push it.

As they crossed the street and headed into the P.D. parking lot, he felt her hand slide into his. He gave her fingers a squeeze, and only then did he notice they were trembling.

He glanced at her, but you'd never guess by her expression that she was rattled. With a firm clench of her jaw and pleasant expression, she walked across the lot toward the police department. No one would suspect she was probably on the verge of bursting into tears.

And if she did, he'd be right there to comfort her.

They stepped into the police station where a twenty-something secretary was focused on paperwork.

"Hi, Audrey," Bree said.

Audrey the secretary glanced up. "Breanna, what are you doing here?"

"There was an accident. I need to give a statement. The chief's outside…." Bree's voice trailed off.

The magnitude of her situation was about to hit her square in the chest.

"Is there a place we can wait privately for the chief?" Scott said.

Audrey narrowed her eyes at him. She didn't like the fact he was here with Bree, probably because Scott had just been questioned by the chief about his real identity.

"He saved my life, Audrey," Bree said. "I really need to sit down."

Audrey snapped her attention to Bree. "Of course, follow me."

Scott and Bree followed Audrey down the hall into a conference room and sat on one side of the table, next to each other.

"Do you want me to call—"

"No," Bree interrupted her. "No need to call anyone. I'll be fine."

With one last narrowing of her eyes at Scott, Audrey went back to her post out front.

"How did it go with the chief?" Bree said.

"We don't have to talk about that now." He took one of her hands in his own and stroked it gently. "You're still shaken up."

"Thanks, but it will distract me from what just happened," she said.

"Ah, so you're using my ill fortunes to distract you from your own? I didn't think you were that kind of girl," he teased.

"Ha ha." She cracked a slight smile. "So, what did I miss when I was on the mission?"

"First tell me how the mission went."

"Good. We found the little girl. She's okay," she said with a faraway look in her eye.

"Breanna?" he prompted.

"That look on her face of complete and utter fear...." She hesitated. "It stays with you for a while."

"But you found her. Everything's okay?"

"Well, everything was okay until Harvey told me you were brought in for questioning. Did they advise you of your rights? Do you need a lawyer? I have a friend who's an attorney. I could call—"

"I wasn't arrested. They thought fingerprinting me might be helpful, so they did. I hope..." He glanced at their hands.

"What?"

"I hope they don't find out I'm a murder suspect or drug dealer or something."

"Hey, don't talk like that. You said you were a cop."

He shrugged. "Even cops go bad."

"Scott, look at me."

He glanced up. She shot him that peaceful, tender smile that seemed to calm every frantic thought in his mind.

"You are not a criminal," she said with conviction.

"Thanks for the vote of confidence, but I can't be so sure. I mean, I had a .50 caliber gun in my room." He shook his head, frustrated. "At least once they run the serial number it might answer some questions."

"We're also sending it to ballistics," Chief Washburn said, coming into the room.

"Ballistics? Why?" Bree said.

"So they'll be able to tell if it was used in any other crimes," Scott explained.

"Oh." Bree frowned.

"Let's focus on what happened just now," the chief said, pulling out a chair and joining them at the table. "The driver of the black sedan threatened you with a gun, Breanna?"

"Yes, sir."

"Did he indicate what he wanted?"

"He ordered me to get in the car."

"Did he give a reason?" The chief jotted something down.

"No, sir."

"I need you to tell me exactly what he said."

"He said 'get in.' When I didn't…" She glanced at Scott and then down at the floor.

"What?" Scott said.

She sighed. "He said if I wanted to know what my boyfriend was into that I'd get in the car and he'd show me."

"Show you what?" the chief asked.

"I have no idea."

Scott stood and paced to the window overlooking the parking lot. "So I *am* into something illegal."

"Wait, you're going to believe the word of a man who tried to kidnap me at gunpoint?" Bree challenged.

"There's no reason to think he's lying," Scott said.

"Actually, there is," the chief said.

Scott turned around.

"I got the report that Scott James has no priors or known criminal activity."

"See," Bree said.

"Maybe I just haven't been caught."

Bree couldn't stand the look in Scott's eyes, one of desperation and shame. But he had nothing to be ashamed of, at least nothing they knew about yet.

She gave him a ride back to the resort and an officer followed close behind. Even though Bree felt confident Scott wasn't the bad guy here, others in the community, especially law enforcement, weren't so sure.

The chief must have notified Aiden about the developments, because he was waiting for them when she pulled into her parking spot.

"He doesn't look happy," Scott said.

She turned off the car and Aiden opened her door. "We need to talk."

"Okay. I was going to walk Scott to his room."

"That's why Officer Carrington is here, right?" Aiden said.

"I was going to check the dressing on his shoulder wound."

"What, are you his private nurse now?"

"Why are you being so rude? Scott saved my life."

Aiden glared at Scott. "You wouldn't have needed the save if he'd never come to Echo Mountain."

"Get out of my way." Bree brushed past him. "Come on, Scott."

When he didn't follow, she turned around. Scott slowly approached her. "I don't want to be the reason that you and your brother fight," he said. "I appreciate you wanting to help, but you've done more than enough for me." With a grateful smile, he headed for the resort. The officer followed him.

It sounded as though he was dismissing her from her duties. But this didn't feel like a duty. It felt right and natural to be helping him.

"He'll be fine," Aiden said.

She spun around. "Why do you hate him so much? You don't even know him."

"And you do?" he snapped.

After the emotional day she'd had, she didn't need her big brother criticizing her. She marched toward her cottage.

"Wait, Bree."

She kept walking, fuming about everything that had happened in the past forty-eight hours, from her brother's rudeness toward a wounded man in need, to a stranger threatening her with a gun.

It seemed strange that Scott's enemies would hang around town considering law enforcement was on the lookout for suspicious characters. Whatever they were into must be incredibly important.

Not her problem or concern. Her only concern was doing right by Scott.

As she approached her home, Fiona rushed the fence and barked her greeting. "Hey, girl," Bree said.

"Bree, stop ignoring me," Aiden said, stepping up beside her.

She opened the gate and let Fiona out to give her a hug. "You could learn some manners from my dog," she said to her brother.

She led Fiona up to the front porch and sat in the rocker. "You want to talk to me? Talk," she said.

"Stop being so angry." He leaned against the porch railing.

"Wow, you're even telling me how I should feel? That doesn't sound like Thomas," she said in a sarcastic tone.

She knew the words were harsh, but couldn't stop them from tumbling out of her mouth. Essentially it was the truth. Aiden was acting like an overbearing, domineering male.

Aiden crossed his arms over his chest. "I guess I deserved that." He glanced her. "But try to understand where I'm coming from. You're obsessed with a guy who's obviously into something dangerous."

"He's not into something dangerous. Danger is finding him."

"It's the same thing."

"No, it isn't."

"I don't want to argue semantics."

"You started it."

"And now we're twelve again," he muttered.

Bree continued to stroke an enthusiastic Fiona, but didn't respond to Aiden. What could she say? He was right. They were fighting like kids.

"Let me try again," he said. "All my life it's been my job to protect my baby sisters. I thought I did an okay job, then you moved to Seattle and I couldn't protect you. And now…this situation with Scott feels like the same thing."

"But it's totally different. Thomas was a manipulating bully who'd convinced me I was a failure without him. Scott is a gentle, wounded soul who needs our help. Have you even talked to him?"

"It doesn't matter." He shook his head. "I failed you with Thomas and this feels like it's happening all over again." He pushed away from the railing and paced to the top of the steps. "Right here in my own resort."

"Aiden—"

"Try to understand, Bree, okay?" he said, not looking at her.

"Sure." She hesitated. "But could you do me a favor and ease up a little? Get to know Scott before you make assumptions?"

"I'll try." He started down the porch steps. "You going by Mom's tonight?"

"No. Chief Washburn is sending over a forensic artist to meet with me and Scott."

"Text me if you need anything."

"Will do, thanks."

Her big brother headed to the main building looking a bit defeated. A part of her understood his need to protect her and she greatly appreciated it, but another part resented the inference that she couldn't take care of herself. She'd done pretty well. She'd saved Scott from the bad guys in the mountains and today she'd avoided being kidnapped. She had Scott to thank for that. If he hadn't come racing across the street to accost the driver Bree might have been forced into the car.

Scott may think she'd done her duty and didn't need to help him any longer, but she disagreed. She would feed Fiona, whip up her specialty, mac and cheese, and head to Scott's room with dinner. The forensic artist could meet her there and the three of them could work on the sketch.

She glanced across the property at Scott's room. The curtains were drawn. She hoped he was resting. Lord knows if she suffered a gunshot wound and mind-

numbing concussion she'd welcome the healing benefits
of sleep. Still, he had to eat. She took Fiona inside and
got to work on dinner.

Scott awakened with a start. He gasped and sat up
in bed, fighting the violent images of a young woman
being tossed out of a moving car onto the pavement.
He rushed to her side, turned her over.

Bree. It had been Bree's face staring back at him.

He flopped back down in bed. "Only a dream."

But it felt real, his panic strangling his vocal cords,
tying his chest in knots and cutting off his ability to
breathe or think straight.

A soft knock tapped at the door. Must be the forensic
sketch artist, either that or the officer telling Scott he
was leaving for the night. They couldn't possibly keep
an eye on him 24/7. No department had that kind of
budget, especially a small department like Echo Mountain P.D.

The tapping grew insistent. Scott sat up a little too
quickly and his head pounded. Time for more aspirin.

"Coming!" he called out.

He stood, surprised that he didn't waver or grow
faint. Man, he hated being this weak, this out of it. He
padded to the door and looked through the peephole:
Breanna smiled back at him. She held a large bag in
her arms.

He pressed his forehead against the door. He wished
he could ignore her or tell her to leave him alone. It was
the best thing for both of them. Well, the best thing for
her, anyway. Scott knew that he had a better chance at
surviving the next few days with Bree in his life.

"You okay?" her muffled voice called through the door.

He swung it open and forced a smile. "Sure, I wasn't expecting you."

"I tried calling but no one answered."

"I unplugged the phone."

An apologetic expression creased her features. "I didn't wake you, did I?"

"Nope."

"I did wake you and you're being nice. I'm sorry."

"No, I was awake, honest."

"Have you eaten dinner yet?"

"No, I thought about ordering room service."

"Not necessary." She brushed past him into the room. "I made sandwiches, green salad and my famous macaroni and cheese." She placed the bag on the table and started pulling out containers. "It would be nice to have company for a change while I eat. I mean, other than canine company."

He stood there, holding the door open. A part of him wanted to convince her to leave because she was putting her life at risk just by being here.

"This is a high-carb meal so we should both sleep great tonight."

He couldn't take his eyes off her carefree smile. You never would have guessed she'd been threatened a few hours ago.

Because of him.

"Bree—"

"Sir," Officer Carrington said, stepping into the doorway, "you should keep the door closed."

"Right, thanks. You're not staying all night, are you?" he asked the officer.

"No, sir. Someone's relieving me in about twenty minutes."

"Come on, before it gets cold," Bree called from the table.

"Thanks," Scott said to the cop and shut the door.

"The weather's crazy outside," Bree said. "The wind's blowing like a Kansas tornado is about to touch down."

"When did that start?"

"Last hour or so. Would you like ham and Swiss or turkey and cheddar?" She held out two foil-wrapped sandwiches.

"Whichever one you don't want."

"That's not an answer. Come on, pick."

"Turkey cheddar."

"Great. Have a seat."

She set the table with paper plates, napkins and forks, put a sandwich on each plate and peeled the lid off a plastic bowl containing a green salad. "Hope you're okay with vinaigrette dressing."

"That's fine." He sat and clenched his jaw against the pain of his bruised ribs.

"Looks like you need a pain reliever." She dug in her purse and pulled out a bottle of acetaminophen. She set it on the table beside her keys. He noticed her key chain read: *Let Go, Let God.*

"It's a gentle reminder when I get frantic," she said, eyeing him.

Frantic because of the mess he'd dragged her into these past few days.

"Help yourself," she said, like they were old friends enjoying a meal.

But they weren't old friends. They were strangers, and she was an innocent bystander threatened by the violence trailing him.

"You shouldn't be here," he said, rubbing his forehead.

"And where should I be?"

"You know what I mean."

"I think I do. What you were trying to say was, 'thank you, Bree, for bringing me a homemade meal so I didn't have to order room service.' Notice how I said homemade, not home-cooked. The only thing I cooked is this." Eyes widening with anticipation, she pulled the top off the macaroni and cheese.

"That smells amazing," he said.

"Makes you change your mind about wanting me to leave, huh?" She smiled and shoved a serving spoon into the pasta.

"I never said I wanted you to leave, but we both know the danger of you being here."

"What danger? We're locked in this room with a cop standing guard outside that door. Relax and enjoy some carbs with me. Wait until you see what I brought for dessert." She rubbed her hands together like a kid on Christmas morning.

Suddenly the lights went out.

SEVEN

"Scott?" Breanna said.

Scott could feel the fear floating off her body.

"Place your hand on the table between us," he said. He sensed her body shift. He reached out and slid his hand over hers. Their fingers automatically curled into a perfect hold.

"It's okay. I won't let anyone hurt you," he said. How was he going to manage that when he couldn't see anything and didn't have a weapon to defend them?

"It's probably the generator," she said with false confidence.

"Has this happened before?" He stroked the back of her hand with his thumb.

"The power has flickered before but it's never gone totally out."

When she squeezed his hand he knew he had to do something to make her feel safe.

"I'm going to check in with Officer Carrington," he said.

"Don't let go."

"Okay, then why don't *we* check in with him?"

He stood and led her by the hand to the door.

"This is awfully creepy," she whispered.

"Yeah." And if it had anything to do with Scott's situation, he was going to figure out a way to check out of this hotel and stop putting these people in danger.

They stepped up to the door. "I'll open the door but you stay out of sight."

"Okay."

He cracked open the door and peered into a pitch-black hallway.

A beam of a flashlight hit Scott square in the chest. "Stay in your room," Officer Carrington said. "I'll find out what's going on. Lock your door and don't open it to anyone but me."

Scott shut and locked the door. Adrenaline coursed through him. He had to get control of this situation, if nothing else, for Bree's sake.

"Wait," she said, "I'm an idiot."

"I'm sorry?"

"I have a flashlight app on my phone."

She dug into her pocket. The glow from her cell phone illuminated her beautiful face. She pressed the screen a few times and a flashlight beam lit the area around them.

"See, not so scary," she said, directing the light into the room.

Something knocked against the window and she jumped.

"Bathroom," he said. With his arm around her shoulder, he led her into the roomy bathroom and locked the door. "Extra precaution," he said. That made two doors someone would have to get through to get to them.

"What now?" she said.

"We wait for the all-clear from Officer Carrington."

"I hate waiting." She sat on the closed toilet seat, shining her light across the sink area where he'd spread out his toiletries. He felt exposed, as if getting a glimpse of his personal things gave her yet a closer look into his soul.

Scott shifted to the floor, pressing his back against the bathroom door. An assailant would have to get through Scott to hurt Bree. Yet how much damage could Scott do considering his weakened physical condition? That got him thinking.

"Can you swing that light across the sink area again?" he said.

She did and he looked for something, anything to use as a weapon. Not much you could do with shaving cream, toothpaste and deodorant. Then he spotted a blow-dryer. He got up and grabbed it, weighing it in his hand.

"What are you thinking?" she said.

"Not sure yet. Trying to get creative in case we have unexpected company." He sat back down.

She pointed the flashlight at the ceiling to light up the bathroom. Even from here he could see her worried expression.

"It's probably an outage from the storm," he suggested.

"That makes sense. It was wild out there."

"Lots of stuff blowing around?"

"Yep. Resort staff were chasing after patio chairs."

"That's probably what hit our window."

"Wait, why don't I call Aiden and ask him what's going on?" She reached for the phone and hesitated. "Probably a bad idea."

"Why's that?"

"He's got enough on his hands without his little sister pestering him."

"He'll want to know that you're okay," Scott offered.

"I guess." She eyed the phone but didn't make the call.

"Breanna, what's the hesitation?"

"He'll freak when he finds out where I am."

"Understandable. Well, I'm not letting you leave until the lights come on and I know you're safe."

"Wait, I can call Harvey, or at least text him." She grabbed the phone and texted a message, then reactivated the flashlight app and aimed it toward the ceiling. "He's probably crazed because of the outage."

A sudden pounding echoed from the outer door. Bree sat straight.

"They can't get in without a key card," Scott assured, but she didn't look convinced.

The pounding stopped. Bree's green eyes widened with fear. Scott got up and rubbed her shoulder. "It's okay."

Someone pounded on the bathroom door and Bree yelped.

"What's going on in there?" Aiden demanded.

"Aiden?" she said.

"Bree? Open the door!"

Bree made a face at Scott. This was going to be ugly.

Scott reached for the door, but she grabbed his shirtsleeve. "I'd better open it."

She took a deep breath, stood and opened the door. Her brother shined a flashlight in her face.

"Hey, point that someplace else," she protested.

He aimed it at Scott, who put up his hand to block the beam. The intense light started to spike a headache.

"What are you doing here?" Aiden said, glaring at Bree.

"Waiting for the forensic artist," she said. "We were about to eat dinner when the lights went out."

"You were about to eat dinner," Aiden said, his tone flat.

"What's with the power outage?" Bree asked.

"If you were about to eat dinner, then why were you hiding in the bathroom?" Aiden said, ignoring her question.

"Scott thought it was the safest place to be. So, is it the storm?"

Her brother didn't answer for a few seconds. Scott couldn't see Aiden's expression because it would require Scott to look directly into the flashlight, but he could guess the guy was shooting him death ray eyes.

"Yes, we think it's the storm," Aiden said. "Maintenance is out there checking the lines." He lowered the flashlight and glared at Scott. "But if it's something else, if someone intentionally—"

The lights popped on.

"That was quick," Bree said.

"Not quick enough," Aiden countered, motioning them out of the bathroom. "We lost all power, even emergency lights. That doesn't reflect well on the safety of our guests."

Scott understood Aiden's anger toward him if this hadn't been a weather-related incident. Scott had already made up his mind he was leaving if that were the case.

Aiden's phone rang and he ripped it off his belt. "What have you got, Harvey?"

As Aiden paced the room, Scott's muscles tensed.

He remembered Harvey was the resort's security manager, so Scott was intent on watching Aiden's reaction to the call.

"Yep, okay. That's good news." Aiden glanced at Scott, then at Bree. She was busy spooning macaroni and cheese onto plates.

Scott couldn't believe how resilient she was, considering only a minute ago she was trembling in a dark bathroom with a stranger. Well, not exactly a stranger. They'd engaged in more than small talk during the past few days.

She must have caught him looking at her because she narrowed her eyes at him. "What?"

"You amaze me."

She blushed and refocused on her dinner.

"Harvey said lightning hit a transformer and knocked out the power, but he's not sure what happened to the emergency lights since they're on a different system. I've got to go talk to guests, give them coupons for free ice cream cones or something." He sighed and ran his hand through thick, blond hair.

"Thanks for checking up on us," Bree said. "We have plenty of macaroni if you want to stop back later."

"How long are you going to be here?" he said, irritated.

"I don't know, a few hours?" she said, unwrapping her sandwich.

"Bree, you know how I feel about…" Aiden cast a quick glance at Scott.

"It's a bad idea to be around me," Scott said. "I agree."

Aiden glanced at Scott as if trying to figure out if he was being sincere.

"I understand, Aiden," Bree said. "And I'm sorry it upsets you, but I'm helping Scott and nothing either of you say will change my mind. So, let's not have this conversation again because it's starting to give me a headache."

She closed her eyes, put her hands together and silently prayed over her meal. A few seconds later she grabbed her sandwich and took a bite. A happy, peaceful expression eased across her features. She'd surrendered, to God, to her taste buds, to the beauty of being in the moment. She definitely wasn't listening to her brother's protests.

Scott looked at Aiden and said, "Sorry."

"You will be if anything happens to my sister." Aiden stormed out.

Adjusting himself in the chair across from Bree, Scott reached over to open his sandwich and winced.

"Do you want me to—"

"Nope." He clenched his jaw and peeled back the foil from his sandwich.

"Apologies for my brother," she said.

"Not necessary. He's looking out for you."

"And I'm looking out for you."

"Thanks, but I'm a big boy."

"A wounded big boy with limited memory."

He picked up his sandwich and put it back down.

"What's wrong, you don't want the turkey, after all?" she asked.

"Tonight might have been an act of nature, but if it hadn't been and anything had happened to you—"

"Don't focus on the darkness. We're safe. We've got shelter and food. Let's be grateful for that and enjoy our meal."

Scott struggled to enjoy a peaceful dinner with the image of Bree's terrified expression and the sound of her anxious voice in his mind.

"'I can do all things through Him who gives me strength,'" she said and glanced up. "*Philippians* 4:13. It's one of my favorites."

"Your faith is important to you," he said.

"It's helped me through some tough times. It can help you, too."

The woman had a kind of courage that mystified Scott. She was still determined to put herself at risk. For him.

That thought made him want to take off, slip out of the resort in the middle of the night and get as far away from Bree as possible. She didn't deserve to be collateral damage to whatever Scott was into.

A knock at the door echoed across the room. Scott got up to answer it. He checked the peephole and spotted Chief Washburn standing outside his door.

"Who is it?" Bree asked.

"The chief." Scott hesitated and glanced at Bree.

She came up beside him and placed a comforting hand on his shoulder.

He wanted to kiss her. In this ridiculously insane moment just before he might be taken away and locked up for good, all he could think about was how soft her lips looked, how much he wanted to taste them.

"You okay?" she said.

He offered a sad smile. "Sure," he said. But he would never be okay because he ached for a woman he could never have.

Scott swung open the door. "Chief, we were expecting the forensic artist."

Chief Washburn nodded at Bree and marched past them into the room. "Can't get one here until tomorrow. I've got good news and bad news."

Scott braced himself against the TV console. Bree came up beside him.

The chief held out a plastic evidence bag with Scott's wallet.

"Your wallet?" Bree said.

Scott nodded, but didn't take his eyes off the chief. The bad news was about to drop. He could feel it.

"That's great," Bree said and glanced at the chief. "Right?"

"You've got two driver's licenses in here, one for Scott James and one for Scott Becket. We ran a background check on Scott Becket and found your employment history with the Chicago P.D. You want to tell me why you checked into the resort using false identification?"

"I have no idea."

"I might be small town, son, but I'm not stupid."

"No, sir, I never thought that."

"Then you'd better come up with some answers, and quick."

"Hang on, the doctors said his concussion was causing his memory loss—"

"Breanna," Chief Washburn said, cutting her off. "You shouldn't even be here so I'd advise you to keep quiet."

She crossed her arms over her chest, obviously not happy with his stern tone. Scott agreed with him: Bree shouldn't be here, especially not now with this new bit of information.

Scott had checked into the resort using an alias,

which meant he didn't want to be found. He was running from something, but was it criminal?

"I honestly don't remember anything prior to coming to Washington," Scott said.

"Could it be an undercover assignment?" the chief asked.

Scott shook his head. "It's anybody's guess."

"That's not good enough."

"I understand your position. You need to lock me up, don't you?"

"Wait, you can't." Bree glanced at the chief.

"I can," the chief said, "but I won't until I know what to charge him with other than using a false ID. He could very well be on the job. First thing tomorrow I'm calling the Chicago P.D. In the meantime, do not leave this room."

"Yes, sir," Scott said.

The chief nodded at Bree. "Pack up your things. I'll escort you home."

"But," she started to protest, then acquiesced. "Okay, give me a minute."

"I'll be waiting in the hallway. I need to speak with my officer." Chief Washburn left them alone.

Bree looked at Scott. "I'm sure there's a logical explanation for the ID thing."

"I have no official jurisdiction here."

"There's got to be a good reason for keeping your identity a secret."

He went to the table to help her clean up.

"I have a friend who's an IT genius," she said. "How about I ask him to—"

"No," he said, "let the chief take the lead on this."

For a second he thought she'd argue with him. Instead, she continued to pack up the containers. "I'll leave some brownies and cookies."

He nodded, stuffing the container of macaroni and cheese into the bag. She placed her hand over his and he looked into her amazing green eyes.

"Why don't you call your sister to help you fill in the blanks?" she offered. "You shouldn't be going through this alone."

"So, you're done with me, then?"

"For tonight. I can argue with my brother and win, but the police chief? Don't want to risk getting locked up," she teased. "I'll check on you tomorrow morning, okay?"

"Perhaps it would be safer if you didn't."

"Friends don't abandon each other, Scott."

Slinging her bag over her shoulder, she stepped around the table and hesitated, as if she was about to give him a hug.

The chief knocked on the door. "Ready?" his muffled voice called.

"Coming!" She redirected her attention to Scott. "Be well, and phone your sister."

She reached out and took his hand. "Focus on the goodness in this moment and surrender your heart to God. It will all work out."

With a squeeze of his hand, she smiled, turned and left. The door clicked shut behind her.

He'd never felt more alone in his life, alone and frustrated. He was potentially facing a world of trouble, yet had no means to defend himself, at least not until he remembered why he'd come to Echo Mountain in the first place.

As he went back to finish his sandwich, Bree's satisfied smile flashed across his thoughts. She'd looked so content, almost euphoric when she'd taken a bite of her macaroni. Scott had never experienced that kind of contentment. He'd always been on edge, hyperdiligent about protecting his little sister or making money to pay for clothes growing up. Becoming a cop only fueled his intensity.

Get the bad guy, lock him up, prevent him from hurting innocents.

Innocents like Bree. Scott had to distance himself if he wanted to keep her safe, yet he needed her like nothing he'd ever needed before. No, he only felt this vulnerable and dependent on her because she was offering solace in a raging storm.

Time to reach out for help, something that felt utterly foreign to him. Although he'd lost his cell phone, he did remember Emily's number. He sat on the bed and picked up the receiver.

He got an outside line and made the call. It rang two, three times, and he wondered if Em was out with friends. He glanced at the clock. It was two hours later in Chicago, which mean it was nearly eleven. He worried that he might wake her.

"Hello?" a female voice said.

"Em?"

"Who's this?"

"Her brother, Scott. Who's this and why are you answering her phone?" He clenched the phone tighter.

"It's her friend Ashley. Emily was in a car accident."

EIGHT

Bree put away the dishes and contemplated a bath with lavender salts and mood-enhancing candles. She loved her nighttime ritual of soaking in the tub while saying her daily prayers. Scott would top the list tonight.

She was about to draw the bath when she realized Fiona hadn't been out since earlier that afternoon. Bree had been so distracted by the day's events she'd neglected her lovable pup.

"Hey, Fi! Let's go potty!" she called, wandering into the living room. Fiona's head perked up from her favorite spot on the couch. "No, I'm not kidding, let's go, silly girl."

Bree grabbed the leash and Fiona catapulted off the couch, rushed Bree and posed in perfect dog sit. "That's my girl."

The bad weather had passed, but fog was rolling in, giving the resort property an eerie feel. Bree walked Fiona around the perimeter of the property to give her a healthy dose of exercise and a chance to relieve herself. "Such a good girl," Bree praised, as Fiona paced alongside her.

A few minutes later Fiona started whining and pulling on her leash.

"What is it, girl?"

Bree was pretty good at reading Fiona's behavior. A stop usually meant she'd caught an odor, and barking meant she sensed something up ahead. But the whining behavior could mean any number of things. Maybe she sensed a skunk in the woods.

Then the whining grew to a frantic bark. Not excited or pleased, but frantic. Worried.

Bree pulled out her phone and hit the speed dial for Harvey. She didn't call Aiden because she'd had her fill of lectures for the day. Besides, the guy needed to enjoy his time off.

"Bree, everything okay?" Harvey answered.

"Oh, good, you're still on duty. I'm walking Fiona and she's acting rather strange."

"Where are you?"

"South end of the property by the barn."

"I'll check it out."

"I'm sorry to bother you so late with this."

"Don't be. Until I get up the guts to retire, this is part of the job. Go on home."

"Thanks." She ended the call and glanced up ahead. That's when she saw it: the silhouette of a man walking away from the property.

A familiar-looking man.

"Scott!" she called out.

He kept walking. This must be what Fiona was upset about. She sensed Scott's presence and wanted to get to him. Well, so did Bree. She wanted to get to him and find out where he was going and why.

She picked up her pace as she and Fiona jogged toward Scott. He'd turned onto the main road leading to the highway, probably to hitch a ride.

"Scott!" She tried again, but the sound of her voice didn't carry far, so she decided on plan B.

She unleashed Fiona and pointed. "Go get him, girl."

Fiona took off and caught up with Scott, barking and dancing around him. He motioned for her to go away, but Fiona wasn't giving up.

Neither was Bree.

Scott turned around and stuck out his thumb, hoping to catch a ride from an oncoming car. Bree jogged toward him. She knew Fiona wouldn't leave his side, which would surely discourage a motorist from picking him up. One passenger was easy, but a man with a dog? That was messy.

At least that's what Thomas had always said: dogs were messy.

Well, apparently so was love.

Bree was closing in on Scott when a car did, in fact, slow down.

Scott motioned for Fiona to go away.

"Hey, be nice to my dog," she said, out of breath as she caught up to him.

The driver of the car poked his head out the window. It was Will Rankin from SAR.

"Hey Bree, I thought that was Fiona," Will said. "What's she doing out here with this guy?"

Bree smirked at Scott. "She knew he was lost."

"You need a ride back?" Will offered.

"No, we're good, right?" she asked Scott.

"Sure, fine," he said in a low voice.

"Say hi to the girls for me," she said.

"Will do. Be safe."

"You, too."

She commanded Fiona to stand beside her as Will drove off. Bree turned to Scott. "What are you doing out here?"

"Leaving town. But apparently the dog has a better chance of hitching a ride than I do."

"Maybe because you shouldn't be trying to leave. Come on." She took a step in the direction of the resort. Scott didn't move. "Scott?"

"I need to go. My sister was in a car accident."

"Oh, I'm so sorry."

"It's my fault," he said.

"How is that possible? You're here and she's…where is she?"

"Chicago."

"Then it couldn't have been your fault. How is she?"

"Okay, I guess. Her friends are taking turns staying with her."

"Did you speak with your sister?"

"No, she was asleep."

"But no serious injuries?"

"According to her friend Ashley, Em's bruised and sore, but okay."

"Good, that's good." Bree sighed. "And you were headed where, without money or ID?"

"I have to get to her."

"Scott—"

He gripped Bree's arm. "I'm all she's got."

Fiona broke into another round of barking, but this was different than before. Fiona's anxious behavior was warning Scott to release Bree.

"I'm sorry." His fingers sprung free of her arm.

"It's okay," Bree said. "Come on, let's go back."

He glanced at the road ahead with a wistful expression.

"Look, if you leave the resort you'll look guilty of something," Bree said. "You said friends are taking care of your sister. You need to take care of yourself."

Instead, he started to walk toward the main road. This time *she* grabbed *his* arm.

"Stop." She held his gaze. "You won't get far without money or identification. You're not thinking clearly."

"It's always been my job to take care of her."

"I understand, but sometimes little sisters have to manage on their own. If she knew about your situation she'd want you to focus on your recovery and resolving your situation, right?"

He shrugged.

"Trust me, she would. The best thing you can do for her is to get better and stay safe."

His gaze drifted to the resort, the massive property surrounded by lush forest. "I guess I shouldn't have taken off."

"You were worried about your sister." She took his hand and coaxed him toward the resort. "Give yourself a break. Your brain's still wonky."

"Wonky?"

"You know, wonky, off-kilter."

Once he started walking she was going to let go of his hand, but she sensed he needed the connection, so she held on. Fiona walked alongside them and it struck Bree how normal this looked: a man and woman holding hands, out for a romantic stroll with their dog.

But this wasn't a romantic stroll. This was a rescue mission of sorts.

"So tell me about your sister," Bree said.

"Emily's great." He smiled. "She's two years younger than me, so I've always been protective."

"You're a good older brother."

"I don't know if she'd agree with that. I was pretty bossy when we were kids, but since Mom was always working I was in charge."

"Why'd your mom work so much?"

"Dad left us, didn't offer any financial support so it was up to Mom. When I was old enough I worked and pitched in. It became my job to take care of them." He glanced sideways at her. "How did you do that?"

"Do what?"

"One minute I'm frantic about my sister, the next you've got me telling my life story."

"It's a skill I developed when I did hair in the city. The things people would tell me…" She smiled and shook her head.

"Like what? It's probably a lot more interesting than my life."

"I doubt it. So, you practically raised your sister then what? Did you go to college?"

"Wait a second, is there something more to this line of questioning?"

"Busted." She offered a pleasant smile. "I thought, maybe if we talked about your family and childhood it could help you remember other things."

"Like why I came to Echo Mountain Resort."

"It's worth a try. Anyway, college?"

He glanced up ahead, still holding her hand. "I went to community college, then transferred and got my bachelor's in psychology. I joined the force and became a detective by the time I was thirty."

"Impressive. But you don't think you're still a cop?"

"No." He got a faraway look in his eye, and melancholy creased his brows.

"I'm sorry," she said.

He snapped his attention to her. "For what?"

"My question made you terribly sad."

"I remembered something about a kid being shot, it's a long story. Anyway, I wasn't the same after that. I took a leave of absence and…" His voice trailed off.

"What is it?"

He hesitated. "I took a job in private security."

"When was that?"

"Last year, I think."

"Great, let's figure out who you work for and maybe they'll know why you came to Echo Mountain."

"No, we can't contact them."

"Why not?"

"I'm not sure."

Headlights pierced through the night fog, aimed directly at Bree and Scott. She realized that although they were close to the resort they were still vulnerable out here in the dark.

The car seemed to be going a bit fast for the damp and misty conditions.

"Get behind those trees," Scott said.

"But—"

"Go!"

"Fiona, heel," she said and darted toward the cluster of trees. As she pulled out her phone to call for help, Fiona nudged her and the phone dropped on the ground. "Nuts," she said, running her hands across the damp earth to find it.

"What are you doing out here?" a worried voice shouted.

She recognized it. Harvey.

"It's okay, Harvey!" she called out. "He's with me."

The resort's security manager got out of his truck and peered into the trees. "What are you doing?"

"I saw Scott out here and followed him. He made me take cover when we saw your truck, and now I've lost my phone."

"We thought you were someone else, so I told her hide," Scott said.

"Let's get you two out of here in case that 'someone else' shows up." Harvey walked over to Bree and pointed the flashlight at the ground. In seconds she found the phone.

Bree encouraged Fiona to jump into the flatbed, then she, Scott and Harvey got into the front seat. Harvey spun the truck around and headed for the resort's back entrance closest to Scott's room.

"You were driving awfully fast," Bree said.

"I was worried about your call." Harvey glanced at her then back at the road. "I won't tell Aiden about this."

"You're the best," Bree said.

"And you—" Harvey aimed a stern look at Scott "—no more late night walkabouts. Got it?"

"Yes, sir."

Harvey parked and escorted them to the door. The cop assigned to watch Scott got out of a nearby squad car and marched up to them wearing an angry frown. "You shouldn't have left the room."

"I know." Scott tapped his head with his fingertips. "The cognitive function is still a little—" he glanced at Bree "—wonky."

"Let's get back inside," the cop said, scanning the property.

Scott nodded at Bree. "Thanks."

"See you tomorrow?"

"Absolutely."

She thought the corner of his lips curled into a slight smile. With a nod, he turned and the cop escorted him inside. Fiona rushed the building, wagging her tail and spying through the glass door for Scott.

"She's developed an attachment to him," Bree said.

"Looks like she's not the only one," Harvey said.

The next morning Scott decided he couldn't continue to live this way, constantly anxious, feeling threatened by the things he didn't remember and therefore couldn't see coming. He also couldn't keep putting Bree at risk. She was the one good thing that had come of this insane situation and he wasn't about to ruin her life because she'd been nice to him.

As he reached for his cup of coffee, he glanced at his hand and remembered how she'd held it last night when she'd stopped him from running away. Running didn't solve problems; it only caused more pain and suffering. Hadn't his father's abandonment taught him anything?

Although it had been Harvey speeding toward them last night, it could have been someone else. Scott was completely vulnerable and helpless until he figured out what had happened during the weeks leading up to his assault in the mountains.

Glancing out the window, he spotted Bree giving directions to a grounds employee. As her gaze roamed the property, it drifted by Scott's window and she smiled, offering an enthusiastic wave. He waved back, remarking how beautiful she looked in her pink fleece jacket and jeans, her blond waves sticking out from a resort baseball cap pulled low to shield her eyes from the sun.

Scott turned away from the window, not wanting to be distracted. He'd awakened this morning with a new goal: piece together his recent past and determine why he'd come to Echo Mountain.

Bree had been on the right track last night. By asking Scott questions and getting him to talk about himself he'd started accessing a part of his brain that could lead him to answers.

Another way to access answers could be through his sister. He needed to call her but had put it off for a full hour, fighting the guilt that he hadn't been there for her, and that somehow her accident had been his fault. Bree had pointed out how implausible that was, but Scott couldn't shake the dread eating away at his gut.

The clock read ten, noon in Chicago. He got an outside line and made the call.

"Hello?"

"Hi, this is Scott, Emily's brother. Who's this?"

"Cassie Marshall, a friend from work. I stopped by to bring lunch."

"How's she doing?"

"Still pretty sore and uncomfortable."

He closed his eyes. His fault, this was his fault. He knew it deep in his core. Somehow his business, his choices had put Em at risk.

"Is she… May I speak with her?"

"Of course, hang on."

He waited a few very long seconds before she came on the line. "Scotty?"

He squeezed the phone at the weak sound of her

voice. "Hey, Em, I called last night but Ashley said you were sleeping. I'm sorry I'm not there."

"It's okay, my friends are taking good care of me."

"I should be there."

"No, it's really okay."

"I'm so sorry, kid."

"It happened two days ago. I left you messages. I thought—" she hesitated "—I thought I'd hear from you sooner."

"I lost my phone."

"Where are you? Ash called your work and they didn't even know."

"Work?"

"Global Resources International."

Okay, now he knew where he'd been working. He jotted it down on a resort notepad.

"Or did you change jobs and not tell me?" Emily asked.

"No, that sounds right."

"It sounds right? Scott, what's going on?"

"I had a hiking accident, hit my head pretty bad and I'm struggling with a mild case of amnesia."

"You're kidding."

"Wish I were."

"Wow, that must be horrible for a control freak like you."

"Control freak, huh?"

"I'm teasing."

But he sensed she wasn't.

"So what happened?" she asked. "Where were you hiking?"

"Cascade Mountains in Washington."

"Why are you out there?"

"Your guess is as good as mine."

"Seriously?"

"I can't remember the accident, or a few months leading up to it. Doctor hopes that will change as the swelling goes down. Anyway, a search-and-rescue team saved me."

More like Breanna McBride saved him.

"Sounds serious if they sent search and rescue to find you. It's just a concussion?"

"And bruised ribs." He didn't want to worry her by mentioning the bullet wound.

"That's a horrible thing to go through by yourself," she said. "I don't know what I'd do without my girlfriends helping me out."

"I'm okay," Scott said. "I've made some friends who are looking after me."

"Don't lie, Scott. It doesn't make me feel better."

"Why do you think I'm lying?"

"Never mind."

"Em?" he pushed.

"You don't do the friend thing, well, except for your partner, Joe. You always said you don't like needing anyone's help, that it makes you weak."

"Well, I'd be a lot weaker without the help I've been getting from the locals."

"Okay, who are you and what have you done with my brother?" she joked.

"Very funny. Tell me about your accident."

"A totally insane driver cuts into my lane and I swerve to avoid a collision, hit a post and the airbag goes off."

"Ouch."

"No kidding. And the jerk didn't even stop. He sped off like he was qualifying for the Indy 500."

"Did you get a good look at the car?"

"A black Lincoln, older model."

The hair pricked on the back of Scott's neck, but he wasn't sure why.

"I gave my statement to the Chicago P.D., so hopefully they'll find the guy. What a jerk. I mean not even stopping to see if I was okay?"

Which meant the driver didn't care if she was okay.

"Scott?"

"Yeah."

"When are you coming back?"

"Not sure. Hopefully soon."

"Are you in trouble?"

"Why do you ask that?"

"I don't know, you seemed more intense than usual these past few months, and now you sound—" she paused "—strange."

"I'm worried about you."

"Don't be. I'm a big girl and my friends are totally smothering me."

Cassie said something in the background to drive the point home.

"I'm glad you called," Emily said. "When you didn't come by to check on me or call I got worried. I thought…"

"You thought I'd left, like him."

"No, I thought—"

"It's okay. I should be there and I'm not."

"Scotty—"

"You should have the number of the resort I'm staying at. Got a piece of paper?"

"No, but I can have Cassie write it down."

"Good. Call if anything changes."

"Sure, okay. Here's Cassie." Emily passed the phone to her friend and Scott gave her the phone number for the resort and his room number.

"Cassie, I can't tell you how much I appreciate you guys taking care of my sister."

"We're happy to do it. That's what friends are for. Bye."

Scott hung up and stared at the phone, concern flooding his chest. Whatever he'd been working on caused the hit-and-run accident that hurt his sister. He could feel it in his gut. But what could he do about it from two thousand miles away?

Friends.

Scott considered calling the one person who'd been there for him when he was on the job: his partner. He slowly pressed the buttons to call Joe, surprised that he remembered the number since he hadn't used it in months. He knew his former partner had a thing for Emily, and Scott hoped those feelings would override whatever resentment Joe felt about Scott leaving the force and abandoning his partner.

"Detective Rush," he answered.

"Joey, it's Scott."

Silence.

"Joe?" Scott pressed.

"What?"

"I need a favor."

"You have *got* to be kidding."

"It's not for me. It's about Emily."

"What about her?"

"She was in a hit-and-run. I think it was intentional."

"Yeah, right, like anyone would want to hurt that sweet girl."

"They were trying to send me a message."

"Great, what did you get yourself into, Mr. hotshot security goon?"

"Joey—"

"I've been waiting for this call, the one where you'd admit you were wrong, that you shouldn't have left the department, but this? You put your sister at risk? What's the matter with you?"

"Joe, I—"

"It's always about you, isn't it? The self-judgment, the blame. You act like you're the only one who was affected by that kid's death, Scott. Aw, forget it."

The line went dead.

"Joey?"

Scott sighed. His former partner had hung up on him. Maybe Scott deserved it, but he hoped the resentment Joe felt for him wouldn't prevent him from checking on Em.

Scott was banking on the fact that the many years of friendship he'd shared with Joe counted for something, because the thought of someone stalking and hurting Emily…

"Please, God," he whispered and caught himself. He wasn't one to lean on God, yet Bree drew so much strength from her faith. It fascinated him. Right now Scott felt so helpless about both his sister's situation and his own personal safety.

He opened the nightstand drawer and pulled out the Bible. Turning to a random page, he landed on *Psalm 57*.

"Be merciful and gracious to me, O God, be merciful *and* gracious to me, for my soul takes refuge *and* finds shelter *and* confidence in You; yes, in the shadow of Your wings I will take refuge *and* be confident until calamities *and* destructive storms have passed."

Someone knocked on the door, probably Bree coming to check on him. He placed the Bible on the nightstand, went to the door and glanced through the peephole. A resort employee stood outside his door.

Scott cracked it open. "Yes?"

"Room service."

Scott glanced at two covered plates on the cart. "I didn't order anything."

"A friend ordered for you, sir," the man said. "She'll be joining you shortly."

Scott smiled to himself. Even when she wasn't here Bree was taking care of him. He'd be able to dive into his investigation more effectively on a full stomach, so he swung open the door and the employee wheeled the cart inside.

Scott glanced up and down the hall, wondering what happened to his shadow cop. Truth was he didn't need full-time surveillance. Like Bree had said, he couldn't get far without a driver's license, money or credit cards.

"Sorry, I don't have my wallet so I can't offer a tip," Scott said, closing the door.

"That's okay, sir. I don't want your money." The guy pulled the cover off a plate and turned.

He was pointing a gun at Scott.

Scott automatically raised his hands.

"I'm surprised you let me in," the man said. He was in his sixties with salt-and-pepper hair and a square jaw. "Although you seemed a little distracted when you were eyeing the hallway. Looking for the cute blonde?"

Scott glared. "I don't know who you're talking about."

"Uh-huh."

This must be one of the guys who'd assaulted Scott in the mountains…and was here to finish the job.

"What do you want?" Scott said.

"Sit." He jerked the barrel of the gun sideways.

Scott sat at the table and lowered his hands.

"You know what I want," the guy said. "The water samples."

Scott had no idea what he was talking about. Now what? He decided to use the truth as his defense.

"Guess you haven't heard, I'm suffering from retrograde amnesia," Scott said.

"Right, and I'm Frosty the Snowman."

"You said yourself that I should have known better than to let you in. Do I know you? Because if I do, I can't remember."

"No kidding," he said, sarcasm lacing his voice. "Okay, I'll play along. You can call me Rich, although that's obviously not my real name. So, Scott, how about you tell me where you stashed the water samples and I'll leave you alone."

"I told you, I can't remember."

Someone tapped on the door. "Scott? It's Bree."

Scott tensed, his eyes glancing at the door, then back at his attacker.

"Maybe she can help you remember," Rich said with a wicked smile.

He must have read the fear on Scott's face.

"Ask her to join us."

"Scott?" She knocked again. "You okay?"

"Well, go on, lover boy," Rich said.

Scott went to the door and placed his hand against the heavy steel. He had to do something to drive her away, and fast.

"I'm not decent."

"But I just saw—"

"Leave me alone!" he shouted.

Silence answered him. His heart ached at the thought that her last memory of Scott would be his cruel tone, since his attacker surely wasn't going to let him live. She disappeared from the peephole. Relief coursed through him.

Without warning, Rich slugged Scott in his bruised ribs. Scott doubled over and fell to his knees, gasping for breath.

"Smart guy, huh?" He leaned close. "It's time you gave up your crusade."

Scott couldn't give the guy what he wanted, but at least he knew he'd been up in the mountains taking water samples for some mysterious reason.

"Maybe if I knock you around, that brain of yours will get back on track." The guy swung the gun at Scott's head.

NINE

Bree jerked away from the door, the hair bristling on the back of her neck.

Scott was in trouble, big-time.

She took off for the security office, hoping to find Harvey, or even her brother. Aiden would probably brush her off, saying she was too sensitive and a man yelling at her to go away wasn't cause for alarm.

But it was. Bree had seen a staff member roll a food cart into Scott's room, so when she knocked on the door only moments later and he claimed he wasn't decent, she knew something was wrong.

Then he yelled at her.

A small part of her brain argued that he'd had enough of Bree, but she shoved that thought aside and focused on helping him.

She rounded the corner at a fast clip and nearly collided with a tall man in a suit walking beside her brother.

"Where's the officer watching Scott?" she asked Aiden.

"This is Officer Willet. I asked them to nix the uniforms so their presence wouldn't alarm guests."

She looked at Officer Willet with pleading eyes. "Scott's in trouble."

"Isn't Officer Jones guarding his room?"

"No. Come on."

The three of them approached Scott's door and the cop motioned for Bree and Aiden to stand aside.

"Why do you think he's in trouble?" Officer Willet asked.

"I just know."

The cop pounded on the door. "Scott, it's Officer Willet. I need to go over a few things with you. Please open the door."

The cop waited. Bree interlaced her fingers together and squeezed.

"Why do you think he's in trouble?" Aiden pressed.

"Because he yelled at me," she admitted.

"Bree," Aiden said in that shaming tone.

She stared directly into his sky-blue eyes. "I know he's in trouble the same way you knew I was in trouble back in Seattle, so don't mess with me."

A crash echoed from the room, then something slammed against the door.

"Key." The plainclothes cop stuck out his hand.

Aiden handed him a master key, and shifted Bree out of harm's way.

"Stay back," Officer Willet said.

The cop withdrew his firearm, swiped the key card and tried opening the door, but something was blocking it. The cop pushed harder and the door swung open. Officer Willet bolted into the room.

"Patio," Scott's voice gasped.

Bree slipped inside before the door closed. The officer rushed out the sliding doors to the patio, and Aiden followed close behind, but didn't go outside. He stood at the glass door barking orders into his radio.

"Bree?"

She glanced down to her left. Scott was sitting against the wall, clutching his rib cage.

"What happened?" She kneeled beside him and searched his eyes.

"You got help?" he said. "After I yelled at you?"

"I knew you didn't mean it."

He tipped his head back against the wall and sighed. "Thank you."

"Where are you hurt?" she said.

"What happened in here?" Aiden said, sliding the glass doors shut and glancing around the disheveled room.

"They sent a guy in a room service uniform to get information out of me," Scott said.

"What kind of information?" Aiden stepped closer.

"Back off, big brother. Let's get him some ice for his ribs," Bree said.

Her brother was wearing that determined look, that *I'm not going to let anyone hurt my baby sister* look.

"It's okay," Scott said, and slowly got up. Bree helped him across the room to sit at the table. "He asked me where I stashed the water samples."

"What water samples?" Aiden asked.

"Have no idea, but at least I have more information than I did yesterday. I found out who I work for, and apparently I have water samples worth killing for. I'll spend the afternoon looking into it. I've got a laptop around here somewhere."

"I can help," Bree said.

"Don't you have to finish putting up Christmas decorations on the south end of the property?" Aiden questioned.

"It's my official day off."

"Bree—"

"The sooner I help Scott figure this out the sooner he'll be gone. That's what you want, right?" she challenged.

"Mr. McBride, this is Justin in Facilities, over," a voice squawked through Aiden's radio.

"Go ahead, Justin." Aiden spoke into his radio, but didn't take his eyes off Bree.

"We've got a problem in the D wing, sir. I think you'd better come."

"On my way." Aiden sighed. "Be careful," he said to Bree.

"I will."

He pointed his radio at Scott. "And no more room service."

"He has to eat," Bree protested.

"I'll send something down for lunch and dinner, but don't answer unless they say it's from me, got it?" Aiden said.

"Okay," Bree said.

Aiden reached for the door.

"Hey, Aiden?" Scott said.

Aiden turned.

"Thanks," Scott said.

With a curt nod, Aiden left.

Scott looked at Bree. "I think he's starting to like me."

"Uh-huh, he'll probably invite you to Christmas dinner," she said teasingly.

"I make a mean cranberry sauce."

"I'll bet." She examined a cut on his cheek.

"How does it look, doc?"

"We should wash it out. You want ice for the ribs?"

"Probably a good idea."

"I'll have the concierge send it over."

"I need to find my laptop." He glanced around the room, as if trying to remember where he'd stashed it.

His curious expression grew frustrated.

"Check the closet," she suggested. "I'll call for the ice."

She called Nia at the concierge desk and ordered ice. Scott searched the closet slowly, as if he didn't recognize his own clothes. He had at least five shirts hanging in the closet, so he'd planned on being here nearly a week.

If he was collecting water samples that could be from the bigger lakes, like Lake Stevens or smaller lakes hidden in the mountains. What she couldn't figure out was why he needed water samples in the first place.

"Are you working for the EPA?" she asked.

He shut the closet door and turned to her. "What?"

"Is that why you need water samples?"

"I don't know." He opened the top drawer on the dresser and moved clothes around. "Here it is."

Laptop in hand, he shifted into a chair at the table and winced.

"I've got pain relievers in my purse," she said, joining him at the table.

"No, I'm good."

"You don't look good."

He glanced up. "Gee, thanks."

"I meant, you look like you're hurting." She certainly didn't mean it the other way, although the truth was she found Scott incredibly handsome. Heat flushed her cheeks in an unwelcome blush.

"What's wrong?" he asked.

"Nothing." She stood and went to the bathroom. "I'm getting a washcloth to clean out your cut."

"Okay, but then I have a job for you."

A job other than nursing him back to health and helping him get his life back? Sure, she would nurse the wounded bird so that he'd be strong enough to fly away. That's what she was doing, right? It's not as though she could have any kind of relationship with this man once he got his memory and his life back.

She ran a white washcloth under warm water and studied her reflection in the bathroom mirror. It was a shame that they'd met under such dire circumstances because she felt a true connection to Scott, an honest connection.

Then again, maybe that was due to his vulnerability. She knew that some confident men—men like Thomas—pushed and shoved until they had you cornered and helpless, willing to do whatever they wanted. Even her brother tended to be bossy and overbearing although she understood he was motivated by brotherly love.

At any rate, she'd appreciate whatever time she had with Scott, helping him resolve his situation and get his life back. She wrung out the washcloth and went into the room. Scott intently studied something on his laptop.

"What'd you find?" she asked, shifting a chair close to him.

She pressed the washcloth against his facial cut. He closed his eyes and she snapped her hand back. "Sorry, does that hurt?"

"No, it feels good."

She continued to clean the wound. It was a small cut, but the skin around it was red and angry. "How's the arm?"

"It's fine."

She dabbed at his cheek for a few seconds, then sat back in the chair. "I think you're good."

"Am I?" he asked, searching her eyes.

It seemed as though he was going to kiss her.

"Scott, I..."

He pressed his forefinger to her lips. "I need to say something, and I've probably said it before, but it's worth repeating." He hesitated. "Breanna, I don't know what I'd do without you right now. I needed you to know that."

"I'm glad I could be here for you."

And I'm starting to care about you, a lot.

She couldn't say the words, words that seemed trite considering they'd known each other only a few days.

"I wish..." he started.

"What?"

He took the washcloth out of her hand and brought her fingers to his lips. A shiver of warmth crept down her spine. She loved the feel of his lips pressed against her knuckles. It was such a delicate, tender touch.

"When this is all over," he said, "maybe we could catch a movie or something?" He looked up, hopeful.

"Even a romantic comedy?"

He smiled. "Sure."

"Wow, I'm impressed."

Someone knocked on the sliding door. "It's Officer Willet," the muffled voice said.

Scott opened the door and let him in.

"He's gone," the cop said. "I'll call it in to the chief. He wanted to be kept in the loop. What'd the guy look like?"

"Older guy, salt-and-pepper hair. Called himself Rich, but said that wasn't his real name." Scott walked him to the door.

"That sounds like the man I saw at the hospital," Bree said.

"Apparently the assailant had a partner who lured Officer Jones away from his post," Officer Willet said.

"Is Officer Jones okay?" Bree asked.

"He's fine." Officer Willet turned to Scott. "Keep the slider and this door locked and secure."

"Yes, sir."

Scott closed the door and double-locked it, then joined Bree at the table. "I shouldn't have let Rich get away."

"You were working at a slight disadvantage."

"That's no excuse."

"Let's focus on what we *can* do." She glanced at the laptop. "You were about to come up with a plan?"

"I got the name of my employer from Emily. I should call and find out what I was working on. Maybe they sent me out here. But it feels strange to call about myself."

"I can call," Bree offered. "What do you want me to say?"

"Ask for me, see if you can find out where I am and when I'm supposed to return."

"Don't you want to speak with your boss and ask him directly?"

His brows furrowed as if he was remembering something. "It's not a good idea. I'm not sure why."

She picked up the phone. "What's the number?"

He handed her the resort notepad with a number on it. That's when she noticed the Bible sitting out on the nightstand. That was certainly a good sign.

She made the call and when the receptionist picked up she asked for Scott Becket's extension. A few rings later a woman answered. "Security."

"Hi, I'm looking for Scott Becket."

"May I ask who's calling?"

"Breanna McBride."

"Hold on."

Bree put her hand over the mouthpiece. "She's acting like you're there and she's going to put me through."

"This is Sue Percy," a woman said. "Scott is out of the office for a few weeks. Can I help you?"

"No, thanks, I'm a friend and wanted to catch up."

"When was the last time you spoke with Scott?"

"Why do you ask?"

"Hang on." A few seconds passed and Bree thought she heard a door shut in the background. Sue came back on the line. "We've been worried about him. He disappeared two weeks ago and hasn't called in."

"Oh, that's odd."

"I know he had vacation time coming, but to leave so suddenly was strange, and then some money went missing from petty cash."

"How much money?"

There was a long pause, then, "I need to go. Goodbye."

The line went dead. "O-kay."

"Why did you ask about money?" Scott said.

"The woman said you stopped coming into work about the same time petty cash went missing."

"What?" Scott stood and paced the room. "That's ridiculous. How much?"

"She wouldn't say."

"Why would I steal from my employer?"

"Don't assume you did."

"But she said—"

"It didn't sound like she thought you stole the money. It sounded like she was touting the company line."

"You got that from one phone call?" he asked.

"I've got good instincts."

Scott iced his ribs and was going through his laptop for clues when the forensic artist showed up. Scott and Bree worked with the artist on a sketch of the man who'd tried forcing Breanna into his car yesterday. By the time the artist was done, Scott felt as though he'd drawn a good likeness of the guy.

"That's pretty good," Scott said.

The forensic artist looked at Bree for confirmation.

"Yes, that looks like him."

The man who'd almost abducted Bree.

Scott balled his hand into a fist and tapped it against his thigh. Bree escorted the artist to the door and thanked him for his service.

Scott wanted answers. He wanted this whole thing over so he could be sure Bree was safe from harm, because by now it was clear she was in this for the long haul and nothing would dissuade her from staying close.

Which was even more motivation for Scott to remember what had brought him here.

He clicked through files on his computer, looking for anything that seemed even remotely related to water, but found nothing. He opened a file titled Lake Trip

2013 and thumbnail photos popped up on the screen.
He clicked one open: it was a shot of Scott with his arm
around an attractive redhead in a bathing suit. Christa.
Right, his…girlfriend?

"What'd you find?" Bree said, approaching him.

"Nothing important. Vacation pictures." He clicked
the picture closed. "There's got to be something on here
that can help us."

He clicked open his email account and scanned
through his sent folder. "Check this out, an email dated
three weeks ago scheduling time off."

As Bree read the email over his shoulder, he inhaled
her floral scent. He loved the way she smelled, the way
she absently placed her hand on his shoulder as she
peered at the screen.

"Open that one," she said, and pointed.

He clicked open an email from the human resources
manager approving his time off.

"Okay, so if they approved it, why did Sue Percy say
you mysteriously disappeared?"

"I can't trust anyone at work," he said.

"Maybe not, but you could retrace your steps."

She let her hand slip off his shoulder and sat next to
him at the table. "Let's figure out where you went from
the time you arrived in town until we rescued you."

"How are we going to do that?"

"It's a small town. Trust me, if someone spotted a
handsome stranger like you, they'd make a mental note.
Plus, when we get your wallet back from Chief Washburn we can go online and check your credit card activity."

"If he gives it back."

"It's not evidence unless a crime's been committed, right?"

"It's called fraud."

She leaned back in her chair and sighed.

He hated that she looked so frustrated. Then a thought struck him. "Hang on, you're on the right track," he said. "How about we start here, at the resort? This place has video surveillance. I noticed it last night. Let's ask Harvey if we can see video from the day I checked in."

"What are you thinking?"

"We'll start at the beginning and build a time line. In the meantime, you can reach out to folks in the community and see if they spotted me and if so, what I was doing."

"Sounds good. I'll start with Mom's book group. They meet every other week. They're pretty tuned into what's happening in town. First I'll call Harvey."

She stood and went to dig her phone out of her purse.

Scott redirected his attention to his laptop. Something in here had to offer a clue as to why he had water samples and who wanted them. Sifting through a few files, it became apparent he was in personal security for Phillip Oppenheimer, owner of Global Resources International—GRI. Scott found daily activity logs that outlined which security agents would be shadowing Phillip and his senior managers. There were at least two bodyguards assigned to the CEO at any given time. Scott wondered why a CEO would need such tight security.

He did an internet search on GRI and a few news stories popped up. Apparently Phillip Oppenheimer was some kind of genius and his company had developed a refinery that converted various types of waste products into diesel fuel.

"Thanks, Harvey," Bree said and turned to Scott, pocketing her phone. "Harvey said as a personal favor to me, he'd let us review the video."

"That's good, that's good," he said, distracted by an article on Global Resources International.

"What'd you find?" She sat beside him again.

"I work for one of the top guys in alternative energy development."

"Nice."

"Maybe I was investigating a competitor or someone who was trying to put him out of business?"

"Could be. What kind of energy?"

"A refining process that turns waste into diesel fuel."

"Wow, that's amazing. I wonder if that has something to do with the new plant up north."

"New plant?" He glanced at her.

"It opened earlier this year, but they didn't hire any locals. We all thought that was weird, but apparently it's automated and needs very few employees to run effectively."

"Huh." He clicked on the GRI website and found a page that identified their production locations. "Is it in Wallace County?"

"Yep."

"That's twenty miles north of here. So, if I'm investigating something related to the plant, what would I be doing in Echo Mountain?"

"Well, there aren't many hotels near the plant."

"Right, but the day you found me I was hiking in Woods Pass, nowhere near the plant. If I could get up to Wallace County and do a little digging…" He sighed. "I need to find my rental car."

"You could call the park service and ask if any cars have been abandoned in the past three days."

A knock echoed across the room.

"Aiden must have sent lunch," she said, getting up to answer the door.

He touched her arm. "No, I'll get it. You stay back."

As Scott went to the door, his mind clicked off possible reasons why he was here in Washington and didn't want to call his boss to tell him what was happening. Scott probably didn't want to disappoint him and risk losing his coveted position. Memories began to surface, like the boost to Scott's confidence when Mr. Oppenheimer had hired him to lead his security team. Scott hadn't want him to think he'd made a mistake by putting Scott in charge.

He glanced into the peephole and saw Chief Washburn.

"It's not lunch," Scott said to Bree, then opened the door. "Good morning, Chief."

Chief Washburn marched into the room and turned to Scott. "The gun you found in your room?" He glanced at Bree, then back at Scott.

Scott pressed his back against the door, bracing himself.

"Go on," Scott said.

"It was used in a shooting two months ago."

TEN

Bree wouldn't believe Scott had anything to do with a shooting, but she knew better than to argue with the chief, so she kept quiet.

"Was anyone killed?" Scott said in a defeated tone.

"No fatalities."

Scott sighed. "So you're taking me in, after all?"

"No."

Scott glanced up.

"The gun wasn't registered to you and the shootings were gang-related so I'm mystified as to how the weapon ended up in your room. It's almost like someone planted it here."

"If it isn't my gun, whose is it?"

Chief Washburn pulled out a small notebook. "It was registered to an Arthur Brown of Chicago, but he reported it stolen a year ago. You know him?"

"No, sir, I don't think so."

"There's more." Washburn consulted his notebook. "I spoke with detective Joe Rush at the Chicago P.D.—"

"My ex-partner."

"He said Scott James was your undercover alias. You

left the department last year to work in private security after the death of a teenager."

The frozen expression of Miguel Domingo still haunted Scott.

"You were cleared of any wrongdoing," the chief added.

Which didn't ease the guilt, guilt for not solving the case fast enough.

"A few months ago the chief of detectives asked Detective Rush for your contact information. When I called to inquire about your alias, Rush said maybe the chief has you working on something." Chief Washburn studied Scott. "Does this ring any bells?"

Scott shook his head. "I wish I could help."

"I've left a message for the chief to get back to me and your partner vouched for you. Apparently you're a good cop." Chief Washburn pulled Scott's wallet out of his jacket pocket. "You can have this back, but use your real identification from now on, okay?"

"Yes, sir. So, am I free to leave the premises?"

"I suppose I can't stop you. That said, I'd rather not have you running around town with guys using you as target practice." The chief glanced at Bree. "And I surely don't want her getting caught in the cross fire."

"No sir, that won't happen."

"You sound awfully sure of yourself."

"I am, sir. Like you said, I was—" he paused "—a good cop. I'll keep her safe. But I have to get out and conduct an investigation in order to solve this."

"I wish I could offer some help, but we're strapped for manpower as it is. I had to borrow from the reserves to keep an eye on you."

"And I appreciate that, sir."

"Where will you start your investigation?"

"First I'm going to retrace my steps beginning with the day I checked into the resort."

With a nod, the chief walked toward the door. "Good plan. But do not go into those mountains without backup."

"You just said you were strapped for manpower."

The chief turned to Scott. "I'll figure something out if you plan to head back up there. We've got some professional climbers in law enforcement who'd jump at the chance to accompany you."

"Thank you, sir."

"Be safe," the chief said, and nodded at Bree.

"Bye, Chief," she said.

Scott turned to Bree, pressing the heel of his palm against his temple.

"Hey, what's wrong?" She went to him.

"Headache's back. Maybe all that computer work." He went to the bed and stretched out on top of the covers.

"I'll get a cool washcloth. When was the last time you took an aspirin?"

"Last night."

"Well, you need one of those, but you should probably have food first. I'll call Aiden."

Scott draped his hand over his face. Bree worried about him, worried that the headache had consumed him so quickly. Perhaps this warranted a trip back to the E.R. After all, the stranger's attack this morning could have exacerbated his head injury.

First things first. She hit speed dial on her phone and called her brother.

"Yes, Bree," Aiden answered, his voice clipped.

"You okay?"

"Toilet broke in 337 and water's been leaking two floors into the rooms below. Not a fun morning."

"Oh, I'm sorry. Is it okay if I order room service for Scott and me? I know you said you were going to, but you sound busy."

"Sure, go ahead. Ask Nia to personally bring it to your room, that way you'll know it's legit."

"Will do. Chief Washburn stopped by with good news. He confirmed with Chicago P.D. that Scott's a good cop, so you can stop worrying about me."

"Sorry, kid, that ain't happening. Gotta go."

"Good luck."

"Thanks, you, too."

She hung up and smiled to herself. Well, at least their conversation was more pleasant than the last time they spoke. She didn't like being at odds with her brother, but wasn't sure how to get him to ease up on the over-protectiveness.

"What do you want for lunch?" she said, glancing at Scott.

"Whatever you're having."

"Soup and sandwich okay?"

"Sounds good."

She placed the order with Nia and asked her to deliver the cart personally. While they waited for lunch, Bree ran a washcloth under cool water and placed it on Scott's forehead.

"How's that?" she asked.

"Good, better." He reached up and placed his hand over hers. "I hate feeling so weak."

"It's okay. Listen to your body. It wants to heal."

"I wish it would heal faster."

"You shouldn't push it. Maybe we should take it easy this afternoon. Not do any running around."

"Can't. Have to figure this out," he said, sounding a little anxious.

"We will, we will," she hushed.

Bree started humming, but this time it wasn't to calm herself. She hoped the sound might give Scott a little peace.

"I know that one," he said, his voice soft.

She realized she was humming "Silent Night," which had been one of her favorites since she was a little girl.

A few minutes later Scott's hand slid off of Bree's and landed on the pillow beside his head. He'd fallen asleep.

"Rest, my friend. Rest and heal." Bree hummed beside him for a bit. She removed the cloth from his forehead and placed the back of her hand against his skin. He wasn't overly hot, so she didn't think he was running a fever.

After rinsing the washcloth under cool water yet again, she reapplied it to Scott's forehead and closed her eyes to say a silent prayer. *Dear God, thank You for this moment of peace, amen.*

Gratitude prayers always seemed to bring balance to a tenuous situation. Even in her worst days under Thomas's thumb, she'd find things to be grateful for: a sun break on a cloudy Seattle day or a little girl pushing her doll in a buggy alongside her mom. Gratitude kept Bree sane during an emotional whirlwind of turmoil.

Eyeing Scott, she wondered what things he had to be grateful for. She sensed there was darkness in his past, but she hoped he'd be able to focus on the light, which would surely help him heal faster.

After a few minutes, she decided to continue his investigation by going through some of the files on his laptop. Since the eyestrain might have spiked Scott's headache, she'd save him that discomfort and take over the project.

She positioned herself at the table and noticed he hadn't signed out of his email. Scanning his inbox, she spotted one from a rental car agency. Apparently he'd reserved a mid-size car for pickup at Sea-Tac airport over a week ago. She jotted down the phone number of the agency and the confirmation number. She'd call to determine what type of car he actually drove off in that day, which would then help them track it down.

Someone tapped at the door. If it was Nia with lunch, that certainly was quick.

She went to the door, glanced through the peephole and spotted Uncle Chuck pacing in the hallway. Terrific. She didn't need another lecture, but wouldn't be rude.

Bree snatched a key card from the nightstand and went to the door. She didn't want to wake Scott.

She stepped into the hallway and quietly shut the door behind her. "Hey, Uncle Chuck."

"Your mom's been worried about you so I said I'd stop by the resort."

"I'm fine, thanks. I talked to Mom last night."

"She told me you're still hanging out with trouble in there."

"He's a cop, maybe on an undercover assignment. Ask Chief Washburn, he'll explain it."

"It's not appropriate."

"Uh, what isn't appropriate?"

"Whatever you're doing with him in there."

"I was putting a cool washcloth on his forehead and

humming a Christmas song. He's still suffering from headaches thanks to the concussion."

"*He* is not *your* problem," he said in a firm voice.

She clenched her jaw against the shame crawling down her back. But this was Uncle Chuck trying to make Bree's mom happy by checking on her daughter. This wasn't about control or manipulation or—

"You need to stay away from him," he continued. "You don't know what he's into or who will come after him next. I heard about the room service incident, and you were standing right outside the door. You could have been seriously hurt."

"But I wasn't. Scott protected me."

"Don't be absurd."

Bree tried not to let the harsh words affect her, but she got that shrinking feeling again, the one that made her feel small and foolish.

No. No one was allowed to make her feel that way again.

She planted her hands on her hips. "I appreciate your concern but this is my business, Uncle Chuck. If Mom has a problem with how I'm conducting myself, she'll let me know."

"She'll be devastated if anything happens to you and it's my job to make sure it doesn't."

"Actually, it's mine," she said with a lift of her chin. "I'm responsible for myself, my decisions and actions."

"You're not thinking straight. That ex-boyfriend of yours has you twisted all up inside."

"Excuse me?" she said, horrified by the reminder.

Uncle Chuck must have realized he'd crossed the line. He sighed and leaned back. "I'm sorry, but I don't think you know what kind of people you're dealing with here."

"Hi, Bree," Nia called as she wheeled a cart toward them.

The concierge couldn't have come at a better time. Bree had had enough of Uncle Chuck's criticism and lectures. He meant well, but his delivery was hurtful.

"Hey, Nia," Bree said, turning to her friend. "Thanks for bringing lunch."

"My pleasure. Hey, Chief," she greeted Uncle Chuck. Most resort employees knew him because Chuck would bring Mom to the resort for dinner a few times a month.

Nia rolled up to the door and waited for Bree to open it.

"He's resting so I'll take it inside," Bree said.

"Great." Nia eyed Uncle Chuck. "What brings you to the resort, Chief?"

"Checking on my friend, here." He nodded at Bree.

"I appreciate the visit," Bree said. "I'll call Mom later." She swiped the key card and pushed the cart into Scott's room. She grabbed the door before it slammed shut, and eased it closed.

With a frustrated sigh, she wheeled the cart next to the dining table. Mom hadn't seemed overly worried last night when they spoke, certainly not worried enough to send Chuck to check on Bree.

Maybe it was Chuck's way of earning points with his girl, at least that's how he liked to think of Margaret McBride. Bree suspected Mom didn't consider her relationship with Chuck a serious one. Mom had shied away from romance ever since Dad passed away, saying she was blessed with true love once and didn't need to go looking for more.

True love. Did it exist in Bree's future? She'd pretty much given up on love after the disaster with Thomas. That nasty experience had proven to Bree that she had the worst judgment where men and love were concerned.

She glanced over her shoulder at Scott—still sound asleep. Talk about bad judgment. She could feel herself starting to care about him more than she should, yet she knew the unrealistic nature of their relationship. She took care of him during a frightening and vulnerable time. After this was over, he'd move back to Chicago and forget all about her.

He may have asked her out for a future date, but she couldn't count on him following through once he got his life back. Still, it was a nice gesture.

She pushed the curtain aside and spotted Ruby, one of the grounds crew, stringing Christmas lights along the split rail fence. The wrong lights. Rats, Aiden had given her specific instructions and she thought she'd clearly explained them to her coworkers. She'd better correct the issue before Aiden got on her case about neglecting her job.

Scott would probably nap for a while, giving Bree time to speak with Ruby and return without him noticing she was gone. Just in case, she left the bottle of pain reliever on the table and wrote him a note. She placed it prominently on the laptop and headed out.

The shrill sound of a siren tweaked his eardrums. Scott opened his eyes and glanced up at the gray sky. Light flakes of snow dropped into his face as he lay flat on his back.

"Help me, somebody help me," a soft, high-pitched voice said.

Scott couldn't move. It was like his body was glued to the pavement.

"Please, won't somebody help?"

He turned his head to the right....

And spotted Miguel Domingo, looking exactly the way he did that cold February night when Scott found him in the street, shot by a gang member's bullet.

A gut-wrenching sob caught in the back of Scott's throat. Why did the kid have to get involved? Scott told him he'd find evidence against the guys who killed his brother, but Miguel couldn't wait.

"How could you let me die?" Miguel said.

"Why, Scott, why?" a female voice said from the other side of Scott.

With great effort, he turned his head to the left....

Bree's beautiful green eyes stared at him. She wore a confused and desperate frown.

"Bree?" he said.

The siren grew louder, the sound making his eyes water with pain. Then Breanna blinked twice and her eyes stayed open with the blank stare of a corpse.

"No!"

Scott sat up, gasping for breath. Searching his surroundings, he struggled to figure out where he was and what just happened. He was damp with sweat and his head pounded. That's when he realized the phone was ringing on the nightstand beside his bed.

Sitting up, he grabbed the receiver. "Yeah?"

"Amnesia? Really?" his ex-partner said.

"Joe?"

"I spoke with the Echo Mountain police chief. So, you're working an undercover gig? For who? I thought you were off the payroll."

"I'm not sure."

"I get it. Need to know stuff. It's cool. I'll stop by your sister's this afternoon."

"Thanks man, thanks," Scott said with as much gratitude as he could muster.

"You think her accident is related to what you're working on out there?"

"It's possible, I'm not sure. My head's still foggy from the assault, and then some guy came after me this morning and whacked me pretty hard."

"Good thing you've got a head like a rock."

"Yeah."

"About before, that stuff I said about abandoning the job—"

"It's fine," Scott interrupted, because he wasn't so sure he hadn't done just that. Scott was confused about some things, but he didn't think his current investigation was part of an undercover assignment.

"Gotta run," Joe said.

"Thanks for calling, Joey."

"Yep."

Scott hung up and stretched out his neck. The headache wasn't as bad as it was earlier thanks to Bree stroking his head with a cool cloth.

Bree. The nightmare.

Panic clenched his gut. He glanced around the room and spotted a note on his laptop. A room service cart was positioned next to the table.

He wondered where she'd gone, but he had no right to expect her to stay close, to continue sitting beside him and stroking his forehead, humming "Silent Night." Yet anxiety tangled his insides whenever she was gone.

He had to figure out how to stop that; stop being so dependent on this woman.

He went to the table and read the note. She was helping an employee with Christmas lights and would be back shortly. Scott downed a few aspirin that she'd left for him. Curious, he took the metal cover off the room service plate to reveal a turkey sandwich. He checked the other one, as well, also turkey. So, she'd left without eating?

The phone rang again. He went to answer it, hoping it was Bree. "I have to let go of this," he muttered, then ripped the phone off the cradle. "Hello?"

Silence answered him.

"Hello?" he tried again.

"You know what we want," a deep voice said. "You've got twenty-four hours."

He gripped the phone. "I can't help you. I can't remember—"

"Figure it out or we'll end that pretty blonde nurse of yours."

Click.

Scott had to get to Bree, warn her and protect her. But how when he didn't even know where she'd gone? She could be stringing lights anywhere on the property.

He called the front desk and asked to be put through to security, hoping Harvey would know her location, but his voice mail picked up.

He grabbed his jacket and a key card off the table and rushed out.

Heart racing, Scott sprinted to the nearest exit and shoved open the door. A cool blast of winter air shocked him fully awake. He glanced up at the gray sky: it looked like snow was about to fall.

Scott scanned the property and noticed an employee stringing lights along a wooden fence. Jogging toward her, Scott's eyes kept moving, seeking out Bree, hoping he'd find her safe and unharmed.

"Good afternoon!" he called out.

The young woman turned to him. She was in her twenties with fair skin and red hair. Her name tag read Ruby.

"Can I help you?" Ruby asked with a smile.

"I'm looking for Bree."

"She was here a minute ago. I think she went to find replacement bulbs for the ones that burned out."

"Where would she have gone to get replacement bulbs?"

"Either the barn, or in the storage locker by the security office."

"Where's that?"

"Inside the south entrance." She pointed.

"Thanks." Scott headed toward the building, shoving his hands in his jacket pockets, focused on finding Bree and making sure she was okay.

She had to be okay.

As he approached the door, Harvey came outside.

"Hey, have you seen Bree?" Scott asked.

"Not since yesterday, why?"

The sound of a woman's scream echoed across the property.

ELEVEN

Chills shot down Scott's spine.

"Help, somebody help me!" Breanna cried.

"The barn!" Harvey said.

Scott took off in a full-blown sprint.

"Wait," Harvey said.

Scott wasn't waiting for Harvey or anyone else. With every pump of his arms, Scott's bullet wound ached.

His heart ached more. He did this. He put Bree in the line of fire.

He got to the barn and slid into the doorway. "Breanna!"

"Up here!"

He snapped his attention toward the second level storage area but didn't see her. Did her attacker have her pinned up there behind the stacks of boxes?

Harvey came up beside him. "Where is she?"

"Up there. Let her go!" Scott ordered.

"I can't let go, I'm stuck!" Bree called down to them.

Scott and Harvey rushed to the far side of the barn and looked up. She was hanging from the ceiling by her ankle.

"How did you—"

"Please get me down," she interrupted Harvey.

Concerned, yet relieved, Scott finally took a breath. She had a mishap, an accident. No one was threatening her with a gun. They hadn't followed through on their threat. Yet.

Scott studied the rope attached to her leg and noticed the other end tied around a cast iron decorative fountain.

"Come on," he said to Harvey.

Scott went to the fountain to untie the rope.

"Here." Harvey pulled out a knife.

"No, then you won't be able to lower her down easy," Scott said. "By untying it we've got all this slack to work with."

"Thanks for not taking any pictures," Bree joked.

Scott looked up at her in question.

"Ya' know, to totally embarrass me on Facebook."

She was being awfully calm considering her position dangling upside down like a turkey ready to be plucked. Then again, maybe the lightheartedness was a cover for the fear that had to be coursing through her body.

It must be terrifying to be strung up in such a vulnerable way. Scott couldn't help but wonder if this was a mere accident or if it was a calculated threat to drive home the caller's message.

Figure it out or we'll end that pretty blonde nurse of yours.

"Almost done," Scott said, loosening the knot. "Harvey, grab hold of the rope and we'll let her down easy."

"Try not to drop me on my head," Bree said.

Harvey grabbed the rope and Scott completely loosened the knot, reaching the rope, as well.

"I can manage her weight," Harvey said. "You get beneath her and cushion her landing."

"My landing? Oh, boy," Bree said.

Scott nodded at Harvey and let go. The older man had a solid grip of the rope and didn't seem to strain against Bree's weight. Although why would he? The petite Bree probably didn't weight much more than a hundred pounds.

"Okay, nice and easy." Scott positioned himself beneath her. Keeping eye contact, he forced a gentle smile to let her know everything was going to be okay.

She jerked down a few inches and flailed her arms. "Yikes!"

"Sorry," Harvey said. "It's like driving a new car. Have to get used to the brakes."

As Harvey lowered her a little more, Scott could tell her eyes were watering. The pain must be worse than she let on. Or was it the fear?

"A little faster." Scott reached out to catch her.

"Yep," Harvey said.

He lowered her in jerky movements, probably trying to balance her weight against his own, until she was only inches from Scott's outstretched arms.

"Catch me," she whispered.

"You know I will," Scott said.

Another jerk and Scott got a hold of her shoulders. He turned her so she was facing him and as her tethered leg lowered to the ground, he pulled her firmly against his chest.

"Okay, I got her," Scott said.

Harvey released the rope. Scott slid his good arm beneath her knees and scooped her up. She wrapped her arms around his neck, burying her face against his shoulder.

"Go ahead and cut the rope off her ankle," Scott said.

"Yep." Harvey cut the rope.

With a shudder, Bree leaned back and looked into Scott's eyes. A part of him never wanted to let her go.

"Thanks," she said.

Scott kneeled and lowered her onto an overturned crate. "Tell me what happened." He didn't let go of her hand.

"I was looking for replacement lightbulbs, but it's a mess back there with garland and lights scattered all over. Then I heard a scuffling sound and thought it was Ruby so I went to call out to her, tripped and went flying up to the rafters."

Harvey analyzed the rope he'd cut off her ankle. "Slip knot. Awfully neat, as if..." he glanced at Scott.

"Someone intended to string her up."

"Why would anyone..." She paused. "Oh."

"This was intentional? To harm Breanna?" Harvey said in a worried tone.

"Could be." Scott pulled his hand away from Bree's and stood. "A man called my room and said if I didn't give them what they wanted they'd go after Bree."

"Then give them what they want," Harvey snapped.

"Harvey," Bree said in a scolding tone.

"What? He gives them what they want and they go away." He nodded at Bree. "They'll leave you alone."

"Problem is, I think I know what they want, but haven't a clue where it is," Scott said. "I'll figure it out. Harvey, you take care of Bree."

"Where are you going?" Bree said, rubbing her ankle.

"I have to leave."

"You mean run away?"

"I mean leave this resort, and you, behind. That way—"

"No." Bree stood and wavered.

When Scott offered his hand to steady her, she pulled away to prove she didn't need his help.

"It won't matter, Scott," she said. "They already have me on their radar. If you're here or not here, I'm still a target."

"Because of me. And that drives me crazy," he said.

She gripped his jacket and looked up into his eyes. "Then fix it. End this thing before something even worse happens."

"But—"

"They're bullies, Scott. As long as you let them stomp all over you they'll keep on stompin'. They'll threaten you and terrorize you and control your life if you let them."

From the expression in her eyes, Scott sensed she was speaking from her heart, from personal—and painful—experience.

"I want you to go away somewhere, for your own safety," he said.

"What will that prove? If they think I'm leverage over you they'll find me. I won't be safe until you find answers and we resolve this situation." She let go of his jacket and stepped around him. "Did you save me anything for lunch, because I think I've earned a turkey sandwich."

He didn't know how to respond to her casual remark. As she headed across the barn, he noticed her limping and rushed to her side.

Bree put up her hand. "Do not pick me up."

"I want to help you," Scott said.

She looked up at him with those expressive and pleading green eyes. "Then stand up to them. Fight them with everything you've got."

Bree thought she did a pretty good job of not letting on how terrified she was when she'd been strung up in the barn; but she guessed Scott knew the truth. She didn't seem to be able to keep anything from him.

Over the course of the next few hours he was attentive to her every need, from offering aspirin for her muscle pain, to heating water for her tea. He didn't even have to ask what she needed; he did what was necessary.

Now if he'd only puzzle through this mystery and put an end to the hidden threat stalking them from the shadows.

At least he'd given up trying to get rid of her. Boy, that sounded pathetic, she thought, eyeing him as he studied the computer screen.

She wasn't leaving his side until they made some headway on this case. The whole bully thing made her crazy in ways that left her speechless. She'd spent months after her break-up analyzing her relationship with Thomas, beating herself up for not standing firm. Whenever she noticed that same bullying behavior in someone else, her anger at the injustice would practically consume her.

That's what these men were doing to Scott. They were threatening him, this guy who was functioning with a head injury, gunshot wound and bruised ribs. She wasn't going to stand for it. No, sir.

As she sipped her tea, she wondered if Harvey had told her brother about what happened in the barn. Probably not or else Aiden would have pounded on the door two hours ago. So Harvey had kept her business private. Either that, or he hadn't run into Aiden this afternoon. Knowing Harvey, it would be a casual conversation, not a specific phone call to tattle on Bree. Harvey was cool that way.

"Bree?" Scott said, studying her.

"Yeah?"

"You okay?"

"Sure, why?"

"You looked worried."

"I was wondering what my brother will do when he finds out about the barn incident."

"You mean, besides kick me out of his resort?" he said. "I'm surprised I haven't received the bill under my door by now."

"Talk about the biggest bully of them all," she muttered.

He took her hand. "Aiden is not a bully. He's a loving brother. You're lucky to have him."

"I guess. Did you find anything in your files?"

"Yes." He released her hand and refocused on the screen. "My phone calendar was synced up to my laptop so I can see what I did the week before I came to Washington, and then once I got here. I was working security for Mr. Oppenheimer, owner of GRI, in Hawaii for a week prior to my trip. Nothing remarkable there. When I got to Washington I had an appointment with someone named C.J. the day after my plane landed."

"Was there a location?"

"Healthy Eats Restaurant. I don't remember if we actually met or not."

"Oh, the new organic place."

"I'd like to take a ride over there to see if anyone remembers me."

"I've been wanting to try their soups." She grabbed her purse and stood.

"What about the Christmas decorations?"

"Ruby's got it covered." She smiled. "Hey, let's bring something home to reheat for dinner later so you don't have to order room service."

"Sounds like a plan. But if we're going out in public I'm going to need your help." He motioned her toward the door.

"With what?"

"Your instincts. Listen to them, trust them. If something seems off or suspicious, let me know, okay?"

"Of course."

"I'm not so sure my instincts are a hundred percent."

She paused and touched his arm. "It will come back to you, your memory, your instincts."

"You always sound so confident when you say stuff like that."

"You have to have faith." She smiled and they left his room.

Bree suggested they stop at her place first to let Fiona out and throw the ball to burn off some of her pup's energy. When they got to her cottage and opened the back door, Fiona bounded outside. Bree shoved a tennis ball in the stick launcher and offered it to Scott.

"Whenever I'm in a bad mood this always helps," she said. "Well, this and baking."

Fiona rushed him as he let the ball fly.

"An important characteristic for rescue dogs is the

high play factor," Bree said. "And their endurance level."

Fiona rushed back to Scott and dropped the ball at his feet, wagging her tail.

"This one can go on for hours, right baby girl?" Bree said.

Scott tossed the ball again and Fiona took off. A warm smile eased across his face. The Fiona mood enhancer was working for him, too.

Bree noted his look of abandon: he was totally lost in the moment playing with her dog. Watching Fiona chase the ball with such joy always brought a smile to Bree's face.

Scott glanced over his shoulder at Bree's home. "Why aren't your Christmas lights up?"

"Aiden's supposed to help but he's been slammed at work, plus helping Mom with some house projects."

"I could help," he offered, and glanced at her, then back at the dog, "if you want."

"That would be awesome."

A sudden image of Bree and Scott sitting by the fireplace in her living room eating freshly baked pumpkin muffins crossed her thoughts. A lovely image indeed.

"You seriously like Christmas, huh?" he said, tossing the ball again.

"What do you mean?"

"The way your face lit up just now when I said I'd help put up decorations. I'll bet you're going to send me up on the roof with boxes of lights."

"Nothing so dangerous."

His smile faded, along with their moods. The word *dangerous* yanked them back to reality. They were no longer a normal couple playing catch with her dog and making Christmas plans.

He was a man being hunted for something he couldn't remember, and Bree was the woman determined to help him.

They played with the dog for a few more minutes, then Bree put Fiona back inside.

She locked up and they got in her SUV. The short drive to Healthy Eats started off quiet. Was Scott worrying about what he'd find out at the restaurant? She noticed he kept looking into the side view mirror.

To ease the tension she clicked on the radio to a station playing Christmas music. The sound of Bing Crosby singing "White Christmas" filled the car.

"This is a fun movie. We watch it every year," she said, casting a quick glance at Scott. "What are your family traditions for Christmas?"

"Don't have any. Mom was always working, Dad was never in the picture, I'm usually working."

"What about your sister?"

"I stop by around the holidays, but she spends Christmas with her best friend, Ashley. She has a big family with lots of kids running around, playing with their new toys. That's more fun for Em than hanging out with me."

"So what do you do on Christmas Day?"

"Relax, watch football if it's on, maybe catch a movie."

"Alone?"

"Mostly." He glanced at her. "What about you?"

"For the past five years Mom's been having an open house. She's got a big old house on twenty acres. Anyone who doesn't have family is welcome as long as they bring a side dish or dessert. Mom provides the ham, turkey and beverages."

"A lot of people show up?"

"Depends on the year. The first few years it was a dozen or so. Last year we had a full house. Aiden counted 35 people, and some stayed until midnight."

"That sounds like quite a party."

She thought about Christmas last year and how embraced she had felt, how loved, in contrast to her Christmases in the city.

"What, did someone break a lamp or something?" Scott said.

"No," she chuckled. "Why did you ask that?"

"Your smile faded."

"It was the first time in a long time that I'd felt part of a community. Living in the city had been an isolating experience for me."

"Because of your boyfriend?"

"Pretty much. He didn't approve of me hanging out with girlfriends or coming back to visit family."

"I take it he didn't attend your family Christmas party?"

"Absolutely not, and he guilted me into skipping it one year, as well."

"The guy sounds like a jerk." He glanced at her. "Sorry."

"It's okay. He was a jerk in the end. He refused to let me break up until I convinced him I wasn't good enough for him."

"You did not," Scott said, disbelief coloring his voice.

"I did what was necessary to extricate myself from a bad situation. It wasn't pretty, but it worked." She sighed, remembering how taken she'd been with

Thomas when they'd first started dating. "He wasn't always a jerk. In the beginning he was polite and sophisticated, intelligent and funny. All the things I thought were important."

"And now?"

"Now, other things are important, like kindness and integrity. But it doesn't matter because I promised myself I wouldn't date for at least a year after that breakup. The whole experience was tough, but I came back to Echo Mountain, adopted Fiona from a SAR volunteer who had to move away and give her up. Training for SAR and going on missions distracted me from my pain."

"And how long has it been, since your breakup?"

"It's coming up on a year."

He nodded and glanced out the window.

Bree realized she hadn't even been interested in dating anyone, not even a little bit and not even the safe men her mom tried fixing her up with.

Until Scott literally fell beneath her tree.

"About this restaurant," he started, "will I have to eat kale and goji berries?"

"Sure, if you want." She winked.

"I'm more of a meat loaf kind of guy."

"I'm sure we'll find something. There it is." She pointed.

"Let's hope someone recognizes me."

She parked and they got out of the car.

The restaurant was housed in a bungalow style building with white trim and multipane windows.

"I've driven by a few times but never had time to go inside," Bree said as they approached the restaurant.

The door swung open and a twenty-something young

man with jet-black hair stepped outside. He glanced at Scott and froze, blocking the door.

"I don't think so."

"I'm sorry?" Scott said.

"Oh, no, not good enough." The young man pulled out his cell phone.

"Who are you calling?" Bree asked.

The kid glared at Scott. "9-1-1."

TWELVE

"There must be some mistake," Bree said.

"No mistake. I told him never to come back. This is a healthy restaurant, we offer a healthy environment as well as healthy food which means no stress, or fighting."

"Look, we need your help," Bree said, hoping to keep him from making the call. "Please? Three minutes of your time. We won't even come inside."

The young man lowered his phone. "Fine."

"Thanks." She extended her hand. "I'm Breanna Mc-Bride, my brother runs Echo Mountain Resort."

"I've heard of you guys, the McBride family."

"And you are…?"

He shook her hand. "Dylan Jones."

"Oh, you're Catherine's son? I met your mom at church a few weeks ago, but I didn't see you."

"I was at work. Hospital shift."

"Dylan, my friend Scott was in an accident and is suffering from a head injury. I'm trying to help him remember things, perhaps by recreating where he's been and who he met with. Obviously you remember him being here."

"Wait, you were the guy that was shot in the mountains?" he asked.

"Yes," Scott said.

"And now you can't remember stuff?"

"Nope."

"Maybe you're better off." Dylan crossed his arms over his chest and leaned against the building.

"Can't argue with you there," Scott said. "Judging by your behavior I have a feeling I'm not going to like what I find out."

"What happened, Dylan?" Bree asked.

"He went nuts on this other guy, grabbed him by the collar and practically threw him across the room."

Dylan's mom pushed the door open. "Dylan, what's going on?" She glanced at Bree and smiled. "Oh, hi, Breanna."

"Catherine, it's nice to see you again."

"Dylan, we're supposed to encourage patrons to come into the restaurant, not keep them out."

"This is the guy, Mom, the one that started the fight last week."

Catherine eyed Scott.

"I'm sorry if I did anything to disturb you or your patrons, ma'am," Scott said. "I wish I had an explanation, but I sustained a head injury which has caused memory loss."

Catherine glanced at Bree.

"It's true," Bree confirmed. "This is the man we rescued from the trail Sunday."

"The one who was shot?"

"Yes."

"Another reason you shouldn't let him into the restaurant," Dylan said. "What if they try shooting him in here?"

"Dylan, don't be so dramatic," his mom said. "Come get something to eat." Catherine held the door open and motioned them inside.

Bree spotted a sheriff's deputy sitting in the corner sipping coffee.

"That's my brother, Nate Walsh," Catherine said. "He stops by on break. Let me introduce you."

"He's got a gun," Dylan threatened, nodding at Scott.

Catherine shook her head. "Nate, this is Breanna McBride and her friend, Scott."

Scott offered his hand. "Scott Becket."

Nate shook Scott's hand and narrowed his eyes. "The hiker who was shot and has amnesia?"

"Wow, word gets around," Scott said.

Nate shrugged. "That was pretty big stuff for this county."

Breanna also shook hands with Deputy Nate Walsh. "So nice to meet you. We were hoping that bringing Scott back to places he'd been to before the accident might help him regain his memory."

"Oh, he was here, all right," Dylan said.

"Hey, kid, can you get me a refill?" Nate held up his empty mug.

"Sure." He sneered at Scott as he passed.

"Well, have a seat anywhere," Catherine said. "This is my slow time of the day."

"Thanks," Scott said. "I hate to press, but it would probably help if your son could give me a play-by-play of what happened when I was here last."

"I'd like to hear that, too." Nate motioned for Scott and Bree to join him in the booth and they did. She appreciated sitting with a police officer, thinking maybe it would keep the bad guys at a distance.

"Well, I have food to prep," Catherine said with a smile. "Keep in mind, Dylan tends to embellish when he has an audience."

"So you don't think Scott got violent?" Bree said.

"I'm sure something happened, but he certainly didn't tear up the place. There was no damage to speak of. Anyway, nice to see you again, Breanna."

"Thanks, you, too."

Catherine disappeared into the kitchen as Dylan returned to the table with the pot and poured coffee for his uncle.

"So, Dylan," Nate started, "tell me again what happened when Scott here tore up the place."

Dylan set the pot on the table. "Are you messing with me?"

"No, I'd like to hear the story again. He got into a fight and what, threw chairs or something?"

Dylan sighed and nibbled at the corner of his mouth. "Not exactly."

"Okay, then what, he made a mess of the table, left you a bad tip?"

"Forget it." Dylan turned to walk away.

"Dylan, please," Scott said. "I could seriously use your help. Anything you could tell me about what I said or how I acted, or anything about the man I was talking to—"

"You weren't talking," Dylan spun around. "You were yelling. The argument started in here, then continued out in the parking lot."

"I didn't do anything violent in the restaurant?"

"You pounded on the table and spilled water everywhere."

"Ah, so you were upset that you had to clean up," his uncle said.

"You didn't see him, Uncle Nate. He looked scary." Dylan glanced at Scott. "Sorry, but you did."

"Don't be sorry. Could you give us a description of the other guy?"

"He was older." He glanced at his uncle. "Even older than you."

"Why, thanks," Nate muttered.

"He had gray in his hair and wore a leather jacket and a blue baseball cap with a red *C* on the front."

Bree gripped Scott's leg. "The man who tried to get to you in the hospital."

"And did get to me in my hotel room," Scott said. "So I knew him pretty well if we met for lunch."

"You might know him, but you didn't like him," Dylan said.

"Go on," Nate encouraged.

"When I was cleaning up your table, you guys kept talking like I was invisible. The other guy said, 'the boss says it's over, then it's over.' You said, 'I'm doing this to save the boss.' You said something about talking directly to your boss and the other guy made a snide comment as I was walking away. That's when I heard a crash and the flower vase hit the floor. When I turned around, you had him by the collar of his jacket. You were breathing fire, man, I thought you were going to strangle him, so I threatened to call 9-1-1 and you left. I watched you guys in the parking lot. He was pretty calm, but you were waving your arms, trying to make your point."

"And you'd never seen the older man before, and you haven't seen him since that day?" Deputy Nate asked.

"No, sir, I'd remember. He was one creepy-looking dude."

"Thanks, Dylan. You've been a big help," Scott said.

Bree puzzled over the conversation Dylan just shared.

"You guys want coffee? It's organic, fair trade," Dylan offered to Scott and Bree.

"Sure, I'll have a cup," Scott said.

"Do you have any tea?" Bree asked.

"I'll bring over the list. It's also organic and loose leaf."

"Sounds great."

Dylan left the table.

"Does that help?" Nate asked.

Scott nodded. "It confirms that I was here for work on a special project for my boss."

"Then why would your boss send the salt-and-pepper haired man to stop you?" Bree asked.

"Maybe he didn't. Maybe Rich was lying."

They three of them sat quietly for a few seconds.

"Well, I'd better get back." Deputy Nate shifted out of the booth. "Watch yourselves and let me know if I can help with anything." He jotted his cell number on a restaurant business card and slid it across the table.

"Thanks," Scott said.

Dylan returned, offered Bree a tea list and poured Scott a cup of coffee.

"Oh, there was one other thing," Dylan offered.

"What's that?" Scott said.

"You asked if I knew where the refinery plant was in

Wallace County. You said something about your GPS not being able to find it or something."

"And did you give me directions?"

"I did. Are you guys ordering food? We have a tasty butternut squash soup that's dairy and gluten free."

"I'll have the paradise green tea but could you give us a few minutes on our food order?" Bree said.

"Absolutely."

Dylan went into the back and Bree placed her hand over Scott's. "This helps, right? Now you know you were headed to the plant."

"I need to get up there."

"It'll be dark in a few hours. Let's go tomorrow."

He looked into her eyes. "I'd rather you stay at the resort."

"And hide? No, thanks. If these jerks are after me, too, then I'd like to be a part of the investigation. Besides, I'm with you until the end of this thing."

"Bree—"

"If you're worried about our safety, we could get one of the SAR guys to come with us, or better yet I'll ask Uncle Chuck to meet us there. It's in his county."

"A cop," he hedged. "I don't know what I'm going to find up there."

"You mean something that will reflect poorly on you?"

"You have such a nice way of saying things. Yes, I'm afraid I've participated in something criminal and it'll come out if I keep pushing."

"I doubt it, but facing your mistakes is the only way to move on with your life or they will shadow you forever."

He cocked his head slightly and a tender smile tugged at his lips. "How did you get so wise?"

"I've had my share of challenges," she said, "but in the end they made me stronger."

"You're amazing."

The words sent a shiver across her shoulders. Thomas used to call her that. Bree leaned back and studied him. Scott wasn't working an angle to get something in return. He sincerely meant it. He considered her an amazing individual.

"Uh, the brain injury has kind of messed with my filter, so was that one of those things I should have kept to myself?" he asked.

"No, actually, I'm glad you didn't."

The next morning Bree got up early and did a majority of her resort work so she could take a long lunch and drive Scott to the plant. She called Uncle Chuck who agreed to meet them, so everything was all set. Since Aiden had business in Seattle he wasn't around to hammer her with twenty questions when she left the resort with Scott.

As they headed north in her SUV she noted that Scott was unusually quiet. "How's your head?" she asked.

"Better than yesterday."

"That's good."

A few minutes of silence stretched between them.

"Are you okay?" she asked.

He glanced at her. "What do you mean?"

"You seem…distant."

"I'm focused on making sure we're not being followed," he said, squinting as he studied the side view mirror.

"How does it look?"

"Good."

Another few minutes of silence. Bree assumed Scott was anticipating the worst; that he wouldn't like what he discovered at the plant.

"It will be okay," she offered.

He nodded and glanced out the window.

"Okay, spill it."

He snapped his attention to her. "What?"

"Whatever's bothering you. I have to know because it's driving me nuts and I'm making up stories in my head."

"Stories?"

"Yes, like you don't want me around, or you remembered something terrible, or—"

"I want you around." He glanced back out the window. "I want this whole thing over."

"It will be. You have to have faith."

"I wish I knew how to do that."

"Just ask."

He frowned at her in question.

"Close your eyes and ask God for guidance in helping you navigate through this challenge."

"I have no right to—"

"You do, Scott. We all do."

With a sigh he closed his eyes for a few seconds, and when he opened them he seemed better, less tense. They still didn't speak much during the ride up to the plant, but she didn't push it.

Thirty minutes later they pulled into a long driveway that led to a large parking lot. There were only a few cars scattered throughout the lot, which seemed odd.

"It's the middle of the workday. Shouldn't there be more cars?" she said.

"You would think."

"There's my uncle's cruiser." She found a spot nearby, but Uncle Chuck wasn't in the car. "Maybe he's already inside."

They shared a concerned look, then got out of the car. As she stepped up to Scott he put out his hand. "Stay behind me."

"Okay."

She appreciated that he was being cautious, but she wasn't too worried since her uncle was here. They approached the main door.

"There's got to be an intercom or something to let them know we're here."

Bree observed that the door was ajar. "Scott." She nodded.

He pushed it open.

The first thing Bree noticed was how quiet it was inside the building, as if it was abandoned. "This is creepy."

Scott pointed at a sign down the hall that read Research & Development. "Let's try there first."

They went down the hall and followed the arrows. Turning the corner, she wondered if this could be considered trespassing. She also wondered what happened to Uncle Chuck. Was he inside speaking with an employee?

"What are you looking for?" she asked, placing her hand against Scott's back.

He pushed open the double doors and froze. "This."

Bree glanced around him into the room. There was

nothing there, no research equipment, computers or even furniture.

"Did they close the plant?" she said.

"Not that I know of."

They wandered around the room looking for something, anything to help make sense of the situation.

"It's almost like it never existed," she said.

"Or everything was destroyed."

"By whom?" she said.

He shook his head. "No clue."

"We should find my uncle."

Scott took her hand and led her out of the empty research room. As they headed back to the main office, Bree peered through office windows as they passed. Desks and bookshelves were empty—no computers, books or supplies. The place was definitely closed for business.

"Hang on." Scott paused beside a set of double doors.

The sign above read Assembly.

He pushed open the doors and they entered a huge room with high ceilings, cement walls and no windows. Twenty-foot metal racks were lined up in rows.

"Where is everything?" he said.

"What should be in here?"

"According to the website, portable refinery containers and braces to hold them in place while the chemical is infused into the containers."

"Maybe they've been shipped out?"

"There'd still be equipment to assemble the product," he said.

Something sparkly caught Bree's attention on the floor. She bent down to pick it up.

A shot rang out.

She instinctively stayed down. Scott dropped to the floor and got in her face. "Stay here," he ordered, shifting her further behind the metal rack.

"Don't—"

He stopped her protest with a kiss. His lips were warm and soft, and she was so shocked by the tender and loving gesture that she couldn't speak when he broke the kiss and took off. Scott darted down the side of the wall, using the metal racks as cover. She guessed he was going after the shooter.

She slipped out her cell phone to call 9-1-1, but realized it would take them too long to get here. She decided to call her uncle instead.

Two more shots rang out. Biting back a shriek, she eyed her phone and willed her trembling fingers to press the right buttons.

Another shot rang out.

Her eyes watered with fear. If anything happened to Scott after everything he'd been through...

She searched her phone's address book for her uncle's number.

A crash bounced off the ceiling and the sound of grunting men echoed through the room. She eyed the door. To get there, to escape, she'd have to expose herself to the gunman.

Bree stuck with plan A and dialed her uncle's number.

Another shot rang out.

Then silence.

She hit Send on her phone.

And the sound of Uncle Chuck's cell phone rang across the room.

THIRTEEN

By the time Scott got to Bree's uncle he was down on the cement floor, gripping his shoulder. Scott pulled him behind the metal rack.

"Go, go protect Bree," Chuck said.

"You're coming with me."

"I'll slow you down."

"Make sure you don't."

Uncle Chuck glared at Scott and Scott glared back, challenging the older man to reach deep down and find the strength to get up.

"Where is she?" Chuck asked.

"Down there by the door. Ready?"

Chuck nodded, his expression unsure.

"On three. One, two, three." Scott shielded Chuck against the wall and they jogged toward Bree's hiding spot.

Scott couldn't move fast enough, but the pain from Chuck's wound was obviously slowing him down. A shot pinged above Scott's head. It wasn't easy hitting a target shielded by metal racks. From this angle, Scott had a pretty good guess where the shooter was positioned.

Scott would get Uncle Chuck and Bree safely to her car; then he'd conceal himself and wait for the guy to leave. Scott wasn't looking for trouble, but this guy was his best lead to figuring out why he had come to Echo County in the first place.

When they got close to Bree, a knot formed in Scott's throat. She was huddled like a little girl afraid of a monster in her bedroom closet.

"Bree, it's okay," Scott said, kneeling beside her. She glanced at him with those big green eyes. "Come on." He helped her up. She noticed Uncle Chuck's bloody hand gripping his arm.

"Uncle Chuck," she gasped.

"I'll be fine once I get you out of here."

A bullet hit the cement wall above them and Bree yelped as they all took cover.

"New plan," Scott said to Uncle Chuck. "I'll draw his fire and you get her out of here."

"Scott, no," she said.

Scott ignored her and nodded at her uncle.

"Let me call it in first." Chuck grabbed the radio on his shoulder and called in the code for shots fired and officer down. That would get local cops and state troopers racing to the scene.

Another shot echoed through the assembly room and Bree leaned against Scott's chest. He gave her a solid hug, waiting until her uncle was ready to make a run for it.

"Why don't we wait for the police?" her muffled voice said against Scott's jacket.

"It'll take too long. Get ready to run."

"I won't abandon you," she said with a tight jaw.

"This isn't your decision to make," Scott said. He

released her and shoved her at her uncle. "If anything happened to you I'd never forgive myself. If you care about me, you won't do that to me."

Her expression softened. "Be careful."

Uncle Chuck grabbed her arm and leaned in the direction of the door. He nodded at Scott. "Whenever you're ready."

Scott took a deep breath, peered around the metal shelves he was using as cover, and took off. He'd had experience outmaneuvering the enemy but this was different. There was more than just his life at stake; Bree's life was at stake, as well.

A bullet pinged the metal behind him, but didn't ricochet and clip Scott. He swerved one way, then the other, focused on the exit, not the marksman. No use letting that image mess with his head: Scott as a duck in a carnival shooting gallery.

He was almost to the door when the shooting stopped. He sprinted outside, finding a spot behind a cluster of trees to wait for the shooter to exit. Struggling against the adrenaline rush, he planned his next move: getting to the shooter without being shot himself.

But the shooter didn't leave the building, at least not through any door that Scott could see. Had he followed Bree and her uncle out front?

"No," he ground out and took off around the perimeter of the plant. When he got to the front, Bree's car was gone.

A door slammed. Scott jerked his head around and saw a short, stocky guy running for a black sedan—the same car that had tried to pick up Bree the other day.

The shooter must have emptied his clip and was fleeing the premises.

Scott charged the guy, tackling him before he could get to his car.

"Why are you shooting at me?" Scott demanded.

"Because I'm bored." The guy struggled against the hold.

"Tell me!"

Instead, he slugged Scott in the stomach.

Scott's grip loosened.

Stocky guy pummeled Scott in the arm where he'd been shot. Scott fought to keep a tight hold, but the guy flipped Scott over and they rolled, Scott fighting the burn of his gunshot wound. He threw a few punches and hit his mark, but was at a disadvantage thanks to his previous injuries.

The shooter nailed Scott in the jaw and he saw stars, but managed to stay conscious. He had to restrain the guy, get him to talk. Scott broke free and reached for a nearby rock to use as a weapon.

Three shots rang out.

Scott hit the ground and scrambled behind a car in the lot.

His arm burned and his jaw ached but it was nothing compared to the fear flooding through his body. Did the guy have an accomplice?

"Scott!" Breanna's voice cried out.

He fisted his hand and slammed it into the quarter panel of the car. Not only did the guy have an accomplice, but he'd also gotten his hands on Bree.

Scott had no choice but to sacrifice himself for Bree's safety. He needed to convince them to let her go.

With a deep breath, he stood and raised his hands in surrender.

Instead of seeing Bree restrained by a heartless

thug, she was running in Scott's direction. Confused, he slowly lowered his hands and spotted the stocky guy sprawled on the ground, blood staining his jacket. In the distance Uncle Chuck clutched his gun, looking a little stunned. Scott wondered if the guy had ever killed a man.

Reality struck hard: if the guy was dead, so was Scott's best lead.

He caught Bree as she launched herself into his arms. "I told you to get out of here," he said.

"Lecture me later. I'm so glad you're okay."

Only then did he realize she was trembling. He held her tight and stroked her hair. "Shh, it's okay."

Scott would have been a lot better if he could have forced information out of the guy lying on the ground.

Chuck went to the body, pressed his fingers against the man's throat and glanced at Scott. "He's gone."

Bree glanced down at the body. "That's the guy who tried to pick me up outside the police station."

Scott turned her away from the dead body.

Sirens echoed in the distance.

"I had no choice." Uncle Chuck stood, looking a little pale.

Scott released Bree. "Hang on, buddy." Scott went to steady Chuck, who started to waver on his feet. "Let's find you a place to sit down."

As Scott and Bree led Chuck to a nearby picnic bench a man came out of the plant. He was in his forties, wore a uniform and winced as he pressed his hand against the back of his head.

"Who are you?" the guy asked.

"Scott Becket, this is Breanna McBride and Police

Chief Trainer." Chuck sat down with a dazed expression.

The uniformed guy joined them. "Police chief?"

"Of Wallace Falls," Chuck said. "And you are?"

"Pete Baker, security guard."

"Where were you when all this was going on, Pete?" Scott challenged.

"Inside. Some guy nailed me in the back of the head and I was out." He glanced at the stocky guy, then back at Scott. "What's going on here?"

"It's a long story," Scott said.

"Scott lost his memory and is trying to get it back," Bree said as she pressed her scarf against her uncle's wound. "Someone told us Scott had been up here so we came to check it out, maybe jar something loose. Do you remember meeting Scott?"

It struck Scott how incredibly trusting she was, and focused. She'd seen a man shot down in front of her but was still on task: she wanted to help Scott remember.

Pete studied Scott. "No, I can't say we've met, but there are five other security guards who work twelve-hour shifts."

"When did the plant close?" Scott asked.

"I'm not sure. I came on board a few weeks ago and the place was already empty."

"Then why hire you?" Bree asked.

"Vandalism," Chuck chimed in. "Bored teenagers get into mischief."

"So far only broken windows." Pete hesitated and glanced at Chuck, then at the stocky guy. "Until today."

"I told you not to hang out with this guy, he's trouble," Chuck scolded Bree.

"Don't get snappy. I'm not the one who shot you,

Uncle Chuck. And Scott saved your life back there," she countered.

Pete eyed them with curiosity.

"Sorry, family spat," she said.

Two squad cars headed in their direction, followed by an ambulance.

Scott took his last chance to get information before local law enforcement shut him out. "You have no idea why the plant closed down?" he asked Pete.

"None."

"Who do you report to? Is he onsite?" Scott pressed.

"No, sir. I work for Magnum Security Service. Companies contract with us for jobs like this all over the country."

Scott glanced at the plant. "Another dead end."

"Hey." Bree touched his arm. "This eliminates one thing off the list and puts us that much closer to the answer."

Bree wasn't going to let Scott drift into that sink-hole of despondence. She knew depression could be a side effect of a brain injury. She'd been there herself once, depressed and pulled down into the darkest corner of her mind, feeling as though nothing would ever work out again.

After being questioned by the local authorities, Bree and Scott were released and stopped by the E.R. to check on Uncle Chuck. He must have called Bree's mom because she was at the hospital by the time she and Scott arrived.

"Oh, honey," Mom said, giving Bree a hug.

"I'm okay." She broke the embrace. "How's Uncle Chuck?"

"He'll be okay. It was a through-and-through." Mom glanced at Scott. "How are you, young man?"

"Fine, thank you."

"You don't look fine." She nodded at his arm. Blood was seeping through his shirtsleeve.

"Come on, let's get that looked at." Bree started to lead him toward the registration desk.

"I can manage. You stay with your mom."

Bree sighed. "I'll be right here."

Scott offered a pained smile and walked away.

"Should I be worried?" Mom said.

"He probably pulled a few stitches," Bree said, watching him disappear around the corner.

Mom touched Bree's shoulder. "I meant, should I be worried about you?"

"No, why? I'm fine. We're all fine."

Mom led Bree to the waiting area and motioned for her to sit down. Bree didn't like what was coming next, undoubtedly a lecture.

"What were you doing up there at the plant?" Mom asked.

"Helping Scott check something out."

"And someone shot at you?"

"Mom—"

"You could have been seriously hurt."

"I wasn't. Uncle Chuck and Scott were there to protect me."

"You wouldn't have needed protection if you weren't trying to help Scott," she countered.

"What was I supposed to do? The guy needs to figure out his life. He doesn't have a car or—"

"He's an adult. He can rent a car," she said. "I think it's something else. I think you're falling for this man."

Bree studied her fingers. *Busted.*

"It doesn't matter," Bree said. "Once he resolves his situation he'll head back to Chicago and I'll never see him again."

"Oh, honey, then why put yourself in emotional and physical danger for him?"

Bree looked into her mother's eyes. "Because he's a good man and I haven't known many of those."

Mom placed her hand over Bree's. "Sweetie, don't let—"

"He needs my help, Mom," Bree said. "I can't turn my back on him."

Bree and Scott returned to the resort around dinnertime. She suggested they order room service, but he said he wanted to sleep and would order it later.

He was dismissing her for the evening, at least that's how it felt. So she went back to her place and straightened up, then took Fiona for a walk on the resort property. She kept Scott's room in her sights as she passed by. A soft glow emanated from behind the sheer curtains. Figuring he was awake, she considered swinging by, but stopped herself. She didn't want to seem desperate, because she wasn't.

He'd been clear that he wanted some space, the night to recover from the day's events. She couldn't blame him.

The resort's Christmas lights clicked on, bathing her in a soft glow of green, red and white.

"Look at that, Fiona," she said. "It's almost Christmas."

"What are you doing out here?" Aiden said, locking the barn and heading toward her.

"What does it look like?" *Ease up, Bree. He's your brother and he loves you.* "Fiona needed a walk. The lights look great."

"Think we need more?" he asked.

Awesome, they were talking about work, having a normal conversation.

"More? Hmm. I think the split rail is perfect, but—" Bree turned and studied the building "—maybe more on the lodge itself?"

"I purposely didn't put a lot up there because the guests can't see it from their windows."

"Yes, but think about how it will look if they take a walk, or even how pretty it would look to frame the outline of the building with a row of icicle lights in front."

"Huh, now there's an idea. I don't suppose you'd want to climb up there and string them along the roof?"

"Not in my job description." She winked.

"Speaking of your job, I heard you took off early to help that guy."

"Scott."

"Whatever. Mom called."

"And we were having such a nice conversation about Christmas lights," Bree muttered.

"I've given up on the lectures."

She smiled at him. "Really?"

"Don't look so pleased. I'm still your boss and you still owe me thirty hours a week."

"I know that, Aiden."

"Good. I'll walk you back to the cottage."

Bree wasn't going to win an argument about wanting to stay out a little longer. Aiden obviously had things to do, but he wouldn't leave her until he knew she was safely home.

Her brother needed a distraction, and not a business distraction. She'd told her friend Billie she planned to play matchmaker with Aiden, only she hadn't found the perfect woman to counter Aiden's strength and obstinate nature.

She'd worry about that later, after Scott's situation was resolved.

"Thanks," she said to Aiden as she approached her porch. She motioned Fiona into the yard and shut the gate. No reason the dog couldn't enjoy another hour of fresh air.

"Be good," Aiden said in that brotherly tone.

"Of course." She went inside.

Locking the door behind her, she realized how much she craved Christmas in her own home. She decided to pull a few things out of her storage closet to get in the spirit of Christmas. Tonight she'd check strands of lights to make sure there weren't any burned out bulbs and who knows, maybe she'd hang some tomorrow. With all the craziness going on, it would be nice to focus on something normal.

Heading for the kitchen, she heard Fiona burst into a round of aggressive barking outside. Must be a bear, or coyote. She went to the sink to pour a glass of water.

And noticed a strange car out back.

Shivers trickled across her back. *Listen to your fear; respect it.* The most important lesson she'd learned in self-defense class.

The floorboards creaked behind her.

A man was in the room.

Focus and visualize your next move. Do not let him sense your fear.

"You need to come with me," a deep male voice said.

She took a slow, calming breath.

"If you come willingly, everything will be okay."

"Who are you?" she said, readying herself for battle.

"I'm a problem solver. Becket's a problem and you can help me solve it."

He touched her shoulder.

She spun around and delivered a palm strike to the nose to disorient him.

"Ah!" The guy instinctively reached for his nose.

She went on the offensive, delivering three quick punches. He gasped and stumbled back.

Bree took off for the front door. Her phone, where was her phone? Racing through the cottage, her heartbeat pounding in her ears, she rushed down the front steps and glanced briefly over her shoulder—

And slammed into another man's chest.

FOURTEEN

"No!" she cried, her eyes pinched shut as she struggled to get away. She would not be brutalized by these men, not in front of her home with her dog on the other side of the fence, and her brother a few hundred feet away.

She slammed her boot against the top of his foot.

"Ouch, Breanna, stop. It's me."

She opened her eyes and was looking up at Scott.

"A man," she gasped, gripping his jacket. "There's a man in my house."

"Get Fiona and go get security."

Adrenaline clouding her thoughts, she didn't move for a second.

"Come on." He led her to the fence and opened the gate. Fiona barked and danced around him. "I know, girl, I know," he said, petting her head. "Go to the resort and find security, now!"

Bree took off, commanding Fiona to pace beside her. They sprinted across the property, Bree panicked not only about her own safety, but also Scott's. She needed to get help, and fast.

She swiped her key card and rushed into the south-east entrance. Grabbing the nearest wall phone, she dialed the security office. No one answered.

She rushed to the front desk, Fiona obediently sticking close, and spotted Nia working on a computer. "Nia, find Harvey, or Aiden, or both."

"What's going on?" Nia pressed buttons on her phone and held the receiver to her ear.

"Someone broke into my place."

Nia refocused on the phone. "Harvey, it's Nia. Someone broke into Bree's cottage.... No, she's here with me."

"Scott's over there," Bree offered.

"Scott Becket is at Bree's—"

"What was he doing there?" Aiden's angry voice said as he approached.

Bree whirled around. "I don't know. I went inside after you left and there was a guy in my kitchen and he said he's a problem solver and Scott's the problem, but I'm the solution and...and..."

"Whoa, take a breath." Her brother pulled her into a hug. "You're okay now."

She pushed against his chest. "Yes, but no, but Scott went inside to check it out and he could be in trouble. You've got to help him, Aiden."

Aiden glanced calmly at Nia. "Where's Harvey?"

"On his way to the cottage."

"Good. Call 9-1-1."

"Yes, sir."

Aiden looked at Bree. "It's handled, okay?"

It wouldn't be okay until she knew Scott was safe. She also knew her brother had combat training and could help Harvey neutralize a dangerous man.

"You have to help them, Aiden."

"Bree—"

"Why won't you help, because it's Scott and you don't care if he gets hurt? How can you be so selfish?"

"You are my priority, Bree, not some stranger who keeps putting you in danger," Aiden said.

"Coward."

Nia gasped. Bree regretted the word the minute it came out of her mouth, but she couldn't control her frustration.

Aiden held her gaze, his bright blue eyes filled with what seemed like shame.

"I'm sorry," Bree said. "I'm upset, please forgive me."

"If you promise to stay here, I'll go help Harvey."

Bree studied him, trying to figure out what was going on inside that head of his.

"I'm waiting," he said.

"I promise."

He nodded at Nia. "Keep an eye on my sister."

"Yes, sir."

Aiden marched down the hall, ripping the radio off his belt. Fiona started to follow him.

"Fiona, right here," Bree said.

The retriever rushed back to her master.

"I shouldn't have said that," Bree whispered.

"No kidding," Nia muttered.

Bree snapped her attention to the twenty-six-year-old concierge. "I'm worried about Scott," Bree said, "and Aiden was an Army Ranger so why wouldn't he offer to help? I mean, what am I missing?"

Nia fiddled with the computer. "Let's see, he was an Army Ranger and now in civilian life he avoids violent situations." Nia glanced up at Bree. "You do the math."

"Wait, you mean he's having PTSD issues?"

Nia nodded.

"How could I not know this? And how did you know?"

Nia shook her head.

"Nia? Tell me."

"A couple of months ago I came in early to work out before my shift and was doing a few laps around the property. I heard a man shouting, a frightening sound. It was coming from Aiden's cottage. His bedroom window was open so I peeked inside." She sighed. "He was having a nightmare. It was horrible."

"What did you do?"

"I pounded on the front door to wake him up. When he finally made it to the door, he looked confused and disoriented. I realized I didn't have a valid reason for knocking."

"His nightmare."

"I didn't want him to know that I'd heard him, so I made something up about the chocolate tour in Seattle for our guests."

Bree glanced down the hall where Aiden disappeared. "You think violence triggers the nightmares?"

"It's a logical assumption."

"He should talk to someone, Reverend Charles, or a counselor."

"Your brother is a proud man. That would be admitting he has a problem."

"No wonder he dislikes Scott."

"What do you mean?" Nia asked.

"Scott represents violence and vulnerability."

"A traumatic combination."

A police cruiser pulled up in front of the resort, lights flashing, but no siren.

Officer Carrington rushed into the lobby. "There was a call for breaking and entering?"

"Yes, my cottage. Come on, this is the quickest way."

"Bree, you promised to stay here," Nia said.

"I'll keep my distance, promise."

Bree motioned to the cop and they headed down the hall and out the back. In the distance, Bree could make out the silhouette of Harvey's security truck, but not much else.

"Is the intruder still on the premises?" Officer Carrington asked.

"I don't know, but I think Scott went inside to check it out and Harvey and my brother went to help him."

"Wait here."

She watched him jog across the property and approach her cottage, withdrawing his firearm. As Fiona danced around her legs, Bree kept her eyes trained to her house. She wanted to go there so badly, but wouldn't break her word to Aiden, especially after realizing what he was risking by being there.

Please, Lord, don't let the intruder hurt Scott or cause my brother any more emotional pain.

Understanding her brother's condition helped Bree make sense of his behavior this past week. It also flooded her with compassion that countered her frustration with his overprotectiveness.

The minutes passed slowly, Fiona anxious to either go for a walk or go home, and Bree anxious to know if the three men she cared about were safe.

Someone got in the truck and it headed toward her.

Harvey pulled into a nearby parking spot. She rushed to the driver's side window.

"It's okay, he's gone," Harvey said. "I think Officer Carrington is going to want a description from you."

"Aiden?"

"He's still there, told me to find you and bring you back."

"And Scott?"

"By the time he got into the house the guy was gone."

She and Fiona climbed into the front seat for the short drive.

"I'm sorry," Harvey said.

"What? Why?"

"I should have told your brother about you hanging from the rafters, but I didn't want to put one more thing on his plate. I should have known they'd come after you in your own place."

"Don't be ridiculous. The only people to blame here are the men after Scott."

They pulled up in front of her cottage and got out. Aiden was waiting on the front porch.

"Your friend is fine," Aiden said.

"Thank you so much." She went up and gave him a hug.

"Pack a bag."

"Why?" she said.

"I want to move you into the resort where you'll be safe."

"No."

"What are you trying to prove here, Bree?"

Scott stepped out onto the porch and she hugged him, as well.

"Are you okay?" she asked.

"Fine, frustrated that he got away, but fine."

"I'm so glad you were here when I came running outside." She broke the embrace and looked at him. "Why were you here?"

"I wanted to apologize for sending you away earlier. I was a little harsh."

"Like that's ever worked with my sister," Aiden muttered.

"She's not buying your idea about moving into the resort?" Scott said.

Aiden shook his head.

Scott tipped her chin with his forefinger so she'd look into his eyes. "We want you to be safe. There's better security at the lodge and—"

"I won't be bullied out of my own home."

"Then you need tighter security," Aiden said. "I'll call Quinn and get his approval to install a foolproof security system tomorrow."

"Until it's up and running, I'm not leaving your side," Scott said.

"If anyone's staying close, it's me," Aiden countered.

"Let's make it three and have a slumber party." Harvey marched up the stairs into the house and Fiona enthusiastically followed him.

"Wait, wait, wait," Bree said. "I don't need all of you here."

"Yeah, well—" Aiden walked up to her and hesitated "—maybe we need to be here." He disappeared into the house.

"Come on, let's get you inside," Scott said, scanning the property. "Officer Carrington is still going through the house, but he'll take your statement when he's done."

"It was the salt-and-pepper-haired guy—Rich."

They stepped into the house and Scott shut the door, took her hands and said, "I am truly sorry for any pain I've caused you."

"It's not your fault, but thanks."

The next morning Scott awoke to the smell of cinnamon and nutmeg. He stretched and opened his eyes.

And saw Aiden glaring down at him holding a cup of coffee.

"Morning, sunshine," Aiden said.

"Yep" is all Scott could get out. He was still a little groggy from his awkward night's sleep on the living-room sofa. Aiden took the second bedroom upstairs and Harvey slept in the recliner.

"Security company is sending someone to install the alarm system today," Aiden said and sipped his coffee.

"That was fast." Scott sat up, gripping his head. The headache was back.

"Coffee might clear up that head of yours, especially Bree's coffee," Aiden said.

"Is she baking?"

"Very astute. Yes, she bakes when she's anxious. We can always tell when she's having a bad day because she comes into work the next day with plates of sweets."

"Today's gonna be one of those days, huh?" Scott rubbed his temples.

"Looks like. Come on, you look like you need a strong cup a joe."

Scott stood up, thankful that he wasn't dizzy and the bruised ribs didn't hurt too much. He had to stay sharp, had to make sure "Rich" didn't get to Bree again.

Scott followed Aiden into the kitchen and hesitated in the doorway. Not only was every counter filled with cookies, brownies, muffins and small cakes, but Bree was nowhere in sight.

"Where's your sister?" he asked.

"Upstairs changing. Guess baking is a dirty business."

"Huh."

Scott poured himself coffee and sipped. The brew tasted delicious, with a hint of something that tickled his tongue.

"Wow," he said, eyeing the mug.

"She's got many hidden talents." Aiden put his mug in the sink. "Anyway, I've got a meeting. She should be down shortly." Aiden started for the door.

"Hey, Aiden?"

"Yep?"

"Thanks for letting me stay."

Aiden glanced at Scott with more of a pleading expression than an angry one. "Figure this thing out so she's safe, okay?"

"That's the plan."

With a nod, Aiden headed down the hall to the front door.

"Hey, you're not leaving without a hug." Bree's voice carried from the top of the stairs. "Thanks again."

"Security company is coming between ten and two," Aiden said.

"But work—"

"Forget about work until this thing is over. I can't have you wandering the grounds, making yourself a target."

"But my thirty hours—"

"Take time for yourself, Bree. Consider it your Christmas bonus, okay?"

"Thanks, big brother."

Scott heard the front door shut with a click, then Bree's footsteps come down the hall. She stepped into the kitchen and froze at the sight of him.

"That bad, huh?" He fingered his hair.

"No I just… I didn't know you were awake."

She went to the stove and put on the teakettle.

"You're not having coffee?" he said.

"Nope, I'm a tea person, remember?"

So she'd made coffee for everyone else. That's the kind of person she was—thoughtful.

"Did you sleep okay?" she asked.

"Sure, you?"

She shrugged.

"Nightmares about last night?"

"At first." She turned. "Then I decided to change my focus and concentrate on the case. So—" she pulled a whiteboard out from behind the table "—I thought we'd play fill in the blanks."

"Board games, great," he said with teasing sarcasm.

"Actually, I'm hoping this game will help us figure out who's after you."

"Okay, I'm in."

Word must have gotten out about the break-in because people kept stopping by to check on Bree. A good thing since she had tons of sweets to unload from her anxiety bake-off this morning. Each time the doorbell rang she'd invite another friend into her home and serve a warm beverage with a scone or piece of sweet bread, then give them a to-go plate of muffins or cookies.

There was hardly time to focus on the whiteboard

with all the people swinging by. By midmorning, Scott decided to go back to his room to change clothes.

He returned in time for lunch and she made grilled ham-and-cheese sandwiches.

"Maybe I need to put a sign on the front door," she said, as she joined him at the kitchen table.

"What kind of sign?"

"Out of Treats. That will give us a few minutes of privacy."

"Uh-oh, am I in trouble?" he teased.

"Eat your sandwich or you will be." She winked.

"You're adorable when you do that."

"Um, thanks." She took a bite of her sandwich and felt herself blush at the compliment. She wasn't used to such honesty, or admiration.

"I've been thinking…."

His eyes were locked on her and she feared blushing again since she secretly hoped he was going to say something profound about their relationship.

Instead, his gazed drifted to the whiteboard. "All roads seem to lead to one thing." He got up and with his back to her made slashing marks on the board. When he turned around, he'd drawn four different subjects in corners of the board with lines going to the center of the board and the word: *water*.

"It's all about the water samples, so let's start there. We'll make a map of all bodies of water near the plant," he said.

She grabbed her laptop off the work desk. "How many miles from the plant?"

"Make it fifty."

He leaned over her shoulder, distracting her focus.

"Why don't you eat your sandwich while I do this?" she suggested.

He sat down and ate his lunch, but she felt his eyes on her.

She looked up the plant's location on the internet and used a map program to draw a fifty-mile radius around the property. "That would be Mt. Vernon to the north and Renton to the south." She turned the laptop around so he could see it. "You were out here at Echo Mountain in Woods Pass, but you wouldn't have been looking for samples there, would you?"

"Are there any bodies of water near Woods Pass?"

She scanned the area. "Doesn't look like it."

"Does any water travel through the pass?"

"Like runoff? Sure, but those won't necessarily be on a map."

"Doesn't the EPA take regular samples of water?"

"Not sure, but I have a cousin whose wife works for the EPA one county south of us. Maybe she has access to statewide information. I could call her?"

"That would be great."

"I'll have to call Mom to get her number." She nibbled her lower lip.

"And you don't want to?"

"She was upset about Chuck's injury and then after last night's break-in—" she hesitated "—you're not her favorite person right now."

"Understandable."

Bree pulled out her phone and made the call, hoping Mom's frustration with Scott wouldn't stop her from helping Bree contact her cousin's wife.

"Hello?" she answered.

"Hey, Mom, it's Bree. How's Uncle Chuck?"

"Better. He's at home resting. And how are you? Did they find the man who broke into your cottage?"

"Not yet, but we're working on it." She realized her mistake too late.

"We?"

"Scott and I are trying to piece together information that might help us figure out why someone's after him, which is why I called, actually. I need Vivienne's number."

"Vivienne? Why?"

"It's complicated."

"I'm a smart woman."

"We think this has something to do with water in the area so it would be helpful to know if there's been any water alerts or strange substances in state water sources. I figured since she works for the EPA—"

"Hang on, I'll get my address book."

Bree gave Scott the thumbs-up sign. Mom seemed awfully supportive, considering.

Mom came back on the line and gave her Vivienne's cell phone number. "Be sure to tell her Aunt Maggie says hi."

"Will do."

"And when things calm down, bring your friend over for apple cider beef stew."

"You mean…?"

"Yes, I mean Scott. Aiden told me Scott came to your rescue last night."

"Yes, he did."

"Well, I'd like to thank him in person."

"Oh, okay."

"Love you, Breanna."

"Love you, too, Mom." Breanna ended the call and smiled at Scott. "Mom invited you to dinner."

"How did that happen?"

"Aiden told her you chased the guy off last night." She shrugged. "I'll call Vivienne."

Bree called her cousin's wife and got the scoop on water sources in the state of Washington. There weren't any reports of tainted water near Echo Mountain, but there were concerns about copper levels in water ten miles south of the plant. Bree thanked Vivienne and said she hoped to see her soon at a family event.

"Okay." Bree pointed to the computer. "Ten miles south of the plant they found odd levels of copper in the water at Lake Hawthorne."

"Odd as in dangerous?"

"Not quite. Sounds like they're going to retest in thirty days and investigate the source. A certain amount of copper comes naturally from the soil but too much can cause health problems."

The doorbell rang. "Must be the security company," she said.

"You going to give them a plate of cookies, too?" he teased.

She glanced at the kitchen counters, still half-full with pans of muffins, scones, cookies and breads. "I think I can spare some."

She snatched a plate of goodies off the counter and headed for the front door. Scott followed close behind.

"Check before you open that door," he said.

She eyed the peephole and saw a tall, redheaded woman on the other side. Bree swung the door open. The woman glanced down at her with a snobbish expression.

"Christa?" Scott said.

"Oh, my God, Scott, you're okay." Side-stepping Bree, she threw her arms around Scott's neck.

FIFTEEN

What was she doing here? As Scott politely returned the hug, he shook his head in apology at Bree for Christa's sudden appearance and public display of affection. Christa's expensive perfume assaulted his nose, triggering a headache.

"How did you find me?" He broke the embrace.

She grabbed his face with her manicured hands and kissed him, hard, as if she were claiming him, branding him.

Letting Bree know he was taken.

Scott grabbed Christa's shoulders and broke the unwelcome lip-lock.

"Christa—"

"I was so worried about you. I called work and they said you'd disappeared from an assignment and I thought you might be having flashbacks from the Domingo case." She glanced at Bree. "He has some emotional issues."

"I don't," he said. "I'm fine."

"That's not what I heard," Christa countered. "Someone told me you were shot. Oh, baby, where are you hurt? Let me make it better."

"Would you like some coffee or tea?" Bree interrupted in an oddly high-pitched voice.

"Espresso?" Christa said with a raised eyebrow.

"Nope, coffee, tea and sweets." Bree shoved the plate at Christa and she reeled as if Bree shoved cow dung in her face.

"I'm off carbs." She turned to Scott and blinked her false eyelashes.

What had Scott ever seen in this woman?

"Come on, babe," Christa said, taking his arm.

"I'm waiting with Bree for a security system to be installed."

"Can't someone else wait with her?"

Bree headed for the kitchen. "I'll call Harvey."

"There, see?" Christa said.

Scott might be a little messed up and confused, but he knew one thing for sure: Christa didn't belong here, not in Bree's charming home.

"Why don't you go to the resort's restaurant and order lunch," he said. "I'll meet you there after Bree's friend shows up."

Christa stuck her lower lip out in a pout. "Baby, I just found you. I don't want to leave."

"Harvey will be here shortly. Go on. I need to talk to Bree."

"If you're not there in fifteen minutes I'm coming to get you, love." Christa gave Scott one last kiss on the lips and left.

He shut the door, remarking how bitter the kiss tasted, nothing like the kiss he'd shared with Bree yesterday at the plant.

With a deep sigh, he headed to the kitchen, wanting to talk to Bree about Christa. What would he say? He hesitated before crossing the threshold. Christa was part of his life, the real world, while Bree was… What? She was his Florence Nightingale; the woman who'd saved him both physically and emotionally during the past week. She'd been thrown into this situation and not by choice. If he hadn't fallen in her path she never would have met Scott, never would have protected him, and his actions never would have put her life at risk.

Reality struck him hard in the chest. Maybe this was the best thing for both of them, waking both him and Bree up to the fact he had another life with another woman. Maybe this would end Bree's need to continue protecting him.

When he stepped into the kitchen he found Bree bagging up more goodies for friends.

"Sorry about that," he said. "Christa can be a little overpowering."

"She was worried about you. Totally understandable." She glanced at him and frowned, then grabbed a paper napkin and wiped at the corner of his lips. She held up the napkin to reveal bright red lipstick. "So, are we done here?"

She quickly turned to pack up more baked goods. He realized she couldn't even look at him, so upset that he'd led her on when he was obviously in a committed relationship.

Yet if that were the case, why did he want to stay here and avoid seeing Christa? Something was off.

"Bree," he said.

"You don't have to wait for Harvey. I'll be fine."

"I won't leave you until I know you're safe."

"Do what you need to do, then."

As she flitted around the kitchen she began humming "Let it Snow." Was Scott making her nervous?

"Stop for a second." He touched her shoulder and she reeled back.

They looked into each other's eyes for a good ten seconds, not saying a word. He searched his mind for the right words, wanting to say something that would ease the tension but he came up empty.

Please, God, help me find the words....

Instead, the doorbell rang.

"That would be Harvey," she said, but didn't move.

"It is real," he said.

"What?"

"What I feel for you, it's real, Breanna."

"That's good to know. But your girlfriend is waiting."

As Christa picked at her green salad, she chattered on about how insanely worried she'd been when Scott didn't return her calls. He was catching about half of what she said, his attention focused out the window overlooking the grounds where employees were stringing more Christmas lights across the split rail fence.

On a normal day Bree would have been out there helping with the decorations. He could imagine her bright smile as she positioned the strands for maximum effect. She loved Christmas, a holiday Scott dreaded due to his family situation. While all the kids got new bikes, video games or baseball mitts for Christmas, Scott and Em were lucky to get one present under the tree. He'd never blamed Mom, but he'd lost faith in Santa at an early age and lost faith in God, as well.

Spending time with Bree had somehow opened his

heart again to the possibility of faith and hope triumphing over desperation.

"Are you listening to a word I've said?"

He glanced at Christa. "What?"

"Let's go. This salad is subpar." She waved her hand in the air as if expecting every staff member in the restaurant to race to the table.

The server came by with the check and she flung a credit card at the girl. Scott excused himself, saying he'd pack while she settled the bill.

He went to his room and appreciated the silence. As he packed up his things, he found a few empty plastic vials in the front pocket of a pair of jeans. Eyeing them, he had a flash of placing two vials in a padded envelope and handing it to someone.

He struggled to capture the image more clearly, trying to figure out to whom he'd given the vials and why. When nothing came, he shook his head and finished shoving his clothes into his duffel.

Glancing once around the room, his eyes caught on the table where Bree had savored her macaroni and cheese. That smile of utter contentment would haunt his thoughts, his dreams for years to come.

With a sigh, he left the room and left the essence of Breanna McBride behind. Or at least that's what he told himself.

Christa was impatiently waiting for him in the lobby. He followed her to a rented SUV and they took off, a knot balling in Scott's chest.

"I'm glad you've given up on your investigation. You're not a cop anymore. You have to stop seeing conspiracies where there are none. These kinds of things are best left to the local authorities and EPA."

"EPA?"

"Yes, you'd concocted this story that someone was sabotaging the GRI plant and toxins were getting into the local water supply. Like anyone would go to those lengths. Seriously, I think you need meds."

If he was mentally disturbed then why were men out to get him, and harm Bree? And if he walked away he'd be turning his back on the possibility of the local water supply being poisoned, of Bree and her family and friends getting sick.

"Stop the car," he said.

"What?"

"Stop!"

"What's wrong, are you feeling ill?" She pulled to the side of the road.

He got out and opened the back door, grabbing his duffel.

"Scott?"

"Go back to Chicago. I've got to finish this."

"You're not thinking straight. Where are you going?"

"Up north, near Lake Hawthorne."

"Okay, I'll drive."

"No, I need to do this by myself." And he didn't want to involve another innocent in his situation. He may not see a future with Christa, but he didn't want anything bad to happen to her.

"Scott, please get back in the car."

"I can't, Christa."

"But how will you get there?"

"I'll walk back to the resort and rent a car. I'll be fine."

"You want to get away from me that badly?" She hushed.

"I'm sorry you went to the trouble of finding me. I'll compensate you for your plane ticket, expenses, whatever."

"Don't be ridiculous."

"Goodbye, Christa."

"You mean, goodbye as in—"

"Yes."

"Oh." She sighed and glanced out the front window of her rental. "At least let me drive you back to the resort—"

"No, I need the walk." He turned and started back.

He didn't want her anywhere near the resort, near Bree. Then again, shouldn't he stay out of Bree's life, as well?

"Hey, wait," she said, jogging up to him on high heels. "At least take some hydration with you." With a sad smile, she handed him a full bottle of water.

"Thanks and… I'm sorry."

"Me, too." She gave him an awkward hug, went back to her car and drove off.

He glanced over his shoulder and saw her car disappear down the highway.

They say brain injuries can change one's personality. Was that what was happening to Scott? Why he couldn't stand being around his girlfriend anymore?

Regardless, he knew he had to finish what he'd started and not run like a coward…like his dad.

This time he'd investigate the water issue without Bree at his side. It was the right thing to do, the best way to keep her safe and out of his dangerous business.

Scott rented a car and made good time to the river leading away from the plant to Lake Hawthorne. He wanted this to be a quick trip: get samples and head back to the resort without incident.

And once he made it back would he see Breanna? Probably not, although his heart ached for her. He couldn't remember feeling this way about a woman, especially not Christa.

With Christa out of his life he was in a position to explore his relationship with Bree.

"Not if you care about her," he muttered, turning the corner of another switchback.

At least he'd achieved his goal and got a water sample from the river leading to Lake Hawthorne. If his suspicions were correct, and the copper content was high, the Oppenheimer refinery plant was most likely the source of the toxins, which meant either one of Oppenheimer's enemies had sabotaged the plant, or employee error had caused the pollution of area water sources.

He'd take the sample to the authorities without involving Bree and putting her at risk.

A little worn out from the afternoon hike, he dug in his pack and grabbed the bottle of water Christa had given him. It had been a nice gesture considering she'd come all this way only to have Scott end their relationship. She had class, he had to give her that.

Something pricked the back of his neck—instinct. Scott eyed the valley below. Sure enough, the salt-and-pepper haired man with the blue baseball cap was headed in Scott's direction. How was that possible? Scott was sure he hadn't been followed.

Scott picked up his pace, following the trail to an overlook where he could watch his pursuer from a hidden spot. A few minutes later "Rich" headed back down. He must have lost Scott's trail and given up.

As Scott started down the trail, a gust of wind nearly took him over the edge. He struggled to keep his balance. His vision blurred and his eyes watered against the chill. Was he dehydrated? He took another swig of water.

In minutes the weather had gone from cool and sunny to cloudy with a wind that sucked the breath out of him. He'd have to take it slow. Staying close to the mountain wall, he took another step but the ground seemed to shift beneath him. Stumbling a few feet, he fought to maintain a sense of clarity, but everything seemed to blur together.

Everything but the image of a seventeen-year-old kid who popped up out of nowhere.

Miguel Domingo.

Scott stopped, unsteady on his feet.

"Miguel?"

"Why did you let me die?"

"I'm sorry, I'm sorry." Scott collapsed.

SIXTEEN

The next morning Bree went into her kitchen and scanned the packages of sweets ready to be delivered. She'd decided to wrap the rest of them in Christmas tissue and make them official presents.

She admitted to herself that she'd hoped Scott would be her Christmas blessing this year. How immature.

He was gone, there was nothing left of him except a pair of wool gloves he'd forgotten yesterday.

Her cell phone rang and her heart skipped, wanting it to be Scott, but she caught herself. He was out of her life. Forever.

She picked up her smartphone. Not recognizing the number, she decided to answer anyway. "Hello?"

"Hi, is Scott there?"

"I'm… No, who is this?"

"His sister. He said he'd be at this number for the next few days."

"Oh, hi, I'm Bree, his—" she hesitated "—friend. How are you feeling?"

"He told you about my accident?"

"Yes, and he was so worried. He wanted to rush back

to Chicago but had some business he needed to resolve here in town."

"May I speak with him?"

"He's not here. His girlfriend came by yesterday and picked him up."

"Wait, Christa?" Emily asked.

"Yes."

"That's not right."

"What do you mean?"

"He told me they broke up last month."

"They didn't seem broken up when she came to my place." And kissed him and hugged him. "I wish I had Scott's cell number but he lost his phone in the fall."

"That's okay. I'm sure he'll check in soon."

Bree heard the concern in Emily's voice.

"If you talk to him, could you tell him thanks for sending Detective Joe to check on me?" Emily said.

"Sure."

"Are you…were you the woman who saved him?" Emily asked.

"Well, I didn't exactly save him, but I was on the rescue team that found him."

"It seems like you did more than that. Thanks, truly. My brother never lets anyone help him. It's nice that he's learning to rely on others for a change."

"It was my pleasure. Take care of yourself."

"You, too."

Bree hung up as Harvey came downstairs. He'd been rifling through her attic for more Christmas decorations.

"Hey!" he called as he placed a box in the hallway. "Did you see the text?"

She glanced at her phone and spotted the alert: 31

yo male hiker missing since night N of Lake Hawthorne meet at Rockland TH.

Lake Hawthorne area? Odd, since that's where she and Scott had been investigating.

"Maybe you should sit this one out considering everything that's going on," Harvey said.

Someone knocked at the door.

"Those vultures still coming by for goodies?" Harvey winked.

"It's Nia! Open up!"

Bree opened the door. "Hey, I already gave you your sweets."

"It's Scott. He's the missing hiker at Lake Hawthorne."

"No, he left for Chicago."

"He came back to the front desk yesterday afternoon, ordered a rental car and asked if I knew the quickest way to Lake Hawthorne. He made me promise not to tell you he was back."

"Why?"

"He was trying to protect you."

"This doesn't make any sense," Bree said, pacing her front hallway. She stopped short, struggling with growing panic and eyed Harvey. "We have to find him."

"I'm not sure you should—"

"Fiona knows Scott and likes him, a lot. We'll find him quicker with Fi on the team, and we can use these to entice her." She snatched Scott's gloves off the hallway table and waved them at Harvey.

"Okay." Harvey put up his hands in surrender. "Get your gear."

Five minutes later, Bree and Fiona were climbing into the front seat of Harvey's truck.

"Be careful," Nia said.

"Will do. You should probably tell Aiden—"

"He knows," Nia interrupted. "He's in the middle of a resort crisis or he'd join you on the mission. He feels horrible about not being there."

"That's silly."

"That's your brother."

"I'll call him on the way."

Bree shut the truck door and they headed for the Rockland Trailhead. She still couldn't believe Scott had taken off for Lake Hawthorne by himself. But then as his sister said, he wasn't one to ask for help.

Yet he'd been able to accept it from Bree.

Bree hoped they'd get to him quickly. She feared another trauma to the head could leave him even more messed up and confused.

Stay positive, she reminded herself.

A definite challenge because she was so worried about Scott.

The man she'd fallen in love with.

The man who could be injured or worse. No, she couldn't lose him this way.

Lose him? She didn't have him. Scott was already spoken for, committed to Christa, at least that's how it had seemed when the redhead with the bright red lipstick and fake fingernails showed up yesterday.

Scott had been on his way back to Chicago with Christa, yet returned to continue his search of mountain water sources. Why? Had he pieced together something else about the case?

Whatever the reason, Bree would rescue him again, make sure he was okay and then say her good-byes, again. Her eyes burned with unshed tears at the thought.

"I'm sure he's fine," Harvey offered.

She sighed, focusing on the mountain range in the distance.

He had to be.

Not only did Harvey partner with Bree to be her map reader, but off-duty sheriff's deputy Nate Walsh, who she'd met at Healthy Eats, also joined them. Nate was an experienced climber and would be an asset to their team, especially if they encountered gunmen in the mountains.

Multiple teams fanned out and began the search. Bree watched Fiona closely for behavioral clues, while Harvey consulted the topographical map to let Bree and Nate know what was up ahead.

A few hours later Fiona's behavior changed, and it wasn't a good sign. She started tasting the fallen brush.

"What's she doing?" Nate said.

"She's stressed," Bree answered.

"Wait, the last time she did that—"

"The victim was deceased," Bree interrupted Harvey. She didn't dare look at him for fear she'd lose it.

Although Mom might consider Uncle Chuck a parental figure for her kids, Bree always felt closer to Harvey in that way. She knew an offer of compassion on his part could make her break down.

They pressed on, Bree fighting the dread filling her chest. A few minutes later Fiona caught Scott's scent so Bree let her off leash. Fiona raced out of sight. Bree, Harvey and Nate followed her off the trail into the brush.

Harvey placed his hand gently on Bree's shoulder. "Maybe I should go first?"

Bree nodded and Harvey stepped around her. He went ahead of them, slogging over fallen branches and tree limbs. Harvey disappeared around the corner. Bree held her breath.

Fiona bolted out of the brush, practically knocking Bree over.

"What, girl? What is it?"

"Over here!" Harvey called.

Bree forged her way to Harvey and spotted Scott, dirty and disheveled, lying on the ground.

"Is he…?"

"He's alive, but unconscious. We might have to carry him out."

"I'm okay, I'm awake, I'm…" He opened his eyes. "How did I get here?"

Bree rushed to his side. "Are you hurt?"

"Breanna, what are you doing here?"

"We came to find you."

"We got an alert from Echo Mountain Rescue," Harvey said.

"Oh." Scott's brows furrowed in confusion.

She didn't like that look.

"Can you stand?" Nate said.

"I think so. Do I know you?"

"We met at the restaurant the other day."

"The restaurant," he repeated. "Right."

Scott seemed unusually disoriented. Had he suffered another blow to the head? He managed to get up on his own but wavered, so Nate offered his shoulder for support.

"It's at least an hour hike down. Are you up to it?" Nate asked.

"Sure," Scott answered.

Nate led Scott out of the brush and back to the trail.

Scott stopped short. "What about Miguel?"

"Who?" Bree questioned.

"Miguel Domingo. He was here…." His voice trailed off as he scanned the forest. "I can't leave him here, alone."

Harvey shot Bree a look of concern.

"Scott, we need to take care of *you* right now," Bree said.

He acted as if he didn't hear her. She framed his face with her hands and turned him to look directly into her eyes. "Do you trust me, Scott?"

"Yes."

"Then trust me when I say we need to get you to the hospital."

"You'll be there?"

"Of course."

"Okay."

A few hours later Bree sat in the waiting area hoping for good news about Scott's condition. Physically he was uninjured. His walking challenges seemed to be more about coordination than an injury to his legs. And the way they'd found him… It had looked as though he'd randomly decided to take a nap in the forest.

Strange, since she assumed he'd gone out there to collect more evidence in the tainted water case. She'd ask him about the samples when he regained some clarity.

Because when they found him, Scott seemed disoriented and foggy. He didn't say much on the hike back to the car, or on the way to the E.R.

It was almost as if his personality was absent, that

he was a blank slate, although he was still determined about wanting Bree to stay close.

Harvey walked up to her carrying two cups. He offered her one. "Got you some tea."

"Thanks."

"What do you think?" he asked.

"About?"

"Your guy in there. He didn't seem right."

"I hope it's not more head trauma," she whispered.

Harvey sat down next to her. "No sense making it worse than it is. Let's wait and see what the doctors say."

She nodded, sipping her hot tea.

Out of the corner of her eye she spotted Uncle Chuck headed her way. "Breanna, what brings you to the E.R.?" he asked.

"A friend."

"Scott Becket?"

"Actually, yes."

"What's he done now?"

"What are you doing at the hospital, Uncle Chuck?" she redirected.

"Getting my gunshot wound checked out," he said, cradling his arm. "Thought I might have ripped the stitches."

"Oh, no, are you okay?" she asked.

"He's tough, right, Chief?" Harvey said.

Chuck frowned at Harvey. "I'm fine. But now that I see Breanna is here I'm worried."

"About?" She leaned back in her chair and sipped her tea.

"Aren't you tired of E.R.'s?"

"Actually, they've got pretty good tea." She smiled,

not wanting to argue with Chuck about her being here for Scott.

"Breanna McBride?" a nurse called from the examining area.

"That would be me." Bree stood and brushed past Chuck to the nurse.

"Scott is asking for you." She motioned Bree into the examining area.

Uncle Chuck tried going with her, but the nurse stopped him. "I'm sorry, sir, just Breanna."

"I'm here if you need me," Chuck offered.

"Thanks," she said and followed the nurse. As Bree approached Scott's bed, he reached out for her. She took his hand and gave it a comforting squeeze.

"Hey," she said. "You scared us."

"Sorry." He glanced at their entwined hands.

"Don't be sorry. I'm glad you're okay." She looked at the doctor. "He's okay, right? No further head trauma?"

"No, although we weren't sure at first because of his impaired cognitive function. I'm running some blood tests to see what's in his system."

"Oh, okay," Bree said, perplexed. Scott hardly took pain relievers for his headaches. Why would the doctors think he was on drugs?

"The doctor says I can go," Scott said.

"Actually, what I said was I'd like to keep him overnight for observation, but I won't force the issue," the doctor said.

"Scott, if the doctor thinks—"

"I want to go home, Breanna. Take me home."

"To Chicago?"

"To the resort."

She studied their hands.

"Unless you don't want me there," he said.

"I have another patient," the doctor said. "I'd advise keeping an eye on Mr. Becket for twenty-four hours."

"Of course," Bree said.

The doctor disappeared on the other side of the curtain.

"It's okay," Scott said, "I understand if you'd rather keep your distance."

"Don't say that. You know how I feel about you."

"But?"

"Your girlfriend showing up kind of threw me off."

"Ex-girlfriend."

"So it's true?" she asked. "You remembered?"

"Remembered what?"

"Your sister called looking for you and said you and Christa broke up last month."

"Then why would Christa…?" He hesitated and frowned. "Oh."

"What?"

"If there are drugs in my system, they got there because of Christa."

"How did that happen?"

"I told her I was heading up into the mountains and she insisted I take her water bottle. If it was laced with something that means she's working with whoever is after me and the evidence. Wow, they even got to her." He leaned back against the pillow. "I don't know which end is up anymore."

"Hey—" she touched his cheek and he opened his eyes "—take a breath." They took a breath together, then another one. "It's okay. I'm taking you home and we'll figure the rest of this out."

* * *

When they got to Scott's hotel room, Bree suggested he stay at her cottage for the day so she could observe his behavior.

"It's not necessary," he said, going through the chest of drawers looking for something. He couldn't remember what.

"I have to insist," she said. "You shouldn't be alone." Her phone vibrated and she snapped it off her belt. "What is the deal today?"

"What's wrong?"

"Another missing hiker."

"You should go."

"I'm not leaving you."

"There's only a few hours of daylight left. They probably need as many volunteers as possible."

She sighed. "You're right. But would you please wait at my cottage for me to get back?"

"Okay." He pulled her into a hug and held on for a few seconds, then released her, looking down into her beautiful green eyes. "Be careful," he said and kissed her. The way she leaned into him, welcoming the gesture, made him feel confident and at peace. When he broke the kiss, she glanced up and smiled.

"That was nice," she said.

"I'm glad you think so."

She gave him the security code and key to her place. "See you later?"

"Yes, ma'am."

After she left he headed to her cottage, hyperaware of his surroundings. But he didn't see anything strange like "Rich" hiding in the bushes. Scott climbed her front steps, pressed the code and went inside.

He hesitated beside the living room, now decorated for Christmas. He could picture her there, surrounded by friends, opening presents and drinking hot apple cider. A smile tugged at his lips.

He wished they'd met under normal circumstances, through mutual friends or church. Scott realized for once he considered going to church if he knew he'd meet Breanna there.

"Stop dreaming," he muttered and headed to the kitchen where she kept her laptop. He wanted to open the map program again, the one that showed a direct line between Lake Hawthorne, the GRI plant and the river where he'd taken a sample yesterday. He tapped his jeans pocket. The vial was still safe and sound.

A knock at the front door echoed down the hallway. Bree must have forgotten something and she couldn't get into the house because she'd given Scott her key. He went to the front door and swung it open with a smile.

And was looking at his boss from Chicago.

SEVENTEEN

"Mr. Oppenheimer, what are you doing here?"

"Good, so you remember me," he joked. "And please, call me Phillip. I'm not that much older than you."

Scott motioned him inside.

"I was in Seattle on business and heard you were in Echo Mountain so I thought I'd track you down," Phillip said.

"How did you know where to find me?"

"The concierge said if you weren't in your room you might be visiting a friend in this quaint cottage. I don't suppose she's got a coffeemaker back there?" He glanced down the hallway to the kitchen.

"Of course." Scott led him back to the kitchen, stunned that the man cared enough to come looking for Scott.

"I'm a bit shocked you're here." Scott motioned to the kitchen table and his boss sat down.

Scott brewed coffee, realizing how odd it felt to be in Bree's kitchen having a conversation with his boss from Chicago. It was as though he was straddling two different worlds.

"I understand you suffered a head injury and have amnesia?" Phillip said.

"Yes, sir, but I'm starting to remember. I think I've found solid evidence of sabotage."

"Excellent."

"I believe someone has been dumping illegal toxins from the plant into natural water sources in the Cascades, then made it look like the plant was responsible," Scott said.

"Yes, and I suspect I know who's behind it," Phillip said.

"You do?" Scott poured two mugs of coffee and slid one to Phillip.

"A competitor from South America," Phillip said. "I actually resolved this issue a month ago."

"But then why did you send me up here?"

"To finish closing the plant. Then you fell off the grid and I sent someone else."

"But men have been after me."

"Probably the saboteurs hoping to stop you from destroying evidence."

"Destroying evidence? I don't understand."

"That came out wrong." He leaned back in his chair. "You were going to supervise the dissemination of equipment and ship it to a new, more secure location in Idaho."

"This was all for nothing?"

"No, Scott. Whatever evidence you have I can take to the feds and clear our company of any wrongdoing. I'd like to get on that as quickly as possible."

Scott hesitated, but realized this was his boss, the man he was trying to protect.

He dug the vial out of his pocket. "I took this water

sample yesterday from a river between the plant and Lake Hawthorne."

"Good, excellent," Phillip said, taking the vial.

Scott considered telling him about the two vials he'd given to someone for safekeeping, but since Scott couldn't remember who had them he decided to keep it to himself so he wouldn't look like an idiot.

"The men who are after me and my friend Breanna—"

"Should leave you alone once I meet with authorities," Phillip said.

"And they were after me because…?"

"They wanted to stop you from gathering evidence that would clear my name. I have some evidence of my own. I'll be going to the feds and ending this within the next twenty-four hours thanks to you." He held up the vial. "You should be very proud of yourself."

"Thank you, sir," Scott said, but for some reason he didn't feel proud. Perhaps because he'd put Bree in the line of fire.

"My senior advisors were concerned about your behavior, but I said you'd come through in the end. Well, I'd better get going. My jet's waiting at Sea-Tac."

Scott walked his boss down the hallway and opened the door.

"Why don't you take another week to recuperate?" Phillip said. "It's invigorating out here."

"Thank you, sir."

They shook hands.

Scott's gaze caught on Phillip's gold, chain link bracelet. A flash of memory rushed through his mind: Phillip slamming his fist on a desk.

Leave it alone, Becket!

But if someone's illegally dumping—
They're not and that's the end of it.

For Scott, it had only been the beginning. Scott ripped his hand from Phillip's.

This man was the enemy.

"Scott?" Phillip questioned.

Now what? If Scott revealed his thoughts, this could go bad awfully fast. Phillip traveled with security, Scott knew that firsthand since he'd been one of them. Security had to be close, waiting for Phillip's signal to swoop in and neutralize the threat—Scott.

"I get these random migraines," Scott said, rubbing his temples for effect.

"From your fall in the mountains?"

"Yes, sir."

"It's a good thing they have a well-trained search and rescue group in Echo County or your injuries might have been much worse." Phillip scanned the mountain range in the distance, then pinned Scott with a serious frown. "Have any of the volunteers ever been hurt while on a mission?"

"Not that I know of."

"That's remarkable considering the rugged nature of the Cascade Mountains. There was commotion in the lobby when I arrived today. Apparently a team was assembling for a mission?"

"Yes, sir."

"Let's hope they all come back unharmed."

Was that a veiled threat?

"They're well trained and experienced," Scott said. "They know what they're doing."

"Yes, but with sudden weather changes I've heard anything could happen." Phillip glanced into Bree's house. "It would be a shame if this lovely girl got caught up in a storm she didn't anticipate." He looked back at Scott. "Wouldn't it?"

So Phillip knew about Breanna. Scott struggled to maintain his self-control, but felt his fingers curl into a fist.

His boss, this entitled, wealthy bully was threatening Breanna in order to keep Scott in line. Had Phillip sent his own men into the mountains as a fail-safe, a way to make sure Scott stayed out of his business? Scott realized that Phillip must have known about the toxic dumping and did nothing to stop it because it would affect the bottom line. The whole competitor from South America story was a lie.

"Scott?" Phillip snapped his fingers in Scott's face and Scott glanced at him.

"Thought I'd lost you there for a minute," Phillip said.

"I'm sorry, sir. I guess I need to lie down."

"Of course. Give me a call when you're ready to return to work." With a victorious smile, Phillip turned and walked to a waiting limousine. "Rich" stood beside it wearing a smirk.

Scott shut the door, paralyzed by the thought of Bree being vulnerable and in danger while on a mission because Phillip's men were sent to hurt her if Scott pointed the finger at the real criminal: Phillip Oppenheimer.

"No," he ground out, as a rush of memory flooded to the surface. He hadn't taken time off to investigate Phillip's enemies, he'd taken time off to prove his theory about Phillip being responsible for the water contamination. Unfortunately Scott had been assaulted in the mountains before he could get the final water samples to authorities.

And now he'd just handed crucial evidence over to the enemy. There wasn't time to get another water sample, not with Bree's life at stake, yet he needed something to neutralize Phillip.

If only he had another sample to turn over to authorities. He fisted his hand, struggling with a memory of who he'd given two vials to for safe keeping.

"Later," he said. Right now he had to protect Breanna, but he couldn't do it alone.

Ten minutes later Aiden showed up at Bree's cottage.

"What's the emergency?" Aiden said, stepping inside.

Scott scanned the area and shut the door. "Your sister's in trouble."

"She's been in trouble ever since you fell at her feet, what else is new?" He went into the kitchen and poured himself a cup of coffee.

"My boss from Chicago was here," Scott said. "I'm pretty sure he's behind the tainted water. He's the one who sent the muscle to neutralize me, and now he's threatening Bree."

"You're being paranoid. He doesn't even know her." Aiden sipped his coffee.

"He's using Bree to keep me from talking to the authorities."

"Bree's with Harvey on a mission. She's fine."

"Don't you understand, he's probably sent his men out there in case I did something stupid. He's a manipulative, dangerous man!"

Aiden raised an eyebrow at Scott as though he was questioning Scott's sanity.

"Look, Aiden, I'll do anything, even promise to stay away from your sister if you'd just take me seriously. Please—" his voice cracked "—you've got to help me protect her."

Aiden cocked his head as if he were putting together a puzzle. "What do you want me to do?"

"Call field command and tell them not to let Bree go on the mission, say there's a family emergency or something. Then go get her and keep her safe."

"What about you?"

"I have to figure out where I stashed the other evidence. I left it with someone but can't remember who."

"Bree's gonna be upset when I pull her off the mission."

"As long as she's safe, she can be furious."

Scott spent the next hour in Harvey's office going through video footage of the resort, hoping to see something that could give him a clue as to where he'd hidden the two vials. They were critical in his investigation; he wouldn't have given them to just anyone.

But he wouldn't have involved the cops, not until he was sure he had enough evidence against Phillip.

Nervous energy drove him to check messages at the front desk, hoping for one from Aiden about Bree being back and safe at the resort.

"Hello, Mr. Becket," a young man in his twenties said from behind the counter. His nametag read Tripp.

"Hi, I'm wondering if anyone's left any messages for me?"

The clerk checked Scott's box. "Nothing up here,

but they could have left a message in your room's voice mail."

"Thanks." He started for his room.

"Mr. Becket?" Tripp said.

Scott turned to him.

"They're serving Baked Alaska for dessert in the dining room tonight."

Scott narrowed his eyes at the guy. "Okay, thanks."

"Baked Alaska," the clerk repeated with a nod.

Scott walked back to the front desk. "And you're telling me this because…?"

"Tripp, do you know if—" Nia hesitated as she came out of the office. "Oh, sorry, I didn't realize you were with a guest. How are you feeling, Mr. Becket?"

"Better, thanks." He glanced at Tripp. "Baked Alaska, huh?"

"Made it two hours ago."

"Tripp, what are you talking about?" Nia said.

Scott figured Tripp was communicating in code, assuming Scott would understand the message.

"Have you got a minute?" he asked Tripp, and motioned him out from behind the counter.

"Can you watch the desk for a sec?" Tripp asked Nia.

Nia raised an eyebrow. "Sure."

Tripp joined Scott in the lobby and they found a secluded alcove near the coffee station.

"I guess you haven't heard, I had a fall and I'm struggling with my memory," Scott said.

"Whoa, when did that happen?"

"Sunday."

"Ah, I was on vacation until today."

"And the Baked Alaska comment?"

"You asked me to hold something for you in the hotel

safe and if anyone inquired about it to let you know by saying *Baked Alaska*."

"Someone asked about it two hours ago?"

"Yes, sir. He said by chance were you keeping anything in the hotel safe? I was going to tell him I'm not at liberty to share information about our guests, but he looked sketchy so I denied that you'd kept anything with us."

"But there is something there?"

Tripp nodded.

"Man, you might have just saved my life. Can you get it and meet me in the men's bathroom?"

"Sure."

Scott went to the men's room and waited. It seemed more secluded than the public lobby, a better place for the exchange. A few minutes later Tripp entered the bathroom and handed Scott a padded envelope.

"Thanks," Scott said.

"Of course. If you need anything else, I work the day shift." With a nod Tripp left and Scott studied the package.

This was it. At least he hoped this was it—the evidence he'd hidden before his hike up into the mountains.

He ripped open the envelope exposing two vials of liquid with OPR and SR, which stood for Oppenheimer Plant Reservoir and Susha River. Bingo. Both were bodies of water that, if tainted, proved the toxins were coming directly from Phillip's plant. Scott also found a flash drive inside the envelope.

"Huh." He shoved the drive into his jeans pocket and slipped the vials into his jacket. It was all coming together.

Anxious to see what was on the flash drive, Scott

walked through the lobby heading back to Bree's cottage. He'd use her laptop to access the information.

As he turned the corner, he spotted Bree's uncle Chuck hovering in the hallway.

"Chief?" Scott said.

"Where have you been? She's been asking for you."

"Who, Bree?"

"Come on." He motioned Scott down the hall.

"Is she okay? Why didn't Aiden call?"

"Now not, not now," he hushed.

Panic knotted in Scott's chest. Had she been hurt? Was Aiden too late?

They went outside and her uncle motioned Scott toward his police cruiser.

"Where is she?" Scott said.

"Stop talking and get in."

Something felt off.

"Hang on, where is Bree?"

"I said, get in!" Uncle Chuck withdrew his firearm and pointed it at Scott's chest. "You wouldn't leave her alone. You had to involve her in this garbage."

He flicked the gun barrel toward the car. Scott knew he wasn't being taken to see Bree. He also knew if he got into the car, he wasn't getting out alive.

"Get in or I'll shoot you where you stand," the man threatened.

"Uncle Chuck, what are you doing?" Bree gasped.

EIGHTEEN

Bree couldn't believe her uncle was threatening to shoot Scott.

"It's his fault, all of this is his fault," Uncle Chuck said in a tight voice she didn't recognize.

"What's his fault?" Bree asked, stepping into his sight line, hoping to dissuade him.

"All this violence is because this man came to Echo Mountain."

"No, the men who were after Scott are responsible for the violence."

"Because of him!" he shouted.

Aiden jogged up behind Uncle Chuck and she put out her hand to caution him to stay back. Her uncle was having some kind of breakdown and she didn't want him to be startled into pulling the trigger.

"Why don't you lower the gun and we'll talk about it?" Bree suggested.

"No more talking." He flicked the barrel of the gun at Scott. "He's got what I want. Let's have it."

Scott pulled something out of his jacket pocket and held it up. Two vials of liquid.

"Give it to me. I'm taking it to the feds and I'll end this thing."

"It's dangerous to have these in your possession," Scott said.

"I can handle this alone."

"But you shouldn't have to," Bree said. "That's what family and friends are for, to help each other fight the hard battles."

He glanced at her with misty eyes and she thought she might have gotten through to him.

Instead, he redirected his attention to Scott. "The vials."

Scott placed them on the ground.

"Back up," Uncle Chuck said.

Scott did as ordered and nodded at Bree to stay back.

Uncle Chuck picked up the vials, but didn't lower the gun. "All this for a little bit of contaminated water."

"How did you know it was contaminated?" Scott said.

"It says so on here." Chuck glanced at the vials.

An odd expression crossed his face, like he'd been caught with his hand in the cookie jar.

"Don't confuse me!" He took a step toward Scott.

Aiden charged Uncle Chuck from behind.

The gun went off.

Scott tackled Bree to the ground. Air rushed from her lungs. "Sorry, you okay?" he said.

She nodded, unable to verbally respond as she gasped for breath.

"Let go of me!" Uncle Chuck shouted.

"Drop the gun!" Aiden countered.

"Stay down," Scott said into Bree's ear and slid off of her.

Bree stayed down all right, she stayed down and prayed. Prayed that no one would be hurt and that Uncle Chuck would come down from whatever anxiety spin he was on.

She also hoped she'd misinterpreted Chuck's reaction and he wasn't part of the master plan to poison the natural water sources in the area. But that's what Scott had implied, right?

Another shot rang out and she gasped.

"The gun," Aiden said.

"Got it."

"Relax, Uncle Chuck," Aiden ordered.

Bree heard the sound of a man sobbing. She glanced to her right. Chuck was chest down with Aiden's knee pressed against his back.

"If I let you go, will you be okay?" Aiden said. "No crazy stuff?"

Uncle Chuck nodded. Aiden helped him sit up.

Scott crouched beside Uncle Chuck. "You knew about the illegal dumping, didn't you?"

He didn't answer.

"I'll call 9-1-1." Aiden stood and pulled out his phone.

Bree kneeled beside Scott. "Uncle Chuck, what's going on?"

Chuck stared blindly toward the mountains. "He said he was going to clean it up, build another plant, employ thousands of locals."

"Did he pay you—" Scott hesitated "—for your co-operation?"

"Do you know how little a municipal police chief makes?" He glanced at Bree. "I wanted to propose to your mom and take her on a nice honeymoon to Greece."

"So you allowed Phillip Oppenheimer to break the law?" Scott said.

Chuck glared at Scott. "Get me a lawyer."

Bree touched Chuck's shoulder and he glanced at her with bloodshot eyes. "Why did you have to find him out there?" he said softly. "He was never supposed to come down from the mountain."

"They're on the way," Aiden said, eyeing Chuck. "I don't get it. You're involved with poisoning your own town, your friends... Mom?"

Uncle Chuck looked away.

"Sometimes money and power are too hard to resist," Scott offered. "Especially when served up by a master manipulator like Phillip Oppenheimer."

Bree spent three hours at the police station giving her statement, first to Chief Washburn, then to federal officers who were taking over the case. Apparently illegal dumping wasn't the only crime committed by the powerful Phillip Oppenheimer, but the feds hadn't been able to charge him with anything else to date.

As she sat in a chair by the chief's desk she felt emotionally and physically exhausted. The most draining part of the day had been the few minutes when she thought her uncle might shoot and kill Scott.

"Hey," Scott said, placing a hand on her shoulder. "It's over."

She glanced up at him. He looked different for some reason, distant, and a little bit like a stranger.

"What about the men who are after you, me, us?" she said.

"Federal officers are detaining Phillip Oppenheimer and his men at the airport," Scott said. "Apparently the flash drive I gave them has plenty of evidence, including emails and voice mails, proving Phillip knew about the toxins."

"Looks like the feds have identified the dead man from the plant as one of Oppenheimer's security agents," Chief Washburn said, walking up to them. "From what we can piece together, Chuck shot him because he threatened to kidnap you, Breanna, thinking you'd be good leverage to control Scott. They were trying to discredit Scott by planting the gun, making the petty cash accusation, among other things. Why was your girlfriend involved?"

"Ex-girlfriend," Scott corrected. "I'd suspected she was on their payroll but couldn't be sure."

"Awfully convenient to have a drugged water bottle in her car before you headed up into the mountains," the chief said.

"She would have drugged me regardless. Another way to make me look mentally unstable so no one would take my claims seriously."

"And the tainted water?" she asked.

"The water council will work on how to purify it before it hits our faucets," the chief said.

Breanna shook her head.

"What?" Scott said.

"I'm having a hard time differentiating between the good guys and bad guys. I mean, Uncle Chuck?"

"That surprised me, too," Chief Washburn said. "But Oppenheimer made promises, convinced Chuck he had big plans for the area. If he'd followed through on those promises, Chuck would have certainly come out the hero."

"Why did Uncle Chuck believe him?"

"Because it's easier to believe you're doing the right thing than to admit you're a part of the problem," Scott offered.

Bree sensed he wasn't talking about Chuck. But why would Scott take on so much personal responsibility about his boss's plans? Scott was trying to bring justice to the situation.

"Can I talk to you outside for a second?" she said to Scott.

"They might need me—"

"I'll let them know where you are," Chief Washburn said.

"Okay, thanks."

Bree took Scott's hand and led him out front. The town's decorations illuminated the street with multicolored bells, stars and snowflakes hanging from streetlights. She smiled at the sight.

Scott slid his hand from hers and she studied him with a heavy heart. She feared what was coming next, so she tried a diversion.

"Isn't it beautiful?"

He shoved his hands into his jacket pockets and glanced down the street, the lights reflecting in his eyes. She was sure he wasn't seeing the beauty of the display as she just had.

"Why do I get the feeling you were talking about yourself when you said it's easier to believe a lie than to believe you're part of the problem?" she asked.

He clenched his jaw.

"Come on, talk to me."

He glanced up. The intensity of his gaze shot a chill to her core.

"It's the truth," he said. "I was a part of the problem."

"You were trying to fix the problem."

"I involved innocent people in the process. Someone could have gotten hurt. You could have been hurt."

"But I wasn't. It's over and everything's okay."

He shook his head. "Chuck was right about one thing—I continually put you in danger."

"Scott, it was those men—"

"If I hadn't asked, make that begged you to stay by me that first night at the hospital you wouldn't have been in danger."

"You were alone and you needed my help."

"Well, I don't anymore."

She tried covering the pain arcing across her chest with a sigh. "It's okay to need someone, Scott."

"Not for me it isn't. I take care of people, I don't put them in the line of fire, like that kid…." He shook his head.

"Miguel?"

He stared at the ground.

"Why do you blame yourself for his death?"

"Because he was killed trying to help me. I didn't ask him to," he said, his voice sounding raw as he spoke. "I told him to stay out of it, that I'd nail the gang for his brother's murder and instead he ends up dead, too."

"He was trying to do the right thing. That was his choice. Not yours."

"It was my fault. If I would have closed the case faster he wouldn't have gone snooping around."

"Scott, we can't take responsibility for other people's choices. I made the choice to help you at the hospital and nothing was going to change my mind. My choice." She took a chance and placed her hand over his heart. "And I'm glad I did."

"Why?" he whispered. "I've got nothing to offer you, no job, no future."

"Hey, we just survived a life-threatening situation. Let's enjoy the moment and not worry about the future."

"I can't help it," he said with incredible sadness in his voice. "I need to know you're going to be happy."

"I'm happy right now." She slid her arms around his waist and looked up at him. "The lights are beautiful and hope is in the air. Mom's open house is tomorrow night and the Christmas tree lighting ceremony is—"

"No." He removed her arms from his waist and looked into her eyes. "This is your world, Breanna, not mine. I come from a violent world and will not infect you with that ugliness."

"Scott—"

He interrupted her protest with a kiss. It was gentle, warm and filled with desperation.

It was a goodbye kiss.

Tears formed in her eyes. Somehow this man didn't think himself worthy of happiness and love.

He broke the kiss and hugged her. "You are...incredible."

He released her and bolted into the police station.

Bree stood there for a few minutes, unsure what to do next. Should she follow him? Confront him with the truth that he was, in fact, worthy of love? Probably not a good idea in front of a room full of law enforcement officials.

She sensed that nothing she said would change his

mind. Somehow he'd have to find enlightenment on his own. Well, not totally alone.

Please, God, help him see he is worthy of Your love.

Glancing up at the dark sky dotted with stars, she considered her next move. Instinct told her to give him space.

But she wouldn't let him leave Echo Mountain without giving him one last gift.

The next day Aiden showed up unannounced at Scott's room to check up on him. Scott hadn't heard from Bree since their conversation in front of the police station.

And the kiss. Scott closed his eyes at the memory of her soft, perfect lips.

"Let me get this straight, my sister helped you out this past week and you're going to leave without saying goodbye?" Aiden said, leaning against the wall, eating an apple. "That's harsh."

"It's better that way."

"Better for…?"

Scott glanced at Aiden. "Her."

"Oh, okay," Aiden said, disbelief coloring his voice. "You still have one more thing to do before you leave town."

"The feds said I could go back to Chicago."

"Not the feds, my mother. She wants you to stop by her Christmas open house tonight. And trust me, you don't want to turn her down."

"I've got a plane to catch."

"Really? After everything you put that woman through?"

Scott glanced at Aiden.

"You practically got her daughter killed," Aiden said. "Then you expose Mom's boyfriend as a criminal."

"So she wants me to come by her party to rip me in front of the whole town?"

Aiden shrugged. "Doubt it. She's about compassion and forgiveness, kind of like Bree."

Bree's compassion had astonished Scott on more than one occasion.

"Are you going to rejoin the force when you get back to Chicago?" Aiden asked.

"I don't know. My heart's not in it."

"Yeah, chucklehead, I know where your heart is," Aiden said.

"I promised you I'd stay away from Bree."

"Hey, don't make me the bad guy here." Aiden pushed away from the wall. "I'm starting to think it's not the worst idea in the world, I mean, you and my sister."

"You're messing with me," Scott said, eyeing Aiden.

"No, I'm not. Bree couldn't trust guys after being with that jerk, Thomas. Then you literally fell at her feet and something changed. Maybe because you were vulnerable and needy, I don't know. But my sister's grown a ton this past week thanks to you. She's got her groove back." Aiden smiled.

"I'm glad." He stuffed a sweatshirt into his duffel bag. "I'm really glad."

"And you really love her."

Scott hesitated as he rolled up his jeans. "It doesn't matter."

"If love doesn't matter then what does?"

Aiden's words haunted him, but Scott knew he was doing the right thing. Letting Breanna go was the true act of love. She'd be free to find another, better man with whom to spend her life.

Scott climbed the steps leading to Mrs. McBride's front porch and reached for the door.

"I wasn't sure you'd come."

He spun around and spotted Bree, bundled up in a fleece blanket, sitting on the porch swing.

"Aiden said not to refuse your mom so…"

"Oh." Bree glanced down.

He instantly regretted his words. He should have said he needed to see Bree one more time, drink in the sight of her face so he'd never forget it.

"I have something for you." She unfolded her legs and grabbed a gift bag from the floor. "It's an emergency kit with everything you need in case you get stuck in the mountains again."

"Thanks."

"Open it."

Scott wandered to a chair and sat down. Excitement danced in her eyes as she watched him. He'd miss that, too, her enthusiasm.

The kit had all the essentials including matches in a plastic bag, a headlamp, pocketknife, mini-first-aid kit, sunscreen, freeze-dried food and a flashlight. Hooked to the flashlight was a key chain that read: *Let Go, Let God*.

"Nice touch." He smiled.

"You'll have to supply the extra clothes and shelter."

"Shelter, even on a day hike?"

"You never know what you'll encounter in the mountains."

Their eyes caught. No, he couldn't have known he'd find the love of his life in the Cascade Mountains.

"There should be one more thing." She smiled, expectant.

He dug into the bag and pulled out a compass. "So I won't get lost, nice."

"Flip it over," she said.

He turned the compass over and on the back was a photo of Bree and Fiona. "Wow, this is great," he said, his heart aching.

"We're always close, Scott. All of us." She went to him and kissed him on the cheek.

He closed his eyes for a second.

And she was gone. The door clicked shut as she disappeared into the house.

His gaze drifted to the photo of Bree and Fiona. How could he leave her?

Aiden was right. Love matters. A lot.

Who would have thought a mind-altering head injury would teach Scott how to trust and love? He'd spent most of his life feeling discarded and unloved. And now, when love was handed to him like a gift, he was going to reject it? That made no sense.

But Breanna did. Everything about her made sense from her gentle way to her determined attitude; her devotion to family and her faith in God.

Leaving Bree would be turning his back on the most amazing thing that had ever happened to him.

He glanced at the key chain attached to the flashlight. "Let Go, Let God," he whispered. He clicked the light on, aimed it across the property and clicked it off. "Show me the way, Lord."

He stuffed the essentials back into the bag and headed for the house, expecting to be shunned by locals and lectured by Bree's mom.

He opened the door and held his breath....

Everyone greeted him as though he were an old friend. Nia handed him a hot apple cider and Grace from the SAR K9 unit offered him a plate of cookies, which he had to put down in order to greet Reverend Charles. The pastor shook Scott's hand and said they could use his help at a fund-raising event next week if Scott was still in town.

Scott felt like a celebrity; he felt as though he belonged.

A new feeling. A good feeling.

Harvey came up beside him and smiled. "Glad you're A-okay."

"Thanks, and thanks for all your help this past week."

"About that—" Harvey hesitated "—I'm worn out from all that horsing around. I need a vacation, or maybe I need to retire, take some trips, go fishing for a week or a year."

Scott chuckled. "Sounds like a plan."

"I don't suppose you'd want to take over as security manager for the resort?"

Scott snapped his attention to Harvey. "You can't offer me your job."

"I didn't, but I think he will." He glanced across the room at Aiden, who cracked a smile and nodded at Scott.

"You mean...?"

"He's willing to give you a trial run while I'm still around to supervise. But let me know in the next 48 hours or else we'll post an ad in the *Echo Mountain Review*."

"Don't post the ad," Scott blurted out.

Harvey burst out laughing, slapped Scott on the shoulder and wandered into the crowd.

Scott had never felt the sense of community he did at this very moment; a sense of belonging. He'd always been the lone wolf, the man of the family who needed to take care of his mom and sister, which didn't leave time for making friends or being part of a community.

Yet somehow he'd found himself surrounded by people who cared, thanks to Breanna's family.

Breanna, the woman he loved with all his heart.

A clinking sound hushed the crowd. Everyone quieted and glanced at Bree's mom. "I'd like to publicly thank our guest, Scott Becket, for exposing the toxic dumping mess and protecting our community."

The group applauded. He scanned the crowd looking for Bree.

"Thanks to Scott—"

"You're back in the dating pool!" Harvey called out. Everyone chuckled.

Scott glanced at Mrs. McBride. "I am sorry about that."

"Don't be. I've been wanting to break it off with Chuck for months but didn't have a good reason other than my gut telling me it wasn't right."

"Gotta listen to those gut feelings," Scott said.

Mrs. McBride raised her cup of cider. "To Scott Becket."

The group cheered, smiles spreading across their faces.

"Thanks, thanks everyone," he glanced down, embarrassed.

"Okay, speech time is over. Let's finish eating all this great food," Mrs. McBride said.

Scott turned to search the back of the house, but Bree's mom caught his arm.

"Maybe you should take your own advice about your gut feelings?" She winked.

"Am I that transparent?"

She smiled and drifted into the crowd.

A crowd noticeably absent of Bree. His heart rate sped up at the thought she'd left, that he wouldn't see her again tonight.

He ambled through the group, shaking hands and accepting thanks, making his way toward Aiden, who was talking to Nia.

"I don't think it's a good idea, Aiden," Nia said.

"You worry too much."

"What's not a good idea?" Scott said.

"He wants to build a camp at the top of Echo Mountain for guests," Nia said.

"It would be a great draw for business," Aiden said.

"It's dangerous up there," Nia countered. "The high winds and steep slopes."

Aiden waved her off and redirected his attention to Scott. "So, you interested in Harvey's job?"

"I am."

"Harvey thinks you're a good fit."

"And what do you think?"

Aiden narrowed his eyes. "We'll see how you do during your probationary period."

"Thanks, and thanks for pointing out the obvious back at the hotel room."

"You mean…?"

"About what matters."

"Anytime buddy, anytime."

"Have you guys seen Bree?" Scott asked.

"I think she went out back to check on Fiona," Aiden said.

"Great, thanks." Scott made his way through the house, smiling at neighbors and friends as he passed, anxious to get outside to find Bree.

He placed the gift bag on top of the fridge as he passed through the kitchen and went out the back door. The crisp winter air filled his lungs and stars sparkled above. He scanned the property and didn't see Bree at first, then he heard her giggling.

Scott followed the glorious sound and found Bree playing ball toss with Fiona on the side of the house.

"Get it, girl. Go get it!" she called.

"Hey," Scott said.

Bree spun around, startled. She swiped at her cheeks and that's when Scott realized she'd been crying.

"It turns out I won't need the compass," he said, approaching her.

"Yeah, why's that?"

"I've found my way home." He reached for her and pulled her into his arms. "And I don't plan on leaving anytime soon."

She studied him with hope in her eyes.

"Your brother offered me a job and I've decided to take it."

"You mean…?"

"I'm yours, Breanna, as long as you'll have me."

She squealed and wrapped her arms around his neck, kissing him with such joy. Scott lifted her up off the ground and twirled in a circle. She giggled against his lips.

Fiona rushed them, bursting into a round of playful barks. Scott broke the kiss and smiled. For the first time since he could remember, he cracked a genuine, heart-felt smile. Bree glanced up at the sky. Soft snowflakes started to fall, landing on her eyelashes.

"Thank you," she whispered.

"For what?"

"My Christmas wish."

He held her tight, thanking God for the wonderful blessing of love.

* * * * *

Elisabeth Rees was raised in the Welsh town of Hay-on-Wye, where her father was the parish vicar. She attended Cardiff University and gained a degree in politics. After meeting her husband, they moved to the wild rolling hills of Carmarthenshire, and Elisabeth took up writing. She is now a full-time wife, mother and author. Find out more about Elisabeth at elisabethrees.com.

Books by Elisabeth Rees

Love Inspired Suspense

Navy SEAL Defenders

Lethal Exposure
Foul Play
Covert Cargo
Unraveling the Past
The SEAL's Secret Child
Innocent Target

Caught in the Crosshairs

Visit the Author Profile page at Harlequin.com.

COVERT CARGO

Elisabeth Rees

I will say to the Lord, my refuge and my fortress,
my God, in whom I trust.
—*Psalms* 91:2

"A good teacher is like a candle—
it consumes itself to light the way for others."
—Mustafa Kemal Atatürk

For Elin Watkins, a head teacher who has guided
countless children to realize their potential and then
encouraged them to surpass it, with love and thanks
from the pupils, staff and governors
at Llansadwrn School.

ONE

The Return to Grace Lighthouse was under familiar attack. A wailing wind whipped around the tower and rattled the windows of the cozy keeper's cottage. Beth Forrester put another log on the fire of her unique home and pulled her dog, Ted, away from the front door, where he whined and scratched, seemingly eager to go out into the wild, dark night.

Ted reluctantly walked toward the hearth, stopping to sniff the cracked remains of an old rowboat that were drying next to the warmth of the flames. The wreck had washed up on the beach a couple of weeks back, broken into two pieces but with the hull intact. After establishing that no one had claimed it, Beth had asked a local fisherman to help her bring the bulky hull inside, where it now lay, ridding itself of the salt water that had seeped into its wooden bones. Beth was in the process of turning the wreck into a bed frame—sanding it down, repairing it, lovingly turning the broken wood into something new and beautiful. Then it would be sold for enough money to keep her going for another couple of months. The pieces of driftwood that washed up on the shore were treasures to her, and she turned them into cabinets, tables, chairs, beds and works of art. Her profession suited her reclusive lifestyle perfectly. This remote lighthouse, standing at the edge of the town of Bracelet Bay in Northern California, had become her sanctuary, her hideaway from the world. She needed nobody and nobody needed her.

A noise outside caught her attention—a high-pitched wailing sound being carried in waves on the wind. Her dog instantly ran back to the door to resume scraping the wood with his paws. The wailing on the other side of the door grew louder.

Beth shook her head, almost disbelieving what she was hearing. "No," she said to herself. "Can that really be what I think it is?" She looked at Ted. "Is there a *child* out there?"

Almost as if he understood her question, Ted barked and ran in circles, clearly agitated. Beth rushed to the closet and pulled on her raincoat, tucking her long brown hair into the hood and drawing it tight around her face. Then she took a flashlight from the shelf and sank her feet into the rain boots she always kept on the mat.

The wind snatched the breath right from Beth's mouth when she opened the front door, and she shone the flashlight into a sheet of rain hammering onto the long stretch of grass that grew on the cliff overlooking the bay. The beam of light picked out a tiny figure emerging from the gloom, arms flailing, bare-skinned and soaking wet. It was a child of probably no more than seven or eight, wearing just shorts and a T-shirt, running barefoot. And there was a look of absolute terror on his face.

Ted raced past Beth's legs, almost knocking her off balance, and she steadied herself on the frame of the door. Then she took off running, following Ted's white paws streaking across the grass. Her dog reached the child in just a few seconds and the boy fell on his behind, obviously startled by the appearance of a big, shaggy dog looming out of the dark night. When Beth caught up with him, she put the flashlight on the ground and reached out to pick up the child, but he scrambled away, crying out in a language that she didn't understand.

"It's okay," she said, taking hold of Ted's collar to keep him back. "We won't hurt you." She looked at the boy's strange appearance, dressed for a summer's day rather than a stormy November night. Squatting to the wet grass and holding a hand out to him, she said, "Where did you come from, sweetheart?"

Another voice floated through the rain-soaked air. This one was deeper, older and louder, belonging to a man shouting words in a foreign language. He sounded angry. When the child heard the voice, he leaped to his feet and took her hand, suddenly eager to go with her.

"Vamos," he said, pointing to her lighthouse. *"Faro."* She recognized the words as Spanish.

When Beth hesitated, the child let go of her hand to start running to her lighthouse, his bare feet splashing on the sodden grass. The older man then appeared from the darkness, dressed in black, agitated and aggressive, waving a knife through the air.

"Leave the boy alone," he shouted in heavily accented English. "He is mine."

The boy called out as he ran, *"El es un hombre malo,"* and Beth delved into the recesses of her mind to dig up her high school Spanish. She realized with

horror the translation of these words: *he is a bad man.*
The child was warning her.

She turned on her heel and started running, calling
for Ted to follow. She concentrated on heading for the
light shining from the window of her cottage. "Please,
Lord," she prayed out loud. "Help us."

The boy reached her front door and pushed it open,
going inside with Ted. He left the door open behind him,
and a shaft of light flowed out onto the grass, giving
her a path to follow.

She picked up her pace and threw herself into her
home, trying to slam the door shut behind her, but
she was too late. The man's fingers curled around the
door frame and gripped tight. Beth pushed with all her
strength, as the child stood shivering on her Oriental
rug, droplets of rain falling from his black hair. Beth
was tall and strong, but she sensed that her power would
not be enough to hold back the danger.

"Give me the child," the man yelled.

Then the door was shoved with such force that Beth
was knocked clean off her feet and sent crashing to the
floor. The door burst wide-open, and the man stood
over her, breathing hard, his big hulking frame drip-
ping wet. The boy screamed and ran to the edge of the
living room, shouting in Spanish. Beth jumped to her
feet and raced to the child while Ted began growling,
standing between her and the danger. The man swiped
his blade at Ted, but her dog dodged out of the way.

Then the attacker suddenly stopped and turned his
head to the old rowboat drying next to the fire. "Where
did you get this?" he shouted. "This boat is not yours."

He walked to the broken vessel and jabbed the blade
of his knife into the wood of the hull and twisted. The

wood seemed to almost squeal, and splinters flew into the air.

The child clung to the hem of Beth's raincoat, cowering behind her. The door leading into the lighthouse tower was just to her right. The tower had been decommissioned many years ago, and she rarely went inside, but she knew that the lantern room had heavy-duty bolts to secure the door from the inside. They would be safe there. With one hand, she made a grab for the child's fingers, and with the other, she snatched her cell from the table. Then she darted to the door, flung it open and plunged into the cool darkness of the tower's circular base. She heard Ted snapping and growling in the cottage, preventing the man from following, but she knew it would be temporary. Ted was a giant schnauzer, large and imposing, but he was old and his teeth were worn. She hated leaving her dog to fend for himself, but the child had to come first.

Beth looked up at the winding, spiral staircase, gripped the boy's hand in her own and began climbing for her life.

Dillon Randall scanned the sea from the Bracelet Bay Coast Guard Station with binoculars, trying to seek out any vessels that might be in need of assistance. The storm had not been forecast, so any boats caught in the swell would be in serious trouble.

As a Navy SEAL, Dillon had welcomed the opportunity to serve a mission for the US Department of Homeland Security, and he had been placed in Bracelet Bay's small coast guard station as the new captain. Nobody in the base had any reason to suspect he was working undercover, trying to crack the largest people-trafficking cartel that the state had ever known. Somewhere along this beautiful stretch of Californian coastline, hundreds of people from South America were continually being crammed into small boats and illegally smuggled into the US. And they had the coast guard chasing their tails trying to capture them.

A young seaman by the name of Carl Holden entered the room, carrying a notepad. "Sir," he said with a note of urgency in his voice. "The police have asked us to respond to a 9-1-1 call they just received from Beth Forrester, who lives at the old Return to Grace Lighthouse. She says she found a child wandering by her home and is now protecting him from a man who's threatening them. The child only speaks Spanish, so I'm thinking he could be one of the trafficked migrants. The police station is more than twenty minutes away, but we can be there in five."

Dillon put down his binoculars. He picked up the keys for the coast guard truck and tossed them to Carl. "Let's go. You drive."

In no time, the men were racing toward the lighthouse, siren blaring. They splashed through the streets, lined with touristy, trinket shops. The summer trade in Bracelet Bay had died away and the town was shutting up for winter. Only the restaurants remained open, bright and inviting on this wild night.

"You really should check out the Salty Dog," Carl said as they passed a large wooden building, painted bright red. The sign hanging above the door swung on its hinges, showing a fisherman casting a line from a boat. Carl flashed a smile. "They got the best seafood in town."

Dillon nodded in response. He didn't much feel like

talking. He wanted to reach the lighthouse quickly and assess the situation. Could this child be one of the many people who were being trafficked along the Californian coastline from South America? People who were sold a dream of a better life only to find themselves working illegally for a pittance, kept hidden under the radar, denied access to education or health care services. The smuggling cartel always seemed to be one step ahead of the coast guard, almost as if they had insider knowledge. When it became apparent that somebody at the station might be providing the traffickers with safe passage, Dillon was drafted in to take charge of the operation. With a staff of just ten, he couldn't afford to trust anybody, not even Carl.

"You don't say much, do you, Captain?" Carl said, leaving the lights of the town behind them and heading along the curved coastal road, which came to a dead end at the lighthouse.

The tower was now clearly visible, perched atop a cliff that hung over the bay—a cliff that looked to have been gradually eroded away by the relentless crashing waves.

"I don't need to say much," Dillon replied, glancing in Carl's direction, "when you're here to do all the talking."

Carl laughed. "I've been told I talk a lot," he said. "But I'm trying to rein it in."

Dillon focused on watching the lighthouse. Its distinctive red and white stripes had the appearance of a candy cane, while the stone cottage was pure white. It had stood overlooking the town for well over a hundred years and would probably stand for another hundred more. But it was a remote and unforgiving place to live, and Dillon began to wonder about the woman who inhabited the old place. What would cause someone to embrace such a solitary life?

Carl seemed to read his mind. "Miss Forrester is a reclusive lady," he said, pulling into a graveled lot next to the cottage where a small Volkswagen was parked. "She got jilted at the altar a few years back. She never got over it."

Dillon pulled out his gun. "As long as she and the child are safe, that's all that matters."

The red and blue flashes from the roof of the truck bounced all the way up the tower and reflected off the Fresnel lenses in the lantern room. Dillon exited the truck and looked up at the tower. The wind immediately yanked down the hood on his waterproof coat, and the rain soaked into his thick, curly hair, snaking down his scalp and into his collar.

"There's a woman in the lantern room," he said to Carl, seeing the silhouette of a female highlighted against the dark sky. "Stay behind me and keep close."

Carl took out his gun and together they approached the front door of the keeper's cottage. There was a driftwood sign above the door with Return to Grace carved upon it, smooth and weather-worn from years of exposure to the elements. As Dillon turned the handle, he felt a shiver of trepidation. It had been many years since he was on an active mission, and the last assignment he had accomplished left a bittersweet taste in his mouth. Along with his SEAL comrades, Dillon had successfully eliminated a terrorist group in Afghanistan four years previously, but he had failed to protect a group of teachers desperately seeking a way of escape from their besieged town.

Local insurgents had been targeting schools that dared to provide an education to young girls, and the SEALs had come across a building that had been destroyed by militants. Those teachers who survived the attack were living on borrowed time, having heard that more militants from the feared group were preparing to come back and finish the job. Dillon had promised to return and help them escape to Pakistan as soon as the SEAL mission was complete. But that was before he met Aziza.

On his return journey to the town, he met a young woman who was fleeing a death sentence handed down by a sharia court. Finding Aziza wandering on a desert plain forced him to make a choice—protect her or protect the teachers. He made the only choice he could. It took him three days to deliver Aziza to a women's refuge in Kabul, and by the time he made it back to the town, the teachers had vanished. He never knew what happened to them. That one distraction had probably cost them their lives. While he saved Aziza's life, he sacrificed theirs. This mission was his chance to make amends. This time, he could save everyone.

The door of the cottage opened straight into the living room, and a large black dog stood in front of them barking furiously. Dillon was unfazed. He held one hand down to the dog's nose and let him sniff, talking softly all the while. The animal responded well, licking Dillon's hand and calming down quickly.

Dillon and Carl entered the cottage back to back, turning in circles to scan the room. There was a good fire blazing in the hearth, casting a glow around the sparsely furnished area. The chairs, cabinets and table all looked to be handmade, crafted from different pieces

of wood. A large Oriental rug lay over the stone tile
floor. The rustic effect was simple and homey. Next to
the fire, an old rowboat lay in two broken sections, taking up a large part of the room with its size.

"Let's get up to the tower," Dillon said. "Keep alert."

The spiral stairs to the tower were dark, and Dillon
could hear the crashing waves outside. The dog followed
them, keeping close to heel, giving Dillon reassurance
that the animal would alert them if the reported intruder
was still inside. The small windows let in a little moonlight but not enough for good visibility, so Dillon activated his flashlight and shone it all around, looking
for the man. The stairwell was empty, and when they
reached the top, he rapped on the door and called out.

"Ma'am, this is Dillon Randall from the coast guard."

He heard the bolts slowly slide across, and the heavy
door opened with an enormous creak to reveal two faces
staring at him. One face belonged to a small boy, barefoot, wearing shorts and a T-shirt. The other belonged to
a young woman, in a large yellow raincoat. Her brown
hair was wet and shone like silk under his flashlight.
He lowered the beam of light and studied the pair. The
boy clung to the woman, and she squatted down to
speak gently to him while her large black dog rubbed
himself against her.

"It's okay," she whispered into the child's ear. "These
are the good guys." When the boy looked at her in confusion, she spoke in faltering Spanish: *"Hombres bue-
nos."*

Dillon watched the way she softly smoothed the
youngster's hair and patted his shoulder before looking up at him and Carl with wide eyes. Even in the
darkness, he could see her high cheekbones and clear,

scrubbed skin. He had not been expecting her to be breathtaking in her beauty and he was momentarily silenced.

"There was a man here," she said, standing up. "But I guess he ran when he saw the lights on your truck."

"Are you and the child all right, ma'am?" Dillon asked.

She smiled. "We are now."

Dillon reached for the child's hand to give him reassurance. If this boy had been trafficked along the Californian coast, it was Dillon's responsibility to find and free the many others who had not managed to escape.

"Let's go make sense of what just happened," he said. "There's a lot of work to do."

Beth stood on the shoreline and inhaled deeply. She loved the smell of the morning air after a storm, new and clean, leaving a sublime taste of fresh oysters in her mouth. The storm had washed up all kinds of jetsam along the beach, mixed with the foam that came in with the tide. The foam caught on the wind and small patches of it swirled in the air, sending Ted into playful mode. He jumped up to snatch at it with his teeth, before bounding off with his favorite playmate, a Jack Russell terrier by the name of Tootsie.

Beth's friend Helen Smith walked on the beach alongside her, keeping to the hard sand where Helen could use her walking cane with one hand and lean on Beth with the other. With her eighty-five years of age, Helen's mobility was failing and she didn't have the stamina that she used to. Beth called at Helen's beachside house at 10:00 a.m. each day, which was just a short walk from her lighthouse on the coastal road. Then they would exercise their dogs on the beach and enjoy the fresh air. Helen was Beth's closest and only friend. Beth knew it must look odd to the townsfolk that she, at the age of thirty-one, was best friends with a lady almost three times her age, but it didn't matter to her. Helen was more than her friend—she was a counselor, spiritual adviser, prayer buddy, confidante and many more things besides. Beth was blessed to have her.

"You're quiet today, Beth," Helen said. "Are you still worried about the child you found last night?"

Beth stooped to pick up a stick to throw for the two dogs, and they raced along the sand. They were a comical sight, one huge and the other tiny, but they were inseparable.

"Yes," Beth admitted. "I know he's being looked after by Child Protective Services, but I wonder how many more children there are like him out at sea." She looked out over the blue water. There was a Jet Ski circling the bay. "I guessed he was being smuggled across the border, but the new coast guard captain was really cagey about it. I think he was hiding something."

"You're always suspicious," Helen replied with a good-natured smile. "Let Captain Randall do his job. I've heard good things about him, and he's made quite an impression on the town already." Her expression turned playful. "I understand that he's also setting a few pulses racing among the single ladies in the town."

Beth let out a spontaneous laugh. "You're not supposed to notice these things."

"Why on earth not?" Helen said with an indignant look on her face. "I may be old, but I'm not dead yet."

Beth's laughter faded away. "I have to admit that he

is a very handsome man, but there's something distant about him."

"How so?" Helen asked.

Beth sighed, not sure she could put it into words. "Even when he was in the room with me last night, it felt like his mind was someplace else." She stopped. The Jet Ski in the bay had cut its motor and the lone man occupying it was staring in her direction. It made her feel uneasy and she turned her head away. "Dillon's a complicated man," she said. "I can tell."

Helen raised her eyebrows. Beth understood exactly what the gesture was saying. "Okay, yeah," she said. "I'm probably just as complicated as he is, but at least I'm honest."

"You don't think he's honest?" Helen asked, clearly surprised. "He's started going to the Bracelet Bay Church, so I sure hope he's an honest and godly man."

Beth waved her hand in the air, worried that she had cast doubt on the character of the new coast guard captain. "I'm sure he's perfectly nice and honorable," she said. "But I'd like to keep my distance from him all the same."

"Oh, Beth," Helen said with a chuckle. "You keep your distance from everybody. Why should Dillon Randall be any different?"

Beth smiled. She couldn't argue with Helen's words. "Did you say he started going to church?" she asked.

"Yes. He fit right in immediately."

"That's nice," Beth said with a pang of sorrow. She had loved being part of the Bracelet Bay congregation. But that was in the past now. She hadn't attended church in five years. Helen stopped walking. "Let me just catch my breath for a moment." She clasped Beth's hand in hers. "You know, there's no reason why you can't start going back to church again. The pastor gives me a lift every week to the Sunday service and he always asks after you. I told him that you and I have our own church of two, taking daily worship together, and he told me to tell you that he keeps you in his prayers." Helen looked hesitant for a moment. "The whole town keeps you in their prayers. You should know that. Five years is a long time to shut yourself away from those who love you."

Beth squeezed her eyes tightly closed. Helen was often trying to persuade her to embrace life again, to return to church, return to her old friends, but she simply didn't have the desire.

"I know you mean well, Helen, but I'm doing fine as I am," Beth said. "I have everything I need right here." She extended her arm out over the ocean, catching sight of the Jet Ski still bobbing up and down on the gentle waves. "What more could I possibly want?"

Helen didn't respond, but Beth knew exactly what answer came to mind: *a husband, a family, a future without loneliness.*

"I often wish I had put more effort into finding someone to share my life with instead of being alone all these years," Helen said. "Don't make the same mistake as me. Nobody judges you for what happened on your wedding day, and nobody is laughing at you. I know you find that hard to believe."

Beth felt the serenity of the ocean breeze ebbing away. "I had to go to the drugstore in town a couple of weeks ago to get some painkillers," she said. "I don't normally use the stores in Bracelet Bay, but I had a big migraine brewing." She looked down at her feet. "I could see everybody whispering and pointing when

I got out of the car—*look, there goes the crazy lady whose fiancé dumped her at the altar.*" She felt her cheeks grow hot with shame. "I left without even buying the painkillers."

"Have you ever considered that people might be surprised to see you?" Helen asked. "They might be staring because they're happy, or because you look pretty." She smiled. "Or because you don't realize you've spilled spaghetti sauce all over your shirt."

Beth laughed. Helen always had the perfect way of uplifting her spirit.

"Come on," Beth said, steering Helen around and changing the conversation. "It's almost time for our daily devotional."

Helen checked her watch. "Oh, so it is." She called for Tootsie to come to heel. The dog stubbornly ran in the opposite direction. "That dog is so disobedient," she said, with a shake of her head. "He's got a rebellious streak."

"Just like me," Beth said. "But you love us anyway."

"I sure do," Helen said, beginning the walk along the sand to her bungalow. "And so do a lot of other people."

Beth nodded, not in agreement but to appease her friend because, in her own mind, she was a laughingstock and always would be.

Before she left, she turned and made one last check on the Jet Ski sitting in the bay. It was still there, and the man was staring intensely at her, wearing a hood pulled up over his head despite it being a bright and clear day. His presence felt sinister in the calm, sunny morning, and she drew her eyes away. She wanted to leave.

"Ted," she called. "Let's go."

Her dog dutifully complied and bounded to her feet, carrying a pebble in his mouth.

"Drop it, boy," she said. "You know those stones wear down your teeth."

Ted released the pebble onto the sand, and Beth gasped in shock at the image with which she was faced. Helen reached for her hand, and they both stared down at the unusual stone, appearing totally out of place among the dull gray shingle and golden sand.

"Ted must have picked it up when he was digging in the dunes," Helen said. "But what on earth is it?"

"I don't know," Beth replied, bending to pick the stone up and turn it over in her hands.

It was a normal pebble, the gray kind found on any seashore, but this one had been intricately painted with an array of bright colors, illustrating a picture of a female skeletal figure, shrouded in a long golden robe. In one hand, she carried a vivid blue planet: the earth in all its glory. In the other hand, she held a scythe with a menacing, curved blade. Beth gazed at the skull protruding from the hooded cloak, the eye sockets painted so well that the stone truly seemed to have been drilled away to reveal deep, dark shafts. The image was both beautiful and terrifying all at the same time.

"Maybe somebody dropped it," Beth said, putting the stone inside her pocket. "Or it got washed up from a boat."

Helen raised her eyebrows. "It's the strangest thing I've ever seen. And a little scary to be honest."

"It doesn't scare me," Beth said, the lie sticking in her throat. "It's just a rock." She attached Ted's leash to his collar. "I'll take Ted home while you wait at the bottom of the steps. He looks exhausted from all this foraging for stones." She tried to sound lighthearted, but inwardly the fear wouldn't budge.

Arm in arm, the women resumed their return walk along the sand. Beth's stomach was swirling with anxiety. She wondered if her discovery of the child and the stone were somehow connected. Had she stumbled into something more sinister than she realized? And was the man on the Jet Ski part of it?

She thought of Dillon Randall, and his assurance that she could call him at any time if she felt troubled. Beth normally shunned the outside world at all costs, but she might have no other choice than to reach out for help.

Dillon spread a large map over his desk, studying the suspected trafficking routes that were marked upon it. The smugglers' boats had been heading up the western coast from Mexico, laden with adults and children from all over South and Central America—people who believed that decent jobs and homes awaited them in the US, but in reality they were destined to be domestic servants, rarely paid or rewarded for their hard work and left with no money to return home. The traffickers seemed to be using flotillas of small motorboats and rowboats for their journeys—vessels that were too small and dangerous for the purpose. One of these vessels had capsized four weeks previously, leading to the deaths of most of its occupants. That was when Dillon was covertly recruited into the coast guard from his SEAL base in Virginia.

There was a knock on the door. "Enter," he called.

Carl came into the room, closely followed by the station's chief warrant officer, Larry Chapman. Larry was five years older than Dillon, and Dillon had felt a considerable resentment from his subordinate officer on their first meeting. He sensed that Larry felt cheated out of the top job at the station—a job that the chief warrant officer felt was rightfully his.

"How are you getting used to being back on the front line?" Larry asked. "It must be difficult to adjust to active duty after spending so many years sitting behind a desk, huh?"

Dillon slowly rolled the maps up on his desk. His cover story involved placing him in the Office of Strategic Analysis in Washington, DC, thereby hiding his true past as a SEAL with almost twenty years' combat experience.

"I'm doing just fine, thanks, Larry," he replied, sliding the maps back into their protective tube. Larry never missed an opportunity to remind Dillon that he didn't believe desk work to be *real* experience. Little did Larry know that Dillon had racked up fifteen active missions, rarely ever seeing the inside of an office.

"Is there anything to report on the traffickers?" Carl asked. "Did the child say something that might help us?"

"The kid's not saying much at all," Dillon replied. "The authorities think he's from El Salvador and they're trying to locate his family."

"And I'm guessing there was no sign of the smugglers when you dispatched the search-and-rescue boat," Carl said.

Dillon shook his head. "No, no sign at all."

Carl let out a long breath. "How do they keep doing that? It's like they know we're coming."

"They'll slip up eventually," Dillon said. "They always do." He turned to Larry. "I'd like you to analyze the data I put on your desk. Your specialist skills in identifying the type of boats being used could be crucial."

"Yes, Captain," Larry said. "I'm on it."

Both men headed out the door just as the phone rang on Dillon's desk. He answered with his usual greeting: "Captain Randall."

The voice on the other end was panicked. "Dillon. Is that you?"

He knew who it was instantly. "Beth? Are you okay?"

Her voice was thick with emotion, and she snatched at her words through sobs. "It's Ted," she cried. "Somebody hurt Ted."

"Ted," he repeated. "Who's Ted?"

"My dog. Somebody tried to get into the cottage while I was out, and Ted must have stood guard." She broke off to catch her breath. "He's bleeding badly."

Dillon checked his watch. "I can be there in ten minutes. Stay exactly where you are, and wait for me, okay?"

"Okay."

He hung up the phone and raced out into the hall, grabbing the truck keys from the hook in the corridor. Once he was in the vehicle, he activated the sirens to reach the lighthouse in extra-quick time, and he found Beth kneeling on the grass outside her home, cradling her limp dog in her arms. The animal was breathing but bleeding from a wound to its rib cage. He looked to have been stabbed, and his shaggy fur glistened with a dark, sticky patch.

Dillon didn't say a word of greeting. He simply bent down, lifted Ted from Beth's lap and carried him to the truck. "Come on," he said. "I'll get him to the vet in no time."

He saw Beth rise and follow, rubbing her blood-stained hands on her light blue jeans. "There was a man watching me from a Jet Ski in the bay earlier," she said, her voice noticeably shaking. "I think he tried to get in while I was at my friend's house. There are pieces of a torn shirt on the floor in my living room, so Ted might have injured the guy before being hurt himself."

"How did the attacker get in?"

"I never lock up when Ted's at home," she replied. "It's usually so safe."

"Go lock up now," Dillon said. "Let's not take any more chances."

He laid Ted across the backseat of the truck and stroked the dog's small pointed ears. "Good dog," he whispered.

He watched Beth turn the key in her front door with shaking hands before she ran to the passenger side and slid into the seat. Her skin was deathly pale and her full lips had been drained of their deep pink color.

"Thank you," she said quietly. "I'm sorry for call-ing, but I panicked and you were the only person I could think of." She looked into the backseat where the dog lay. "Ted means so much to me."

He shut the passenger door and went around to the driver's seat. "Don't ever apologize for calling me," he said. "The most important thing is that you're safe."

He switched on the siren and raced back along the coastal road, heading for the veterinarian's office in the town. The fact that Beth's house had been broken into so soon after she saved the young boy was no co-incidence. He suspected that the cartel was responsible, and he needed to find out why this woman was of interest to them. Had she been targeted for elimination because she had seen the face of one of their men the previous evening?

He glanced over at her. She had turned her body to the left, to reach an arm around and stroke the dog's head. A tear slipped down her cheek. This young woman was in danger. He didn't know how or why, but he knew it wasn't good to be on the radar of a Mexican cartel. She would need protecting.

This situation just got a whole lot more complicated than he would have liked.

TWO

Beth felt helpless. She had been sitting in the waiting room of the vet's office for two hours. She looked around the room, with its bright strip light shining on the metal chairs and coffee table, piled high with various pet animal magazines. Before buying the lighthouse and changing professions, she had been a real estate agent and had shown the young vet, a red-haired man named Henry Stanton, around the building several years ago. He had purchased the property, set up his practice and the rest was history. And now that same man was trying to save the life of her beloved dog.

Dillon sat opposite, flicking through a back issue of *Dog News*. He had insisted on staying with her, despite her protests. She was grateful for his help, but she didn't want to spend time alone with him. She felt awkward in a man's company. She'd gotten too used to her solitary lifestyle. Dillon seemed to read her mood perfectly, and he stayed quiet, occasionally taking a whispered phone call in the corner. She knew he wanted to quiz her about the man she had seen on the Jet Ski in the bay, but for now he kept his questions to himself. Various customers from the town had come and gone, bringing a range of animals, but now the waiting room was empty and the receptionist on a break. The silence lay heavily in the air, loaded with anxiety and unanswered questions. All the while, Beth was conscious of the bulk of the stone in her jacket, weighing down her pocket and her mind in equal measure.

The vet entered the waiting room and sat down on a chair. He had a smile on his face, and Beth's heart lifted with relief. Henry wouldn't be smiling if the news were bad.

"Ted is fine," Henry said. "But he'll need to stay in for observation, probably no more than a day or two. He suffered a wound to his liver and I want to make sure he doesn't have an infection." He looked between her and Dillon. "Is this okay with you both?"

Beth suddenly realized that Henry thought she and Dillon were romantically involved. She considered explaining the situation but decided against it. It was too complicated.

"Can I see him?" she asked.

"Ted is highly sedated at the moment," Henry replied. "If he sees you, he may get overexcited and try to stand. It's best that you leave a visit until tomorrow."

Beth felt her shoulders sagging. The thought of returning to the lighthouse without Ted was horrible, but it was made worse by the fact that she couldn't even see him.

Dillon noticed her sadness and stepped into the conversation. "Thank you for all your help, Dr. Stanton," he said, rising. "We'll come back tomorrow and see how Ted's doing."

The vet stood also, and the two men shook hands. "Please call me Henry," he said. Then he looked at Beth.

"And can I say how pleased I am to see you, Beth? It's been too long."

She forced a smile. She was too ashamed to admit that she normally used the veterinarian who lived in the next town, but she guessed that Henry already knew. Nobody could keep any secrets in a town like Bracelet Bay. She stood, pulling her long sweater down to cover the bloodstains on her jeans. She thanked Henry and headed for the door.

A light rain was falling outside and the temperature of the earlier sunny day had dropped away. Beth pulled up the hood on her raincoat and felt the painted stone hanging in the pocket. Dillon stayed by her side, his face a picture of tension. The air seemed to feel different, as though particles of fear itself were being swept on the wind over the water. Ted's stabbing had struck deep into her psyche. She was too numb to even cry.

"This incident changes everything," Dillon said, standing so close that she could see his curly hair collecting tiny droplets of water, as delicate as a spider's web. "You can't be alone at your lighthouse anymore."

Beth took a deep, steadying breath. "There's something else you need to know," she said, curling her fingers around the stone hidden beneath her coat. "Ted found something on the beach this morning."

His eyes widened and he steered her toward the truck, checking their surroundings before bringing his attention back on her. "What?"

Beth slowly pulled the smooth stone from her pocket and held it in a flat palm. The skeletal figure seemed to have become even more sinister, even more ominous since she had last looked.

Dillon took the pebble and studied it hard, his

eyebrows crinkling in concentration. "This is Santa Muerte," he said finally. The way he said the words struck dread into Beth's heart. His tone was grave.

"Who is Santa Muerte?" she asked. "And what does this mean?"

Dillon seemed reluctant to answer, and Beth's heart began to hammer. "Ted found it on the dunes right by my house," she said. "I think it may have been left there by the man on the Jet Ski in the bay." She looked up into his face. "If you know what it is, please tell me."

He swallowed hard. "Santa Muerte is a saint worshipped in some parts of Mexico, where she is also known as Our Lady of the Holy Death."

Beth clamped a hand over her mouth and closed her eyes. The mention of death was chilling. The significance of this find was worse than she'd thought.

Dillon opened the truck door and gently guided Beth onto the passenger seat, but he remained standing in the lot, his outstretched arm resting on the open door as though he were holding a shield. "Santa Muerte is particularly revered among Mexican drug cartels, who pray to her for protection, for guidance and to grant them a painless death. People also sometimes ask her to grant them success in eliminating targets." He looked down at the stone. "They often perform a ritual to Santa Muerte when a target has been identified."

"Is this a ritual?" Beth asked, unable to keep her eyes off the bony image staring up at her from Dillon's hand. "I'm the target, aren't I? That's why the stone was placed by my home. They want to eliminate me." She realized that her voice was becoming quick and breathless, so she tried to steady it. "The cartel wants me dead, right?"

Dillon said nothing, but his silence was answer enough.

"Why me?" she asked, rubbing her moist palms on her jeans. "What did I do?"

Dillon shook his head. "I don't know. Not yet anyway. But I'll need to assign you protection." He held up the bright stone. "This is too serious to ignore."

Beth thought of her tranquil little cottage, cramped with people allotted to look after her. She and Ted had gotten used to a quiet life. Could she handle the intrusion of others sharing her space? But she knew that Dillon was right. This ritual to Santa Muerte was far too serious to ignore. She turned her head to look over the ocean.

"Okay," she said quietly. "Who would be staying with me?"

"I have a friend—Tyler Beck—and I've already put in a request to transfer him into the Bracelet Bay Station to assist us with some duties. He's a surveillance expert working for the Department of Homeland Security on the East Coast. If you'll allow us to create a lookout post in your lighthouse tower, Tyler and I will set up home there until the cartel members are in custody and no longer a threat to you."

"You do realize how small the lighthouse tower is, right?" Beth asked. She imagined two big men bedding down for the night in the tightly curved space, dominated by the huge lenses of the disused beacon. "It'll be a really tight squeeze."

Dillon smiled. "Tyler and I have worked plenty of missions in the past where space was limited. We'll manage just fine."

"Missions?" she questioned. "You make it sound like a military operation."

"The coast guard is a branch of the US armed forces," he replied. "Not many people realize that we *are* part of the military. The coast guard is trained in reconnaissance, search and rescue, maritime law enforcement and many more things besides. And these are all very good reasons why you should place your trust in us to keep you safe."

Beth rubbed her hands together, creating friction to keep them warm in her lap. Dillon's words and tone sounded formal, and they made her feel even more ill at ease. Her safety seemed like a military mission to be accomplished, and the severity of her situation had hit home.

"So you and Tyler would be with me twenty-four hours a day?" she asked.

"I'll be continuing to work at the station during the day while staying at the lighthouse during the night," he answered. "Tyler will take the lead in providing protection for you." He must have noticed a look of disappointment sweep over her face. "Tyler is a highly trained individual. You can rely on him."

"Of course," she said. "It's just that I kind of figured you would take charge of things." She felt awkward and uncomfortable asking him to take the lead, but if she must accept somebody being responsible for her safety, she would at least prefer it was someone she was already on a first-name basis with. And although she didn't want to admit it, he radiated a strength that reassured her. She felt secure with him.

Dillon kept his fingers gripped firmly around the painted pebble as he spoke. His face had lost the previous expression of concern and was replaced by one of detachment. "I'm afraid it's not possible for me to take my focus away from my job and put it onto you. I'll do whatever I can to assist Tyler, but I need to keep my sights elsewhere." He cast his gaze out over the ocean as if to emphasize his point. "I can't afford to let myself be sidetracked."

Beth watched Dillon's eyes scan the ocean, darting back and forth across the waves. He always seemed to be searching the sea, permanently on the lookout. His awareness was constantly heightened, and she wondered whether his single-minded focus was the reason he'd been given the top job at the coast guard station. He had an important smuggling assignment to oversee, and her situation must be like a thorn in his side. She suddenly saw herself as he did: as a nuisance and a distraction. It made her defensive streak rush to the surface and prickle her skin.

"I've been managing by myself for five years," she said, crossing her arms. "Once Ted has recovered from his surgery, I'm sure we'll be able to cope alone. I really don't want to divert resources from your day job."

He clearly guessed he had hit a nerve. He took his eyes away from the ocean and settled them on her. "Ensuring your safety is as important as any task I need to accomplish in my day job, but I can't take personal responsibility for protecting you." He sighed. "It's complicated."

She looked him full in the face. She figured he was casting her off with excuses, trying to make her feel better about being such a drain on his brand-new job as station chief. She also knew that all her insecurities about being a burden shouldn't be laid at his feet. They had been stored up nice and tight for a long time.

"One thing I've learned over the years," she said, "is that things are always complicated."

He leaned in close to her on the passenger seat. "I know that you're an independent woman who's going to struggle to adapt to a couple of big men lumbering around your little lighthouse like giants." She smiled in spite of her swirling emotions. "And I also know that you're more than capable of taking care of yourself under normal circumstances," he continued. He uncurled his fingers from the stone and held it in his palm. "But these are not normal circumstances. Although I won't be the person taking overall responsibility for your security, I will make absolutely sure that nothing bad happens to you." He laid a hand over hers. "You deserve all the resources we have, and you're worth the effort. You should know that."

His words almost took her breath away. Had he been able to guess that she saw herself as worthless? That she felt of little value to anyone? Had he seen through the air of confidence she had created to hide the pain of being publicly rejected?

She finally found her voice after being stunned into temporary silence. "When would you want to move into the tower?"

"Tyler should be here tomorrow evening, so for tonight it'll be just me staying with you." He checked his watch. "Let's get back to the lighthouse so I can measure the tower room for equipment. I'll have Carl deliver it later on."

"How long do you think this will take?" Beth desperately wanted to know when the acid taste of fear would leave her mouth and when she could return to her normal life again. "How close are you to catching these cartel guys?"

Dillon pressed his palms together and brought them to his face with a sigh. Before he could give an answer, a crashing sound cut through the air, carried from the open kitchen door of the Salty Dog, which could easily be seen from the high vantage point of the vet's parking lot. The noise was quickly followed by angry, raised voices and the banging thuds of a brawl. Dillon took Beth's hand.

"I should go check that out," he said, pulling her from the seat, close to his side. "But don't leave my sight, whatever you do."

Beth glanced over to the Salty Dog, the last place on earth she wanted to go. But she steeled herself, took a deep breath and allowed Dillon to lead the way.

The restaurant was busy, yet nobody was prepared to step in and separate the two fiercely fighting men, seemingly fused together in a ball of flailing arms and legs. One of the men was wearing a white T-shirt and jeans. And the other guy was taller, leaner and fitter, wearing navy blue clothes exactly like Dillon's.

"It's Larry!" Dillon exclaimed, guiding Beth to stand by the wall out of range of the ruckus.

"The other guy is Kevin," Beth said, wide-eyed. "He owns the place. He and Larry are brothers."

Dillon pressed her against the wall. "They sure don't seem to be feeling any brotherly love right now. Stay here while I pull them apart."

He approached the men with a barking order. "Break it up, guys. That's enough."

Neither man made any attempt to stop brawling, so Dillon was forced to grab Larry by the collar and yank him away sharply. Larry continued to throw wild punches and kick the air, forcing Dillon to place him in an armlock. Larry cried out but immediately stilled under the firm grip of his superior. Dillon pushed the subdued man to an empty chair and made him sit while his brother hauled himself to his feet with a groan.

Dillon quickly checked that Beth was still standing against the wall. She had wrapped her arms around her waist and bowed her head as if trying to hide away. But nobody's attention was on her anyway—it was on the two breathless men glowering at each other with wild, dark eyes. The explosion of violence was jarring against the family-oriented restaurant, busy with people enjoying a quiet lunch. This was definitely not the kind of place where brawling was commonplace.

"Okay, everyone," Dillon called out to the crowd of onlookers while righting some upended chairs. "Show's over, folks. You can all get back to your meals and eat in peace."

Amid murmurings and mutterings, the diners gradually pulled their gazes away and resumed their lunches, while Larry and Kevin regained their composure and breath.

"Now," Dillon said, looking between the pair. "I understand that you two are brothers. So what on earth has turned you into enemies?"

Neither man spoke. A tall, dark-haired woman stepped out from behind the serving counter. "Larry came bursting in here about five minutes ago," she said, "and he was mad as a hornet at Kevin. I've never seen them fight like that before."

"And who might you be, ma'am?" Dillon asked.

"I'm Mia," the woman replied. "Mia Wride-Ford. I'm a waitress here." She looked around the restaurant, and Dillon noticed her do a double take on seeing Beth standing just a few feet away. She turned and smiled at Beth, giving her a small wave. Beth raised a weak smile in response, obviously embarrassed to be in public view.

"And what was the argument about?" Dillon addressed the question to nobody in particular, hoping that someone would give a straight answer.

"You know Larry," Kevin replied, straightening out his rumpled clothes. "He's always got a beef about something. He's a loose cannon."

"*I'm* a loose cannon?" Larry said, widening his eyes and letting out a snort. "That's rich coming from you."

Kevin narrowed his eyes at his brother. "You had no right coming in here, shooting your mouth like that. If we weren't family, I'd call the police and have you arrested for assault."

Larry rose to his feet and, in a theatrical gesture, pointed to a pay phone attached to a wall. "Go right ahead, Kevin, call the police and file a report." He crossed his arms. "I won't stand in your way."

Kevin stood for a few seconds, hands on hips, looking between Larry and the pay phone.

"Would you like to report this matter to the local sheriff?" Dillon asked. "If Larry attacked you without provocation, you have a roomful of witnesses to back up your story."

Kevin bent over and rested his hands on his knees like a deflating balloon. "No. There's no need to involve the police. We're family. We'll deal with it our own way."

Larry began to walk to the door. "If it's all right with you, Captain, I'll get back to the station."

"Sit down, Larry," Dillon ordered. "I want some answers from you before you go anywhere."

Larry stopped and cast a sly eye over to Beth, who had partially hidden herself behind the large wooden menu that stood by the front door. Dillon guessed that the next words out of Larry's mouth would be mean. He was right.

"Well, I figured that you'd want to get back to your date," Larry said with a curled lip. Then, under his breath, he muttered, "Looks like somebody managed to thaw the ice queen."

Dillon rested his hands on the waistband of his pants. "What did you just say?"

Larry shrugged. "Nothing, sir."

Dillon walked to within a couple of inches of Larry and pulled himself up to full height. "You're sailing very close to the wind, Chief Petty Officer Chapman," he said in a low voice. "I expect a better standard of behavior from an officer of the coast guard. Get yourself back to the station and I'll deal with you later."

Larry saluted, spun on his heel and strode from the restaurant.

The door leading to the kitchen then swung open and a petite blonde woman came out. "Has Larry left?" she asked, darting her eyes around.

Kevin put his arm around her shoulder. "Yeah, he's gone and good riddance to him." He turned to Dillon and held out his hand. "I'm Kevin Chapman, owner of the Salty Dog, and this is my wife, Paula. I'm guessing you're Dillon Randall, the new coast guard captain."

Dillon shook Kevin's hand and smiled warmly at

Paula. "That's right. I'm pleased to meet you both. I only wish it was under better circumstances."

"I'm so sorry for the trouble, Captain Randall," Paula said. "It's normally really quiet and peaceful in here."

Dillon looked around the restaurant. The nautical theme was a little overwhelming. There were fishing nets, helms and plastic crabs attached to the wooden walls and overhead beams. Even the tablecloths had anchors on them, and the salt and pepper shakers were tiny fisherman.

"Yeah," he said. "This isn't the kind of place I'd normally expect to break up a fight." He turned his attention from Paula to Kevin. "Are you ready to explain to me what that was all about?"

Kevin rolled his eyes to the ceiling. "Larry's a hothead. It was nothing. Just a stupid argument about nothing." He pointed to the kitchen. "I've got to get back to my stove." He gave himself one final brush down, as if dusting off his brother's fingerprints, and walked through the swinging door, sending the aroma of garlic and herbs blowing into Dillon's face.

Paula smiled nervously. "Thanks for dealing with those two, Captain Randall. Would you like some lunch on the house? It's the least we can do."

"Thanks for the offer, Mrs. Chapman," he replied. "But I've got some business to attend to. I'll come back another time."

"Please do," she said. "We don't want to leave you with a bad impression of the town." As she walked back into the kitchen, she turned her head and said, "Welcome to Bracelet Bay, by the way. Mia would be happy to give you a coffee to take out if you don't have time to stay."

The waitress smiled and picked up a paper cup from the counter. "Decaf or regular?"

"Regular please," he said. "But you'd better make it two."

"Is the other one for Beth?" she asked. "It's so good to see her in town again." Her mouth turned down at the corners. "It's been years since I last talked to her." She looked behind Dillon's shoulder to the front door where Dillon assumed Beth was still waiting for him. "I wish she'd stuck around to say hello."

Dillon spun around. Beth was gone!

He swiveled back to face the waitress. "Where did she go?"

Mia pointed to the door. "She left right before Larry. She looked a little hurt by what he said."

Suddenly a flashback struck Dillon. He remembered Aziza wandering alone in the desert, at the mercy of those who wanted to harm her.

"I gotta go," he said, racing for the door, hearing Mia calling after him, "You forgot your coffee!"

He burst out onto the street. He saw Larry ambling back to the station, but no sign of Beth. How could she have been so stupid to have left without him? He had expressly warned her to stay close. The stone in his pocket jumped around with his movement, reminding him of the level of danger she was facing.

He ran to his truck in the vet's parking lot and his heart leaped with relief on seeing her standing by the passenger door. He found it difficult to contain his frustration when he reached her side.

"You shouldn't have run out on me. You can't go taking risks like that." He heard the harshness in his voice and tried to soften it. "Anybody could be lying in wait for you." He quickly checked their vicinity as if his words might be proven correct.

Then he unlocked the truck and opened the passenger door for her. "I'd feel a lot safer if you weren't out in the open. Get in and I'll take you home."

Once they were both settled in their seats, Dillon started up the engine and pulled out onto the quiet street that ran through the town. Bracelet Bay's location, a couple of miles from Highway One, put it off the beaten track, and it retained a quaintness that had surprised him. He loved the way the narrow, winding streets of the town's center suddenly opened up onto a wide road that ran alongside a vast and crystal-clear ocean. The sandblasted, weathered houses in varying pastel shades reminded him of picture postcards, and the seven hundred or so residents were fortunate to live in such idyllic surroundings. Yet he guessed that, at this moment in time, Beth felt anything but fortunate to be among the Bracelet Bay inhabitants. She was silent, staring into the distance through the windshield, lost in her thoughts.

"I apologize if I was a little hard on you back there," he said, glancing over at her. "But I wanted you to understand how serious it is for you to put yourself at risk."

Her voice was small. "I heard Larry call me the ice queen, and I just had to get away. I'm sorry."

Dillon clenched his jaw. "I'll be speaking to Larry about that. I won't stand for bullying on my watch."

"I don't expect you to step in and defend me," she said. "You don't want to make yourself unpopular when you've only just arrived in town."

"I don't much care for popularity contests," he said. "I prefer to do what's right instead."

Beth twisted in her seat to look at the town that was

now stretching into the distance as they made their way to the lighthouse. "It was hard being back in the Salty Dog," she said. "I guessed I might get a nasty reaction like that from somebody."

"Don't let Larry's childish comment get to you." Dillon remembered the waitress and her kindness. "There was a young woman in there named Mia who was pretty happy to see you. Is she an old friend of yours?"

Beth nodded. "She was my bridesmaid." She tried to laugh, but the sound seemed to get stuck in her throat. "Or she was supposed to be my bridesmaid anyway. It turned out that she wasn't really needed." Her voice became high and strained. "Actually it turned out that I wasn't really needed either."

Dillon wasn't sure what to say. "I know about your wedding," he said gently. "Carl mentioned it."

Beth let her head fall back onto the headrest with a long exhalation. "I'm sure he did."

"From what I've seen and heard in the town, everybody wishes you well," Dillon said, switching on the wipers as the light drizzle became heavier. A dense and moist fog often rolled into the town, and the damp air clung to everything it came into contact with. The air in this town seemed to brush gently against the skin like a caress, and he liked it. He reckoned that Bracelet Bay was a place that worked its way into your heart and took up residence pretty quickly.

"Mia was sorry that she didn't get to talk to you today," he continued. "Once this situation is behind you, maybe you should think about contacting her." He smiled, unsure if he was overstepping. "She clearly misses you."

Beth looked out the window. "I miss her too sometimes, but my life is different now. I'm happier this way."

"As a recluse?"

She didn't answer.

"No man is an island, Beth."

She turned her head from the window to face him. "What does that mean?"

"It's an old poem from England," he said, quoting the lines, "'No man is an island entire of itself. Every man is a piece of the continent.'"

"I never knew you were so cultured," she said in a teasing tone. "But I still don't know what it means."

The truck hugged the shoulder of the road as they neared the lighthouse, shrouded in swirling fog. "It means that we all need connections to others to make us strong and healthy. God made us as individuals, but that doesn't mean He intended us to be alone."

The teasing tone disappeared from her voice. "I don't know what God intends for me, but right now I'm happy alone."

He knew this wasn't true. He knew it was an act, perfected in order to push people away and bolster her lack of confidence. But if that was her choice, he wouldn't push the matter.

"If you're happy to put your faith in God's path," he said, "then you can't go wrong."

She smiled, and the way she tilted her head to brush hair from her neck reminded him of Aziza. It was just a flash of something, a split second of familiarity that transported him back four years to a hot and arid plain in Afghanistan. At that time, he was driving along a dusty road to Kabul with a young woman escaping certain death. And now he was back in the same situation, forced to choose which innocent lives to save. As soon as Tyler arrived, he would relinquish Beth's safety to his good friend and fellow SEAL. Then he could get back to work.

As the truck neared Beth's home, Dillon saw that the fog surrounding it appeared thicker than before, curling around the tower like smoke. When an acrid smell began filling his nostrils, he realized that it *was* smoke.

"I think we may have a problem," he said, hitting the gas pedal hard to pick up speed.

Beth placed her hands on the dash, leaning forward and letting her mouth drop open in confusion and disbelief.

"My cottage," she exclaimed. "It's on fire!"

THREE

Beth kept her hands on the dash of the truck as Dillon sped to her home.

He handed her his cell. "Call 9-1-1."

She fumbled with the phone, barely able to form her words in coherent sentences. How could this day be any worse? It was like all her most terrible nightmares rolled into one. She managed to give her details to the operator, all the while watching her lighthouse come into clearer view. A pungent smell of burning wood invaded her nostrils, and as soon as the truck skidded to a stop on the graveled parking area, she flung herself from the passenger seat and started to run to the cottage. The front door of the keeper's cottage was fiercely ablaze and smoke was eddying around the tower, rising and falling with the wind. Yet the windows were intact, with no smoke leaking through—this meant she might be able to save the contents inside. Her entire life was in the cottage, including all the handcrafted furniture she had spent hundreds of painstaking hours making.

She felt a strong arm curl around her waist and pull her back. It was Dillon.

"Stay back," he ordered. "I'll try and stop the flames from spreading."

She felt helpless as she watched him pick up one of the buckets she kept by the front door for retrieving small pieces of wood from the beach. The buckets had filled with rain overnight and he threw the water at the door, dousing the flames as best he could. She noticed that the door had almost burned away and she could see right through into her living room.

"It looks like somebody dumped a bunch of trash by your front door and used gasoline as an accelerant to set the whole house on fire," he shouted. "The fire's taken a hold of a china hutch along the wall."

"No!" Beth said, hearing the sound of her plates cracking and dropping to the floor as the wooden shelves gave way. "That was the first piece of furniture I ever made."

She tried hard to stop herself from sinking to her knees. It felt as though the whole world were against her.

Dillon saw her distress. "I'll see if I can save what's left. At the very least, I should be able to do enough to stop the fire from spreading."

Dillon picked up the second metal bucket by the door and briefly turned to her. "Now, stay as far away as—" He stopped as the bucket flew out of his hand, sending the water splashing across the stones. In an instant, he threw his body toward her and tackled her to the ground.

"Somebody's shooting," he shouted. "Keep down."

Beth's mind was awash with confusion. She was dazed. Dillon sprang to his feet but crouched low. He pulled out his gun with one hand and grabbed her arm with the other. Together they crawled to the truck and Dillon positioned Beth against the driver's door.

"Are you okay?" he asked, kneeling beside her, checking her over.

"I'm fine," she said breathlessly.

Another shot rang out, zipping through the air and hitting the roof of the truck. Dillon shuffled to the front wheel and used it for protection while he tried to spot the shooter.

"I see him," he yelled. "Do you still have my cell?"

She slipped the phone from her pocket with shaking hands. "Yes."

"Call 9-1-1 again. Tell them that the fire truck will need police protection."

Another shot hit the truck's hood and she let out a yelp. The fire looked to be taking tighter hold inside her house. Smoke was billowing out the door and the sound of smashing crockery falling from her china hutch made her jump. She found it hard to believe what was happening. It was like the scene of a movie. She watched the smoke sweeping out over the bay and imagined her quiet, sedate life being carried away with it.

"Beth!" Dillon's voice brought her out of her trance. "Make the call."

She punched the numbers into the keypad and waited for an answer. She saw the lights of the Bracelet Bay Fire Department truck flashing some distance away. They were on their way already.

"Dillon," she said, her voice betraying her rising panic. "The fire truck is coming."

"I can't let them drive into an ambush," he said. "I'll go take care of this guy myself. Stay right here and wait for me to come back."

Then he was gone. The emergency operator on the end of the line had to repeat her question twice before Beth remembered what she was meant to do. She requested officers from the sheriff's department in the town of Golden Cove, the closest law enforcement station. The operator said there would be a wait of twenty minutes. Beth wondered if that would be too late. But there was no other choice. She hung up the phone and watched the fire truck making its way toward the lighthouse. Sporadic shots pinged through the air, but none seemed to be close. She pressed her hands together, closed her eyes and said, "Please, Lord, keep Your servant, Dillon, safe as he faces the forces of evil."

She kept her head bowed until she heard the sound of the fire truck's siren become louder. Then she lifted her head, realizing that she could no longer hear the gunshots. Somewhere down on the beach, beneath the cliff, the sound of a power boat or maybe a Jet Ski roared to life. Then the motor streaked over the water, echoing across the bay.

The fire truck was within a half mile of her home. She didn't know whether to run and stop it or to sit and wait. She couldn't make a decision. She was overwhelmed with a sensation of helplessness and despair, a feeling she had not experienced since her ill-fated wedding day.

"Come on, Beth," she said out loud, rallying herself. "You're tougher than this."

With renewed strength, she rose from her position behind the coast guard vehicle and began running toward the fire truck, waving her arms to flag it down. She couldn't allow the firefighters to drive into a gun battle. She had to take control. The truck stopped right in front of her and one of the men jumped from the vehicle. It was the long-serving station chief, who had known Beth since she was in elementary school.

"Beth," he said. "We need to get to your home. You're blocking our way."

"No, I can't let you pass," she said, realizing that she sounded crazy. But what did it matter? They all thought she was crazy anyway. "It's too dangerous."

The fire chief spoke to her in a gentle tone as if she were a child. "We're specially trained for this. We're used to the danger."

"This is more than a fire," she said. "Somebody is shooting a gun. The police are on their way, and we should wait for them."

Then she heard Dillon's voice behind her. "It's okay, Beth, you can let them through." She turned around and saw him standing at the side of the road, looking disheveled and covered in sand. "The guy escaped on a Jet Ski."

He walked over to the fire chief. "The fire is in the living room. Please be careful and save everything you can."

He steered Beth to the side of the road and they watched the red truck rumble past. He then turned her toward him and put both hands on her shoulders.

"I'm sorry the guy got away," he said. "I really wanted to catch him this time."

Beth found herself unable to contain her emotions any longer. "Why me?" she asked with a wavering voice. "Why would somebody hurt my dog and try to destroy my home?" Tears began to flow, and she was powerless to stop them. She gritted her teeth. She hated to cry. She'd spent too much of her life crying, and she was done with it.

Dillon pulled her into an embrace. His skin was warm and slightly damp from the exertion of running. He smelled like a mixture of wood smoke and soap, and it was strangely comforting. But she hadn't been in the arms of a man for a very long time and she stiffened against his touch. This only caused him to draw her in tighter.

"We'll figure this all out together," he said. "I'll find you a safe place to stay in the town while the damage is repaired."

She pulled away in one quick movement, her mood swiftly changing from fear of the unknown to a fear of returning to live in Bracelet Bay. "No. I don't want to move into the town."

"Beth," he said. "Your home isn't secure."

She wrung her hands together. In her peripheral vision, she saw the firefighters bringing the smoking remains of her china hutch out onto the gravel. "I don't want to move into the town," she repeated. "Even for just one night. I can't. I really can't."

"I'm afraid there really is no other choice."

A thought struck her. "I have a friend who lives close by. Her name is Helen. I'll stay with her."

Dillon ran his hands through his dark curly hair. Sand fell out onto the shoulders of his jacket and he brushed it off. "Which house is hers?"

Beth pointed to Helen's small wooden bungalow a half mile away. The place was old and ramshackle, with wind chimes and streamers hanging from the porch.

"That place doesn't look very secure to me," he said. "And I'd feel a lot better if we didn't involve anybody else in this matter. Another person would simply be another liability."

Beth cut him off. "A liability? Is that what I am?"

"No, that's not what I meant," he protested.

"That's exactly what you meant," she said angrily. She knew that her anger was borne out of shock, fear and distress. She had temporarily lost Ted, lost her home and was rapidly losing hope. The only person she could attack for this pain was Dillon.

Obviously seeing her determination to remain close to home, he relented. "I'll arrange for somebody to stay with you at your friend's house," he said.

She nodded mutely.

He rubbed her shoulders as if he was trying to warm her up, and she realized she was shivering. "I know this is hard for you, Beth," he said. "You're a private person who didn't ask for any of this, but you have to stay strong."

He put an arm around her shoulder and started walking to her house, where the fire had now been extinguished and the firefighters were assessing the damage. "You'll get through this," he said gently. "I won't let anything happen to you. I promise."

Beth silently balked at his words. Promises rolled off a man's tongue like raindrops from petals. Promises were cheap, even those from supposedly good men.

Dillon wiped the last of the sooty residue from the inner walls of Beth's living room. She had been fortunate that the fire hadn't spread beyond her large china hutch. The thick stone walls weren't a good conduit for flames and, therefore, the most damaging effect of the fire was from the smoke. Beth's misery had been obvious and she had insisted on trying to clean the house immediately. His only option was to assist her, leaving Larry, Carl and the rest of his staff holding the fort at the station. He hadn't yet had the opportunity to speak to Larry about the incident at the Salty Dog, and this troubled him. He felt as though he were juggling too many balls, and he didn't want to drop one. He needed Larry working at full capacity, not brooding on a petty argument with his brother.

Both Dillon and Beth had worked hard all afternoon to remove the traces of soot. They began right after the local sheriff's deputies had taken statements and left to begin their investigation. Dillon had given them the best description he could of the gunman, but he got the feeling they would struggle to find the culprit—the attack had been well prepared and was indicative of a professional criminal. This guy would be safely hiding away by now.

Beth came into the living room carrying two mugs of hot chocolate. "Thanks for helping me get things straight again," she said, handing one of the mugs to him. "It'll be getting dark soon. We should finish up."

He took the cup and warmed his frozen hands on it. The door had totally burned away, and he had placed a temporary board over the empty space, but the air had chilled right through. He had put Larry on lighthouse lookout duty over at the coast guard station, keeping watch for anybody approaching Beth's cottage, but this would be an impossible task as soon as darkness fell. Any attack she was likely to face would come from the sea, and at night the ocean was an immense and murky hiding place. They would need to be gone by nightfall.

"I've arranged for two members of my staff to stay

at Helen's house with you tonight," he said. "They'll be there by seven." He raised his eyebrows at her. "You *did* call her, right?"

"Yes, I called her and asked to stay the night, but I didn't want to worry her, so I didn't tell her about the gunman."

"You need to tell her, Beth. She should know the risk of allowing you into her home."

"I know," she said. "She's already guessed something is wrong anyway, and once two coast guard members arrive with toothbrushes and sleeping bags, she's bound to ask a ton of questions."

"Well, I won't be far away if anything happens," he said. "I've decided to stay here for the night. If the gunman comes back, then I want to be ready and waiting for him."

Beth held her mug close to her chest. "You mean, if the gunman comes back looking for me."

"Yes. I don't know why the cartel has you in their sights, but I intend to find out."

"Is it because I saved the boy?" she asked, hooking her hair behind her ear. Her cheek had black streaks on it, where grime had rubbed off. "And because I can identify the man who was chasing him?"

"Perhaps," he said. "I think the arsonist assumed you were home when he set the fire. I noticed some blood on his pants as he escaped, so I'm reckoning that Ted injured him earlier this morning. He obviously came back a second time to finish the job properly."

"What job was he looking to finish?" Beth asked. "Burning down my home or shooting me?" She broke off to compose herself. "Or both?"

Dillon tried to phrase his reply carefully because he simply didn't have any definite answers.

"When the gunman returned and found your house locked up, I assume he set the fire to flush you out into the open."

"To take his shot?"

"Yes." There was no way of softening his words, but he tried anyway. "This is all just guesswork. The gunman may have a whole other agenda."

"It's pretty obvious that his agenda is to hurt me," she said quietly. "Possibly to punish me for saving the boy and to stop me from helping others. I know you probably can't discuss the matter in detail, but are there lots of people like him being smuggled over the border out at sea?"

She was right about one thing. He couldn't discuss the matter in detail with her. "The coast guard has seen a small rise in people trafficking activity lately." The word *small* didn't even come close to describing the unprecedented levels of smuggling over the last two months. "We're hoping to make a breakthrough soon."

"What kind of people would put a child in a boat and transport him through a raging storm?" she asked. "Do you know much about the gang responsible?"

Dillon wished she would drop the subject. She was already in grave danger, and the less she knew the better. He needed to keep his focus firmly on the trafficking cartel and not protecting her. He was already concerned enough about her safety to sleep in her unsecured house overnight. That was as far as he wanted to go.

"Don't start asking too many questions," he said. "The coast guard is tracking the movements of these smugglers and we hope to make some arrests soon." He drained his cup. "You already know too much, so it's best to leave the investigation to the professionals."

She looked a little hurt and he wished he hadn't spoken so severely. But it was in her best interest. Driving Aziza to safety in Kabul had prevented him from helping others who needed him, and had resulted in their probable deaths. If Beth learned more information, then she would be even more at risk and would demand even more of his time. He felt as if he were walking a tightrope—one wrong move and someone would die. But who would it be?

"Okay," she said. "I get it. I'll butt out from now on. You're the expert, after all."

He looked at her gray eyes, startling in their clarity, and saw intelligence within. She was perceptive.

"So what's your background?" she asked. He suspected she was fishing for more details on the case. "Carl said you came here from Maryland. I'm guessing Washington, DC."

He had learned his cover story down pat. "Yeah," he said. "I was working a boring desk job in the Office of Strategic Analysis, and I wanted to get back on the front line." The act of lying to her again didn't sit well with him, so he mixed in some truth. "For a long time, I couldn't move away because I was taking care of my father, who was suffering with Alzheimer's disease. After he died, I decided to make a change and take a new post." He smiled. "I figured that moving over two thousand miles away was enough of a change."

In reality, he had been based in Little Creek, Virginia, taking care of his father in Pittsburgh on weekends, while his sisters picked up the slack during the week. It had been hard work, but he was glad he did it. His father had spent the last few months of his life being looked after by those who loved him.

"That's an honorable thing to do," she said, clearly surprised. "Not many men have such a strong sense of family commitment these days."

He noticed the way she flinched when she said these words, no doubt remembering the man who had so spectacularly dishonored her by abandoning her on their wedding day.

"There are plenty of honorable men around," he said, thinking of the five men he had served with in Afghanistan during the Dark Skies Mission. "You just need to know where to look."

She folded her arms across her chest. "I'm not looking."

"I guessed that," he said, placing his mug on the coffee table. He couldn't blame her for deciding never to trust a man again. Any woman would probably do the same in her position.

"I'll arrange the delivery of a new door from the hardware store tomorrow," he said, inspecting the frame. "I'll buy one as similar to the old one as possible, and once you put a new coat of paint on the walls, you'll be almost as good as new."

"Let me know how much everything costs," she said, not looking him in the eye. "I'll pay you back in full."

He guessed that she was already concerned about the vet's bill, and this was another expense that she just didn't need. "We don't need to talk money now," he said. "You should go pack a bag. I'll drive you to Helen's house and stay with you until the protection team arrives."

"Okay," she said, turning to go through the door that led up a small flight of stairs to her bedroom. She looked back. "I appreciate everything you're doing for me," she said awkwardly. "It's really kind of you to help me like this."

He was surprised at her sudden and uncomfortable show of gratitude. He guessed that social interactions didn't come naturally to her. "You're welcome," he said. "I'm glad to be able to do it."

She smiled and disappeared through the door. He sat down on one of the chairs and let out a long, slow breath. He felt like a fraud for lying to her, especially considering she had commended his honor in taking care of his father. Being with her unsettled him. Just like the town of Bracelet Bay, Beth was beginning to creep into his affections, and he needed to put an immediate halt to it. He had no intention of getting too involved with her, and he couldn't let her safety override the safety of the vulnerable people being trafficked into a life of misery. All he needed to do was keep an emotional distance, maintain a level head and stay resolute. How hard could it be?

As he mulled over these thoughts, his radio crackled to life on the belt around his waist. It was Larry's voice.

"Unidentified vessels spotted out on the ocean, sir. We need you back at base right away."

Helen took Beth's hands in hers over her kitchen table and squeezed tight. "Oh, Beth," she exclaimed. "I can't believe this is happening. Whoever in the world would want to hurt somebody as kind as you?"

Beth glanced through the kitchen door into Helen's living room. Carl was deep in conversation on his cell phone while his coast guard colleague, Clay, was setting up a telescope by the large window that looked out over the bay. Beth knew Clay from years back, when she was active in the church of Bracelet Bay.

"You need to know the kind of risk involved in allowing me to stay the night here," Beth said solemnly. "Once my front door is replaced tomorrow, I can go back home. But if you feel nervous or frightened in any way, please tell me, and I'll leave immediately." Even as she said these words, she had no idea where else she would go. She would rather sleep in her car than surround herself with the gossipers of Bracelet Bay.

"Nonsense," Helen said, gripping her hands even tighter. "You will stay here and we'll let the Lord take care of us. He is our refuge and our strength. Never forget that."

Beth bowed her head. God had been her constant source of support during the last five years, and she was thankful He had provided a companion like Helen to bolster her faith whenever it was weakening.

"I feel like a ship on the ocean in a storm," Beth said. "I'm being tossed around like a cork, and I have no control over my journey."

"You just need to find a safe harbor," Helen said with an encouraging smile.

Beth sighed. Her safe harbor had always been her lighthouse. Now that it had been infiltrated by a sinister force, she was lost.

Helen seemed to read her mind. She always could. "Maybe God is leading you to find a safe harbor elsewhere, asking you to place your trust in people again." She patted Beth's hand. "A girl like you shouldn't be alone all the time."

"I'm not alone," Beth protested. "I have you."

"Oh, Beth," Helen said. "I won't be around forever. You need to be with people your own age, people who want to help you."

"People like Dillon Randall, you mean?"

"Yes," Helen said. "And people like Henry Stanton, the nice young vet. He asked me about you today when I called him to order some medicine for Tootsie. And I also heard from Mia that you were in the Salty Dog earlier. She wanted to know how you're doing. She misses your friendship an awful lot."

"Wow," Beth said, leaning back in her chair. "It really is impossible to keep any secrets in a town like this, isn't it?"

Helen leaned down to hand a dog treat to Tootsie underneath the table. "We're a community. Where you see gossip, I see concern. Where you see nosiness, I see love. Don't push it away."

Beth didn't want to continue this conversation. She was happy alone and didn't need to hear these things. She steered the conversation in another direction. "Did Mia also mention the fight between Larry and Kevin in the Salty Dog?"

"Yes, she did," Helen replied. "It sounds like those two need their heads knocked together. Kevin's wife told Mia it was a fight over money." She threw her hands in the air. "Brothers should never fight over money. Let's hope they patch things up and put it behind them." Her face broke into a smile. "But I was pleased to hear that Dillon defended your honor when Larry made a snide comment."

"He called me the ice queen," Beth said quietly.

"Take no notice of Larry Chapman," Helen said with

a wave of her hand. "He's always been jealous of Kevin's success with the Salty Dog and he really wanted the coast guard chief's job just so he could go one better than his little brother. He's a sore loser and he's taking it out on everybody else. I'm glad Dillon put him in his place."

Beth was intrigued. She had left the restaurant as soon as Larry made the remark. "So what did Dillon say to him?"

Helen thought hard. "I forget what Mia told me, but he's a good ally for you, Beth, and a good man."

"Would you stop trying to set me up with Dillon Randall?" Beth said in exasperation. "It's never going to happen."

"Maybe not," Helen replied, rising from her seat with creaking bones. "But at least I've taken your mind off the man who wants to hurt you and put it on the man who wants to protect you."

Beth laughed. Helen was right. Her mind *had* been distracted and she felt a lot better.

"Now," said Helen. "It must be time for our walk. It's ten o'clock."

"It's ten o'clock in the evening, not morning," Beth said. A seed of concern planted itself in her belly. Helen had been making mistakes like these on a regular basis recently. "We had our walk this morning, remember? We found the painted stone."

"Oh yes," her friend said, shuffling to the kitchen counter. "So we did."

Carl appeared in the doorway. "Sorry to interrupt you two ladies, but there's some important business that I have to attend to on the coast guard search-and-rescue vessel." He looked as though he was in a hurry, and he pulled on his coat as he talked. "Clay will stay here to take care of you, and I'll be back as soon as the boat returns to the harbor. Keep the house locked up while I'm gone and don't leave, okay?"

"Is everything all right, Carl?" Helen asked. "You look worried."

"There's some serious activity out at sea," he said, giving very little away. "And we need all hands on deck. Clay is more than capable of holding the fort until I get back."

He began to walk to the front door. "Is it the smugglers?" Beth asked. "Are they on the move?"

Carl turned around. "I can't say too much, Beth, but Captain Randall wanted me to reassure you that you'll be perfectly safe." He opened the door to the pitch-dark night. "I'll be taking the coast guard vehicle, so please promise me that you won't go anywhere."

"We won't," Beth said. "It's not like I've got a bunch of parties to attend anyway."

Carl smiled, stepped onto the porch and closed the door behind him. Helen shuffled to Beth's side and Beth automatically extended her elbow for her friend to lean on.

"There's no reason why we can't have a little party of our own," Helen said. "How about a game of Scrabble and some iced tea?"

"Sounds wild," Beth replied with a laugh, trying to allay her fears for Dillon and his crew out on the ocean. She didn't want to care so much about his well-being, but she couldn't stop herself. His face snuck into her mind like an advancing tide.

Together they walked into Helen's small living room. The thermostat was always turned up high in the elderly woman's home and Clay had removed his sweater to compensate for the heavy heat. He sat in his T-shirt by the window, face pressed against the sight of the telescope, unmoving in the low light of a table lamp.

Helen turned on the overhead light.

"Please shut it off," Clay said with a raised hand, keeping his eye trained on the telescopic sight. His voice was kind but firm. Helen flipped the switch down again.

"What's wrong?" Beth asked, walking to the window and squatting down next to him. "Is something out there?"

Clay didn't answer right away, and Beth's heart began to race.

"It's nothing," he said, pulling his face away from the telescope. "Just a dog sniffing around the lighthouse."

"A dog?" Beth exclaimed, standing up sharply. Could Ted have escaped from the vet's office? If her dog had managed to find a way out, he'd head straight home without a doubt. "What does he look like?"

Clay bent his balding head back to the scope. "Kinda big, black, shaggy, scruffy-looking."

"That sounds like Ted. I have to go check it out."

Clay stood up. "I'm afraid that's impossible, Miss Forrester. I'm under strict instructions to keep you inside."

Beth walked to the door and picked up her coat. "Ted has just undergone some major surgery and he might have run away from the vet without anybody realizing. He could be confused and in pain. I'm not leaving him out there all night."

"Wait a minute," Clay said, rushing to try and prevent her from pulling on her coat. "Let's call Henry and find out."

"The vet's office closed hours ago." She opened the door and a sound of barking could be heard. It sounded like Ted, but a little higher pitched. "You can come with me or you can stay here."

"Well, it's clear that you're going whether I like it or not, so I guess you made the decision for me," Clay replied, reaching for his coast guard jacket on the hook. He checked his weapon holstered around his waist before turning to Helen. "We'll be right back, Miss Smith. Don't go anywhere."

Beth stepped outside and began walking swiftly along the road, forcing Clay to run in order to catch up. She walked even faster, covering ground quickly.

"Stay behind me," Clay said, activating a flashlight as they approached the lighthouse. "I see the dog." He pointed to a patch of drooping flowers close to her cottage. "He's in among those beard tongues."

Beth rushed forward, calling Ted's name. She saw a big black shape come trotting out of the foliage, instantly recognizing that this dog wasn't Ted. It wasn't even a schnauzer. It was a retriever of some sort, most likely a stray. The unkempt dog took one look at Beth and Clay and tore past them, racing down the street, clearly frightened by their sudden presence in his quiet foraging.

"It's not Ted," she said, uncertain whether she should feel gladness or disappointment.

Clay seemed eager to turn around and go back. "So let's leave."

Beth looked over at her cottage. "Now that we're here, there's an item I'd like to collect from my bedroom. It won't take a second."

Clay let out a long breath. "Boy, you sure aren't making things easy for me." He checked his watch. "You got five minutes. I'll check the place out before you go inside and guard the door while you get what you need."

"Thanks, Clay," she said, heading for the temporary board covering the doorway. "I wouldn't ask if it wasn't important."

Clay looked around furtively. "Captain Randall told me you could be a handful. And I can see what he means."

Aboard the coast guard search-and-rescue vessel, Dillon navigated his way expertly through the harbor and opened up the throttle once he was out on the open water. Larry had earlier spotted a flotilla of at least ten small boats on the radar heading straight for the rocks. Dillon figured that the inhabitants must be in trouble, unable to steer. And there was no doubt in his mind that this was the cartel trying to bring another shipment of people across the border illegally.

The coast guard boat jumped over the waves, and the salty spray peppered Dillon's face. He felt invigorated and energized, ready to do the job he was trained for. With a full boat crew of eight, he felt sure that this time the smugglers wouldn't evade capture.

Pretty soon, the small boats came into view on the dark horizon. They were wooden rowboats, without oars, all tied together with rope. And they were drifting aimlessly, being carried by the current, bobbing silently in the darkness. Dillon cut the motor, switched on the searchlight and cast a bright glow on the vessels, waiting to see the many faces of their cargo. He saw nothing but emptiness. For a moment, he was confused. And then realization dawned.

That was when he understood he'd been duped. Somebody must have been watching the lighthouse, and this was their way of luring him away. He'd fallen for it hook, line and sinker.

And he had left Beth with just one man guarding her.

FOUR

Beth pulled open the top drawer of her bedroom bureau and rummaged around inside for the small white box hidden beneath her folded clothes. The air was still tinged with a faint aroma of smoke, and the smell grew stronger as she lifted up her woolen sweaters. She would need to wash everything she owned in order to make her house normal again. But at least she would have a new front door the following day and she could secure her precious furniture. She knew it was ridiculous, but she was more concerned about her home-crafted items than her own safety. She didn't place much value on her own worth at all.

Her grasping fingers finally found what they were searching for, and she pulled the box out into the frigid air, shivering slightly. Without the hearth fire, her cottage had developed a deep chill all the way to its core, and this lack of comfort combined with Ted's absence made her home seem sinister and unwelcoming. She placed the box on the bureau and opened it up. The hinge was stiff and creaky, but the unworn yellow gold ring inside looked as shiny and polished as the day she had bought it. The fact that she had been required to purchase her own wedding band should've set alarm bells ringing, but she had been naive and trusting. Her fiancé had taken no interest in the details of the wedding, and she'd been too wrapped up in her own excitement to notice his lack of enthusiasm.

The ring glinted at her, filling the room with a heavy sense of sorrow and regret. She ran an index finger along the smooth, cool metal before teasing it out of its velvet bed. Then she carefully slipped it inside her jean pocket and placed the box back in the drawer. She instantly felt better, stronger and tougher, secure in the knowledge that this ring was far better off any place other than on the third finger of her left hand.

This was a ritual she performed every time she felt her resolve weakening. Whenever she felt herself contemplating allowing another man into her heart, she would take the ring from its box and carry it with her as a constant reminder of the pain that her last relationship had caused.

"Never again," she muttered, patting the pocket where the ring lay.

She took a deep breath and pushed all thoughts of Dillon Randall from her mind. His appearance in her ordinary, sedate life had caused her dormant desire for companionship to reawaken, and Helen had no idea of how her light teasing had hit the mark. Beth didn't want to be attracted to Dillon, yet she couldn't stop herself from noticing his strong, firm torso and rough, weathered hands. And yet, in spite of his ruggedness, he was gentle and caring. He had even put his own needs aside to care for his sick father in the twilight years of his life. A man as decent as Dillon Randall had every right to feel smug, but he wasn't. He was humble, kind and modest: qualities that Beth had once dreamed of finding in a man. All of these swirling emotions were the reasons why she wanted to retrieve the ring—she needed to remind herself of where that kind of thinking would lead. It would lead to heartbreak.

She slid the pine drawer back into place and turned to leave the room. She instantly froze. The moonlight streaming in from the window behind her was casting a glow through her open bedroom door and onto the stairs leading down to her living room. And highlighted in the glow was the unmistakable shadow of a man, elongated on the white wall, his limbs stretched to giant proportions. He was standing at the bottom, hidden out of her sight, with the foot of one bent leg resting on the first step.

It must be Clay coming to see where she was. She called softly into the darkness, "Clay, is that you?" In her head she added the words, *Please let it be you.*

There was no reply, but the shadow began to walk slowly up the stairs, each footstep creating a creak in this old, well-worn cottage. The movements were deliberately slow and laborious, sending her heart rate soaring with panic. She rushed to the window and craned her neck to see as far down to the ground as she could, trying to spot Clay's upright figure guarding the entrance to the cottage. All she could see was a pair of legs lying half out of the doorway. She recognized the navy combat pants as those worn by the coast guard, and she knew instantly that it was Clay, incapacitated and helpless.

She dashed to her bedroom door and slammed it shut, turning the old-fashioned key in the lock. Trying to control her soaring anxiety, she patted down her jeans, searching for her cell. It wasn't there. She spun around in blind panic, imagining the fate that awaited her. Then she remembered she'd placed her cell in her jacket, and she fumbled in the deep pockets, grasping the solid object she found inside. All the while, the creaks grew louder on the stairs. The only two rooms upstairs were her bedroom and a bathroom. She had no place to run. She was trapped.

Her head swam with alarm. Hadn't Dillon promised she would be safe? And now his promise was proven to be as wafer thin as she'd predicted. She hit the redial button on her cell. She knew that Dillon's number had been the last one she'd called. In fact, it was the only number she'd called in weeks, and she impatiently waited for the tinny ring to start.

The man reached the top of the stairs. She heard the loose board squeak underneath the carpet as he stood on it, and she knew exactly where he was. He was close.

Dillon's phone began to ring, but no answer came. Then she heard the roar of a boat's engine and, turning to the window, she saw the coast guard vessel streaking over the bay, heading back to harbor. The boat was illuminated with bright lights and many figures were standing upright as it leaped over the water. The figure at the helm was unmistakably Dillon's, and she knew there was no way he would be able to hear his cell above the noise of the motor.

A recorded message was playing in her ear: Dillon's voice inviting callers to leave their details. She almost shouted into the speaker: "I need you at the lighthouse right away. I'm in trouble."

As if sensing her plea, Dillon suddenly looked up at the lighthouse, raising his face against the wind. She imagined that she could hear his voice inside her head: *I'm coming to you, Beth. I'm almost there.*

The handle of her bedroom door started to turn, and was rattled when it failed to open. Beth picked up a heavy, cast-iron sculpture from her dresser. It was in the shape of a ship's helm, with many spokes sticking out from a central wheel. The door rattled once again, this time more insistent and menacing. She felt the weighty weapon in her hands and took a step forward. Whoever wanted to hurt her certainly wouldn't find a shrinking violet behind the door. She intended to stand her ground and not be cowed. She would fight back with all the strength in her body.

Dillon jumped from the boat even before it was fully docked. He called out to Carl as he ran down the harbor deck, instructing them to secure the vessel in its berth. He had more important matters to attend to, and there was no time to lose. He felt a vibration in his pocket and yanked his cell out. The display told him that a message had been left three minutes ago. Beth had tried to call. As he ran to the truck, he listened to the message and was prompted to pick up the pace by hearing Beth's pleading words: *I'm in trouble.*

He should never have left her being guarded by just one man. Should he have put Beth first just as he had done with Aziza in Afghanistan? Had he made the wrong call?

As he reached the truck, he heard Carl's voice shout, "Hey, Captain, where you going?"

He only had time to yell, "Lighthouse," before starting up the truck and speeding from the parking lot. The harbor was close to the lighthouse, just a five-minute drive, but he felt each second ticking by as he raced along the coastal road, trying not to imagine the scene that would await him when he arrived.

The lighthouse was in total darkness as he approached, and he parked under the cover of a tree on the opposite side of the road. He wanted to remain out of sight and retain the element of surprise. Stepping out of the vehicle, he moved soundlessly across the road, keeping close to the exterior wall of the cottage until he reached the doorway. That was when he saw Clay, lying sprawled on the ground, silent and unmoving. He squatted down next to his colleague and took his pulse. He was still alive. Grabbing Clay by the collar, Dillon dragged him away from the door to a more shielded position. Clay let out a muffled groan and tried to speak. He looked to have been hit with some force on the back of the head, clearly taken by surprise.

Dillon propped up the injured man with his back against the outside wall. Clay shook his head, seemingly trying to rid himself of dizziness. He waved his superior officer away. "Go," he said. "Go get Beth."

Dillon didn't need telling twice. He pulled out his flashlight and entered the cottage, quickly searching every inch of the living room and kitchen. He had to stop himself from calling Beth's name, unwilling to give his position away to any intruders. But it was difficult. He was experiencing the same sensation of urgency as he'd felt upon finding Aziza in the desert. Her tragic story had pushed his protective instincts to the fore, and he knew he wouldn't have rested until she was safe in Kabul with people who would guard her from the barbaric sharia ruling of her hometown. He never wanted to feel that way again, but it looked as though he had no choice in the matter.

A thud sounded overhead. With lightning movements, he ascended the stairs two at a time and saw Beth's open bedroom door. Lying halfway through the doorway was person wearing jeans and brown boots. From this angle, he couldn't determine who it was.

He muttered the word *no* under his breath. Was he too late? He raced to the room, raising his flashlight and gun out front, ready to apprehend the attacker. Yet the beam of light picked out only Beth's shocked face looking down on a man who was spread-eagled on her bedroom floor, passed out cold. By Beth's feet lay a cast-iron sculpture of an old-fashioned ship's wheel.

She brought her hand up to her face in shock. "I hit him," she said shakily. "Hard."

Dillon holstered his gun and switched on the overhead light. The room grew bright and he was able to assess the scene clearly. The man lying on the ground was facedown, a trickle of blood clearly visible on his temple where the heavy object had landed a firm, well-placed blow. The rise and fall of the man's lungs let Dillon know that he was still breathing.

"Are you okay?" he said to Beth, stepping over the man's prone figure. He placed his hands on either side of her shoulders, stopping himself from embracing her, despite her looking as though she needed it.

"I'm fine," she replied, looking into his eyes with panic. "I didn't kill him, did I? He's okay, right?"

"He's alive," Dillon replied. "But I don't want you worrying about this guy. You did the right thing in protecting yourself. I'm proud of you."

Beth summoned up a weak smile, but she couldn't

mask her anxiety. "Clay!" she exclaimed. "I forgot about Clay. He's outside."

"I saw him. He'll be okay." Dillon looked down at the man. "Is this the same guy who tried to come into your home to take the child?"

She nodded. The man was heavyset, with dark wiry hair and a trimmed beard. While he was out cold, Dillon patted him down for weapons, finding a curved knife in an inner pocket.

"It's the same knife he was carrying the night I found the boy," she said. "He tried to stab Ted with it."

Dillon held the weapon carefully between his forefinger and thumb and placed it on the bedside dresser. "I'll get it forensically analyzed to see if it contains any traces of your dog's DNA," he said. "I suspect this is the same person who hurt Ted, set fire to your home and used us for target practice earlier today."

He unclipped the radio from his belt and made a request for the police and an ambulance. Once this intruder had recovered from his injury, he would hopefully provide the answers to a lot of important questions.

Dillon bent down and hauled the man up onto the bed. He then pulled some cuffs from his back pocket, securing one ring around the man's wrist and the other to the solid wood bed frame.

Beth picked up the heavy iron sculpture from the floor and placed it back on the dresser.

"The police may need to take that as evidence," he said. "But I'll get it returned as soon as possible."

She flinched, jumping back from the sculpture as if it had burned her. "Sorry," she said. "I should've left it where it was. I forgot that my house is a crime scene now. Will the police want to question me?" She let out a gasp. "Will they charge me with assault?"

He approached her slowly. "Yes, the police will want to question you, but I'll make sure that any investigation is carried out jointly with the coast guard." He put a hand on her cheek, wanting to keep her calm. "You won't be charged with anything. This is a clear case of self-defense." He brushed her smooth skin with his fingers. "Don't worry. I'll stay with you the whole time you're questioned."

His touch seemed to open up a crack in her defenses and allow a vulnerability to slip through. She melted into his arms and buried her face in his torso. This close contact was definitely going beyond his call of duty and he knew he should pull back, yet he couldn't.

"I can't do this anymore," she said. "I just want Ted back. I want my life back."

He curled his arms around her waist. "You'll get your life back. I promise."

"You can't promise anything," she said through muffled sobs. He felt her breath coming in quick puffs. "You can't back them up."

"I messed up this time," he said, bringing his hand to her hair and stroking it lightly. "I should never have left you with only Clay to guard you. I won't make the same mistake twice."

His whole body tensed with conflict: an inner battle between his desire to personally keep Beth safe and his sense of duty to those being trafficked. As he held Beth in his arms, he was scanning the sea, wondering where the traffickers were now, wondering how many people were crammed into filthy, unsanitary boats. He couldn't abandon them to take care of one woman, no matter how much he wished he could.

He pulled away from her. "What are you doing here anyway?" he asked. "You should be at Helen's house."

"There was a dog here and I thought it was Ted, but it was just a stray, or maybe a decoy to lure me to the lighthouse." She moved her hand nervously to the pocket of her jeans. "And I wanted to pick something up while I was here."

"Well, I won't let you out of my sight for the rest of the evening," he said. The man shackled to the bed began to stir and Dillon led Beth out into the hallway. "I'll hand over any remaining tasks to the search-and-rescue crew so I can stay ashore."

"I don't want to disrupt your work," she said. "You've done far too much for me already."

A flashback rushed into his mind, reminding him of similar words that Aziza had spoken as he was preparing to leave the women's refuge in Kabul: *you have done so much for me*. Aziza had no idea of the lives he had sacrificed in order to guarantee her safety. If Dillon shifted his attention to Beth, how many might die? He couldn't allow that on his conscience.

But relinquishing her safety to others was not as easy as he'd imagined. He was between a rock and a hard place. For one night, he would stay close and watch over her. Tomorrow would be different. Tomorrow he would back off again.

Beth watched Helen busily making coffee, using her best china cups. She then laid out warmed homemade cookies on a plate, adding a sprinkling of powdered sugar before placing them on a tray.

"You really don't need to go to all this trouble, Helen," Beth said. "You're not entertaining the Queen of England. It's just the coast guard captain."

"Hush, now," Helen said. "As it says in the book of Peter, *show hospitality to one another without grumbling.*"

Beth pursed her lips together, taking the deserved rebuke. Helen struggled to pick up the tray, so Beth stepped in front of her and carried it to the fireside, where Dillon was sitting with Tootsie curled up on his lap. When the dog heard Helen's distinctive, hobbling footfall, he lifted his head sleepily and then resettled himself on the lap of the visitor who had given him plenty of fuss and attention.

"Tootsie is never usually this welcoming of strangers," Helen said, leaning her cane against the wall and sitting in the chair opposite Dillon. "You're very fortunate, Mr. Randall. He normally would be biting your ankles by now."

"He's a great dog," Dillon said, brushing at the knees of his pants. "But he sure does leave a lot of fur behind."

Helen laughed. "It's his scent marker. You belong to him now."

Beth felt awkward hovering between the pair, holding the laden tray. Dillon suddenly noticed her predicament and placed the dog on the floor, before rising to take the tray from her hands.

"Let me get this," he said, searching for a place to put it down in Helen's cluttered home.

Beth lifted the piles of books from the coffee table and placed them on the floor. Once a large enough space had been cleared, Dillon slid the tray onto the surface and began to pour out three cups from the china pot.

Beth remained standing, aware of the fact that Helen's small living room contained only two chairs.

Dillon gesticulated to the chair he had just vacated. "Please sit, Beth."

"No," she protested. "That's your seat. I'm okay to stand."

Dillon's eyes darted around the room, coming to rest on a footstool in the corner. He picked it up and brought it close to the two upholstered chairs. Then he perched on it, looking ridiculously oversize for the small piece of furniture.

"I have a seat right here," he said with a smile. "Please sit down, Beth. It's been a stressful evening for you, and you need to relax."

She sat, taking a cup from Dillon's hand. She felt uncomfortable, unable to relax as Dillon suggested. The room was too warm and Dillon's proximity too close.

He seemed to sense her discomfort and he shifted on the stool, trying to move back a little. "The man who attacked you has received twelve stitches to a wound on his head, and he's currently under observation at the hospital. I'll be interviewing him in the morning right after the police finish their questioning."

"I'm so proud of you, Beth," Helen said, punching a puny fist into the air. "You showed him, huh?"

Beth didn't feel much like smiling, but she tried anyway. Helen was clearly trying hard to be upbeat, attempting to revive her flagging spirits. Despite the very late hour, Helen was still perky and energetic, but Beth was exhausted, particularly after another session of intense police questioning.

"What about Clay?" Beth asked. "Is he okay?"

"He's fine. He went to the hospital just as a precaution. He's already home."

"And I can go home tomorrow as well?" She realized it may sound ridiculous to want to return to a place where she had faced such danger, but she felt hemmed in at Helen's cluttered bungalow. "I hope to get Ted back tomorrow, and I'd really love to be able to take him straight home."

Dillon put his cup down on the tray and turned toward her. "I know that you really don't want to leave your cottage, but would you reconsider moving into the town for a while?"

Beth didn't even need to think about it. "No."

He nodded as though he had expected that reaction. "Your lighthouse is remote, dark and wide-open to the sea. Even just one of these things is enough to make me nervous, but all three is a perfect storm."

Beth thought of the many solitary nights she had spent curled up with Ted, listening to the waves crashing on the shore outside. She thought of the peacefulness, the seclusion, the knowledge that she was entirely alone.

"I already told you that moving into Bracelet Bay isn't an option," she said. "I thought I made myself clear."

Helen entered the conversation. "Please don't take Beth's harsh tone personally, Captain Randall. The problem with living a solitary lifestyle is that even a small town like Bracelet Bay becomes a little claustrophobic." Helen looked at Beth in much the same way as a teacher reprimanding a student. "And loners sometimes forget how to be polite in social situations."

"I'm sorry, Dillon," Beth said. "I didn't mean to be

rude, but Helen's right. I'd feel claustrophobic in the town." She closed her eyes. "The lighthouse is the only place where I can properly breathe."

Dillon regarded her with thoughtful eyes. "Okay. I can see how strongly you feel about it. I'll make sure the door is replaced first thing tomorrow morning and you can move back in by the afternoon. I'll also add some extra security features. If you insist on staying there, the least we can do is get the place locked up tight. I've posted a couple of guards there for tonight to make sure your possessions stay safe."

She cast her eyes downward. "Thank you."

"I must say," said Helen, feeding Tootsie a piece of cookie. "It's nice to have a man around to take care of these types of things, isn't it, Beth?"

Beth knew exactly what Helen was up to. "It's only temporary, Helen," she said. "Now that somebody is in custody, all this might be over soon."

Dillon rested his forearms on his knees and leaned forward, tensing his biceps to keep his balance on the small stool. "This is a very serious time for you, Beth," he said. "Just because a man has been captured doesn't mean we can afford to take any chances, and we have no idea how long you'll need to be under the protection of the coast guard. Somebody will stay close to you until we're absolutely sure you're out of danger."

"Oh, that reminds me," Helen said, pushing herself up to stand. "I need a big strong man to lift the camp bed out from the storage cupboard. I'm afraid I don't have the room for another guest, so you'll be sleeping in here. Is that all right, Captain…um…" She had forgotten Dillon's name.

Dillon stood with a smile. "Randall," he reminded

her. "It's Dillon Randall, and I'm happy to sleep any-where, Miss Smith. Thank you for your hospitality."

"Please," Helen said, reaching for her stick. "Call me Helen."

"In that case," he replied, "you must call me Dillon."

Helen giggled like a schoolgirl with a crush. "You're a welcome addition to the community, Dillon. I hope you'll decide to settle here. You know what they say about Bracelet Bay—every year it adds a new charm."

"That's certainly sounds like it would be true," Dillon said. "I like it here a lot."

Helen beamed at Beth. "I'm pleased to hear it. Now all we have to do is find you a good woman to marry, and you'll be set for life."

Dillon gave a throaty laugh. "One step at a time, Helen. My work keeps me pretty busy, so I don't have a lot of time to meet that one special lady."

"Who's to say you haven't met her already?" Helen said with a mischievous grin.

Beth jumped from her seat. "I'll take this back into the kitchen," she said, picking up the tray while shooting Helen a warning expression. "It's late, and we should all turn in for the night."

As she walked into the kitchen, the wedding band in her pants dug slightly into her hipbone, and she bal-anced the tray on one hand to tuck it deeper down into the corner of the pocket. Her past was contained in that one small pocket, reminding her that it was still there, still powerful and still able to teach her a lesson about allowing someone to get too close.

Dillon slid the door open leading into the unheated sunroom and relished the coolness flowing over his face. Helen's home was like a hothouse and he desperately needed some cold air. Stepping into the room, he closed the door behind him and pulled out his cell to call his old friend Tyler Beck. He and Tyler went back a long way, all the way to the Dark Skies Mission in Afghanistan four years ago, when a team of six Navy SEALs had been asked to terminate a dangerous insurgent group. After Dillon had returned to the US, he'd turned to Tyler for support, to help him come to terms with his failure to remove the teachers from danger. Only Tyler knew how much Dillon had been affected by his decision to get Aziza to safety. Only Tyler knew of Dillon's feelings of guilt and betrayal toward the people he subsequently failed to save.

Tyler answered his cell quickly. "Hey, Dill," he exclaimed. "I've been waiting for your call. I was assigned a new mission today, and it was your name on the papers."

Dillon decided to cut the small talk. "Did you get all the details? Is there anything you want to ask before you leave Virginia?"

"The mission brief was very thorough," replied Tyler. "I think I'm pretty well prepared. I leave at 09:00 tomorrow so my ETA is about 18:00. I gotta say that I'm looking forward to working together again. It's been a long time."

"Yeah, it has," Dillon said, thinking of the years that had passed since Dark Skies. "Just remember your cover story when you arrive. You're a coast guard surveillance expert transferring from Florida to help with the smuggling investigation. We never met before, right?"

"Sure thing. I know the drill." Tyler's voice turned

serious. "Are you okay, buddy? You sound kinda downbeat."

"It's complicated."

"Isn't it always?" Tyler replied. "What kind of complicated are we talking about here? Mission complicated or woman complicated?"

"Both."

"Is this woman somebody you care about?"

"No," Dillon said. "I mean yes, but not like that."

Tyler let out a low whistle. "Oh boy, it really is complicated. Out of interest, is she blond, beautiful and single?"

Dillon couldn't help laughing. "Yes, she's all of those things, but that's not why it's complicated, so quit joking around."

Tyler feigned offense. "Hey, I'm not joking around. I'm just getting some background details so I can be prepared."

"I'll brief you when you arrive tomorrow," Dillon said. "You don't have a problem with heights, right?"

"No. Why?"

"You'll be living in a lighthouse tower."

"I've slept in caves, ditches, trees and even in the water, but never in a lighthouse. I'll look forward to it."

"That's what I thought," Dillon said. "Call me when you get to town."

A scraping noise alerted Dillon to Tootsie's presence behind the door. The dog paced back and forth scratching at the floor, trying to gain access to his new friend.

"I gotta go," Dillon said. "Tonight I have a hot date with an amazing eighty-five-year-old lady and a tiny dog that covers me in fur."

Tyler laughed. "Nobody can say that the life of a SEAL isn't glamorous."

"You know it."

After hanging up the phone, Dillon stayed in the sun-room gathering his thoughts. Beth and Helen were putting sheets on the small camp bed in the corner of the living room, but he didn't relish the thought of spending the night there. He wanted to be at the station, working late into the night, planning surveillance stakeouts. Beth was taking up precious time and valuable resources. She was clouding his mind with distractions. When he closed his eyes, it wasn't the trafficking vessels he saw, it was her face.

As soon as Tyler arrived, Dillon intended to let his Navy SEAL colleague take control of Beth's safety. The most painful lesson Aziza had taught him was that his loyalties could not be divided again. He had to pick a priority and stick to it. And his priority could not be a woman. Not this time.

FIVE

Dillon smiled warmly at the gruff-looking man sitting across from him, who was wearing handcuffs chained to the table. Dillon often found that a wide smile was a useful weapon, disarming and unexpected, catching any hostile people off guard. The man shifted back in his seat, looking confused, uncertain how to react. This man was wearing a prison issue orange suit, the short sleeves exposing dark tattoos: scorpions, spiders and silver daggers. The tattoos snaked up his neck, ending just below his Adam's apple. There was also a swelling to his temple, where an angry gash had been expertly stitched. But he had been declared medically fit to be questioned, and Dillon wanted some straight answers.

He opened a paper file on the table in front of him, containing all the details that the police department had compiled. Thankfully the guy was already on their records, having skipped town while on bail two years previously, so the file gave Dillon a lot of background information.

"It's nice to meet you, Mr. Olmos," he said. "Your name is Miguel Olmos, right? And you're originally from Mexico but became a naturalized American citizen three years ago, back when you had no criminal history."

He did not reply, so Dillon continued. "Since that time, you've become a people trafficker, using the Californian coastline as a point of entry for illegal crossings into the United States of America. My best guess is that you applied for your American citizenship with the full intention of using it to aid and abet your cartel friends back home."

Miguel raised his eyebrows high in false astonishment. "I don't traffic people," he said in accented English. "I am just an ordinary fisherman."

"Drop the pretense, Mr. Olmos," Dillon said. "All those distinctive tattoos on your arms and neck identify you as a member of the most feared cartel in Central America. We know that you've been smuggling people right under our noses, and we also know you've been getting some insider help from the Bracelet Bay coast guard."

A flash in Miguel's eyes let Dillon know that his assumption had been correct. There was a spy in the coast guard ranks. But who was it?

"Do you want to tell me the whole story?" Dillon suggested. "Starting with the night you forced your way into a woman's home while she was protecting a young child?"

Miguel tried to affect a blank expression. "I have no idea what you are talking about. Maybe she is mistaken."

Dillon placed his hand on the open file resting on the table. "I understand that you're facing some serious charges relating to offenses you committed here in California two years ago." He looked over the notes. "Drug dealing, smuggling illegal firearms, harboring illegal aliens, threats to kill, assaulting a police officer…" He raised his head. "Shall I continue?"

Miguel Olmos tilted his head to one side. "What do you want?" he said, looking Dillon up and down. "You are a coast guard, yes? Shouldn't you be on the sea looking for fish or something?"

"That's funny," Dillon said with a straight face. "But do you know what's funnier? Thirty years in a US federal prison. How old are you, Mr. Olmos?"

"Forty-two," came the reluctant reply.

"By the time you're released, you'll be over seventy years old." Dillon leaned back and crossed his arms. "You'll be an old man, all washed up in the cartel business. What you gonna do then, Miguel? Go back to being a *fisherman*?"

Miguel leaned forward and looked Dillon squarely in the eye. "The cartel looks after its own."

Dillon let out a snort. "You think so? I don't notice them rushing to help you, do you?" He looked toward the door. "Where's your cartel-hired lawyer? Is he on his way?"

Miguel looked down at his chained hands, biting his lip. "I already told the police that I don't want a lawyer." He forced a smile. "You are trying to scare me."

Dillon pointed to the stitches on the wounded man's head. "That's a nasty cut you have there. You got more than you bargained for when you went into Beth Forrester's home last night, am I right?"

When Dillon was faced with silence, he continued. "Do you make a habit of targeting vulnerable young ladies? Is that the kind of man you are?"

These words seemed to have the desired effect. "I'm

not like that," Miguel said, raising his voice angrily. "I don't like to hurt women."

"Is that right?" Dillon said sarcastically. "I guess you just stab their dogs and set fire to their homes instead. We got your fingerprints on a gas can that was used to set fire to Miss Forrester's home yesterday." He narrowed his eyes. "So I know exactly what kind of a man you are, Mr. Olmos."

"You know nothing about me."

"I know that you hid your links to the cartel in order to gain American citizenship," Dillon said. "In which case, there's a chance it could be revoked. So you're looking at jail time *and* potentially being deported back to Mexico afterwards."

Miguel's head snapped up sharply. He was rattled. "This is not possible. I am American now."

Dillon smiled. "Oh, it's entirely possible. You were given a chance to make something of your life here, but instead you used your opportunity to hunt a young woman and terrify her."

Miguel lifted his chin. "I am not proud of these things. I didn't want to hurt that woman, but I had my orders. I tried to help her by asking Santa Muerte to grant her a quick death."

Dillon remembered the painted stone in his pocket. He pulled it out and placed it on the table. "Did you leave this on the beach by the lighthouse?"

"Yes."

"Why?"

"Our Lady of the Holy Death can make any death painless," Miguel said. "I bought this stone from a witch doctor who guaranteed that my prayer would be granted. I prayed for a quick death for the lighthouse lady." He leaned back and smiled as if these words affirmed his status as a good man. "You see, Mr. Coast Guard, cartel members are not all bloodthirsty savages."

"Why must Beth Forrester die?" Dillon asked. "Why did the cartel put a hit on her?"

Miguel sniffed and ran his eyes around the small, bare room. "I don't know. I was not told why."

"Is she a threat because she saved the boy who escaped from you?" Dillon asked. "Is that it?"

"No. The boy was trouble for us anyway. He was scared by the storm and jumped overboard. The sea was so brutal I was certain he would drown, but the waves somehow carried him onto the shore." He raised his eyes to the ceiling. "God was looking out for that child, I am sure of it. I was supposed to get him back before he made contact with anyone on the mainland, but the woman got to him first." He laughed loudly and punched a fist onto his chest. "She protected him like a lioness. The boy can have his freedom. The woman won it for him."

Dillon was finally getting some answers but not the ones he had hoped for. "So why is the cartel continuing to pursue Miss Forrester? Does she have information that can harm you?"

When he was met with yet another wall of silence, Dillon slammed his hands onto the table, making Miguel jump in surprise.

"What do you want with her?" Dillon demanded. "I need to know."

A slow smile spread across Miguel's face, creasing his craggy features and revealing his sharp teeth. "You like her," he said mockingly. "You like her very much, I think."

Dillon rubbed a hand down his face in frustration. Miguel's words got underneath his skin, and he hated himself for rising to the provocation. He took some deep breaths.

"I can help you, Mr. Olmos," Dillon said calmly. "If you cooperate with the coast guard, we can cut you a deal with the federal prosecutor regarding the numerous charges you're facing, and your citizenship will remain safe. I've been granted special privileges to offer you incentives to talk."

Miguel narrowed his eyes. "You can keep me out of jail?"

Dillon shook his head. "Oh, you're doing jail time, but we could reduce the sentence to ten years if you lead us to the rest of the trafficking gang."

"Ten years?" Miguel repeated, rubbing his stubbly beard.

Dillon let this idea sink in for a few moments. "Think about it, Miguel," he said. "You could be out of jail at fifty-two years old or seventy-two. It's your choice."

"I want a lawyer."

Dillon smiled. This was a good sign. "I'll get one assigned to you right away."

Miguel leaned over the table, dragging the chained cuffs along the wood. "Is that lady still at her lighthouse?"

Dillon thought of Beth in the living room of her cottage, where he had left her that morning, sanding down the old rowboat she had salvaged. She was being guarded by Carl and Larry, who were overseeing the fitting of a new door to her property. "Why do you want to know? Is there something you want to tell me, Miguel? Is another attack planned?"

"She is not safe. I am certain that the cartel will send another man to her house. And soon. Take my advice and trust nobody."

"What do you care?" Dillon asked coolly. "She means nothing to you."

Miguel looked at the painted stone sitting on the table. "Another cartel member might not have the respect for Santa Muerte that I do. I don't want an innocent woman to suffer before death. She doesn't deserve that. She doesn't know what she has done."

"What *has* she done?"

Miguel leaned over the table, his dark eyes darting and shining like a crow's. "She has information which somebody in the cartel wants to keep secret. This is all I know. I was told to burn her cottage to the ground after killing her. I was instructed to destroy everything."

These words chilled Dillon to his very core. "This woman is a total recluse. What information could she possibly have on a Central American cartel?"

Miguel closed his mouth and crossed his arms. Dillon could almost see the shutters being pulled up in the terrified man's mind. He clearly didn't intend to say any more, fearful of the repercussions that would be served to him by the gang masters.

"I will say nothing until I see a lawyer," he said. "Then I will consider your offer of a deal."

Dillon picked up the stone and slid it back into his pocket. Then he stood, walked to the door and rapped on it loudly, waiting for a uniformed officer to open up.

He turned back to Miguel Olmos. "You can stop saying your prayers to Santa Muerte now," he said. "Beth doesn't need or want them."

"But without the guiding hand of Our Lady of Holy Death, she might suffer in death."

"Don't you see how perverse it is to pray for someone to die?" Dillon asked incredulously. "What kind of faith is that?"

"It is the only thing protecting this woman right now," Miguel said, eyeballing him. "It is all she has."

"Oh no, it isn't," Dillon said as the door was opened up and he stepped into the corridor. "She has her own God keeping watch over her. And she also has me."

Beth was knocked off her feet by the exuberance of Ted, who was clearly overjoyed to see her after his overnight stay at the vet's office. Henry, the veterinarian, helped her to her feet and held Ted by the collar, using his obvious skill with animals to calm the dog down. Henry had kindly delivered her dog to the lighthouse, and if he wondered why Seaman Carl Holden from the coast guard station was busy installing window locks on her cottage, he maintained enough politeness not to ask.

"Ted's recovered well," Henry said, giving a final check to the neat row of stitches on the dog's abdomen. "The fur will grow back soon enough, but the wound might itch, so make sure he doesn't bite at it. The only other option is to put a cone over his head."

"No," Beth exclaimed. "He would hate that. I'll keep a close eye on him to make sure he leaves it alone." She held out her hand. "Thank you, Henry. You've done a fantastic job taking care of him."

"He's a great dog," Henry said, shaking her hand vigorously. "I've really enjoyed his company." He laughed awkwardly. "Does that sound weird?"

"Not at all," she said. "I feel the same way. How

much do I owe you for his treatment?" She opened a drawer to pull out her checkbook. Hopefully there would be enough in her account to cover this unexpected expense. She'd planned to have turned the old rowboat in her living room into a bed frame by now. The client was paying over two thousand dollars for that particular piece of furniture, and she badly needed the money.

Henry held up his palms. "The bill is all settled. There's nothing to pay."

Beth shook her head in confusion. "There must be some mistake."

"No mistake," Henry said. "I took a credit card payment over the telephone earlier this morning."

"From whom?"

"Captain Randall."

The surprise on Beth's face must have been evident.

"I'm sorry," Henry said. "I assumed you'd be okay with that. I mean…" He looked embarrassed. "I thought you were a couple."

"We're *not* a couple," she said strongly. "He had no right to pay on my behalf. I'd like to settle the bill myself, please."

Henry clasped his fingers together. "I can't take a payment from you without refunding Captain Randall's money, and I'd rather not do that without speaking with him first."

Beth heard the crunch of tires on the small stones that covered the ground next to the cottage. It was the coast guard truck.

"Ah, here's Captain Randall now," Henry said, clearly relieved to be able to avoid a difficult conversation. "Maybe you should discuss it with him."

Through the window, she saw Dillon step from the truck and come to her newly fixed front door. He knocked loudly and she opened up, letting him inside while Henry took the opportunity to make a quick exit.

"You got Ted back," Dillon said with a smile. His face showed signs of his poor night's sleep on a rickety camp bed in Helen's living room. His hair was a little unkempt, with a curled lock falling over his forehead, and his olive-toned face looked paler than usual. But he still managed to produce a tug somewhere deep inside her chest, a yearning not felt for years. He smiled broadly, and she remembered how it felt to have a man notice her, to feel like a real woman instead of an eccentric collector of sea junk. She was dressed in her favorite old jeans teamed with a pink turtleneck sweater, but his smile made her feel as though she were wearing a ball gown. It was almost enough to make her forget why she was mad at him.

"You paid Ted's bill." Her tone was accusatory.

"Yes, I did," he said. "Ted was injured by a criminal gang member who I was supposed to be tracking. It's my responsibility to pay for his care." He said these words very matter-of-factly, as though it was a subject not up for discussion. It irritated Beth even further.

Dillon dropped to his knees and extended a hand to Ted. The dog looked up at his mistress for affirmation that he was allowed to take affection from this new man in his life. When Beth gave a small nod, Ted bounded over to Dillon and nuzzled his hand before dropping to the floor and exposing his belly to be tickled. Dillon duly obliged, being careful of the stitches, and the dog kicked his back leg in delight.

"You should have asked me first," Beth said, trying hard not to sound whiny and sullen. "I know you wanted to help, but it makes me feel…" She couldn't find the right word.

"Indebted?" Dillon offered.

"Yes. Exactly."

He stood. "I don't expect, or want, anything in return, Beth." He looked exasperated. "I simply wanted to help you as a friend. I think you've been cooped up in this lighthouse for too long and you've forgotten how to accept an act of human kindness."

She was taken aback by his reprimand. And a little hurt. "Thank you for the advice," she said tersely. She noticed Carl casting a glance her way, no doubt agreeing with Dillon's judgment.

Dillon saw her embarrassment. "Carl, why don't you go join Larry on lookout duty up in the tower? I want a full three-hundred-sixty-degree surveillance. If any boats, vehicles or people come heading our way, inform me immediately."

"Yes, sir." Carl crossed to the winding staircase and closed the door behind him. Beth heard his heavy footsteps on the wrought-iron steps, curling round and round.

"I'm sorry that I didn't ask you before settling the vet's account," Dillon said, putting his hand on the small of her back and leading her to sit on a chair. "But can we just put that matter to one side for now? There's something more important we need to talk about."

Beth felt her stomach lurch. "What happened?"

He held up his hands. "Nothing happened," he said gently. "But the man we currently have in custody has given us reason to believe that you are in possession of information that can seriously harm the cartel."

"How?" she asked in disbelief. "I do nothing but mind my own business. What could I possibly know about a criminal gang?"

"That's the exact same question I've been asking myself," Dillon replied. "Do you think that somebody from your past or present might have cartel connections, or brought you into contact with a cartel member?"

Beth let out a burst of laughter, partly from surprise and partly from fear. The implication that she was somehow connected to a dangerous, criminal organization was ludicrous. She couldn't think of a serious answer. "Well, I've had a suspicion for a long time that Helen is a cartel gang master," she said. "And Tootsie is her drug mule."

Dillon rolled his eyes to the ceiling. "This isn't a joke, Beth. These people want to kill you, and you're taking a huge risk by staying here at the lighthouse. There *will* be another attack, and we have to figure out exactly why the cartel is coming after you. Otherwise they won't stop until the job is done."

Beth took a sharp intake of breath. Dillon's voice was hard and stern, letting her know exactly how grave the situation was. She had been kidding herself that having a man in custody meant the danger had passed. Dillon was right. She had let down her guard.

"I'm sorry," she said. "I didn't mean to be flippant. I just can't think of any way I would be connected to a cartel."

"Have you come into contact with anybody new recently? Maybe on the beach?"

She thought hard. "No, except for the occasional fisherman I don't make contact with anybody. The only person I spend any real time with is Helen."

"What about somebody from your past?" He looked uncomfortable. "I understand you were almost married some years ago. Could your ex-fiancé have somehow brought you into contact with any members of a cartel that you were unaware of?"

Beth stared at him, eyes widened in surprise at the boldness of the question. She never talked about Anthony, her ex-fiancé, not even to Helen. Not because she still cared for him, but because he reminded her of her foolishness.

"Anthony was an accountant who was so much of a coward he was scared of his own shadow," she said. "When faced with trouble, he would turn and run the other way. One time Ted was attacked by another dog on the beach, and he hightailed it back to his car, leaving me to protect Teddy all by myself." She closed her eyes, remembering the day when it had finally dawned on her that the man she would marry was weak in thought, word and mind. "So I very much doubt that Anthony had any links to a smuggling gang. He's not the type."

She opened her eyes to see Dillon studying her face closely. "I see," he said. "Would you mind if I asked a personal question, Beth?"

She guessed what it would be. "Go ahead."

"This guy sounds like a real jerk. Why did you want to marry him?"

She shrugged. "I've asked myself the same question hundreds of times over. I met him right after my parents moved to Oregon to be closer to my grandma, and I think I was lonely." She met his eyes. "I just wanted to be with somebody."

He nodded, seeming to understand. "We all feel like that sometimes."

Beth felt a floodgate opening. "I wish I'd had the courage to walk away from him when I realized I didn't love him. I wish I'd called off the wedding instead of allowing him to run away like the coward he was. I wish I'd never let him humiliate me in front of my family and friends." She buried her head in her hands. "I wish I wasn't too embarrassed to now return to the town where I was born and raised." She took her hands away and looked at Dillon in earnest. "Isn't is crazy that I would rather stay at a lighthouse, where men with guns and knives will come to find me, instead of going to stay in Bracelet Bay like you suggested?"

"No, not crazy," he replied. "I'd call you defiant, stubborn and determined but not crazy."

She managed to smile. "You're just being kind. You don't really know me."

"Oh, I think I do," he said. "I see the beautiful furniture you create and the simple way you live. I see how you love Ted and how you help and care for Helen. I saw the way you tenderly held the boy you found on the beach." He tapped the side of his nose. "I see more than you know. You're a good, decent person, Beth, and I think everybody in Bracelet Bay agrees with me. But I understand why you don't want to leave the lighthouse. It's become your sanctuary from pain. I get that."

"You do?" she said with surprise. Nobody had ever managed to articulate her feelings so well before. Her parents had often tried to persuade her to move to Oregon to make a new life with them, but they had never understood her deep connection to the lighthouse. They couldn't see why she felt at peace there. But after only two days, Dillon seemed to be able to grasp the reason she felt so strongly about her seaside home.

Dillon reached out and took her hand. His fingers felt large in hers. "Sometimes tragedy can make us retreat to a place of safety, and what safer place is there than a lighthouse that has stood for over a hundred years, being battered by storms and waves? Not even a hurricane can get though these thick walls. Nothing can hurt you here, right?"

She found herself transfixed by his words. She didn't realize that he was so insightful, that he was able to see through the strong defense she presented to the world.

"This tower and cottage were built in 1871," she said. "But before that, many boats were wrecked on the rocks, and lots of sailors were lost. Do you know the story of the lighthouse?"

Dillon shook his head. "Not yet, but I have a feeling you're about to tell me."

She smiled. "Have you seen the statue in the center of the town, next to the grocery store?"

"Yeah," he replied. "It's a lady holding a lantern, but I haven't really had a chance to study it."

"Her name was Grace Haines, and it's all thanks to her that this lighthouse exists. One afternoon in 1865, a ferocious storm hit the town and Grace's husband was caught out at sea with his crew on a fishing boat. When darkness fell Grace lit a kerosene hurricane lamp and went to stand on the cliffs to warn him off the rocks. So the story goes, she stood there all night through the raging storm, and when the morning came she was so weak that she had to be carried from the cliff top. As she lay dying in her bed with pneumonia, her husband returned. He'd seen her light shining in the darkness and had managed to steer away from the rocks." Dillon's hand remained in hers as she spoke. "After Grace died, her husband petitioned to have a permanent light-house built on the site where she stood with the lamp. And when the tower was completed, it was named Return to Grace, to commemorate the sacrifice she made to guide her husband and his crew home."

Beth realized that tears were pricking her eyes. This story had always captivated her, imagining a young woman standing firm and strong in the storm, sending a beacon of hope out into the night, determined to save the man she loved. As a younger woman, Beth wondered whether she would ever experience the same intensity of love that Grace felt for her husband. Now, at the age of thirty-one, she had all but given up on that dream. Despite her untimely death, Grace was one of the fortunate ones. How many people found that kind of love in their lifetime?

"That's a beautiful story," Dillon said. "I can see why the lighthouse is so precious to you. It's the perfect place of refuge, and it will never let you down." He squeezed her fingers. "Almost like God Himself."

"Yes," she said in a whisper. "That's exactly how it feels. As long as I'm here, I feel that nothing can hurt me, and God can protect me from anything."

Dillon said nothing for a few moments, obviously trying to find the right words to say. "But God is in here," he said, putting his free hand over his heart. "He doesn't live in a lighthouse or on the rocks or out on the sea. He goes wherever you go. You carry Him with you. *He* is your refuge and your strength, not a building made of stone."

Beth realized that he was quoting the same verse as Helen had recited the previous night, and she wondered if he and Helen had planned this together. Had they conspired to take down her defenses using scripture?

She pulled her hand away. "I feel closer to God when I'm in the lighthouse," she said. "And I'm happy here. This is the way I choose to live my life, and I don't care what anyone else thinks."

Dillon made his voice softer. "I'm not judging you, Beth."

"Maybe not," she said. "But it still feels like you're trying to persuade me to leave."

"I would prefer it if you moved away from the source of danger," he said, "but I won't try and force you. We're in the process of setting up the most wide-ranging surveillance equipment we have in the tower. If you want to stay, we'll make sure no harm comes to you."

Beth felt a small surge of gratitude. She stroked Ted's head where he had laid it in her lap, sensing her sadness. "Can I get back to my work now?" she asked, looking at the wooden boat that had been sanded to a pale brown shell, marled with darker colors. Tiny particles of dust still hung in the air from her morning's hard work with the sander. Usually she performed this type of task outside, but, unable to leave the cottage, she had worn a mask while doing the work indoors and made Carl do the same. "I need to have this piece of furniture finished soon."

"But we're no closer to solving the mystery of your connection to the cartel," Dillon said, pulling a notepad from his jacket pocket. "It would help if we went over your history since you purchased the lighthouse, and I'll look for any possible links."

Beth sighed. She imagined Dillon filling up the pages of his notepad with her life story, making a permanent reminder of her failure to live like a normal person.

"Okay," she said. "What do you want to know?"

He clicked the top of his pen. "Why don't we start at the beginning?"

Dillon knew that Beth's spirits were flagging. He had asked her a series of probing questions about her life and had drawn a blank each time. Her contact with the outside world was minimal, and aside from Helen, she spent her days almost entirely in her own company. He suspected this wasn't healthy for a young woman like her, but he said nothing. He knew better than to tread on her toes any more than he had done already. Her attachment to the lighthouse was strong, and her eyes had taken on a wistful quality when she was telling him the story of Grace Haines and her cliff-top vigil to save her husband. It was clear that she was spellbound by the tale, and she wrapped herself in its romanticism like a cloak. The lighthouse was far more than a home to Beth: it was her armor against the harsh reality that a pure and unselfish love like Grace's would never be hers.

He shut his notepad and slid it back into his pocket, feeling disappointment settle in his gut. He was no nearer to solving this mystery, and no nearer to achieving closure for Beth. The capture of Miguel Olmos had only served to create more questions than it answered. Dillon had not yet managed to weed out the mole in the coast guard, and this knowledge was disturbing. He had almost grown to fully trust both Carl and Larry, but Larry's erratic behavior in the Salty Dog had caused Dillon to look at his subordinate officer in a different light. Larry had called Dillon's cell early that morn-

ing to apologize profusely and assure his captain that
an incident like this would never happen again, but it
had soured their working relationship. A man capable
of such a public show of aggression was not in charge
of his temper, and therefore a potential liability, but
Larry's skills and expertise were badly needed at this
moment, so Dillon had no choice but to keep him on
active duty.

And in the midst of all this uncertainty was Beth,
battling bravely to remain in her home and defy those
who had placed her in their crosshairs. He wished she
would agree to leave, if only for a short time, so he
could transfer all his efforts to the traffickers. The cartel's illegal sea activities had been limited these last
twenty-four hours, no doubt thanks to the vigilance
of the coast guard, but they would resume again soon,
and he needed to be ready for them. Right now Beth's
lighthouse felt just like the desert in Afghanistan where
Aziza had been walking, exposed and vulnerable. The
terrain might be very different, but the sense of obligation to a woman in need was exactly the same. If this
story was to have a different ending, he would have to
pull away from Beth and stop himself from doing what
came naturally—shielding her from harm.

"Okay," he said. "I think we're done. Thanks for talking so openly, Beth. I know it was hard."

She rose from the couch and ran her hands through
her hair. Her sweatpants and T-shirt were covered in
dust and she picked up a mouth mask from the coffee
table.

"I really need to get back to work now," she said. "If
you'll be staying, I'll get you a protective mask."

He stood, tilting his head to hear a shout that he

thought was coming from the lighthouse tower. "Did you hear something?"

Suddenly footsteps could be heard running down the curved iron steps, heavy and urgent. Carl's voice cut through the air.

"Chief, a powerboat is heading our way at high speed. I see three men, all armed, ETA thirty seconds."

Dillon grabbed his weapon and prepared himself for the most audacious attack he had ever faced.

SIX

Dillon took Beth's hand and led her to the base of the tower.

"Go to the lantern room with Ted," he said. "And stay there until I give the all-clear."

She didn't argue. She hooked her finger into Ted's collar and guided him up the staircase, just as Larry and Carl came bounding down, weapons drawn. Their faces were apprehensive, looking at Dillon for guidance, awaiting orders.

Dillon rushed to the kitchen window, which gave him a good view out over the beach just yards from the lighthouse. He saw a small inflatable powerboat being guided by a black-clad man glide onto the sand and come to rest. Then the three occupants leaped from the boat and began to run to the steps that led up the cliff side. They would be there within a minute.

"Larry," Dillon called. "Go upstairs to Beth's bedroom and train your weapon out the window. Shoot on sight. Carl, stand guard at the tower steps. I'm going outside to try and keep these guys from reaching the cottage. Bolt the door behind me."

Then he grabbed the radio from his belt and tuned

it to 9-1-1 emergency dispatch. He spoke into it as he walked through the front door and positioned his back flat against the exterior wall.

"This is Captain Dillon Randall from the Bracelet Bay coast guard requesting immediate assistance at The Return to Grace Lighthouse. Three armed and hostile attackers have been sighted incoming from the sea." He broke off to glance around the corner of the cottage, seeing nothing but a perfect view out over the waves. "I repeat, immediate assistance required from a police SWAT unit. We have a civilian to protect."

He clipped the radio back onto his belt as a man's voice sounded in response through the speaker. "Message acknowledged, Captain Randall. Help is on the way. Hold tight."

Dillon raised his eyes to the sky. He didn't have any other choice than to hold tight. With Beth hiding in the tower, it was a straight-up match of three against three. He raised his weapon to his shoulder and crouched to the ground, peering out from his protected position toward the steps that led down to the beach. He waited for faces to emerge or for gunfire to pierce the air, but neither came. The only sound to be heard was the gentle lapping of the waves on the shoreline and the squawk of the gulls overhead.

He maintained his position, unwilling to move in case he was then caught out in the open when the men finally did emerge. Where were they? There was no way to ascend the cliff face other than the steps. Unless…

It suddenly occurred to Dillon that perhaps these men were throwing a decoy and heading for the road instead, intending to attack from a different angle. A little farther down the coastal road was Helen's bungalow, which stood level with the sand. At that point, anybody could access the beach from the road and back again.

He ran to the edge of the cliff and dropped to his belly, peering carefully over the edge of the rock. Small stones, loosened by his forward shuffling, fell from the top and bounced all the way to the bottom, scattering on the deserted beach like a spray of water. The men were nowhere to be seen. Only their boat lay empty and still by the water's edge, its cargo dispatched to a hiding place until ready to launch an attack.

A holler rose from somewhere inside the keeper's cottage. Either Larry or Carl was sending a warning shout. An explosion of gunfire suddenly echoed across the bay, bouncing off the opposite cliffs and magnifying its sound. The sound of return fire could be heard immediately, coming in rapid bursts.

Quick as a flash, Dillon jumped from where he lay and raced around the cottage, keeping low, but finding little coverage in the wide-open space. He saw two men making their way up the road, running quickly, shooting all the while. Both men were dressed in black, but with faces uncovered, and Dillon could clearly see the same distinctive tattoos as Miguel Olmos snaking up their necks. Their shots were wild and reckless, pinging off the curved, thick stone of the tower or missing their target altogether. Dillon's heart pounded as he watched them advance. Where was the third man? He knew there were three.

Despite the return fire being rained down from Larry and Carl inside the cottage, the men's speed and movement clearly made it difficult to achieve a direct hit. Dillon planted his feel firmly on the ground, raised his weapon and began to empty his bullets from the chamber, directing them as accurately as he could, trying to halt the men's progress to the lighthouse. He saw one of the men jerk backward with a jarring motion, as he looked to have caught a bullet in the arm. One of them was now injured, a grimace of pain spreading over his face as he continued to run. This should have brought Dillon some relief, yet his mind was still on the missing third man. He couldn't fight a man he wasn't able see.

The two attackers reached a roadside rock jutting up from the ground like a flame of granite, and they took shelter behind it. They were now within fifty feet of the lighthouse, and this was way too close for comfort. This attack was bold and daring, taking place in broad daylight with no regard for any passersby who might find themselves entangled in a gun battle. It was a sign of desperation on the part of the cartel. They wanted to get to Beth at all costs.

Dillon deliberated his next move. The two men were now hidden behind the rock, gunfire ceased. Should he try and capture these two men or look for the third gunman? He turned in circles, trying to seek out the elusive man. No sign.

Larry's voice cracked over the radio. "What now, sir? Targets are out of sight."

Dillon unclipped his radio. "Keep watch over that rock, Larry. If anything moves, shoot it."

A quick darting movement caught his attention. At first he thought it was a bird flying from the cliff, but it was a man coming from the steps leading to the beach. It was the third gunman! And with a series of shots from his gun, he had blasted open the cottage door to give himself clear access inside.

"No," Dillon muttered under his breath, sprinting

after him. He thought of Beth in the tower, taking refuge from the danger.

He saw the gunman disappear inside the cottage and immediately dashed in after him. The pair instantly collided, as the gunman appeared to change his mind and attempt to beat a hasty retreat. Dillon grappled with the man, and their guns were both knocked from their grasp. Carl stood in the kitchen doorway, weapon raised, unable to take a clean shot on the dueling men for fear of hitting his captain.

The attacker hollered and kicked, seemingly desperate to make a getaway, and Dillon watched in horror as the man opened his clenched fist and a small, black device, no bigger than a tennis ball, rolled from his fingers onto the rug.

Dillon released the man instantly and jumped to his feet, hollering at the top of his voice.

"Grenade!"

Beth saw the bright flash of the explosion before she felt the ground shake around her. The lighthouse tower vibrated with an almighty tremor, and she dropped to the floor, covering her head in case any parts of the huge Fresnel lenses decided to fall down at the moment. Ted pressed his body tightly against hers, and she felt the dog's cold, wet nose on her cheek.

"It's okay, boy," she said gently, but she knew she was attempting to reassure herself more than Ted. What on earth was happening?

She remained on the floor, lying motionless, until someone rapped loudly on the door.

"Beth. It's Dillon. Are you okay?"

She jumped to her feet and slid back the bolts on the

door, opening it and taking in Dillon's tousled appearance. His uniform was dusty and rumpled.

"What happened?" she exclaimed. "I heard an explosion."

"One of the attackers threw a grenade into your living room," he replied. "I managed to grab a hold of it and throw it outside, where it exploded about thirty feet away. It's left a pretty big crater in the ground, and one of your windows got blown out, but thankfully everybody is okay."

Beth felt her mouth drop open. "A grenade?"

"Yes." He stepped toward her and put his hands on her shoulders. "These guys mean business."

"Where are they now? Please don't tell me they got away."

Dillon sighed. "Once the grenade was deployed, I had to focus all my energy on getting it away from the house. In the chaos, the attackers managed to flee back to their boat and escape via the sea. I've canceled our police SWAT request and dispatched an armed coast guard vessel to search for them instead."

Beth could hardly believe what she was hearing. Her home had been turned into a war zone. And she was the enemy's number-one target.

"I never expected anything like this," she said, putting a hand over her belly where a feeling of sickness had settled. "I mean, I knew I was in danger, but this goes beyond my worst nightmares." She looked up into Dillon's face, which was etched with concern. "You were right about me staying here. It just isn't safe."

"I don't think any of us expected such a daring attack," Dillon said. "It's as if the cartel doesn't care about their members being seen or captured. It tells me that they're pretty desperate to get to you and will keep on coming until the job is done." He bent his knees a little to be on her eye level. "Don't you see how dangerous it is to remain here?"

She dropped her head low. "Yes."

"Will you agree to leave until we're certain the danger has passed?"

Beth bit her lip to prevent the tears from flowing. She had assumed she would fight tooth and claw to remain in her secluded home, but she couldn't ask Dillon's men to put themselves in the firing line for her. It wasn't fair. As much as the thought of returning to the town of Bracelet Bay pained her, she had no other choice.

She lifted her head. "Yes. I'll leave."

As if overcome by relief, Dillon drew her into an embrace and held her tight. "I'm really pleased to hear it, Beth," he said. "That's a big worry off my mind. Tyler will be arriving soon, and with you someplace safer, I can get back to concentrating on catching the bad guys."

She pulled away from him. "Where exactly is *someplace safer*?"

"My apartment seems like the best option for now."

"And where is that?"

"It's part of a complex called Harbor View."

"I know it," she said, closing her eyes and envisioning it in her mind. "It's between the grocery store and the library."

"You got it. It's secure, with a double-entry door system, a good view out over the sea and an enclosed yard at the back where you can walk Ted."

On hearing his name combined with the word *walk*, Ted pricked up his ears and jumped against Dillon, pawing at him. Beth grabbed him by the collar and pulled him away, irritated by Ted's sudden allegiance to a brand-new person. She knew she should be pleased that Ted was happy and comfortable in Dillon's presence, but it felt as if she was losing all things precious to her: her home, her work, her dog. And worse than that, she couldn't blame Ted for being fond of the new coast guard captain. Despite all her best efforts, she found herself liking Dillon more and more, particularly his commitment to keeping her safe. Compared to Anthony, Dillon was a knight in shining armor. He was decent, dependable and gentle—all those qualities she had wanted to see in Anthony but never did.

"I should go pack a bag," she said, turning to look out over the water and commit the breathtaking view to memory. She didn't know how long she would be away, and she wanted to make sure she could recall the lighthouse view whenever she needed. "I guess we'll have to leave right away."

"Carl and Larry are clearing up the glass downstairs," he said. "We'll need to make more repairs to your front door and get a new window fitted, so it's not really safe to hang around. It's best to leave now and Larry will get to work getting the place straight again."

Beth thought of all her pieces of handcrafted furniture. She also thought of the bed frame that she would be forced to leave behind, delaying her deadline for the client, and therefore delaying the payment she would be due. She would be forced to dip into her savings in order to make the mortgage payment that month.

"What about my things?" she asked. "My entire life is here. It might be destroyed by the men if they come back."

"A guard will be posted to your home twenty-four hours a day," Dillon replied. "Try not to worry about material possessions. The most important thing right now is you. Items can be replaced, but you can't."

For a second, it sounded as though he actually cared about her in a way that went beyond his job as a coast guard captain. "I need to go explain the situation to Helen," she said. "She'll worry if I don't see her before I go."

"We'll drop in on her along the way. And I'll make sure somebody checks on her every day while you're away."

Beth smiled. "Thank you." She guessed that the years Dillon had spent caring for his father made him more sensitive to the needs of the elderly. "She's not so agile around her home, and she forgets things, so she sometimes needs help with cooking and laundry."

Dillon nodded. "I did that kind of stuff for my dad. Please leave it all to me."

"And she needs help to walk Tootsie—"

Dillon cut her off. "Beth, you're just delaying leaving." He put a hand on her shoulder and she felt the warmth of it through her sweatshirt. "Let's go. We should keep our intended location a secret for now, so don't give anything away to Carl or Larry."

She knitted her eyebrows together. "You don't think you can trust them?"

"I don't know who I can trust," he said. "So I'm being extra cautious."

Beth gave one last glance at the wide blue sea, sparkling into infinity, and she hooked her finger through Ted's collar to lead him from the tower and into a temporary new home.

* * *

Helen was unwell. Dillon was dismayed to see her looking frailer than usual and gaunt in the face. Her normally coiffured hair was lying limp and flat, and the rouge she so carefully applied each day was nowhere to be seen on her cheeks. She was sitting in a recliner in her living room, holding a cup of previously hot tea that looked to have gone cold some time ago.

Beth took the cup from Helen's fingers and set it down on the coffee table. Then she pressed a palm onto Helen's forehead and gave a gasp.

"Helen, you're freezing cold," she said, grabbing a blanket from the back of the recliner and laying it over her friend's knees. "And you look so pale."

"I'm perfectly fine," Helen said with her usual note of cheerfulness. "My old joints get a bit stiff now and again." She looked up at Dillon. "Could you turn the thermostat up a degree or two? I think the outside temperature has dropped low today, and I'm pretty sure I heard thunder a little while ago." She splayed her fingers out wide in the air. "There was a huge rumble, but no sign of the rain just yet."

Beth dropped to her knees to kneel by Helen's chair as Dillon adjusted the thermostat in the already warm room. He removed his jacket and hung it up by the door, staying back to give Beth and Helen some privacy but still able to observe the affectionate interaction between the pair.

"That wasn't thunder, Helen, that was an explosion," Beth said. "My lighthouse was attacked again and one of the men threw a grenade." Helen's eyes widened in shock, so Beth made her voice softer. "Everybody is okay. The only damage is to the keeper's cottage, but

I've been forced to accept that it's too dangerous for me to stay there." She put a hand on top of her friend's. "I'm leaving for a while."

"*You're* leaving the lighthouse?" Helen questioned. "This must be serious to force you out of your home." She gripped Beth's fingers in her own. "I don't think you've spent a night away from that lighthouse in four years."

"Five years," Beth corrected. "It's been five years now."

Helen could obviously see what a wrench this would be for her friend. "This must be so hard for you, Beth. Are you okay with leaving? Where will you go?"

"Yes, I'm okay," Beth replied. "I don't want to leave, but it's for the best." She looked over at Dillon. "Captain Randall is taking me and Ted somewhere safe until it's okay for me to come back."

A look of relief swept over Helen's face. "Oh, good. Captain Randall will look after you. I know he will. I can always tell who the good ones are, and he is one of the best. I hope he restores your faith in men."

Beth looked embarrassed. It was clear that Helen had forgotten Dillon was in the room. He stepped forward and coughed.

"Thanks for the compliment, Helen," he called. "If I can help restore Beth's faith in men, then I'd be glad to help."

Helen turned her head in surprise. "Oh, I'd forgotten you were here, Captain…um…"

"Randall," he said. "It's Captain Randall, but I thought we'd agreed on first-name terms, so please call me Dillon."

The way the elderly woman looked at him with a

vacant stare, trying to process this information as if it were new, set an alarm bell ringing in his head. He recognized the confusion, the forgetfulness, the lack of interest in her appearance. It seemed highly likely that Helen was in the early stages of dementia, most likely caused by Alzheimer's disease.

"Helen," he said, walking to her recliner. "How are you feeling today? Have you eaten?"

Helen thought for a moment. "Well, I usually have my breakfast at nine and then Beth comes to take me for a walk on the beach with Tootsie at ten, and then we have our daily devotional before lunch." She looked up at the clock, which showed almost 3:00 p.m. "But my routine is all out of sorts today."

"I'm sorry," Beth said, brushing a strand of hair from Helen's face. "I couldn't do our walk today." She looked up at Dillon, clearly feeling the same sense of alarm as he. "Dillon says that he'll send somebody to check on you every day while I'm gone."

Dillon could see the strong bond that existed between the two women, and he found himself feeling a kinship with Beth. Beth had not realized how important her routine with Helen was to her elderly friend. To a person whose mind was failing, performing the same tasks each day was vital to their sense of identity. It grounded you in real life, enabling you to take part in activities that were familiar, repetitive and comforting. Dillon knew this only too well from his experience with his father. As soon as a routine changed, a mind affected by Alzheimer's disease struggled to comprehend a new system. Without Beth's daily visit, Helen had become confused and a little muddled. But he wasn't sure how advanced her dementia was. In the early stages, it tended to be very subtle, with highs and lows. She might simply be having a bad day today.

"Have you ever considered moving to a retirement home, Helen?" Dillon suggested. "There's a nice one overlooking the Golden Cove Harbor."

Helen's hand shot into the air, palm flat and straight. "No chance," she said with a firm edge to her voice. "I've lived here for over fifty years, and this is where I'll stay." She pointed toward the door. "The only way I'm leaving this house is in a box." She gave a chuckle. "I'm a stubborn woman, you see, just like Beth."

Dillon smiled. Helen's reaction told him everything he needed to know. She might be forgetful, but she was strong-willed and resilient.

"I'll send somebody from the coast guard station over this afternoon to help you prepare a meal," he said, knowing that this obligation went way beyond the scope of his job responsibilities but guessing that any one of his team would be happy to help out. Helen was both well-known and well loved by the townsfolk. "And I'll come over at 10:00 a.m. tomorrow to take you and Tootsie out for a walk."

By that point, his Navy SEAL buddy, Tyler Beck, would have settled in and Dillon would be able to breathe easier, knowing that Beth would be securely guarded. Dillon had fallen way behind on his paperwork because of Beth's situation, and he desperately needed to schedule another interview with Miguel Olmos. The cartel member currently in custody was the coast guard's best chance of cracking the trafficking ring. Whatever emotions he felt for Beth, he must relinquish her care to someone else. He had to keep telling himself that she wasn't his primary concern.

"Thank you, Dillon," Helen said, pushing herself up to stand. "Now, why don't I make a pot of coffee for us?"

"I'm afraid we don't have time," Dillon said. "I'd like to get Beth set up in her new home as soon as possible."

"Of course," Helen said, with a small shake of the head. "Beth is leaving the lighthouse." She turned to Beth and extended her arms. The women embraced and Dillon saw tears prick Beth's eyes. He guessed she was upset for a reason other than saying goodbye. This was probably the first time Beth had clearly seen the signs of Helen's decline in mental health. And he knew exactly how she felt.

"Now, you let this nice young man take good care of you, Beth," Helen said. "You'll be in safe hands with him."

"It won't be for long," Beth said, glancing over at Dillon for confirmation that this statement was correct. He could give no assurances. Beth forced a smile. "I'll be back before you know it."

Helen's face turned serious for a moment. "Promise me one thing, Beth."

"Anything."

Helen leaned in close and dropped her voice. "Get rid of that ring."

Dillon saw Beth's body give a jump of surprise and she looked like a cornered cat. "What ring?" she asked.

Helen smiled knowingly. "The one you carry around in your pocket like a penance. Throw it away. You don't need it anymore."

Beth's hand brushed the pocket of her jeans. "I don't know what you're talking about. I don't carry a ring."

"My mistake," she said with a wink. "I must be getting confused."

Helen then spoke to Dillon. "I hope you realize how precious this woman is," she said. "I've prayed every day for the last five years for God to send a man worthy of her hand." A sparkle had returned to her eyes and she seemed to be more like her old self. "And I'm so pleased to see that my prayers have now been answered."

Dillon looked down at his feet, feeling his color rise. He saw no point in contradicting Helen, so he simply smiled and said, "I'll take good care of her, I promise."

Helen reached for her stick and began walking toward her bedroom. "If I'll be having a visitor from the coast guard this afternoon, I really should fix my hair." Tootsie ran circles around her ankles as she walked. "And put on some face powder."

Beth went to stand by Dillon's side and touched his arm. "Thank you," she said. "Thank you for everything you're doing for Helen. I can't tell you how much I appreciate it."

"No thanks necessary," he said. Beth's face was close to his, close enough for him to see the fine lines on her plump lips suddenly smoothed out by a wide smile that revealed her gleaming teeth. He tried very hard not to lose his concentration. "What was Helen saying about needing to get rid of a ring?" He thought of the stone painted with Santa Muerte. "Is that something else you found by your house?"

"No," she replied quickly, stepping back and busying herself by folding the cast-off blanket neatly on the chair. "Helen was confused. There's no ring."

"Okay, then," he said. "Let's take one final check on

Helen in her bedroom and get going." He looked at Ted curled up on the rug, sleeping soundly. "Ted, let's go."

The dog instantly bounced up from where he lay and ran to Dillon's heel, before sitting obediently. Dillon saw Beth's shoulders tense, and he guessed she wasn't happy with his newfound authority over her dog. He tried to see it from her point of view. It must seem as though he was inviting himself into all aspects of her life, taking over, forcing her from solitude into the community. He was even becoming a master to her beloved Ted.

Well, she needn't worry. He would shortly be able to stop his constant intrusion. And it couldn't come a day too soon. Beth's dangerous circumstances could prevent him from achieving a successful mission in Bracelet Bay, and he would never live with himself if he allowed innocent people to die again.

Beth felt like a fish out of water in Dillon's apartment. It was comfortable and well furnished, but it wasn't to her taste. She preferred the natural look of sanded wood, cotton throws and rustic sculptures, whereas Dillon's taste was clearly more manly. His couch was an old beat-up leather one, obviously well loved, and his tables were functional rather than beautiful. She walked around the living room, looking at the pictures on the wall—the generic kind that can be found in any department store.

"I guess the place could do with a woman's touch," Dillon said with a laugh. "I don't really have an eye for interior design."

Ted slunk around the room, sniffing in the corners, checking out his new surroundings. Finally he jumped up onto the couch and settled down, closing his eyes for a nap.

"Ted!" Beth admonished. "Get down."

"He's fine to stay there," Dillon said. "Please, I want you and Ted to treat this place like your own while you're here."

Beth found herself thinking that she would go out of her mind with boredom stuck inside all day with nothing to do, but Dillon had obviously thought of that possibility already.

"I'll be transporting your boat wreck and tools from your living room to the basement here tomorrow. Every apartment in the complex is allocated an underground garage, but I don't have a car, so the space is empty. I thought you might want to carry on with making that bed frame for your client. It's safe and secure and Tyler will always be with you, wherever you are in the building."

Beth felt a lump rise in her throat. Dillon's thoughtfulness and attention to her needs made her want to rush over and hug him.

"Thank you," she said. It seemed like the hundredth time she had thanked him that day.

Dillon sat next to Ted and stroked the dog's head. "I'll show you to your room in a minute or two and let you get settled, but first I wanted to ask you about Helen."

Beth went to stand by the window, where she could see her lighthouse like a matchstick in the distance, standing guard at the edge of the world. Helen's bungalow was too small to be seen from this distance, but she knew it was there. She and Helen were the only neighbors each other had. They were at least three miles from the nearest house.

"She has Alzheimer's, doesn't she?" Beth asked, keeping her body turned to the window. She felt Dillon move behind her and guide her away, leading her to the couch.

"It's best if you stay out of sight," he said. "I haven't told anybody you're staying at my apartment, not even the crew from the station, so let's not advertise your presence here, okay?"

"You didn't answer my question," Beth said. "Helen has Alzheimer's, right?"

"I think so. I recognize the symptoms. Have you ever noticed her being forgetful, confused or disoriented recently?"

"Yes," Beth admitted. "But I just put it down to old age. Some days she's as sharp as a tack, but other days she struggles to remember what she's eaten for dinner. I started helping her more and more over the last twelve months." She sighed. "I think deep down I knew something was wrong, but I didn't want to accept it. I didn't want to face the fact that I might be losing her."

"You've helped her in more ways than you can possibly know," Dillon said gently. "You've given her a stable routine and taken her out for regular exercise. These things are really important to a person in Helen's condition, and if you hadn't been there for her during the last five years, she probably wouldn't still be in her own home."

"How much longer will she be able to stay in her bungalow?" Beth asked. She knew that Dillon had plenty of experience in this area and she assumed he would have the answers to all her questions.

"I don't know," he replied. "Everybody is different, and some people's progression of Alzheimer's is a lot slower than others. We just have to take it one day at a time. We should schedule an appointment with her doctor as soon as possible to get her assessed."

Beth met his gaze. His eyes were a rich dark brown, flecked with traces of amber. They reminded her of knots she often found in wood she worked with, pitted and imperfect, yet beautiful in their naturalness. She knew that these eyes would never hide the truth from her, no matter how brutal.

"But she won't get better, will she?" she asked.

"No, she won't get better. She'll only get worse from here onward."

Beth buried her face in her hands. This wasn't what she wanted to hear. She wanted Dillon to tell her that Helen would be fine, that she'd carry on for another twenty years, cracking jokes, teasing Beth with her gentle humor, making silly words with her Scrabble tiles. She couldn't lose Helen. What would she do?

Dillon saw her anguish. "All you can do is carry on being a friend to her and help her deal with the symptoms as they develop."

Beth removed her hands from her face. "How can I do that when I'm stuck here on the other side of the bay?"

"I've arranged for Janice from the coast guard station to go visit at 6:00 p.m. She'll make sure Helen has a hot meal and company."

"But it's not enough," Beth protested. "Helen needs me."

Dillon seemed to be considering his words carefully

before speaking. "Does Helen need you?" he asked. "Or do you need Helen?"

Beth was silenced. Dillon had exposed the fact that Helen had become an emotional crutch over the last five years. The older woman had filled every empty gap in Beth's life, providing the love and support that most people get from several different people. Beth had put all her eggs in one basket. And now that basket was unraveling. Without Helen, Beth had nothing.

She stood from the couch, feeling tears sting her eyes.

"I need to use the bathroom," she said, rushing from the room.

Shutting the door behind her, Beth sank to the floor, knees drawn against her chest and cried, contemplating the reality that she would have to live her life entirely alone.

And there was nothing she could do about it.

SEVEN

Dillon gave his old friend, Tyler, a warm hug and took the large backpack from his hands, resting it up against the wall in the hallway.

"So you found the place okay?" Dillon said. "Sorry I couldn't come get you from the airport. I can't leave the apartment at the moment."

Tyler cast his eyes around Dillon's home. "Correct me if I'm wrong," he said, "but this doesn't look much like a lighthouse to me."

"We had to leave the lighthouse this morning because of a serious attack. Beth will be staying here for the time being."

Tyler crouched down as Ted came ambling into the hallway, and he greeted the dog with affection. "I'm guessing this is Ted."

"Yeah. He's a giant schnauzer and he looks big and scary, but he's a softie really."

Dillon led Tyler into the living room, where he had put a pot of coffee awaiting his friend's arrival. His SEAL comrade seemed to have changed little in the ten years they had known each other. His light brown hair was still neatly cropped, and his skin was always tanned, no matter the time of year. The guys from their unit always teased him for being baby-faced, but his looks belied his true character. Tyler was tough all the way to his core.

"Where's Beth?" Tyler asked, walking around the room, checking out the visibility from the window, familiarizing himself with his surroundings.

"She's taking a bath," Dillon replied. "She's struggling to adjust to a new place, so she needed some time to herself to relax." He kept his voice low, as though he didn't want Beth to overhear. "She's been living a very reclusive lifestyle over at the lighthouse and she's gotten a little too used to her own company."

"You mentioned something on the phone about her being left at the altar on her wedding day a few years ago," Tyler said. "That's gotta hurt."

"Yeah, it did," Dillon said. "She shut herself away and turned her back on the community, so it's hard for her to return to the town, even though nobody knows she's here."

Tyler raised his eyebrows. "Nobody?"

"Nobody but you and me. Word will probably leak out eventually, but I decided not to give any information to the crew at the coast guard base." Dillon poured a couple of coffees from the pot. "I have my suspicions that somebody is feeding information to the people traffickers, helping them gain access to Beth. I still don't know why the cartel wants her dead, but I can't take any chances with her safety. You're the only person I can trust to guard her right now."

"You got any suspects?" Tyler asked, sitting next to Dillon and taking a cup from his hands.

"Not yet, but there's a chief petty officer by the name

of Larry Chapman who's a bit of a loose cannon. I had to break up a fight between him and his brother in a local restaurant yesterday, and although he's apologized, it seems to have affected him. His mind isn't totally on the job."

Tyler nodded, understanding the issues at stake. "When you're protecting a civilian, you need to have total faith in your team." He took a gulp of his coffee. "You know that better than anyone."

Dillon knew exactly what Tyler was referring to: Aziza.

"I never wanted to be in this position again," Dillon said, staring into his cup. "When I found Aziza running from the sharia court, I felt torn between two camps. By saving her, I left those teachers to die."

"Hey," Tyler said. "You don't know that those teachers died."

"That's the most likely explanation, right?"

"They could have gone into hiding," Tyler suggested. "Or gotten help from somewhere else to escape into Pakistan. We just don't know what happened to them, and probably never will." He set down his cup. "It was chaos in Afghanistan back then, with bombs being detonated without warning, but there were still plenty of people who made it to places of safety. You were put in a difficult situation, and you made the right call, even if it doesn't feel that way. Aziza is alive and well thanks to you."

Dillon rubbed a hand down his face. "It's impossible to protect people in two different locations. Somebody will always pay the price."

"And that's how you feel about Beth's circumstances?" Tyler asked. "You think she's like Aziza?"

"I do." Dillon cast his eyes toward the window, where the ocean lay out in a vast expanse. "I'm here to save people from human traffickers. Every day there could be hundreds of people being smuggled right in front of my eyes, led into a life of misery. My focus has been taken away from them because of the fact that I have to protect a vulnerable young woman who has no one else to take care of her."

"But that's why I'm here," Tyler said. "Right?"

"Right. I need to step away from Beth and get back to the job I was drafted here to do."

Tyler smiled. "I'm guessing that isn't as easy as it sounds."

"It's not," Dillon said. "There's something about Beth that draws me in and holds me there. It's like…" He struggled to find the words. "It's like I can't stop worrying about her."

"I see," Tyler said slowly. "I think your feelings for this woman have gone beyond just wanting to protect her. It sounds like you're starting to fall for her."

Dillon shook his head vigorously. "That's ridiculous," he said. "I'm in Bracelet Bay to complete a mission and move onto the next one. I'm too professional to allow any personal emotions to creep into my work."

"Okay, if you say so," Tyler said. "But feelings have a habit of finding their own way out of a person, and sometimes they can't be contained by a professional attitude."

Dillon decided to move on from this subject. "I have a coast guard uniform for you to wear and a standard-issue weapon. If you come into contact with anybody from the station, or any locals, just stick to the cover story. Beth and Ted are set up in the spare room, and you'll be sleeping in my room."

"Where will you be?"

"I've decided to move into the lighthouse while Beth is here," Dillon said. "I'm guessing that the cartel will come after her again, so I can be ready and waiting for them."

"We should have a thorough briefing session so I can be sure of my duties," Tyler said.

"I already thought of that. We'll go through the plan after dinner. I ordered takeout from a local restaurant called the Salty Dog." He checked his watch. "It should be delivered any minute now."

Beth's voice called from the hallway. "Did I hear somebody mention takeout from the Salty Dog?"

Both men rose as Beth entered the room. She was rosy-cheeked after her bath, and was wearing black sweatpants and a sweatshirt. As she smiled at Dillon, his stomach flipped in a way that took him by surprise and he averted his gaze. He realized he was looking at Beth in a new and deeper way—his affection for her was developing into something even more meaningful. Tyler had called it, and Dillon had denied it, but he silently admitted that she was becoming more than a protection assignment.

She extended a hand toward Tyler. "You must be Tyler. I'm pleased to meet you."

Tyler smiled. "Likewise, ma'am."

"Please call me Beth," she said. She looked at her dog, sitting at the feet of the two men. "And I see you've met Ted already."

"Yes, I have. He's a great dog."

A buzz rang out in the apartment. It was the external

doorbell, and Dillon hooked his finger through Ted's collar. "Let's get you two in your bedroom while I answer that." He guided Ted out the door. "Do you think you can keep him quiet, Beth?"

"Sure," she said, brushing past him as she went into her room, sending a scent of cocoa butter and vanilla into his nostrils. "We won't make a sound."

Dillon pressed the intercom system and heard the words "Salty Dog delivery." He buzzed the external door open while he did one final check of the apartment. He didn't want any missed items to give away the fact that he had a female guest.

When the knock came at his front door, he used the peephole to assess who was there. It was Paula Chapman, looking slightly apprehensive, holding a brown paper bag. He opened the door and she smiled politely.

"I have your takeout order," she said. "We're short-staffed this evening, so I have to do some deliveries myself." She handed the bag to Dillon, and his mouth watered with the wonderful aromas of chowder, shrimp and garlic. "There's an awful lot of food here. Did we make a mistake with your order?"

"No," he said with a smile, checking the corridor each way just to be on the safe side. "I have a friend over for dinner."

She peered around his shoulder, trying to catch a glimpse of this mysterious guest. "A lady friend, by any chance?"

Dillon rolled his eyes to the ceiling. Why did the townsfolk of Bracelet Bay seem to be so concerned with his relationship status? "No, it's not a lady. It's a new member of staff who will be starting work at the coast guard station."

Paula looked disappointed at the dispelling of her assumption that the coast guard captain might be having a romantic evening. "Well, I hope you enjoy your meal," she said, turning to leave.

"Paula," he said, calling her back. "How are things between Larry and Kevin after their fight yesterday?"

Her expression slid downward. "Not so good. They're still not talking, and I can't get through to either of them."

"Do you know why they were fighting?" he asked. "Larry refuses to discuss the reason with me."

She shook her head. "Kevin says it's private, so I don't pry, but I'm hoping they'll both swallow their pride and make up soon."

"Me too. Thanks for the delivery. I appreciate it."

Paula smiled and said goodbye, disappearing into the elevator while he kept watch until it was making its downward descent. Then he closed the door and double-locked it from the inside. As he turned away from the door, he noticed that Ted's leash was dangling from a peg in plain sight. He shook his head in annoyance and pulled it from its resting place, opening a drawer in the hallway table to hide it away before calling out the all-clear.

Beth appeared from around the corner, her damp hair piled loosely into a bun on top of her head. There it was again—that flip in his stomach, which he was powerless to control.

"Something smells good," she said. "I'm starving."

"Well, then, let's eat," he said, taking the bag into the kitchen.

As he plated up the food, he reminded himself that there was still plenty he needed to do this evening. This dinner would simply be a short respite from work. After eating, he would brief Tyler on his duties, telephone the jail to schedule another visit with Miguel Olmos, check on Helen, prepare an assignment update for his superiors and, finally, make the journey to the lighthouse to bed down for the night.

With so much activity going on, he surely wouldn't have time to worry about Beth—or think about his attraction to her—would he?

Beth leaned back in her chair, satisfied after her delicious meal. She sat opposite Dillon in his kitchen while Tyler took the opportunity to unpack.

She rubbed her hands over a slightly protruding belly. "That was fantastic. I forgot how good the food at the Salty Dog is."

"It sure is," agreed Dillon. "Kevin is a fantastic chef."

"He's been cooking ever since he was a kid," Beth said. "The Salty Dog has been in the Chapman family for generations, and we all assumed that Larry would take over the reins one day, but it was Kevin who showed the most culinary talent and business sense, so their parents trained him to take over the restaurant when they retired."

This obviously piqued Dillon's interest. "Did it cause any friction between them?"

"A little," Beth said. "Larry hated the fact that his younger brother would be taking over the family business, and he bad-mouthed him all over town for a while. But he accepted it in the end, which isn't surprising when you consider that he owns a fifty percent stake in the restaurant, and Kevin's superb cooking got business booming."

"So a career in the coast guard wasn't Larry's first choice?" Dillon asked.

"I don't think so," Beth laughed. "He tried to get into the police force, the fire department and the army before finally settling on the coast guard. I think he had an attitude problem, which the coast guard somehow managed to knock out of him."

Dillon looked intrigued. "I wonder whether a little bit of that attitude got left behind," he said. "What do you know about Larry?"

"Not much. He's ten years older than me, so we never mixed in the same social circles, but he was quite a troublemaker when he was a teenager. My mom always told me to steer clear of him. She said he was bad news. But when he came back to Bracelet Bay after completing his coast guard training, he'd calmed down a lot. Then he got married to a local girl, had a couple of kids and started earning everybody's respect. I admire him for turning his life around, and he was man enough to apologize to me yesterday for making that nasty comment in the Salty Dog." She looked down at her hands in her lap. "It must be hard to prove yourself to a town where everybody has already made up their mind about you."

Dillon smiled. "I guess Bracelet Bay is a very forgiving town, always willing to welcome its prodigal sons and daughters back into the fold."

"I don't think many people would welcome me if I came back to the town," she said, trying to cover up her sadness with a laugh. "It's been too long."

"That's not true," he said strongly. "Both Henry and Mia were really pleased to see you yesterday. I know everybody likes you. You grew up in this town, right?"

She nodded. Her first memory was of toddling along

the beach, picking up stones to throw into the water. All her childhood memories were filled with sun, sand and laughter. It had been a perfect childhood in an idyllic town. But it seemed like such a long time ago now.

"I was born and raised in a house not far from here," she said. "I went to the local school and church, and I was really happy. After graduation, I thought about going to art school, but I didn't want to leave Bracelet Bay, so I got a job in the real estate agency on Main Street. I loved working there. I got to drive for miles around, showing people properties with the most spectacular views over the ocean."

She sighed, remembering how she had felt honored to showcase her beautiful town to incomers seeking to be part of their tight-knit community. Bracelet Bay was described in brochures as "the hidden jewel of the Californian coast," and she used to be proud that her roots were embedded in the richness of its soil. She had assumed she would raise her own family here and continue her ancestral line, which she could trace back to the area for several generations. She had never envisaged being a hermit, shunning the world to take solace from her pain and humiliation. She had ceased to be a real person and had become a caricature instead.

"Don't you miss the town at all?" Dillon asked. "You talk about it with a lot of affection. Surely there must be a part of you that wants to come home?"

She didn't want to relive these memories, but she knew it was cathartic to talk about them. "After my wedding day ended in disaster, I shut myself away in my house for weeks with only Ted for company. I didn't want to talk to anyone, not even my best friend, Mia. The more time I spent alone, the harder I found it to reenter the town again. Every time I tried to go out, I thought I could hear people snickering and whispering, and I would get dizzy and have palpitations. So in the end I just stopped going out altogether."

Dillon moved his chair closer to hers. "It sounds like you were suffering from anxiety attacks."

"Looking back on it, I think that's probably the most likely explanation," she said. "But at the time, all I could think about was escaping the town. It felt like I was being closed in, like I couldn't breathe, like nobody understood me."

Dillon nodded his head in understanding. "That definitely sounds anxiety related to me, Beth. Why didn't you get some therapy or counseling?"

"My family and friends tried to persuade me to get some help, but I thought I had the perfect answer." She smiled, remembering the day she had seen the old Return to Grace Lighthouse come up for sale and was instantly drawn to the idea of total solitude. "Being in real estate, I had made some good investments in property," she continued, "and I was able to free up some capital fairly quickly. I made an offer on the lighthouse that was accepted immediately and I suddenly found myself in possession of a beautiful tower and keeper's cottage. The lighthouse was decommissioned over twenty years ago, so it was all mine, with no intrusions, no neighbors and no people staring at me."

"And that's when you started collecting driftwood to make a living?" he asked.

"Yes. I knew I could never go back to my job in real estate, but I needed to earn some money, especially as maintenance costs on a lighthouse are so high, so I figured I would go back to my first true love, artistry. I'm pretty good with my hands and I can make anything out of broken wood, so it was the perfect career change." She looked toward the kitchen window, imagining she could smell the seaweed and clean air, hear the boats chugging into the harbor, see the sun dip behind the horizon. "But best of all, I don't have to explain myself to anybody. I can be free."

"Freedom is a state of mind, Beth," Dillon said, leaning in close. "You can be free anywhere as long as you believe you are. If you're running from something, you'll always be in chains."

"You make it sound so easy," she said with a laugh. "Are *you* free?"

He tilted his head to the side. "I think so."

"So there's nothing in your past that you regret? Nothing you're running from? You're happy with every single choice you've made, huh?"

She knew that she sounded a little defensive, but Dillon had suddenly gotten way too close. Without realizing, she had opened up to him and revealed more than she ever had to anybody before. Not even Helen knew about her panic attacks following her failed wedding day. She had been ashamed of her inability to cope with her crippling anxiety, so she'd kept it hidden away and revealed it to no one.

"No, I'm not happy about every single choice I've made," Dillon replied. "And there are plenty of things I've done that I regret, but I accept them and try to move forward." His face took on a melancholic expression for a moment. "Some things are harder to accept than others, but what's done is done. Nobody's perfect." He smiled, obviously trying to lift the mood. "Not even me." He leaned in closer and his eyebrows did a dance. "But I'm getting there."

His playfulness soothed her irritation, and she took a deep breath, feeling a little lighter after unburdening herself. She had refused offers of companionship for so long that she'd forgotten the joy that a long conversation could have on her spirit. Helen wasn't able to concentrate for long periods of time and would often grow tired, so Beth hadn't spoken to anybody at length for many years. And her interactions with Dillon reminded her of what she was missing. She reluctantly and silently accepted that she was lonely.

"Trust me," she said. "No man is perfect."

Tyler chose that moment to poke his head around the door. "I can't believe what I'm hearing," he said, flashing a grin. "Did I just hear a woman say that no man is perfect?" He stepped into the kitchen. "And here I was, thinking that women assumed *all* men were perfect."

"No, Tyler," Dillon said with a teasing tone. "Not all men are perfect, just you and me."

Beth found herself laughing along. "Well, for the only perfect men in the entire world, I'm guessing that you two must be in high demand."

"Of course," Tyler said. "We have women fighting over us constantly, isn't that right, Dillon?"

"Absolutely," Dillon replied. "Some mornings, I can't even get outside my front door."

Beth glanced at Tyler's left ring finger. It was bare. "And yet the two of you are single, right?"

Dillon raised his eyebrows in a theatrical way. "It's not easy being a perfect man, you know," he said. "We have to wait for the perfect woman to come along."

"That's true," Tyler said with an exaggerated nod.

"I've been waiting for over ten years, so I've had lot of practice."

Dillon laughed hard. "Ten years is nothing," he said. "Try waiting almost twenty."

"Now, *that's* true commitment," Tyler said, sitting on a chair at the table. "You see, Beth, men like Dillon aren't only perfect, handsome and kind, but they're incredibly patient too."

Beth felt herself blush. It seemed that Tyler was trying to set her up with Dillon and persuade her that he was good husband material. She rose from her seat to fill a glass of water and hide her embarrassment.

"You guys obviously go back a long way," she said. This kind of easy, natural conversation only ever existed between men who had a strong, unshakable connection, and the bond between these two friends was rock-solid. She could see that even after such a short time. "It's good to be able to laugh despite everything that's going on. I appreciate the way you've both tried to cheer me up."

Dillon stood, the playfulness dropped, replaced with somberness. "Now it's time for me to get back to work. I need to talk with Tyler, make a few phone calls and then get going to the lighthouse for the night."

"You're going to the lighthouse?" Beth asked in surprise. "I assumed you'd be staying here."

"It makes sense for somebody to be ready and waiting in case any attackers return," he replied. "Carl and Larry are still there, and I told them I'd take over by 10:00 p.m."

Beth felt her stomach drop away. It was a sensation of worry. She was concerned about Dillon and realized that she didn't want him to leave. For such a long time,

Helen had been the only person in her life that she worried about. Now, apparently, she was forming an unintended attachment to Dillon, and she didn't like it. Her life was complicated enough right now. The last thing she needed was a man occupying her thoughts. Yet she couldn't help it. Her whole being was craving Dillon's attention, despite her resistance.

"Are you sure you'll be okay there?" she asked, watching him holster his weapon around his shoulder. "I know you said that the coast guard is part of the military, but it's pretty dangerous for you to stay by yourself in a remote lighthouse that might come under attack at any moment. It's not like you're a Navy SEAL or anything."

She saw Dillon exchange a quick glance with Tyler and a small smile passed his lips.

"I'll be fine, Beth," he said. "Try not to worry about me."

That was easier said than done. "Can you send a message to let me know everything is okay once you're there?"

"Sure," he replied. "If it helps, I'll text you to put your mind at rest."

"Thanks." She eyed the clock on the wall. "Now I think I might hit the hay. It's been a really long and stressful day and I'm exhausted."

"Sleep well, Beth," Dillon said. "And if you're concerned about anything, Tyler will be here to take care of it."

She nodded, whistled for Ted to come to heel and made her way to her bedroom. Tyler instilled a sense of security in her, but she found herself wishing it were Dillon protecting her through the night. She wanted to know he was close by, and not across the other side of the bay, alone in her lighthouse, open to all kinds of danger.

"Stop it," she muttered under her breath, as she closed her bedroom door behind her. "You shouldn't be thinking about Dillon like this."

She settled Ted down on the old blankets that had been laid in the corner for him and busied herself folding some clothes she had left lying on the bed. Yet, try as she might, she found herself unable to stop worrying about Dillon's welfare. Would he return safe and well in the morning? And why did she care so much?

She sighed and dug into the pocket of her sweatshirt, finding the gold band she had placed inside. Pulling it out into the open, she held it between her thumb and forefinger, remembering Helen's words: *Get rid of that ring*. Despite Helen's occasional confusion, her old friend was still capable of being sharply observant and perceptive at times.

Beth wasn't yet ready to let go of the band. It served a valuable purpose, reminding her that loneliness was a small price to pay to avoid the kind of heartache a man brings into a woman's life.

She slipped the ring under her pillow, feeling strengthened by its message. Now was not the time to discard it. Helen was wrong on that matter. She would keep hold of it for just a while longer.

Dillon walked across the deserted street toward the coast guard truck, which he always kept parked outside the station, just a short walk from his apartment complex. By now, most of the staff members would have gone home and just one night watchman would remain, keeping eyes on the sea for signs of any activity. Tonight was meant to be Clay's shift, but he was still recovering from his recent head injury, so Dillon had assigned a replacement officer. Not being certain of who he could trust inside the station made Dillon's job almost impossible, but without any evidence of the culprit he was forced to utilize all the crew members at his disposal.

The only sound he could hear above the lapping of the sea was the echo of his own footsteps in the street, which glistened with wetness from a recent rain shower. It was a calm and mild night, with only light rain, perfect for the traffickers to make a journey. Yet they had shown no movement for the last two days, despite the weather conditions being perfect for seagoing vessels. Maybe they were gearing up for a big shipment. He had already scheduled another meeting with Miguel Olmos for the following day, and this would hopefully give him some clues regarding the intention of the cartel.

He glanced back to his apartment, noticing that the light in the spare room was still illuminated. Beth wasn't yet sleeping. Would she be lying awake worrying about him perhaps? He smiled to himself, knowing he shouldn't feel happy that Beth was concerned for his safety, yet he couldn't help enjoying the sensation anyway. He had never felt this important to a woman before. He was always the soldier departing for overseas assignments without the embraces and weeping that he witnessed between other soldiers and their wives. He didn't know how it felt to be waited for, to be worried about, to be missed. The note of anxiety in Beth's voice and her care for his welfare gave him a warm glow inside. It pained him to think that he would be spending less time with her now that Tyler had arrived. He was starting to enjoy being with her, and he sensed she felt the same way. But he was all too aware of his responsibilities and his duty to others who needed him much more than a lone, young woman from Bracelet Bay. Beth was now safe with Tyler, and he was free to get on with his job.

He stopped in his tracks. The sound of his footsteps seemed to be matched by another set, walking in rhythm with his.

He spun around, instantly reaching for his weapon. The town was dark, the streetlamps giving only a soft and minimal glow. He saw nothing.

"Hello," he called. This could be just someone out on a night walk, but unlikely. The dark November evening was chilly. Most of the townsfolk would be keeping warm indoors. "Is anybody there?"

He waited for a reply, but none came. A cold wind blew in from the sea, brushing over his skin and sending prickles to the surface. He kept his hand on his holstered weapon beneath his jacket, wondering if he was imagining things. Maybe the footsteps had merely been an echo of his own.

Then a sudden and darting movement flashed in his peripheral vision. Somebody was running in the shadows, scurrying between buildings, hiding from view. He saw something move under the canopy of the grocery store, the figure stopping briefly, before resuming his path on the sidewalk. This person looked to be heading for Dillon's apartment complex.

He pulled his weapon from its holster and silently gave chase.

EIGHT

Dillon's feet moved soundlessly on the pavement, and he had raised his gun to his shoulder, following the shadow as it jumped over the fence that led to the communal backyard for the residents of the Harbor View apartments.

He didn't want to waste time or give away his position so decided against using his cell to warn Tyler of a possible intruder. Instead he vaulted the fence, landing silently on the other side and darting down the pathway that led alongside the apartments. Staying close to the wall, he kept the suspect in his sights. At closer range, he could see that this was a heavyset man wearing rain gear, with the hood pulled up tightly around his head. As the man moved toward the back of the building, his clothing rustled, mingling with the swishing sound from the trees overhead.

The man disappeared behind the corner and Dillon hung back, waiting to see where he was going. The Harbor View building was very secure, with no means of access through the front door without authorization from a resident. The figure walked across the lawn, keeping to the edge where flower beds lined the grass, ducking low under the trees, possibly searching for the perfect hiding spot. Then he pulled something from his pocket, and Dillon saw a glint of metal flash in the darkness. The man crouched low, almost crawling into the shrubbery, hiding himself totally from sight. Could he be shielding himself from view with a gun, hoping to take the perfect shot at Beth when she emerged from his apartment, perhaps to exercise Ted in the yard?

Dillon raised his gun and strode across the yard. "Stay right where you are," he bellowed. "And come out where I can see you."

His barking orders caused a lot of rustling and movement in the shrubbery as the man seemed to react in a panicked way.

"I said come out where I can see you," Dillon repeated. "And I want your hands in the air."

A familiar voice called from the leaves, "Captain Randall, is that you?"

"Who's there?"

A face emerged from the darkness and stared up at Dillon with wide, fearful eyes. It was Kevin Chapman from the Salty Dog, crouching low in the flower bed, his clothes now streaked with mud.

Dillon didn't lower his weapon. "Kevin, what are you doing crawling around in the dirt in my backyard?"

Kevin slowly rose to his feet, hands aloft, and Dillon saw that the flash of metal he had observed was part of a dog leash held in Kevin's right hand.

"I was looking for Sailor," he replied, his eyes fixed on the barrel of Dillon's gun, pointing right at his chest. "I'm sorry, I didn't mean to scare you."

Dillon lowered his gun but kept it in his hand. "Who's Sailor?"

"My dog." Kevin put his arms by his side. "He ran off and jumped the fence into your yard." He jerked his head toward the apartment block. "Some of the residents have complained that he digs up the shrubs, so I wanted to make sure I got him back as quickly as possible." He attempted to smile, but his nerves were clearly frayed by the surprise Dillon had just sprung on him. "Did you think I was an intruder or something?"

"Technically you *are* an intruder," Dillon said, while scanning the lawn. "So where's the dog?"

Kevin let out a low whistle and called, "Sailor, come here, boy."

Both men waited in silence for the dog to come to heel, but there was no sign of him.

Dillon narrowed his eyes at Kevin. "I didn't know you had a dog," he said. "What kind?"

Kevin gripped the leash tightly in his hands, twisting it as he spoke. He seemed uneasy in Dillon's presence, and this made Dillon wary. The story about looking for a dog could easily be a cover. If Larry was the mole in the coast guard, he might have recruited Kevin to do the bidding of the cartel also.

"Sailor's a German shepherd," Kevin said. "I use him as a guard dog at the restaurant, just in case anybody gets any ideas about trying to steal the takings." He bent his knees to look in the foliage. "But for such a big dog, he's pretty good at hiding himself."

"Yeah," Dillon said. "It would appear that way. You look tense, Kevin. Is there something else on your mind?"

"Well," Kevin said, shifting on his feet. "I'm always nervous when talking to a man holding a gun."

Dillon holstered his weapon and stood with his arms crossed. "Is that better?"

Kevin nodded. Then he whistled again, and a big, shaggy shape came bounding across the lawn, tongue rolling from its mouth. Kevin dropped to the ground and greeted the dog with a smile of relief.

"Sailor, you're a bad dog," he said, attaching the leash to his collar. "You almost got me into big trouble there."

Dillon looked up at his apartment. The light in Beth's bedroom had been turned off.

"So I'm guessing you'll want to get home now," Dillon said. "Just in case Sailor decides to go exploring again."

"That sounds like a good idea," Kevin said, leading the dog toward the gate that opened onto the street. "Do you think you could punch the access code into the gate? It would help if you let us out."

"Sure. Follow me."

Dillon started walking to the gate, burying his cold hands deep into his pockets. His fingers curled around the stone that he had not yet found time to log into evidence at the station. It reminded him of the words that Miguel Olmos had spoken about the cartel sending another man to attack Beth: *trust nobody.*

"What do you know about Beth Forrester, who lives at the Return to Grace Lighthouse?" Dillon asked, making sure he studied Kevin's reaction carefully.

Kevin blinked quickly. "Not much. I haven't seen her in years. Our waitress, Mia, talks about her sometimes. They used to be best friends." He shrugged. "From what I hear, the only person who sees Beth these days is the old lady in the beach house."

"So you haven't seen her recently?"

"No."

"You didn't see her in the restaurant yesterday when you and Larry were fighting?"

"No, but if you recall the situation, I was a little preoccupied."

"I remember," Dillon said. "Has anybody other than Mia talked about her, either in the restaurant or anywhere else in the community?"

Kevin shook his head. "Why do you ask?"

"No particular reason," Dillon said, pressing numbers on the keypad to release the gate. "She's been helping the coast guard with some investigations and I was just wondering if Larry mentioned anything about it."

Kevin's face darkened. "Larry?" he questioned. "We're not talking right now, so Larry's mentioned nothing to me about nobody."

"Okay," Dillon said, leading Kevin and Sailor down the narrow path alongside the apartment building toward the street. "I was just wondering."

Kevin's face lit up as though an inspired thought had suddenly occurred to him. "Oh, I get it now," he said with a smile. "You're interested in Beth Forrester." He let out a laugh. "I can see why. She's a beautiful woman, but I think you're onto a losing streak with that one. She's a total loner." He leaned across conspiratorially. "I think she's probably gonna turn into a crazy cat lady."

Irritation tingled over Dillon's skin. Kevin had no idea of the kind of person Beth was. He was simply making assumptions based on his limited knowledge of her life, no doubt gleaned from gossip and rumor.

"Actually," Dillon said, "she isn't crazy and she doesn't own a cat."

Kevin must have guessed he'd hit a nerve, and he didn't argue the point. "Sorry for Sailor's intrusion on your evening," he said. "Good night, Captain Randall."

Dillon watched Kevin stride across the road, heading back to the Salty Dog, and he kept his eyes trained on him until he rounded a corner and was out of sight. Then Dillon resumed his walk to the coast guard truck, all the while mulling over the stark warning from Miguel Olmos: *trust nobody.*

He intended to take that advice to heart.

Beth couldn't sleep. She lay in bed staring up at the ceiling, listening to the rumbling snoring of Ted in the corner. Dillon had promised to let her know that he was safe inside her lighthouse, yet the clock had passed midnight and there was still no word. She sat up, closed her eyes and bowed her head, intending to ask for the Lord's protection over him.

As if her unsaid prayer was already answered, her cell lit up, illuminating the nightstand with its soft glow. She snatched it from the bedside and saw a message from Dillon on the screen: All quiet here at the lighthouse. Sleep tight. X

Beth read the message three times and then found herself staring at just one letter: the X that Dillon had tagged onto the end. It made her heart skip like a child's at Christmas, and she wondered if he had meant it to signify a kiss. Maybe he ended all his text messages with this note of affection. Maybe it meant nothing. And why did it matter so much to her anyway?

She tapped the keys, sending an immediate reply: Glad to hear it. What about Helen? She deliberated about whether to also include the X on the end of her message. Would he read too much into it? Would it constitute flirting? She decided on the safest option and left it out, hitting Send and waiting for a reply to ping back.

She didn't need to wait long. His response buzzed through within seconds: Helen is fine and ate a good hot meal. Will check on her in the morning. It's late. You should go to sleep.

She tapped her reply: Can't sleep. Too much to worry about. She looked at Ted lying peacefully asleep in the corner, and tried to lighten the message by adding But Teddy is snoring like a walrus.

His response made her chuckle: Are you sure Ted isn't an actual walrus? After these words, he had added, Try to sleep and not worry. Tyler is an excellent bodyguard.

She knew this was true. She had heard Tyler's movements throughout the apartment, double-checking the locks and bolts. He was a good protector, but he wasn't Dillon. With this weighing on her mind, she quickly wrote her reply before she changed her mind: Tyler's a great bodyguard, but I wish you were here with me instead.

Immediately after pressing Send, Beth regretted her words. She tried to retrieve the message before it flew across the bay and into the lighthouse, but it was too late. It had gone. She stared at her phone, feeling embarrassment creep up her torso, along her neck and flush across her face. Why had she said that? Now Dillon would think she was flirting with him. He would assume that she was interested in him romantically. It had been so long since she experienced this level of interaction with a man, she had made herself look foolish by being too open with her feelings. She put the cell back on the nightstand, assuming that she had brought an end to their text exchange with her cringe worthy honesty.

Settling back onto her pillow, she heard a buzz vibrate the nightstand and she sat up, steeling herself before picking up the phone to read the reply.

It was just two words: Me too.

Beth hugged the phone tightly to her chest, beaming widely. This short text message made her feel happier than she had ever been in her entire life, and she knew it was ridiculous that she, a grown woman, should feel this degree of joy from just two words. But the sensation in her belly was like fire catching throughout her body, and she couldn't contain the excitement that only comes from making a meaningful connection with somebody special. She guessed the feeling wouldn't last, but for that moment, she wanted to enjoy the fluttering butterflies.

She tapped a reply, and this time she included the kiss: Good night. X.

After that, she snuggled down under the sheets and closed her eyes, finding that sleep came surprisingly easier than a few minutes ago.

Just as she was drifting off, a final message buzzed through and she reached for her cell with heavy lids. Dillon's final words to her that evening were Sleep tight. X.

Dillon had a fitful night's rest in the lighthouse. He had made a bed up in the corner of the living room, hidden behind a screen so that he couldn't be spotted with prying eyes from the outside. He had made the front door as secure as possible, but bullets had destroyed the locks and splintered the wood, so the wind was able to whistle through the gaps with an eerie whine. Today he would ask Carl to fit yet another brand-new door and contact a glazier to replace the shattered windowpane.

As he had lain on his makeshift bed, Dillon imagined Beth sleeping alone in this remote place for five years, and he found a new admiration for her. She obviously had a lot of courage and determination to live perched on the cliffs, being battered by the elements on a daily basis. The noises throughout the night had kept him on the edge of wakefulness and each time he opened his eyes, he checked his cell phone for any new texts from Beth, feeling slight disappointment when the screen came up blank.

Their exchange of text messages the previous night had clearly veered into a far more intimate territory than they had ever gone before. And he found himself enjoying the feelings it stirred in him. But he knew he was on dangerous ground, especially considering that he had promised himself to step away from her and her protection detail. He was forced to concede that the tug he felt in his chest, drawing him to Beth, had become a problem. He must allow Tyler to do the job he was drafted into the town to carry out, and not interfere.

Dillon had risen, eaten breakfast, checked on Helen and was preparing to move Beth's half-finished bed frame onto a trailer attached to the coast guard truck by the time Larry and Carl arrived to take the daytime shift. Carl jumped from their vehicle to help Dillon carefully position the old boat onto the trailer and tie it down with ropes. The vessel was now in one piece, having been expertly repaired by Beth with rivets and panels, and was sanded and buffed smooth. She was obviously in the process of making storage drawers beneath the hull, and the small size of the frame could only mean it was for a child. Whoever the child was, he would be one fortunate kid. Dillon knew that the finished product would be beautiful and unique.

Larry watched from the sidelines, running his eyes over the old boat with interest. "What are you doing with this, Captain?" he asked.

Dillon decided to bend the truth. "Beth is worried about the damp conditions in the lighthouse while the window is out," he replied, tightening a knot in the rope at the hull. "So she asked me to remove this work in progress and store it someplace dry."

Larry walked around the trailer. "And where are you taking it?"

"I'll store it in my basement for the time being. It's also a good idea to get it out of the living room. It gives us more space to move around."

Larry nodded in agreement. "So where is Beth holed up?"

Dillon stopped what he was doing and stood up straight. Larry knew that this information was confidential, even to the coast guard staff. "She's gone out of town for a while," he lied. "To visit her parents in Oregon."

Larry seemed to be far too interested in this information for Dillon's liking. "She's gone out of town?" he asked in surprise. "You sure about that? I didn't think she would ever leave Bracelet Bay, not for anything."

"Yes, I'm sure," Dillon said, watching Larry's eyes dart around with suspicion. "And while she's gone, it's our job to try and keep her home exactly as she left it." He made a snap decision, based on his gut instinct about Larry's trustworthiness. "It doesn't need the two of you on lighthouse duty, so why don't you work from the station on search and surveillance today, Larry? We might get a breakthrough after I meet with Miguel Olmos, so there will be plenty to do. I'll give you a ride back to town."

"I hear we have a new crew member due to start working with us," Larry said. "I saw his name on the staff list, and I assumed he was drafted in to help guard Beth. Now that she's decided to go to Oregon, will the new guy be leaving?"

Dillon narrowed his eyes. "How do you know the new guy has even arrived?"

"Paula mentioned something about you getting take-out last night for a new recruit."

Dillon rolled his eyes. "This town does a better job of reconnaissance than any expert I ever met. Don't worry about the new guy, Larry. He won't interfere with any of your duties, and you won't even know he's here." He looked out over the calm ocean, shimmering under the winter sun. "It's all quiet here, but I got a feeling the cartel is working its way up to something big, so let's keep our eyes peeled and our senses alert. There's a lot at stake and people's lives depend on us."

Dillon slid into the driver's seat of the truck and waited for Larry to join him. The chief petty officer's questions had aroused suspicion in him, but he didn't have good enough reason to take him off active duty. He would limit Larry to station duties for the time being, and monitor his work for signs of anomalies or deliberate attempts to mislead the coast guard search.

Dillon carefully backed up the vehicle onto the road, with Larry silently sitting beside him, and began the journey back to the coast guard station. His mind was running with questions to answer, tasks to be carried out, charts to check, plans to make and people to monitor.

With forced determination, he tried to push Beth totally from his mind. He would check on her just one time, but after that, he would concentrate on the tough day ahead.

Beth found herself feeling shy and uncomfortable when Dillon entered the apartment at lunchtime. He locked eyes with her and smiled, and she gripped the edge of the kitchen door frame, dropping her gaze to the floor.

"Did you sleep well?" he asked, removing his coat and hanging it up.

"Yeah," she replied. "Best night's sleep in a long time."

"Good."

They stood in awkward silence for a few seconds, each waiting for the other to speak and maybe acknowledge the moment that had passed between them the previous evening. But neither was willing to broach the subject, and Beth concluded that it was a momentary lapse for both of them. Neither she nor he wanted to take the next step on this newly forged intimate path.

"Everything okay here?" Dillon asked, walking into the living room and acknowledging Tyler with a nod.

Tyler glanced up from his seated position by the window, overlooking the yard. "There's been no sign of any danger," he replied. "Although I did notice a guy entering the yard last night just after you left." He smiled. "But you dealt with him pretty well from what I saw. He looked scared stiff when you pointed your gun at him."

Beth's stomach dropped. "Who was there? You didn't mention it in your messages."

"It was Kevin Chapman, looking for his dog," Dillon said.

Beth knew the animal well. Sailor and Ted used to be great friends, seeking each other out whenever possible. She suddenly found herself thinking of all the things she had deprived Ted of by moving him away from the town. He used to enjoy the sights, sounds and smells of the various stores, and the owner of the butcher shop would give him tidbits from under the counter. She wondered if Ted remembered these things. Five years was a long time to a dog.

"I thought Ted was a bit too interested in sniffing around the flower beds this morning," Beth said. "I was watching him from the window and I was sure he could smell something. He must've picked up Sailor's scent."

She bent down to stroke the dog's head, hearing him whining softly under her touch. He was restless.

"Ted isn't used to being cooped up like this," she said. "Tyler exercised him in the yard this morning, but he normally has a wide-open beach to run along. I think he's going a bit stir-crazy. To tell you the truth, so am I."

"Your boat bed frame is on a trailer in my basement garage, and your tools are in the truck," he said. "I guess that ought to keep you busy for a while."

She smiled, feeling her heart lift. Dillon had made good on his promise, and she was grateful. "Thank you. I'm way behind on that project, so I really appreciate it."

Tyler stood and stretched himself out. Dillon guessed he had been sitting window-side for quite some time.

"What are you doing here anyway, Dillon?" Tyler

asked. "Aren't you supposed to be out there catching the bad guys and leaving the protection stuff to me?"

"It's just a quick visit," Dillon replied. "I'll grab a coffee and unload the trailer, then get on my way."

"I'll go make a pot," Tyler said, walking through to the kitchen. "I could do with a caffeine boost, as well."

When she and Dillon were alone, Beth felt the tension between them rise again. She decided to take the bull by the horns and bring up the topic they had both been skirting around.

"I hope you didn't read too much into my texts last night," she said. "I'm really grateful for Tyler and what he's doing for me, but I guess I wanted a familiar face like yours around."

Dillon smiled. "It's odd to hear you describe me as a familiar face," he said. "We only just met, after all."

She realized, with surprise, that he was right. It seemed as though they had known each other for years, not just a few days.

"Well, it certainly feels like your face is familiar," she said. She laced her fingers together in front of her waist and twirled her thumbs. "And I'm starting to be comfortable around you, which isn't an easy thing to achieve for somebody who's used to spending most of their time alone."

His smile didn't fade. "I'm glad you finally feel comfortable with me. It means a lot to hear you say it."

She swallowed away her nervousness. "So that's what I meant when I said I wished you were here instead of Tyler." She avoided his eyes. "I don't want you to think that I was flirting or anything like that." She laughed to cover up her discomfort. "Not that I would know anything about flirting. I barely talk to anybody, let alone single men." She realized she was rambling and she promptly shut her mouth tight, in case she embarrassed herself even further.

"It's okay," Dillon said kindly. "I didn't get any ideas about romance if that's what you're worried about."

She breathed a sigh that she assumed was one of relief, but the tightness in her chest refused to shift.

"Good," she said with a bright smile. "I'm glad we cleared that up."

He looked into her eyes for a few seconds, saying nothing, but studying her intently. He exuded a kind of magnetic power over her, and her words belied the way she truly felt inside. The more she saw of him, the more she wanted to be with him, but it was futile to think that they could have a future together. What man would be interested in a crazy hermit lady living in a lighthouse with a shaggy, old dog? Even if she were confident enough to act on her feelings, she would simply be kidding herself to think that Dillon would return them.

Dillon broke the silence first. "I need to borrow Tyler to help me unload the bed frame from the trailer. He'll only be gone for five minutes and we'll watch you shut the door and lock up behind us so we know you're safe inside. It makes sense for you to stay here while we're distracted with the trailer. Is that okay?"

"Sure," she said, glad to be moving the conversation along. "I have my cell if anything happens."

Dillon brushed past her and spoke quietly to Tyler in the kitchen, and Tyler then walked into the living room and handed her a cup of coffee.

"We'll be back before you finish this," Tyler said.

Beth went out into the hall as both men approached the front door of the apartment. Dillon looked through the peephole and opened the door, checking the corridor both ways. Then he turned back to her.

"See you in five," he said, before adding with a smile. "Don't go out for a walk or anything, okay?"

On hearing his favorite word, Ted leaped up from his sitting position at Beth's feet and knocked her coffee cup from her hand. The hot liquid splashed all over her pants and the carpet.

"Oh no," she cried. "I'm so sorry." She turned to Ted and wagged a finger at him. "Bad dog!"

Ted slunk away, hiding beneath the hallway table. She picked up the empty cup from the floor and brushed at her pants, shaking her head. "Look at the stain on the floor. I'll clean it up."

"It's fine," Dillon said soothingly. "Are you all right? Are you burned?"

"No. I'm okay."

Tyler took the cup from her hand and set it on the kitchen table.

"Why don't you go change your clothes while Tyler and I see to the trailer?" Dillon suggested. "Leave the carpet. It's really not important."

"If you're sure," Beth said. "I'd like to put these pants to soak before the stain sets."

"Make sure you lock up behind us," he said, leading her to the door. "We'll stay here until we hear the bolts put in place."

Once the men were in the hallway, Tyler called the elevator while Dillon watched her close and lock the door. Then she checked beneath the table where Ted had been hiding. He was gone and had no doubt crawled into his bed by now to serve out his punishment. She walked into her bedroom, muttering her annoyance with him.

While she pulled on a fresh pair of jeans, she spoke in an admonishing tone.

"Ted, that was a bad thing you did. We're not in the lighthouse now, and there's no space to jump." She turned around, expecting to see his doleful eyes looking up at her from his bed. But he wasn't there.

"Ted," she called, going back into the living room. "Are you hiding from me?"

She checked all the places that a large dog could go, and her heart began to hammer as each one turned up empty. Ted was gone! Then she realized that he must have snuck past them when the door was open, using the distraction of the spilled coffee to make his escape.

Beth put a hand over her mouth, wondering what to do. It had been five years since Ted was in the town of Bracelet Bay. He might not remember his way around. He might end up on Highway One, dodging the trucks and cars speeding along the ocean road. She needed to find him fast. She pulled out her cell and hit the redial button to call Dillon. The line went straight to voice mail, and she suspected that cell reception in the basement would be patchy. She hopped from foot to foot, knowing that she would be unable to wait for their return to begin her search. Ted had only been gone a few minutes and she was the best person to find him. Hopefully he would still be somewhere in the foyer, unable to get out of the main front door.

Having made the decision to go, she left the apartment with no time to lose, grabbing her coat along the way. Having a dislike for small, enclosed spaces, Beth shunned the elevator and ran down the stairway, calling Ted's name all the while. She met a young man walking up the other way.

"Did you see a dog come through here?" she asked breathlessly. "A big black one."

"Yeah," the man replied. "He ran outside when I opened the door."

Beth raced down the flight of stairs, hearing the man call out behind her, "I'm sorry, he pushed right past me."

When she reached the main front door, she looked out of the glass, trying to spot Ted sniffing around the sidewalk or ambling across the street, but she saw only people going about their daily business.

She rested her head on the cool pane, closing her eyes as images of her beloved dog, scared and hurt, flooded her brain. She would have to find him before that happened. Where would he be? Where would he go if he remembered the town from years ago? She mentally checked off the list of places in her mind and opened the door to step outside. She instantly felt fear invade her senses, almost forcing her back. Not only was she afraid of encountering an attacker from the most feared cartel in Central America, but she was afraid of the town itself. The familiar sensations of panic gripped her tight: rapid breathing, palpitations, sweaty palms. The old fears of the past still held sway over her and she had to force herself forward, calling Ted's name, ignoring the dread in her chest.

Whatever happened to her, she had to find Ted.

NINE

Beth stumbled toward the first place she thought Ted might go: the butcher shop. It had always been his most favorite place in the world with its array of meat smells and the promise of scraps. She pulled her coat tightly around her torso and walked across the road, failing to notice a car heading her way. The honk of the horn caused her to jump and stop dead, feeling like a rabbit caught in headlights.

The car came to a halt and a man stepped from the vehicle. He was coming toward her, and she couldn't control the explosion of panic inside. Had she stepped straight into the path of an attacker? She willed her body to move, to put one foot in front of the other and take herself away from the potential danger, but her legs simply refused to work.

"Are you okay?" the man called to her. "Do you need some help?"

She let out the long breath she had been holding. "No," she managed to say. "I'm just looking for my dog."

"Beth Forrester?" the man said. "Is that you?"

She looked at him, recognizing his long, thin features. It was her old math teacher from high school. A familiar face from the past made her limbs free up in an instant, and she ran across the street, wanting to flee the inevitable interest that her presence in town would generate.

"I gotta go," she called, keeping her eyes focused on the red-and-white-striped sign of the butcher's shop. She didn't look back.

The butcher, a middle-aged man with a big, bushy beard, seemed hardly surprised to see her when she burst in through the door. "I thought you must be back in town," he said with a beaming smile. "When Ted came walking in here like he owned the place, I guessed you wouldn't be far behind. It's great to see you after so long."

"Ted was here?" she asked quickly. "When? Did you see where he went?" She spun around, hoping to catch a glimpse of him disappearing into another doorway. "I lost him."

The butcher came out from behind his counter. "I gave him a sausage like I always used to and he put it in his mouth and trotted back outside. Don't worry, Beth. I think he knows the town well enough to be safe."

"But he hasn't been here in such a long time," she cried. "He might get lost and end up on the highway."

"Would you like me to make a few calls?" the butcher offered. "We'll have him back in no time."

Beth began to retreat out the door, imagining the grapevine of Bracelet Bay being set in motion on the telephone, and news of her return to the town spreading like wildfire. The gossiping and whispering would be rife. It was too much to contemplate.

"No, thanks," she said, stepping out onto the sidewalk. "I'll keep looking."

Then she turned and began running to the Salty Dog, where she knew Ted might be led by the familiar scent of his old friend Sailor. She ran past a whole host of faces that she recognized: the librarian who always waived the late-return fees on her books, the grocery store worker who once helped her rescue Ted when he got into trouble swimming in the ocean, the pharmacist who tested her on various treatments for her allergy to pollen until he identified the perfect one, the couple who sent her flowers after she found them the ideal family home. These people all smiled in pleasant surprise to see her, and they waved, calling after her, but she continued running, feeling too many eyes upon her. She was only just managing to contain her rising panic, but began to be vaguely aware of a person keeping pace behind her.

On entering the Salty Dog, she was rosy-cheeked and moist with perspiration. Mia looked up from the counter with a huge smile and rushed over to envelop Beth in a hug before she even had a chance to speak.

"Beth," her old friend exclaimed. "I hoped you'd come back in soon. I saw you here with Captain Randall yesterday—"

Beth cut her off. "Have you seen Ted?"

Mia pulled away, looking confused. "No. Has he gone missing?"

"Yes, he escaped and ran off," Beth replied. "And I'm so worried that I might not find him." Aside from Helen, Ted was the only constant companion in her life, and he hadn't left her side during the years of self-imposed exile. A sob broke through her voice. "If he comes in looking for Sailor, please keep him here and don't let him leave. Can you do that?"

"Of course," Mia said gently. "Why don't you sit down and I'll bring you some hot tea? I'll make some calls and we'll get Ted back in a jiffy."

"No," Beth said quickly and loudly, causing diners to turn and stare. "I can't wait." She headed for the door. "Maybe he's trying to get back to the lighthouse."

"Have you tried the vet's office?" Mia called. "He was there recently for an operation, right? He might remember the place and head there."

"Of course," Beth said as she opened the door. "Thanks Mia. I'll give it a try."

Once out on the sidewalk, she wiped her brow, enjoying the cool breeze rushing over her warm skin, and started running again, keeping her eyes to the ground, still feeling an uncomfortable sensation of being followed. She turned and craned her neck to look down the street but saw nobody suspicious tailing her. She shrugged off the feeling, knowing that her aversion to the bustle of the town would induce mild paranoia. After all, she thought everybody was watching her every move. She kept telling herself that she was safe; nobody had known she was at Dillon's apartment, so there surely couldn't be anybody lying in wait.

She pushed open the door of the vet's office and rushed inside, instantly colliding with Henry, forcing him to place a steadying hand on the wall. Much to her huge relief and thankfulness, Henry was holding on to a leash that was firmly attached to the collar of her big, disobedient dog, who was sitting at the vet's feet panting happily after his short excursion around Bracelet Bay.

"Oh, Ted," she said, dropping to her knees and wrapping her arms around his neck. The smell of his damp fur brought tears to her eyes. "You bad dog." Ted's ears pulled back and his head bowed. He knew he was in trouble, but she couldn't stay mad at him. She touched noses with him and he gave her cheek an affectionate lick. "Don't do that again," she said. "You gave me such a scare."

Henry bent down to be level with her. "I heard Ted whining at the door to get in, and when I opened the door, he jumped up on me like a long-lost friend." The vet rubbed the smooth patch of fur between the dog's ears. "Ted and I are good buddies now, aren't we, Ted?"

"He must remember you as somebody who gave him food and lots of attention," Beth said, standing up to take the leash from Henry's hand. "Could I borrow the leash for a day or two? I'll return it."

"Keep it," Henry replied with a wave of the hand. "I have a million of them."

"Thanks." She started pulling her dog toward the door, although he seemed reluctant to leave his new friend and strained on the leash. "And thank you for looking after Ted. He obviously likes you."

Henry beamed. "I like him too." He shifted uncomfortably on his feet and ran his hands through his auburn hair. "Um… Beth…before you leave, could I ask you something?"

Beth thought of her need to get back to the apartment before Dillon and Tyler noticed her absence, but she owed Henry some gratitude.

"Sure," she said. "But I have to leave pretty quickly."

He took a deep breath. "Would you like to have dinner with me sometime?"

Beth felt her eyes widening in shock. Was she being

asked out on a date? Was Henry not aware of her status as a crazy recluse, who lived in a lighthouse and scoured the beach for pieces of old wood?

She was silent for a few seconds and racked her brain for something to say. Henry tried to make light of his offer in the face of almost certain rejection.

"It's no big deal," he said, backing away to the door of his office. "I didn't mean to put you on the spot." He looked down at his feet. "It's just that you're the nicest woman I've met in a while."

"Me?" she questioned. "But you hardly know me."

He smiled. "Sometimes you just know," he said as his color rose. "I liked you when I met you five years ago, but I missed my chance to ask you out back then. I didn't want to miss another one."

"I'm sorry, Henry," Beth said, opening the door to leave. "You're a great guy, but I don't think we'd be right together." She gave a little tug on the leash to encourage Ted to move outside. Then a thought struck her. "But I have a feeling you'd get along really well with Mia, the waitress from the Salty Dog." Helen often mentioned Mia's continuous search for Mr. Right and Beth thought that Henry just might fit that bill. "Why not see if she'd like a coffee after her shift?"

Henry looked eager to make a quick getaway. "I might do that. See you around, Beth."

She pulled Ted out into the pale sunshine, fading under the thickening clouds, and hurried along the steep, narrow lane, anxious to return to the apartment. Henry's office was set high up behind the main street, away from all the stores and shoppers, so her immediate surroundings were empty. She picked up her pace.

She had now advertised her presence in town to

many of its residents, so she had jeopardized the plan to keep herself hidden away. She wondered with dismay whether she would have to move again. Dillon's apartment might not be perfect, but she felt safe there.

As she pondered these thoughts, a van skidded to a halt alongside her, splashing her with water that had gathered in the gutter. Her heart leaped into her mouth, as the flash of gray metal filled her vision. She turned to run, but the sliding door whooshed open and a strong hand gripped her arm. She twisted her body and cried out, trying to alert the people who she had previously wanted to shun. She needed them now.

"Help!"

She let go of Ted's leash and used both hands to fight with all her strength. Ted barked and jumped around, getting his feet tangled up in his leash and immobilizing himself. In a matter of seconds, Beth was encased in darkness and pushed to the hard, metal floor. Then she heard the door slide back into place before her hands and feet were bound together and a strip of silver tape placed over her mouth. In her peripheral vision, she saw the man climb into the driver's seat and heard the squeal of rubber tires on wet pavement as the van sped from the scene, leaving her with nothing but stone-cold fear.

Dillon ran from room to room in his apartment, shouting Beth's name, but no replies came. She was gone!

"Where did she go?" Tyler asked, opening the closet to pull out the clothes and take a thorough look inside. "We were only gone a few minutes and the security locks haven't been forced, so she must've left of her own free will. Why?"

The answer came to Dillon instantly. "Ted!" he exclaimed. He sprinted for the front door. "Ted must have escaped while we were distracted and she went out after him."

He yanked his cell from his pocket and called Beth's number, waiting impatiently for a reply. When the call finally went to voice mail, he knew she might be in trouble.

"Let's go," he said. "We should be able to find her quickly if we split up."

Dillon bounded down the stairs, feeling Tyler close behind. When they reached the sidewalk, he turned to Tyler and said, "You take the harborside part of town, and I'll take Main Street. Call me immediately if you spot Beth or Ted."

"Dillon," Tyler said, pointing into the distance, where Main Street curled out of town. There, attempting to run, legs tangled in his leash, was Ted. But he was alone on the road, and Dillon knew in his heart that something sinister must have happened to Beth.

"Ted looks like he's chasing after something," Dillon said, pulling the coast guard truck keys out of his pocket. "Maybe he's trying to get to Beth." He handed the keys to Tyler. "Go fetch the truck and drive it here. It's parked outside the station, right on the edge of the harbor. I'll go to Ted and see if I can spot anything."

Tyler didn't waste a moment in tearing off down the sidewalk in the direction of the harbor, dodging between the shoppers milling around in his path. Meanwhile Dillon kept his eyes focused on Ted, pumping his feet and arms in rhythm, trying to control his soaring pulse. He veered between fear and annoyance. Beth knew how dangerous it was for her to leave the apartment. Why hadn't she called him if she'd discovered Ted missing? But he also knew that Beth was sensible. She probably thought it would be a simple case of retrieving the dog with no harm done. After all, the town was busy on this sunny afternoon. Anybody would feel safe on the pretty, picture-postcard streets.

When Dillon reached Ted, the dog wagged his tail and whined in frustration at being unable to free himself from the tangled leash. Dillon unwound the rope and unclipped it from Ted's collar. Then Ted started running up the hill, obviously trying to continue his journey to Beth.

"Ted," Dillon called. "Come back here."

Ted stopped abruptly and immediately returned to Dillon but continued to stare at the road that led out of town and toward Highway One. If Beth had been abducted, Highway One would be the point at which she would be lost to him. Without knowing the vehicle he was looking for or its destination, time was of the essence if he was going to catch up with her.

Just then, Tyler screeched to a halt alongside him and opened the passenger door, allowing Dillon to jump inside. Ted leaped up onto his lap before scrambling into the backseat.

"Head outta town," Dillon said. "I think Beth's been taken by somebody."

Tyler floored the gas pedal and screeched from the roadside. Ted struggled to stay upright in the back, sliding over the leather seats, trying to look out the window, softly whining the whole time.

"What are we looking for?" Tyler said. "Do we know?"

Dillon ran a hand down his face. He had been determined not to let his panic levels rise, but it was proving impossible. He was forced to admit that his concern for Beth's well-being went way beyond the ordinary.

"Your guess is as good as mine," Dillon replied. "Let's just check every vehicle we see in the hope we spot her."

Tyler pushed the truck to its limits, hurtling along the road, which was thankfully free of traffic. Soon a dark gray van came into view, traveling above the speed limit but not recklessly so.

"Could this be our guy?" Tyler asked. "Shall we pull him over?"

Dillon unclipped the radio from his belt. "I'll see what I can find out first." He spoke into the radio, asking Clay to run a check on the dark van with tinted windows and California license plates. He relayed the number.

Clay's voice came back quickly. "The vehicle belongs to a man named Gerardo Hernandez, sir. He's a known accomplice of Miguel Olmos and there's a warrant out for his arrest. This vehicle has been involved in a number of robberies in the San Diego area."

Dillon pulled out his weapon. "That's our guy," he said, activating the blue lights and siren on top of the vehicle. "Whatever happens, let's keep Beth unharmed. Don't shoot without thinking about it carefully."

"Dillon," Tyler said with a note of exasperation in his voice. "I know you want to be super cautious about protecting Beth, but I'm a trained SEAL just like you. Trust me."

"Sure," Dillon said. "I'm sorry." The van ahead of them picked up speed and veered between lanes. "This guy's clearly not gonna stop. Let's try and force him off the road before he reaches the highway."

Tyler waited for a suitable moment and maneuvered the truck alongside the van. The metal of both vehicles crunched and scraped as they collided, and Tyler used his skill to quickly right themselves on the road. The driver of the van didn't possess the same level of driving experience, and the gray vehicle began to veer out of control, losing traction on the asphalt.

In the next moment, the wheels left the road and began bumping along the grassy verge, slowing its path and sending the back end bouncing up into the air.

"Take us in front," Dillon ordered. "And be ready for anything."

Tyler brought the truck to a quick halt as the van shuddered to a stop in the grass. Both men then jumped from the truck, and Dillon quickly closed the door to keep Ted inside. The dog barked furiously, desperate to break free and assist the rescue.

"Out of the vehicle," Dillon yelled at the van. "All of you in the open with your hands in the air."

The driver of the van had his head bowed over the steering wheel, unmoving. It appeared as though this man was the only suspect in the vehicle, but Dillon couldn't be sure. Anybody lying on the floor in the back was out of sight.

"Get out," Dillon repeated, concerned that if he allowed too much time to pass, they could use the time to hurt Beth.

Dillon approached the front windshield with caution. The man had raised his forearms across the wheel and buried his head between them. For a second, Dillon wondered if he might be crying. His position was almost one of mourning.

"I'll count to five before I shoot," Dillon shouted, aiming his gun at the window. "He began the count. "One, two…"

Slowly, almost imperceptibly, the man began to raise his head. Dillon waited. This guy certainly was in no hurry.

When Dillon saw the driver's face come into clear view, he realized why this man had shown such reluctance to reveal himself: the face belonged to Larry Chapman.

Beth rubbed her wrists where the rope had cut into the skin. The soreness would heal, but the terror would remain. For those few minutes when she was imprisoned inside the dark van, she had imagined her life ending and wondered who would miss her presence on this earth. Aside from her mom, dad and Helen, Beth's existence was barely noticed by anybody. The experience had terrified her in more ways than one because it forced her to question exactly what she was living for if she could slip away from the world unnoticed. She was certain that God didn't want her to die lonely and afraid. Her near-death experience had affected her profoundly.

"Are you sure you're okay?" Dillon said, sitting next to her in his office at the coast guard station. "No feelings of dizziness, nausea or confusion?"

"No," she said. "If anything, I'm thinking clearer than I have done in a very long time."

"I've left Ted with some of the guys in the break room," Dillon said with a smile. "He's in his element. They're all making a huge fuss over him."

"That's good," she said, trying to muster up some positivity. "I'm so glad he's okay. I know I shouldn't have left the apartment to go looking for him, but where Ted is concerned I tend to lose my common sense."

"I understand," Dillon said gently. "You had no reason to suspect that a member of the coast guard was tracking you. I suspect Paula from the Salty Dog saw the dog leash hanging in my hallway and mentioned it to Larry." He shook his head angrily. "I had my doubts about Larry, but I never imagined he would do something like this." Beth noticed Dillon's fists clench up tight. "Everybody in the station is ashamed of him. Whatever story he comes up with to defend himself, he's finished in the coast guard and probably finished in the town of Bracelet Bay."

"When I saw Larry in cuffs after you freed me, I was totally stunned." Beth remembered the icy sensation that had started in her shoulders and slithered down the entire length of her body, making her immobile with shock. She could scarcely believe it was Larry who had bound her wrists and ankles and taped her mouth. They had exchanged a glance while standing on the side of the road, and Larry had looked at her with a mixture of pity and sorrow, but remained silent, refusing to meet her eyes again. "Has he said why he did this?"

"Not yet," Dillon replied. "We've got him locked up in a holding cell at the County Sheriff's Office. Officers from the Coast Guard Investigative Service will be here tomorrow to interview him, and NCIS are also sending some men our way. If Larry won't talk to me, then I'm hoping he'll play ball once the big boys get here."

Beth struggled to comprehend why Larry would get involved with a cartel, especially after he had gone to great lengths to turn his life around and become a re-spected member of the coast guard. "It doesn't make sense," she said. "Larry can be hotheaded, but he's not a bad person." How could she have gotten it so wrong?

Dillon smiled. "After what he just did to you, I'm amazed that you can still see some good in him." He brushed her cheek. "That takes a lot of humility."

Beth's cheek burned under Dillon's fingers and she dropped her head, hoping to hide her strong reaction to his touch. "I guess I never learn," she said quietly. "I never was any good at sorting the good men from the bad. I obviously made a poor judgment call on Larry."

"You're not the only one. He fooled a lot of people."

"What about his wife?" Beth asked, remembering that he had two small children. "He has a family, you know."

"Yeah, I know," Dillon replied softly. "Don't worry about that. The coast guard is taking care of them. Our priority is making sure you go back into hiding. Now that the entire population of Bracelet Bay has found out you're back in town, we'll have to move you some-place else."

Beth felt her heart sink right down to her feet. "I thought you might say that. I really would like to stop running, but I guess I have no choice."

He cradled her hands in his. "The van that Larry was driving has been linked to several cartel activities close to the border with Mexico. The fact that it's now in Bracelet Bay tells me that somebody from the cartel has driven it here. And I want to know where that car-tel member is now. He was obviously too clever to get involved in your kidnapping and is lying low, waiting for the next opportunity to attack. We have to make sure he doesn't get the chance."

Beth sighed. "Where would I go?"

"I've got Tyler on the case right now. We're looking for a place to stay that's set out of town, maybe in the hills overlooking the ocean so we get a nice elevated position. Tyler knows what to look for. He's trained in guerrilla warfare, so he'll pick the perfect place."

Beth could hardly believe her ears. "He's what?" she questioned. "I thought he was a surveillance expert."

Dillon closed his eyes for a split second, looking as though he was composing himself. "It's just a figure of speech," he said. "What I meant to say is that he understands how the cartel thinks. When you're tracking hardened criminals, it can sometimes feel like guerrilla war." He smiled. "I hope I didn't alarm you by my choice of words."

"No, you didn't alarm me," she replied. "But why do I get the feeling you're not telling me the whole truth?"

Beth felt that she had gotten to know Dillon's personality well, and she believed she could trust him with her life, but something didn't feel right. For some reason, she thought she could smell a lie. And the last thing she would ever do again in her life was accept a man who lied to her.

"Beth," Dillon said, looking uncomfortable. "I'm telling you the whole truth."

"Are you sure?" she asked. "Because sometimes it feels like you and Tyler aren't like other members of the coast guard. You seem to be…" She couldn't think of the right words to describe Dillon and Tyler's relationship, the way they seemed to be so in tune with each other, speaking in hushed, coded words. "More like army soldiers."

Dillon's face gave nothing away. "Tyler and I go back a long way," he said. "We've worked a lot of important assignments together, so I guess we might have developed a regimental way of working that looks more military based than other people." He smiled. "But we're still regular members of the coast guard, just trying to do our job and keep the seas safe for everybody."

"But there was something else..." she started to say before stopping. She was ashamed to reveal that she had eavesdropped on his conversation, albeit unintentionally.

"What else?" he asked. "You can tell me."

She decided to come right out with it. "While I was in the bathtub yesterday, I overhead some things you and Tyler said to each other after he arrived. I'm sure I heard you mention Afghanistan, and something about bombs being detonated." She had only caught snippets of the discussion and had tried very hard not to listen, but the more words she made out, the more she was intrigued. "And it seemed like you were comparing me to a woman called Liza, or it may have been Alicia, I'm not sure. But this woman had been in some sort of trouble." She looked straight into his eyes, seeing the flashes of recognition register in them. "It just didn't seem like the kind of conversation two members of the coast guard would normally have, so I started wondering if there was more to your history than meets the eye."

Dillon rubbed his fingers hard across his forehead as if ironing out a headache. He took his time to reply.

"Tyler has some friends in the marines," he said. "The facts we were discussing didn't directly relate to us—they were details of a mission involving some buddies of his who had been serving overseas."

"In Afghanistan?"

"Correct."

"But I thought that US troops had withdrawn from Afghanistan a few years back."

"That's right," he said. "We were discussing a mission that happened four years ago."

"Why?"

He seemed to clam up in an instant. "I'm afraid I can't discuss that with you."

"Why not?"

"It's confidential."

Beth narrowed her eyes in suspicion. "Yet Tyler was openly discussing these confidential things with you in your living room?"

"That's different. He thought that some aspects of this old mission could be relevant to the current people-trafficking situation. If I'd known you could overhear our conversation, I'd never have talked so freely."

Beth wasn't convinced by the story, yet she knew how decent Dillon was, and how he valued honesty and integrity above all else. After finding out that she had misjudged Larry so wildly, she really needed to reassure herself that Dillon was the man he claimed to be.

"So you're not hiding anything from me?" she asked. "You promise?"

He smiled, yet the look seemed unnatural. "Please trust me, Beth," he said. "I only have your safety at heart."

She fixed her eyes on his. "You didn't answer the question. I asked you to promise that you're not hiding anything from me."

He kept his gaze on hers. "I promise."

She smiled. It was a weight off her mind. The affection and closeness she had developed for Dillon were growing stronger, pushing her further into his arms like a powerful tide. Her mind had even begun to contemplate that she might actually have a future with him, and her recent terrifying experience had given her an urge to seize life by the horns again. Maybe she could finally trust a man and love him with a pure heart. And maybe that man was Dillon.

A rap on the door caused them both to sit up straight. The knock was loud and urgent.

"Enter," Dillon called, rising to stand.

Clay opened the door and came inside.

"Miguel Olmos wants to move up your meeting time today," he said. "And he says you definitely want to hear what he has to say."

TEN

Miguel Olmos looked to have aged ten years since Dillon had seen him just a day previously. His eyes were ringed with dark circles and his dark hair was unwashed and matted, revealing thinning patches on his scalp. At his side sat a court-appointed lawyer, acting harassed and distracted, repeatedly checking his watch as if he needed to be someplace else.

"I heard about the attack on the lighthouse," Miguel said. "The grenade took you by surprise, huh?"

"What do you know about that?" Dillon asked.

"My lawyer has told me that you are hoping I will be able to provide information about the attackers." Miguel laughed. "I also heard that the lady at the lighthouse has been moved to a secret location and is under your protection." He smiled in a sleazy way. "So it looks like you got the girl after all."

Dillon ignored the comment. "I was told that you wanted to make a deal. If that's the case, then you'd better start talking because I'm not in the mood to be messed with."

Miguel looked at his lawyer, awaiting the nod of approval to start talking. When he received it, he leaned across the desk and spoke quietly. "The cartel is changing routes. Apparently the Californian coastline is too hot right now with coast guard trackers, so the cartel is switching to land vehicles for a while. But before they do that, they have one last shipment of over two hundred people to transport via the sea. The drop is due to take place tomorrow night, and some high-ranking gang members will be on board to oversee the operation."

Dillon had no way of verifying Miguel's story. "How do you know this?"

"I was told of this plan a few days ago before I ended up here," Miguel answered. "I heard it straight from the…how do you say it?…from the horse's mouth. If you agree to cut my sentence to five years, I'll supply you with times, coordinates, weapons on board and exact numbers of people."

"The agreement was ten years," Dillon said. "You're facing some pretty serious charges, Mr. Olmos."

At this moment, the lawyer put his hand up to prevent Miguel from answering and spoke on his behalf. "Captain Randall," he said with a false smile. "My client is taking a huge risk by agreeing to provide you with this information, and he'll no doubt be forced to serve his prison sentence in solitary confinement to avoid being attacked by an inmate acting on the orders of the cartel seeking retribution. We think that the offer of a five-year prison sentence in exchange for data that will lead to the potential capture of several important cartel members is a very good offer. And, of course, two hundred people will be prevented from illegally entering the United States, sending a clear message to other ocean traffickers that the US Coast Guard is a force to be reckoned with."

Dillon sighed. He hated dealing with lawyers—they always sounded insincere. But Miguel was holding all the cards, and he knew it. Dillon stared at Miguel with mistrust. "If this information turns out to be false or a trap, the deal is off the table and we'll seek the maximum penalty plus extra years for reckless endangerment of the coast guard."

"This information is not false," Miguel answered. "It's one hundred percent true. And this is your last chance to catch the cartel ringleaders because, after tomorrow night, they will stop using the coastal route and you will lose them."

"Tell me something, Mr. Olmos," Dillon said. "Does the reason the cartel is switching routes have anything to do with the fact that they were concerned about losing their inside man at the coast guard?"

Miguel looked puzzled. "What man is this?"

"Chief Petty Officer Larry Chapman. He was arrested for the attempted kidnapping of Beth Forrester earlier today."

"Larry Chapman," Miguel repeated, rolling the name on his tongue. "I have never heard this name before."

"Aw, come on, Miguel," Dillon said, trying hard to maintain a cool head. "If you're prepared to give up members of the cartel, you're surely prepared to give up their accomplice? If you agree to give evidence against Larry Chapman at his trial, I'll approve the five-year sentence."

"Like I said already, I do not know this Larry Chapman," Miguel replied. "So I cannot agree to give evidence against a man I never met."

Dillon narrowed his eyes and felt frustration bubbling up in his chest. "Then the deal is off." He was bluffing, but he hoped it wasn't obvious. "I want details of the cartel's informant included in any negotiations on a reduced sentence."

Miguel leaned across and spoke quietly to his lawyer, communicating in fast-paced Spanish. Then he turned back to Dillon with a solemn face. "I cannot agree to this, because I do not know anything about the cartel's snitch. His identity was always protected, and nobody but the big bosses know his name." He began to rise from his chair in a big fake gesture. "So if the deal if off, then I shall leave, yes?"

"Sit down, Miguel," Dillon said, knowing he had to batten down this contract before anything could ruin it. "I want all the information you have regarding the shipment of people coming in tomorrow night, and I'll cut your sentence to eight years. Do we have a deal?"

Miguel again leaned across and whispered to his lawyer in Spanish, taking his time to deliberate this new offer. Finally he turned to Dillon and said, "This is acceptable to me. I agree."

"Good," Dillon said, pulling a portable recording device from his black backpack and placing it on the table. "Then start talking."

Dillon parked his coast guard truck in a secluded spot on the roadside and then walked through the trees to access the property where Beth and Tyler were waiting for him. Tyler had rented a vacation cottage called Ocean Vista, perched high up on a cliffside with a sheer drop leading to the water. There was certainly no danger of any sea attack from this vantage point, and the house was set in steep, hilly terrain that would make it difficult to approach the property on foot, particularly at night. Plus, the place was alarmed and modern, with extra-strong windows that could withstand the battering northwesterly winds that often blew in. But, as an extra precaution, Dillon had insisted that no vehicles should be driven on the narrow lane leading directly to the cottage. This way, they could ensure that nobody would be able to follow them without being spotted. It was far easier to notice a pursuer when walking through the quiet trees than in a vehicle on a winding road.

The sun had almost disappeared over the horizon, leaving a murky and patchy light to guide his way, but he was using the old-fashioned method of map and compass to ensure that he found the coordinates. The tree-sheltered cottage was not easy to find unless a person knew the landscape, and its seclusion was an advantage.

When Dillon reached the front door, Tyler was already there to open it, having spotted him approach. Both men instinctively checked the immediate vicinity before stepping inside and locking up behind them. Through the open kitchen door, Dillon saw Beth sitting at the breakfast bar, Ted curled at her feet, looking perfectly comfortable in his new home already. She caught his eye and waved before turning her attention back to the window, which had a sweeping view out over the ocean. She seemed sad and distracted, yet stoic in the face of adversity. It certainly was an improvement on her earlier state of mind. Maybe these beautiful and tranquil surroundings were having a positive effect.

"So what did Mr. Olmos have to say?" Tyler asked. "Are you finally making progress with him?"

Dillon gave Tyler a quick summary of Miguel's words regarding the final big shipment of trafficked people due to sail along the coastline the following day.

"I think he's telling the truth, so we don't have much time to prepare our special-purpose boats. We've had to requisition some extra help from the San Francisco coast guard to make sure we've got enough capacity to rescue the two hundred migrants we might find. It's a huge operation and there's a lot of organizing to do."

"Then what are you doing here?" Tyler asked. "We have everything we want and I got a panic button linked directly to the local police station. We don't need you." He laughed. "I hope that doesn't make you feel unwanted."

"I came to visit Beth," Dillon said. "I had to see for myself that she's okay."

"Ah," Tyler said. He winked conspiratorially. "I understand."

Dillon walked into the kitchen, stopping in his tracks and looking around the large, airy room. The dining table and four chairs had been pushed aside to accommodate the bed frame that he had already transported to his apartment from her lighthouse.

Dillon turned to Tyler. "How did you get this here?"

"I decided to move it at the same time as Beth," he replied. "I didn't want to risk her being seen in the truck, so we managed to get the boat on the back of the truck and she hid underneath it, surrounded by a lot of padding."

"But you parked the truck a half mile away," Dillon said. "I saw it at the side of the road."

Beth rubbed her upper arms and grimaced. "We carried it here together," she said. "My arms are aching like crazy. But at least this gives me something to work on while I'm here. This place is absolutely beautiful, but being confined indoors twenty-four hours a day will make it seem like a prison without being able to occupy myself."

Dillon sat on a high stool at the breakfast bar next to Beth. "We've had a major development on the people trafficking case," he said. "And I'm hoping this will give us the breakthrough needed to remedy your situation. Tomorrow night, if all goes according to plan, I should be capturing several members of the cartel and I'm hoping that one of them will cut a deal in exchange for information regarding the hit that's been placed on you. If we can find out why they want you dead, we can put a stop to it."

She smiled and touched his arm. "That sounds like music to my ears, Dillon. Thank you."

He watched the way her fingers lingered on his forearm, alternating between firm and gentle pressure. It caused goose bumps to spring up on his skin, and he thought he understood what this simple touch was saying. Beth was letting him know that she was opening her heart to him, trusting him, giving him permission to explore the possibility of taking their relationship further. It should be something that made him happier than he'd ever been, but the knowledge was bittersweet.

Earlier in the day he had lied to her, deliberately and blatantly. He had looked her in the eye and promised that he was telling her the whole truth. He had seen no other choice. His status as an undercover Navy SEAL must remain top secret until he could be sure that there were no more informants in the coast guard. The town of Bracelet Bay had eyes and ears everywhere. Secrets were impossible to keep once word was out, and one wrong move could see him unmasked in a matter of minutes. If his true background was revealed, he would be removed from the mission immediately and sent all the way back to Virginia before he could even take a breath. He couldn't take that chance, not even with Beth, and his lies had stuck in his throat like glue, clogging his mouth with guilt and shame. He was on the verge of falling for this woman, yet he had started a possible romantic relationship by lying to her. Would she forgive him when she found out? Had he destroyed the fragile roots of their possible love before it had even been planted? And, more to the point, was he on the right track with his theory that she was inviting him to take the next step?

"I'm only here for a short visit," he said. "I need to prepare for the important assignment tomorrow evening, but I wanted to see you beforehand."

She let her fingers remain on his arm, pressing gently on his skin. "You did?"

Tyler shifted awkwardly, sensing the change in atmosphere. He looked relived when his cell began to buzz in his pocket. "I'll take this in the living room," he said, heading out the door. "And leave you guys to talk."

Dillon picked up Beth's hand and placed it in his own, curling his fingers around hers. "If the assignment is successful, and we manage to smash this trafficking cartel, there's a chance I might be moved onto a new coast guard station."

He saw her eyes widen. "Really? But I thought you'd been placed in Bracelet Bay for the long term. Why would the coast guard move you when you only just arrived?"

"It's only a possibility at the moment," he said, knowing for sure that it was a certainty. "The coast guard is always looking for troubleshooters to help deal with illegal smuggling activities, and my success at Bracelet Bay will make me a prime target for relocation to an area suffering with a similar type of organized crime."

He watched her carefully, looking for signs of her innermost feelings. Her eyes searched the white tiles of the floor as she seemed to struggle to find the right words. "Do you want to leave Bracelet Bay?" she asked.

Her hand was warm in his. "No."

She smiled. "I don't want you to leave either," she said. "I kind of got used to having you around."

"So it's okay with you if I stick around?" he asked, leaning over the breakfast bar to bring his face closer to hers. "Because you're the main reason I want to stay."

She tilted her face to the side, obviously expecting the kiss to come, and Dillon put his hand on her cheek, brushing her long silky hair to one side.

Just as their noses touched and he felt Beth's breath on his lips, Dillon became aware of Tyler's presence in the doorway. He quickly pulled away and gave his attention to his SEAL comrade, trying to regain a professional posture. He was embarrassed at being caught out.

"I'm sorry, guys," Tyler said, realizing he had interrupted an intimate moment. "But that phone call was urgent. It was Janice calling from Helen's house."

Beth's hands flew to her face. "Is Helen okay?"

Tyler clearly didn't want to answer. "She's really sick, I'm afraid. She's asking for you."

Beth jumped from her stool. "How sick is she? Should I take some aspirin? Does she have a fever?"

"Beth," Tyler said. "I don't know how to break this to you, but Helen is dying."

* * *

The woodland that led to the road was filled with strange noises, as nocturnal creatures began their night-time rituals. Tyler lit the way ahead with a powerful flashlight and Beth clung to Dillon's hand, occasionally stumbling and being firmly held in his strong grip. The fear that she would have expected to feel at being out in the open in the dark was not there, replaced by a sense of urgency that rose with each step she took. A sense of unrealism hung in the air, as if she were in an alternate world. If only she could find the doorway back to her own reality, she would be back in her lighthouse, making tea for her and Helen before settling down to a game of Scrabble.

She spoke her thoughts out loud. "None of this seems real."

Dillon brought his index finger to his lips and made a whispered "sshh" noise. They were supposed to maintain total silence on this short journey to the truck, making it even more torturous for Beth. She needed support, comfort and reassurance that Helen would be fine. Instead she was faced with a black and lonely silence. Only Dillon's hand in hers gave her something to hold on to.

When the trio finally reached the black-and-yellow truck, Beth was forced to huddle down in the foot well, hidden from view, just in case any eagle eyes spotted her. Even though she couldn't see the road whizzing past, she knew the bumps, the turns and the dips, so she predicted when Helen's house was near.

Dillon turned around from his position in the passenger seat. "Stay low," he said. "And I'll give you the all-clear to come inside."

Beth lay down across the seat, allowing the familiar smell of the sea air to calm her senses. She was sure that each beach had its own distinctive odor, and Bracelet Bay was her favorite—salty, bitter and briny, yet fresh and clean, with an underlying sweetness that blew in from the town's restaurants and cafés, where cotton candy hung in bags for the tourists.

The truck door opened and Dillon's voice called her out. He put an arm around her shoulder, pulling her close and then rushed her inside Helen's home. The temperature was high, as usual, and Beth removed her jacket, wondering if this would be the last time she would ever visit Helen. She took a deep breath, refusing to allow herself to accept such a devastating outcome. Helen was tough. It wasn't her time. Not yet.

Janice from the coast guard appeared in the hallway, closing Helen's bedroom door behind her.

"Helen has suffered a stroke," she whispered. "I found her when I came to prepare her evening meal. She can speak, although her speech is slurred, but she can't do much else."

Beth felt irritation rise. "Why didn't you call an ambulance? She should be in the hospital. They could have started treatment hours ago."

"I called an ambulance as soon as I arrived, and the paramedics assessed her condition," Janice said. "She's suffered a massive stroke that will be fatal without urgent care, but she refused to go to the hospital. She sent the paramedics away." Janice's voice was gentle. "She said she wants to die in her own home with her dog by her side and not hooked up to machines and drips."

Beth would not accept this. "Helen is often confused. She sometimes doesn't know what she wants."

Janice looked sympathetic. "In my opinion, she seems to know exactly what she wants, and it's our moral obligation to respect her wishes." She touched Beth lightly on the shoulder. "I'm so sorry, Beth. I think she's been holding on until you arrived. Why don't you go in and see her?"

Beth could hold back the emotion no longer and allowed the tears to fall freely down her cheeks. Dillon took her hand, squeezed it tight and led her along the hallway.

"We'll get through this," he said, opening the door to reveal Helen's frail figure propped up on pillows on the bed, with Tootsie sitting on the mattress by her feet, watching his owner patiently. The room was peaceful, dimly lit only by a small bedside lamp. It felt like a haven of tranquility from the danger she'd known the last few days.

"Hi, Helen," Beth said softly. She had to break off to compose herself. "It's me, Beth."

Helen's eyes sprang open and she tried to move, but the effects of the stroke were clear to see. One side of her body was completely immobile, while the other had limited movement.

"Beth," Helen said with slurred speech. One side of her face had drooped and she dribbled slightly. "I'm so glad you're here. Come sit with me."

Beth walked to the bedside and sat on the chair, picking up a tissue from the nightstand and wiping Helen's mouth. "Would you like some water?"

Helen shook her head. "Did you bring Ted?"

"No, we left him behind. We thought he might be too boisterous for you."

Helen blinked slowly, yet only one eyelid functioned

correctly. "Will you look after Tootsie for me? He'll be happy with you and Ted, and he won't miss me too much."

Beth grabbed hold of Helen's hand and pulled it to her damp cheek. "Don't talk like that, Helen," she said. "If you fight hard, you'll recover from this."

Helen let out a laugh, half strangled in her throat. Her words were spoken slowly, with care taken to enunciate as best she could. "Even if my body recovered, my mind would soon be gone. You must have noticed how I forget things." She stopped abruptly. The effort of speaking was clearly draining her energy, but she recovered and continued. "The Lord is calling me home before I forget your name, Beth." She gave a lopsided smile. "I'm ready."

Beth couldn't stop herself from saying the first words that entered her head. "But I'm not ready."

Helen smiled in an enigmatic way. "Yes, you are." She struggled to lift her head from the pillow. "Yes, you are."

Dillon had remained standing by the closed door, clearly trying to give Helen and Beth some privacy together. Now he stepped forward. "Is there anything practical you would like me to do for you, Helen?"

"Just one thing," she replied. "Take good care of Beth."

"You got it."

Beth looked up at Dillon. "Could you give us a minute alone?"

"Sure. I'll be right outside in the hallway." He slipped through the door, softly clicking it into place behind him.

Then Beth moved her chair as close to Helen's bed

as possible, leaned across and laid her head next to her old friend's on the pillow.

"I think I might have fallen in love," she whispered. "You were right about Dillon Randall. He's a good, kind man, and I just might be ready to take a chance on trusting somebody again."

Helen smiled weakly, but her eyes lit with joy. "I knew already," she slurred. "I knew from the start."

Beth brushed her fingers against Helen's forehead. "I'm so thankful that you've stuck with me all these years," she said. "When I felt like I had nobody to turn to, God gave me a true friend, and you've helped me more than you can possibly know. Thank you."

Helen's breathing began to change, becoming rattle-like and raspy. Beth suspected that the end was near, and she leaned across to give her old friend a kiss on the cheek as Tootsie made his way up the bed to settle next to Helen's pillow, head resting on his owner's shoulder.

"Goodbye, Helen," Beth said. "Sleep well."

Beth sat back up and clasped Helen's hand in hers, listening as her breathing grew more labored, more raspy and less frequent. Eventually the breaths stopped coming entirely and Helen's chest failed to rise. Tootsie, sensing a change in his mistress, raised his head and whined before settling back down.

Beth stood, deciding to leave Tootsie with Helen for a while longer. She opened the bedroom door to see Dillon standing on the other side, awaiting the inevitable news with a solemn face. She could hear Janice and Tyler talking in hushed voices in the living room, looking through Helen's address book in an attempt to find any family members. Beth knew they would come up blank. Helen had no family except the church.

"She's gone," Beth said. "Janice was right. I think she'd been holding on for me to say goodbye."

Dillon wrapped his arms around her shoulders, and Beth buried her face in his torso, allowing the grief to overtake her body, and her chest jerked with sobs.

She allowed her sobs to subside before lifting her head and trying to talk. "Helen has been my only friend for the last five years, and it's hard to imagine her not being here anymore. Apart from Ted, she was the only constant in my life. I know it's selfish of me to want her to live forever, but I feel like I lost my right arm." She took a steadying breath that hiccupped in her chest. "She was so much more than a friend."

Dillon held her even tighter, pressing her cheek onto his chest. "Don't think of this as an ending," he said softly. "Think of it as a new beginning. Helen said she felt God was calling her home, and she obviously wanted you to embrace life without her. She loved you very much, Beth, and she knew you could cope. She knew how strong and capable you are." He stroked her hair. "She knew you were ready to move on."

Beth considered the prospect of moving on without Helen's wise counsel. Who would she go to for support and advice? Who would pray with her when her spirits were low? Suddenly the strength that Helen had instilled in her began to evaporate, leaking through her pores like mist. The tears returned with force.

"It's okay," Dillon soothed, pulling her in tight again. "I promised Helen that I'd take care of you and I meant it."

Beth wondered if Dillon was simply paying lip service to an elderly woman's dying request rather than genuinely agreeing to such a huge commitment. "So you've decided to stay in the bay?" she asked. "For good?"

"I've never felt more at home than in Bracelet Bay," he said. "And now that I've made an important promise to Helen, it seems to have sealed the deal. I'll speak to my superiors and do whatever it takes to secure a permanent posting here."

Beth smiled and wiped her cheeks. Could Dillon be right in thinking that Helen's passing heralded a new beginning? Beth had never believed in love at first sight, but Helen clearly did, and had steered her toward Dillon in the certain knowledge that they were meant for each other. It was her final act of kindness.

Beth decided to be bold. The chance of happiness had given her a desire to seize the moment, and the air around her felt charged with electric particles. "Are you staying because you want to be with me? I mean *really* want to be with me?"

"Absolutely," he said with a smile. "I've developed feelings for you that have totally blown me away. I tried to ignore them and focus on the job, but it's just too difficult. A woman like you is impossible to ignore."

Beth felt her heart swell and rise. The mixture of emotions swirling within was juxtaposed—deep grief combined with joyful elation.

"I'm glad," she whispered. "I hoped you felt the same way as me."

"I do," he whispered back. "But I need to put this conversation on hold until tomorrow's assignment is completed. I have to keep my focus on the traffickers and put a stop to the attacks on you. Do you think you can wait a day longer before we discuss the possibility of *us*?"

"Of course," she said. "As Helen would say, patience is a virtue."

Thinking of Helen's body growing cold in the bed beyond the door set Beth's lip wobbling, and she took a deep breath, running her fingers through her hair.

Dillon's face was solemn, and the overhead bulb illuminated the crease that always developed between his eyes when he was under stress. "We mustn't forget that your life is still in grave danger, Beth," he said. "I know that Helen's passing will have a deep effect on you, but let's stay on our guard." He pulled her back into his arms. "If we're going to have any sort of future together, I need you to be strong and vigilant, and to keep yourself safe."

"I will," she whispered. "I promise."

As their lips touched, Beth allowed herself to believe that she and Dillon were only hours away from perfect happiness. Once he had smashed the people-trafficking gang, it surely would mean her safety was guaranteed. He would return to her like a triumphant warrior after battle.

She might have lost Helen, but for the first time in many years Beth felt a ray of hope. And she convinced herself that nothing could snuff it out.

Yet the ring remained tucked deep in her pocket, taunting her with its misery, its mocking words repeating in her head: *he's lying.*

ELEVEN

A low rumble of thunder echoed across Bracelet Bay the following night, ominous and foreboding on a dark, stormy night with no moonlight to illuminate the way ahead. Dillon felt the wind pick up speed, and his boat began to bounce heavily over the waves, forcing him to plant his feet far apart and steady himself at the wheel.

Carl came into the cabin where Dillon and Clay were navigating. "There's been a power outage in the town," he yelled above the wind, closing the door behind him. "Look." He pointed into the darkness, where Dillon would usually expect to see an array of twinkling lights dotted along the hillside. He saw nothing but empty black space. "Lightning struck the main power plant."

The boat that Dillon was captaining was the first in a line of coast guard vessels making their way toward the coordinates given to them by Miguel Olmos. The sea had been forecast to be choppy, but the sudden storm sweeping in from the north had taken them all by surprise.

Dillon's crew was a small one—just himself, Carl and Clay. The other three flotilla boats, and associated crew members, had been supplied by the San Francisco coast guard. These other vessels were cutters, much larger and better equipped to ride over the rolling waves than Dillon's all-purpose utility boat. Dillon's vessel was built for speed, stealth and agility, not stormy seas. He had been given extensive sailing training before taking up his position with the coast guard, and was using all those skills to good effect, but the presence of forked lightning on the horizon was an added worry. A lightning strike was the last thing the coast guard needed on this important assignment. The electrical storm had already taken the town out and would wreak havoc with the GPS on a boat.

"Sir," Clay said, not taking his eyes from the binoculars trained in the distance. "I see three large boats, all tethered together and possibly in trouble. It's too dark to assess the occupants, but this looks like our traffickers."

Dillon sounded the horn, signaling to the other coast guard vessels, and they went into their planned formation. Dillon hit the throttle, pounding over the swell of the waves and reaching the beleaguered migrants in a matter of seconds. He switched on the searchlight to assess the situation. The boats were packed with people, hundreds of them, all forced to sit or lie out in the open air while the sea rose and rolled around them. The wooden boats pitched and lurched, taking on water, and many people were vomiting or hunched over, simply trying to stay in one position. Some bravely attempted to bail out the seawater sloshing at their feet, but it was futile. Without immediate assistance, they stood no chance of reaching land without major damage and loss of life. The scene was pitiful.

Miguel had informed Dillon that armed guards would be on board, but it was impossible to distinguish who these cartel members were. Everybody seemed to be desperate to be rescued, reaching out their arms, wailing, begging. The storm had stolen the fighting spirit of the guards and they had hidden themselves among the migrants, probably hoping to blend in as they saw the coast guard approach.

Dillon picked up his radio to speak to the captains of the cutters. They had already decided on a plan to transfer the people from the cartel-controlled boats onto the coast guard vessels, but the ferocity of the storm now made this scenario impossible.

"I recommend we tow these boats into port and disembark there," he said. "Let's move fast. This weather front is worsening."

As he relayed the instructions to the crew, he watched the lightning streaking from the sky to the horizon like plant tendrils seeking soil. The darkness was closing in all around, and he had no idea in which direction the port was, but they would rely on modern technology to guide them home. Many years ago, the Return to Grace Lighthouse would have been the only landmark to protect sailors on a night like this. Now GPS had replaced the old-fashioned ways.

Attaching tow ropes to the smugglers' vessels proved to be an arduous task, and crew members from the coast guard were forced to make the perilous journey from their cutters to the cartel's boats, causing many heart-stopping moments when the sea rose to try and snatch another victim into her watery depths. But their prayers were answered when the ropes were securely fastened and their homeward journey could begin. Just at this point the sky opened and dropped its heavy cargo onto the sea in big, fat drops.

"The towing vessels should lead the way," Dillon said into his radio, switching on his wipers. "And I'll follow on to make sure nobody gets lost overboard. Good work, everybody. We saved a lot of lives today. Let's go."

Dillon's boat, small in size relative to the leading cutters, climbed the steep waves and lurched over the other side, sending his belly into free fall. But despite the nausea, he grinned from ear to ear. This mission looked to be a success, and he could feel proud of his actions in rescuing vulnerable people from the clutches of evil. With continued help from Miguel Olmos and possible testimonies from the migrants, he might have enough evidence to put these dangerous traffickers behind bars. He allowed himself to hope for a positive outcome for the migrants and for Beth. Neither would have to pay the price for the other's safety.

Dillon finally accepted that he would never know the fate of the teachers in Afghanistan, but he forgave himself for the choice he made. Aziza was living a free life because of that choice, and he felt the guilt lifting.

Now he could return to Beth and make plans for his future in Bracelet Bay. He knew it was a long shot, but he would put in a request for a permanent transfer from the SEALs into the coast guard. If his request was denied, the only way for him to remain in Bracelet Bay was to leave the SEALs and forge another career path. He loved his job, but he loved Beth more.

As he was mulling over this possible perfect conclusion to his mission, a blinding flash filled his vision and he felt the air around him charge with positive ions. A bolt of lightning had struck the boat. All three men instinctively dropped to the floor, hoping to evade the creeping electrical energy. The vessel was fitted with a Faraday cage, a metal safety structure that allowed electricity to ground itself beneath the boat and therefore leave its occupants unharmed, but this structure could not protect the instruments or the GPS.

"Is everyone okay?" Dillon called as the men slid around the floor, being tossed with the force of the waves.

When both Carl and Clay gave affirmative replies, Dillon stood up to assess the damage. The navigational instruments had been shorted and the engine cut. As he looked out the window, he saw the cutters sailing farther and farther away, towing the migrants to safety. He automatically picked up the radio before realizing that it was fried. He placed it back in its cradle. Even if he were able to call the cutters back, he wouldn't do it. It was too dangerous, and the storm's intensity was increasing.

"What do we do now, sir?" Carl said, pulling himself up to stand and holding on to the control deck for balance. "We're totally blind." He picked up the portable compass, which had been securely attached to the deck in a holding case. "Even the compass is cooked."

Clay added a more important point. "And we have no engine."

Dillon thought for a moment. Nothing on this earth was going to prevent him from returning to Beth. He grabbed a rope from the storage box and fastened the harness around his waist, clipping it securely. He then handed the other end to Carl.

"Tether me to the deck," he said. "I'm going to fix the engine and take us home."

Beth stood in the large living room staring out the window, which gave her no view except a black hole.

The room was dark and cold, with no power for light or heating. She held a cup of sweet, iced tea in one hand and her cell phone in the other, nervously awaiting a phone call from Dillon to let her know that he had safely arrived back in port. Yet time was dragging on and her anxiety was growing. All grief regarding Helen's recent passing had been replaced by concern for Dillon, and she was unable to stop pacing on the wooden floor, with Ted's paws clipping alongside her as he kept pace with her feet.

She had prayed until the words would no longer come. The waiting was torturous. Tyler was trying to keep her spirits buoyed, but he knew it was pointless. Beth's connection to Dillon had now gripped her heart entirely, and the thought of losing him was terrifying.

Tyler came into the room with his eyes downcast. Immediately Beth feared the worst.

"Sit down, Beth," Tyler said. "I have some news."

"What?" she asked quickly. "What happened?"

"Sit down," he repeated.

"Just tell me," she said, raising her voice. "I have to know."

"The San Francisco coast guard cutters returned to port with the rescued migrants." He stopped to take a deep breath. "But Dillon didn't make it back."

Beth sat down, fearful that her legs would give way. "What do you mean he didn't make it back? He has to make it back."

"When he failed to return, the coast guard tried to raise him on the radio, but it's not working. They managed to reach Carl via cell phone and he says that they suffered a lightning strike. Dillon is repairing the engine, but the instruments are shorted and they're sailing blind."

"So the coast guard is sending a helicopter for them, right?"

Tyler cast his eyes over to the window. "Listen to the storm, Beth," he said. "It's gale force. There's no way the coast guard can send a helicopter out in this."

"But they can send a boat."

"Dillon, Carl and Clay have all agreed that no search-and-rescue boat should be dispatched for them. They don't want anybody risking their lives." He wound his fingers tightly together as he talked, clearly deeply affected by the news that his friend was in serious trouble. "Dillon's a strong character. He'll make it back eventually. Don't worry."

Beth sprang to her feet. "How can I not worry?" she said. "He has no way of navigating. Without the lights of the town to guide him, he'll have no idea where the rocks are." An image of his boat, smashed into pieces and scattered along the shore, came to mind. "There's not even a working lighthouse anymore." She stopped. An idea hit her with such force that she put a hand to her forehead to suppress the dizziness. "Of course!" she exclaimed. "The lighthouse. I could take a light and shine it from the cliffs to warn him." She spun around as her thoughts spiraled in her head. "We need flashlights." She rubbed her chin, thinking. "I have a powerful one at the lighthouse, and I can shine it behind my big, Fresnel magnifying glass to create a spotlight. Dillon gave me a key for the new front door so I can get inside. And we can use the truck headlights." The plan was coming together. "We should leave right now."

Tyler stood up. "Beth, that's a very noble idea, but

you can't go outside, especially in this storm. Dillon would never allow it—"

The window behind her suddenly shattered with a huge bang and the glass exploded onto the floor. Tyler threw himself at her and dragged her to the floor. Together they scrambled behind the couch, closely followed by Ted, where Tyler grabbed his shoulder and winced in pain.

"You've been hit," she cried.

"It's not bad," he said, pulling his gun from its holster. "Go lock yourself in the basement like we agreed until I deal with this."

Beth knew she could never cower in a basement while Dillon was out on the stormy sea. "I have to save Dillon," she said. "I'm leaving."

Tyler closed his eyes for a second, clearly deliberating whether there was any point in trying to change her mind.

"I'm leaving," she repeated. "I'm sorry."

Another shot zinged through the air, hitting the arm of the couch. Tyler reached into his jeans pocket and pulled out the keys to the truck Dillon had allocated him on arrival to Bracelet Bay. "Take the truck," he said. "The shooters are out front, so leave via the back door and take a wide path around the house. I'll provide cover fire as you leave so they don't suspect anything, and I'll keep them busy. You remember the way to the main road, right? Head for the sound of the sea and make sure you're going down the hill, but watch out for the cliff." He pulled a gun from his pocket. "Take this, and use it if you have to."

She took the weapon in her hand. "Thank you. Please stop Ted from following me. I can't take him with me."

Tyler took hold of Ted's collar and smiled at her. "Dillon's found a powerful ally in you, Beth. Go save him." Another shot rang out. "Go."

She scrambled across the floor and into the kitchen, pressing the police panic button on her way. She didn't know how long it would take for help to arrive, but at least it would come. Opening the back door onto the veranda, she felt a sheet of horizontal rain hit her in the face.

Then she took a deep breath and disappeared into the unforgiving night.

Dillon battled to keep his vessel afloat, hearing the engine struggle under the strain of his temporary repair. He steered out into what he hoped was open water to move them behind the weather front battering the town. If he accidentally strayed onto the rocks, the boat would go down and all crew lost. He could see the electrical storm fading into the distance, the thunder becoming less and less audible as time ticked by. Clay and Carl scanned their surroundings as best they could with binoculars, but their task was too difficult. The darkness combined with the tossing movement of the boat meant that spotting rocks was impossible until they loomed upon them.

Then Clay shouted out in alarm, "Cliffs directly ahead!"

Dillon snapped his eyes up from the deck and followed Clay's pointed finger. He saw a series of lights shining out from the cliff top: at least four of them, possibly two car headlamps included. It told him that their boat was heading straight for the rocks, and he yanked the wheel with full force, turning them sharply in the swelling waves. The boat's engine whined and whirred, but held firm.

"There must be somebody at the Return to Grace Lighthouse," Carl shouted above the engine. "It's like the old story is repeating itself."

Dillon knew the story well. He remembered the wistful tone in Beth's voice when telling him of Grace Haines saving the man she loved by standing out on a cold stormy night atop the cliffs. Was Beth now following in those footsteps, putting herself in mortal danger to send a beacon of hope out into the darkness and guide him to safety?

But he knew how that tale ended: Grace sacrificed herself so that her husband could live.

Please, Lord, he prayed silently in his head. *Be her refuge and her fortress, because she has been mine.*

Beth didn't know how long she had stood on the cliff top, but when the sun's first rays rose from the horizon she realized that hours must have gone by. Her arm muscles ached with the strain of holding her high-powered flashlight behind the large, Fresnel sheet she normally used to magnify sections of wood for intricate work. The combination of the two had sent a strong beam, like a searchlight, over the wild sea, and she prayed that Dillon had seen it. The storm had passed, leaving behind a feeling of newness as though the winds had swept the bay clean. The truck she had parked with its headlights shining on high beam now had a dead battery, and the lantern she'd put on the sill in the lighthouse tower had long since burned up.

She sank to her knees with fatigue, looking at her lighthouse with its old weather-worn Return to Grace sign hanging above the cottage door. Was this how Grace Haines felt after that stormy night in 1865? Did Grace know the same sensation of longing and despair, wondering if her all-night vigil had steered the man she loved to safety?

A little way behind her stood two coast guard members, sent there by Tyler during the night to watch over her as he battled with the gunmen, finally repelling them in a fierce battle. She had since heard that Tyler was now in the hospital, having his gunshot wound attended to, and Ted was being cared for by Henry. Her two guards had tried to encourage her to go into her cottage as the storm died away, but she had refused, needing to stay outside as long as the darkness remained a threat.

Then she saw a truck heading along the coastal road, and she recognized the familiar black-and-yellow markings of the coast guard. She rose, her legs feeling a little shaky from the effort of standing firm while being buffeted by the gale. As the truck came closer she allowed herself to feel more and more hopeful.

When Dillon's face finally came into view at the wheel, Beth broke into a run and forced her tired legs to carry her forward to greet him as he stepped onto solid ground, looking exhausted and bruised, but in one piece.

She flew into his arms. "You made it!" she cried.

"Thanks to you," he said, squeezing her so tight, she thought her lungs might burst. "I saw the lights and you guided me away from the rocks. You're amazing to think of it when nobody else did."

She pulled away and smiled. "Somebody else thought it before me," she said. "I just borrowed the idea."

"We got eight cartel members in custody," he said. "And hundreds of people saved. At least three of the men are prepared to turn against their bosses for a plea bargain. I'm hopeful we can finally find out why you've been targeted and put a stop to it once and for all."

"I hope so," she replied. "I really do."

"And I'll be putting in for a transfer from the SEALs to the coast guard—"

She sprang back from his arms, cutting him off mid-sentence. "What?"

He must have realized his mistake and closed his eyes, pinching the bridge of his nose. "I'm sorry. I'd planned to tell you later."

She folded her arms. "Tell me what?"

"I'm not a member of the coast guard. I'm a Navy SEAL based in Little Creek, Virginia. I was drafted into the Bracelet Bay coast guard as an undercover operative to take over the people-trafficking investigation." His face looked to be cracking as he spoke. "I couldn't tell anybody the truth, not even you."

She was too stunned to speak for a little while and she walked away from him, deliberating her words. When she turned back around, there was a pain building in her chest. "And Tyler? Is he a SEAL too?"

"Yes."

A spear was delicately poised over her heart, the tip pressing into it, waiting to penetrate through to the core. "And you never worked in Washington, DC?"

"No."

The spear was making its way inside, piercing her with the barbs of broken promises and a thousand lies. "And I suppose that story about your father was all made up?" she challenged. "All those things you said to me about Helen were false. You never understood how I felt about her developing Alzheimer's." She wanted to scream out loud, but she kept her voice low. "You lied."

"No," he said strongly, moving toward her. "Everything I told you about my father and my family is true. It's all true."

"How can I ever believe you?" she cried. "If you can lie about who you are, how can I trust anything else you say?"

He held out his hand. "Beth, please, I couldn't tell you I was a SEAL. It was for your own protection."

She let out a snort. This sounded like a likely story. "I almost married a man who lied to me for months," she said. "It's taken me five years to finally trust somebody again." She covered her mouth to stop a sob from escaping. "And yet you lied to me so easily."

"It wasn't easy," he said, keeping his hand extended toward her, encouraging her to take it. "It wasn't easy at all. I hated keeping information from you, but I never lied to you about my feelings. And I promise from the bottom of my heart that I will never lie to you again."

"You looked me in the eye and told me you weren't hiding anything from me," she said. A sensation of hopeless despair crept up her spine. She'd been knocked all the way back to her failed wedding day and she wanted to run and hide away. "You're a different person to me now." She turned her back. "How can we have a future together when I feel like I don't even know you?"

He came to stand close behind her and touched her shoulder. She tensed up and he removed his hand. "You *do* know me," he said. "I think you know me better than anybody. You know that my faith in God keeps me sane, you know how I nursed my father in the final years of his life, you know how much I love living by the ocean, you know how much I love *you*."

Beth dropped her head and watched her tears fall onto the small, gravelly stones beneath her feet. Anthony had told her he loved her on the eve of their wedding. It was the biggest lie she had ever been told.

"I want to believe you," she said quietly. "I really do, but I refuse to start a relationship built on false promises. I can't be with you, Dillon. Please leave."

She felt his breath leave his body in a big whoosh and caress the back of her neck. "I can't leave you, Beth," he said. "You know that. The cartel still poses a major threat to you, and it's not yet safe to resume your normal life."

"I don't want you or Tyler to protect me," she said, turning around. "You can both leave Bracelet Bay and go back to Virginia." She looked over at the two coast guard members who were standing on the grass overlooking the cliffs. "There are plenty of other people who can keep me safe." She cast her eyes to her cottage, feeling a deep-seated urgency to retreat within its thick walls. The door and window had been replaced, and it was ready to be lived in again. "I'll be moving back into my lighthouse today with Ted."

"You shouldn't come back here just yet," he said. "Not until we can be certain no more attacks will come."

"I don't care if more attacks come," she said, raising her voice. "I would rather live on my feet than die on my knees. Clay or Carl can come stay with me if necessary, but I intend to get back to living a normal life and forgetting that you were ever part of it."

Dillon's face crumpled. "You don't mean that."

It was true. She didn't mean it. She would never forget that Dillon had swept into her life, stolen her heart and made her smile again. But she could recover in time. She'd done it once. She could do it again.

"You can leave now," she said. "I'll be fine here with these two coast guard officers. I'd also be grateful if you could arrange for Ted and all my personal items to be brought here this afternoon. I really need the bed frame that's currently in the rental house. I should be getting back to work."

He looked crestfallen. "I'll bring them here myself."

"No. Please send somebody else. I don't want to see you again."

With that, she turned and walked slowly into her cottage, closing the door behind her. Only then would she allow the dam to be breached and the torrent of tears to come. She didn't want Dillon to see the tears she was shedding over him. It was best to make a clean, quick break.

She was back where she belonged. Nobody needed her, and she needed nobody.

Dillon continually glanced at his cell as he carried out some final paperwork at his office in the coast guard station. It had been seven days since Beth rejected him so painfully after learning of his dishonesty regarding his background. With each waking day, he had held out hope that she would change her mind and pick up the phone, but the call never came. And he was forced to accept that it never would.

Beth was adamant that she would remain at the lighthouse, and her safety continued to worry him. She had made it clear that she wanted no contact with Dillon, but he was not prepared to remove her protection detail and had assigned Carl as her guard. No more attacks had occurred, and he was hopeful that the capture of several high-ranking gang men would spell the end of danger, but he had not been able to answer the question of why she was on their hit list. The cartel men in custody either wouldn't or couldn't shed any light.

His eyes traveled to his packed suitcase, sitting by the door, awaiting his departure later this evening. Both he and Tyler had received their orders to return to the SEAL base in Virginia, as the Department of Homeland Security was now satisfied that the mission had been accomplished. Hundreds of lives had been saved, the cartel operation effectively shut down and Larry Chapman was facing some serious charges. Dillon should have felt pleased at his success, but he felt like an empty shell, sucked dry of his previous happiness.

There was a knock on the door. "Enter," he called.

A smartly dressed man stepped into the room, wearing an ID badge bearing the letters NCIS. "I'm sorry to bother you, Captain Randall, but my name is Agent Liam Griffiths, and I'm in town working on the cartel case. Larry Chapman has asked to speak with you privately. He says it's very urgent and can't wait."

Dillon looked at his watch. "I'll be leaving in two hours to catch a flight. A meeting with Chapman is out of the question, I'm afraid."

"Yes, I thought that might be the case, which is why I brought him here." Agent Griffiths stepped aside and revealed a downcast Larry, handcuffed and flanked by another agent, in the hallway. "He refuses to talk to anyone but you. Shall I send him in?"

After the shock of seeing Larry standing there in the station wore off, Dillon was surprised to find himself feeling some sympathy for his subordinate. "Yes," he said. "Handcuff him to the metal cabinet and you can leave us alone."

Larry shuffled forward, his leg chains clunking on the floor. The agent handcuffed him as instructed and left the room, leaving Dillon and Larry regarding each other with mutual curiosity.

"What do you want to say, Larry?" Dillon asked. "Because I don't have much time."

"I'm not a traitor," Larry said strongly. "It wasn't me feeding information to the cartel."

"Uh-huh," Dillon said, not believing him for one second.

"What's more," Larry said. "The hit that was put on Beth Forrester was placed there by somebody local— somebody who's been working with the cartel for a few months and has a lot of influence in its activities."

Now Dillon's attention had been captured. "If this is the case, Larry, then can you explain to me why you were found at the wheel of a van that had Beth tied up inside?"

"I was *saving* her," he replied. "I learned that a cartel van had been sent to Bracelet Bay to help facilitate Beth's abduction, so I stole the van and got to her before they did."

"You didn't think it was better to go get her in a coast guard truck?" Dillon asked incredulously. "Or bring her into the station for safety?"

"I had to act quickly," Larry said. "The two cartel men were just about ready to make their move. These guys saw me take the van and they were coming after me on foot, so I only had a minute or so to get to Beth and take her out of the danger zone. I know how feisty she can be, so I didn't think she'd ever go with me willingly. That's why I tied her up to stop her from running straight into the path of the cartel." He looked down at his chains. "But it looked bad."

"Larry," Dillon said. "If you know the person helping the cartel to traffic people and target Beth for elimination, then why didn't you come to me sooner? Why have you said nothing for days?"

Larry was reluctant to answer. "It's not as straightforward as it seems," he said. "My loyalties were divided."

"Loyalties?" Dillon questioned as he began to guess where the finger might be pointing. "Do you mean family loyalties?"

Larry nodded. "Why do you think me and Kevin were fighting? I found out he'd been copying confidential paperwork relating to the trafficking investigation from my office. That's how the cartel always knew our plans. I didn't want to see Kevin go to jail. He's my brother and I love him. But sitting in jail for a week has forced me to reassess my priorities and I'm not gonna take the rap for this."

Dillon realized that Larry's explanation was actually plausible. "But what did Beth ever do to Kevin? Why would he want her dead?"

"I don't know for sure," Larry replied. "But he's been pretty interested in that boat she picked up from the beach a few weeks back, so I'm reckoning it's important and may even link him with the cartel." He looked Dillon squarely in the eye. "Did you know that cartels sometimes use secret compartments in boats to hide information that they want to exchange with associates?"

Dillon reached for the phone, suddenly incredibly

anxious to know that Beth was okay. "Carl," he said, as soon as the young seaman answered his cell phone. "Is Beth okay?"

"I think so," replied Carl. "But I'm on my way to the sheriff's office in Golden Cove, just like you asked."

"What?" Dillon said, rising to stand. "I didn't give that order."

Carl hesitated before answering. "I got a call from NCIS. Somebody said that Larry had managed to escape and you had ordered all personnel to report to the Golden Cove Sheriff's Office immediately to begin a search."

"No!" Dillon exclaimed. "Why would I take you off lighthouse duty?"

Carl's voice dropped as he realized his terrible mistake. "A guy calling himself Agent Stokes said my replacement was just minutes away and not to worry. He sounded so plausible. Captain, I'm sorry—"

Dillon hung up the phone, grabbed his coat and flew out the door, past the surprised faces of the NCIS agents. He yelled out behind him, "Make sure Larry is secured and meet me at the lighthouse."

Beth stood back and appraised the finished bed frame. It was beautiful, gleaming with varnish and finally ready to accommodate its small occupant. Yet the accomplishment brought her no joy. She had been bereft these last few days, her thoughts turning to Dillon constantly. The only person who could counsel her through this was Helen, and her bungalow now lay empty and cold. The funeral was scheduled for tomorrow, and Beth didn't know how she would face it without Dillon by her side.

A knock at her front door caused her to jump in alarm. Ted and Tootsie began to bark, running in circles, eager to sniff the outdoor scent of the visitor. Carl had urgently left the cottage a half hour ago, promising that a replacement would arrive within minutes, but no one had turned up. Maybe this was the new guard. She walked to the door and used the peephole, standing back in surprise when she saw the callers on the other side.

"Hi, guys," she said opening up and inviting Kevin and Paula Chapman inside. "What brings you all the way to this part of town?"

Paula cast her eyes around the room and pointed to the finished bed frame in the corner of the living room. "We'd like to make you an offer for that beautiful piece of furniture."

Beth smiled politely. "I'm sorry, but it's already been promised to a local man who commissioned it for his daughter."

Kevin pulled out a tightly packed roll of bills. "But we can give you a very good price." He began to peel off some notes. "What do you think is fair? Ten thousand?"

Beth gasped. That was four times what the client was paying. "I'm sorry," she repeated, beginning to feel a little uncomfortable. "It's not for sale."

Paula grasped her by the arm. Her touch was a little too firm to be friendly. Kevin stepped farther into the cottage and closed the door behind him.

"Everything has a price, Beth," Paula said sweetly. "You name it."

"No," Beth said firmly. "This bed is not for sale." She tried to twist her arm to release Paula's grip, but the older woman simply tightened her fingers. "Please leave. I'm expecting a visitor any minute now."

Paula sighed. "I'm afraid we're not leaving until you sell us that bed, so why don't we stop playing games and make the deal."

Beth looked at Kevin pleadingly. "What is this about, Kevin? You're scaring me."

Kevin cast his eyes down to the floor. "I'm sorry, Beth, but trust me when I say you should sell us the bed. You can make another one."

Beth yanked her arm free. "You can't have it."

Paula let out a moan of exasperation and shoved her husband toward Beth. "I told you this wouldn't work," she hissed. "Now we have no choice. If the memory stick inside the hull of that bed is discovered, we're dead in the water."

Kevin's face darkened, and he flung himself around to challenge his wife. "You've just gone and told her exactly why we want it."

"It's too late to care about that now," Paula said with a raised voice. "If Beth won't sell us the boat, we'll have to take it from her by force. And then she'll go to the police. So it's time for you to step up and be a man." Paula jerked her head toward Beth. "Get rid of her."

Beth backed away from the arguing couple, terror rising in her throat.

"Why do I have to do the dirty work?" Kevin spat out his words in anger. "This is all your fault in the first place."

Paula raised her voice even louder. "That's not fair."

"It's totally fair!" shouted Kevin. "If you hadn't run up hundreds of thousands of dollars in gambling debts, we wouldn't have been forced to sell information to the cartel just to keep our heads above water."

He smiled sardonically. "And we wouldn't be in this position, would we?"

Beth began to understand just how she had become a target for attack. There was something inside that boat—something that would reveal Paula and Kevin Chapman's involvement with the trafficking cartel.

"Okay," Beth said, trying to remain calm. "You can have the boat." She gesticulated toward it, knowing that offering it to them was her only hope of survival. "Take it."

Paula's smile sent a chill through the air. "It's too late for that, Beth." She sat on a chair and crossed her legs. "You see, there's a memory stick inside the hull of that bed which contains the bank details of several offshore accounts that can all be traced to Kevin and me." She tapped one foot impatiently on the floor as she spoke. "The cartel was meant to have disposed of you already, but I guess we'll have to do that job for them."

Beth shook her head. "You can't be serious."

Paula stood and walked slowly toward her. "Now that old Helen Smith has died, you've got nobody. Wouldn't it be better for you to end your life quickly and pain-lessly? Nobody will miss you, after all."

Beth darted her eyes around the room. She was frozen with fear. This was all like a bad dream from which she couldn't wake.

"No!" she exclaimed, holding out her palms in a pleading gesture. "Somebody will miss me. I know they will."

Kevin lunged at her and she turned on her heel to run, but it was too late. He pounced and pulled her to the front door.

"No!" she screamed, lashing out. "Please don't do this, Kevin. Please."

Beth felt the cool outside air on her face and the small stones dragged underfoot. She was being taken to the edge of the cliff. Ted and Tootsie were barking from behind the door where Paula had prevented them from following.

"I'm sorry, Beth," Kevin said. "But Paula's right. Nobody will miss you. You don't have much of a life really, so we're just putting you out of your misery. Shh, don't struggle. It's much easier this way."

Beth thought of the opportunity she had just wasted: the chance to be happy with a man who loved her. Her fears and insecurities had prevented her from accepting God's blessings, and she would now die on a lonely and isolated beach, deprived of the chance to put things right.

But she hadn't counted on Dillon's perseverance. She saw a flash and heard a crack, and there he was, standing tall and erect on the cliff top, pointing his gun in their direction. Kevin's limbs slackened in an instant and he slumped to the ground, blood oozing from a wound to his back.

Paula ran from the cottage, screaming Kevin's name and racing to him, dropping to her knees to cradle him in her arms. Beth took a while to realize what had just happened. A black SUV skidded to a halt beside the cottage and two men jumped from the vehicle like a scene from a movie. And in the midst of it all was Dillon, gun still midair, his face stony and determined, locking eyes with her as if she were the only person he could see. As they stared at each other, he slowly holstered his weapon and smiled, sending her heart into free fall. He had come for her, and she was alive because of him.

She sprinted to him, wrapping her arms around his neck, and he lifted her into the air, holding her tight and kissing her face with light, fluttering lips.

"I love you," she murmured. "So very much. I don't care where you came from or who you are. I just know that I love you."

He squeezed her in a hug. "And I love you too." He put his arm around her shoulder and led her away from the cliff, where the men were stabilizing Kevin Chapman and comforting a hysterical Paula.

"Wait," Beth said, remembering something important Helen had told her to do. "I'll be right back."

She took small steps toward the edge of the cliff, rummaging in her pocket for the wedding band that she had been carrying for too long. Pulling it out, she let it lie in her palm before tossing it with all her might into the sea below. She imagined the gold metal sinking into the murky depths, landing in the silt and being lost for an eternity.

Then she turned to Dillon and said, "I'm ready."

EPILOGUE

Dillon adjusted the bow tie on Ted's collar, making it straight. Both Ted and Tootsie were looking impressive in bow ties and waistcoats, patiently awaiting Beth's walk along the sand to join her husband-to-be at the beautifully simple altar she had made from pieces of driftwood.

The beach setting was perfect, and the whole town had come out to join them in the joyous occasion. Beth's best friend, Mia, now had the chance to fulfill the role of bridesmaid, and she rushed up to Dillon with a flower in hand.

"Beth told me that you forgot this," Mia said, threading the flower through his buttonhole. "She's on her way, so look sharp."

Dillon peered over her shoulder. "I see that you and Henry are looking very much in love. Will you be next perhaps?"

Mia blushed and slapped his shoulder. "Today is all about you and Beth, not me and Henry."

Dillon glanced down at Tootsie and Ted, who panted in the summer sun. "Well, that told me, huh?"

Tyler elbowed him in the ribs. "She's here. Eyes front, Captain."

As the Wedding March played, Dillon beamed from ear to ear. His request for a transfer into the coast guard had been granted, Paula and Kevin Chapman were soon to face trial for numerous charges relating to their illegal activities and Larry had quit the coast guard to take over the running of the Salty Dog. But best of all, Beth had opened a gallery in Bracelet Bay where she was showcasing and selling her beautiful wooden sculptures and furniture, leading to her becoming quite famous in her hometown. She hadn't given up the lighthouse, but it was no longer her fortress. After marriage, they planned to set up home together in the cottage and raise a family in its idyllic setting. Dillon had already begun to build the fence that would enclose a yard and prevent toddling feet from straying too close to the edge of the cliff. And his crew had offered to help him convert the tower into extra living space for a growing family. He was blessed beyond measure.

Then Beth was at his side—her beauty radiating right across the bay.

"Hey," she said, taking his hand and squeezing it tight.

He smiled. "Hey, yourself."

The pastor opened his Bible and began to read the pre-agreed verse: *He is my refuge and my fortress, my God, in whom I trust.*

* * * * *

SPECIAL EXCERPT FROM

Love Inspired.
SUSPENSE

When her son witnesses a murder, Julia Bradford and
her children must go into witness protection with the
Amish. Can former police officer Abraham King keep
them safe at his Amish farm?

Read on for a sneak preview of
Amish Safe House *by Debby Giusti,*
the exciting continuation of the
Amish Witness Protection miniseries,
available February 2019 from Love Inspired Suspense!

"I have your new identities." US marshal Jonathan Mast
sat across the table from Julia in the hotel where she and
her children had been holed up for the last five days.

The Luchadors wanted to kill William so he wouldn't
testify against their leader. As much as Julia didn't trust
law enforcement, she had to rely on the US Marshals and
their witness protection program to keep her family safe.
No wonder her nerves were stretched thin.

"We're ready to transport you and the children,"
Jonathan Mast continued. "We'll fly into Kansas City
tonight, then drive to Topeka and north to Yoder."

"What's in Kansas?"

Jonathan pulled out his phone and accessed a
photograph. He handed the cell to Julia. "Abraham King
will watch over you in Kansas."

Julia studied the picture. The man looked to be in his midthirties with a square face and deep-set eyes beneath dark brows. His nose appeared a bit off center, as if it had been broken. Lips pulled tight and no hint of a smile on his angular face.

"Mr. King doesn't look happy."

Jonathan shrugged. "Law enforcement photos are never flattering."

Her stomach tightened. "He's a cop?"

"Past tense. He left the force three years ago."

Once a cop, always a cop. Her ex had been a police officer. He'd protected others but failed to show that same sense of concern when it came to his own family. The marshal seemed oblivious to her unease.

"Abe is an old friend," Jonathan continued. "A widower from my police-force days who owns a farm and has a spare house on his property. He lives in a rural Amish community."

"Amish?"

"That's right."

"Bonnets and buggies?" she asked.

He smiled weakly. "You'll be off the grid, Mrs. Bradford. No one will look for you there."

Don't miss
Amish Safe House *by Debby Giusti,*
available February 2019 wherever
Love Inspired® Suspense books and ebooks are sold.

www.LoveInspired.com

WE HOPE YOU ENJOYED THIS BOOK!

Love Inspired®
SUSPENSE

LISHALO2019